Further praise for

THE CHINCHILLA FARM

"[An] elegiac novel. . . . Verna is a rare creature, a reliable female narrator, whose preoccupations are with what she sees and learns about the world instead of with the resolution of her own story."
—Diane Johnson, *New York Review of Books*

"Incidental to this novel is a plenitude of facts more wonderful than fiction . . . lyrical but tough-minded . . . extraordinary."
—*The New Yorker*

"A tremendous coup for a first novel, for any novel. Freeman introduces us to an America of transcendental landscapes, cultures like forgotten flowers and festive, fierce cities. . . . Freeman brings her richest gifts to literature."
—Pagan Kennedy, *The Nation*

"Judith Freeman, raised as a Mormon herself in Ogden, Utah, tenderly creates a world both magical and stark. She is wonderful at describing the 'specialness' of Mormons. . . . Freeman's Verna Flake [is] a wonderful heroine with wry humor and a generous spirit."   —Fern Kupfer, *Washington Post Book World*

ALSO BY JUDITH FREEMAN

Family Attractions: Stories
Set for Life
A Desert of Pure Feeling
Red Water

THE CHINCHILLA FARM

Judith Freeman

W. W. Norton & Company
New York London

First Norton paperback edition 2003

Copyright © 1989 by Judith Freeman

For information about permission to reproduce selections from this book, write to Permissions, W. W. Norton & Company, Inc., 500 Fifth Avenue, New York, NY 10110.

Excerpt on page ix from "Moving Ahead," from Selected Poems of Rainer Marie Rilke, edited by Robert Bly. Copyright © 1981 by Robert Bly. Reprinted by permission of Harper & Row, Publishers, Inc. Lyrics on page 229 from "Honky Tonk Merry-Go-Round," written by Stan Gardner and Frank Simon. © 1983 Acuff-Rose Music, Inc. P.O. Box 121900, Nashville, Tennessee 37212-1900. International Copyright Secured. Made in U.S.A. All Rights Secured. Lyrics on page 232 from "I've Loved and Lost Again," written by Eddie Miller. © 1982 Acuff-Rose Music, Inc. P.O. Box 121900, Nashville, Tennessee 37212-1900. International Copyright Secured. Made in U.S.A. All Rights Secured.

Library of Congress Cataloging-in-Publication Data
Freeman, Judith, 1946–
The chinchilla farm: a novel / Judith Freeman
ISBN 0-393-32426-5 pbk.
I. Title
[PS3556.R3915C47 1990]
813'.54—dc20   90-50117
CIP

W. W. Norton & Company, Inc.
500 Fifth Avenue, New York, N.Y. 10110
www.wwnorton.com

W. W. Norton & Company Ltd.
Castle House, 75/76 Wells Street, London W1T 3QT

1 2 3 4 5 6 7 8 9 0

For Anthony

CONTENTS

Once more my deeper life goes on with more strength as if the banks through which it moves had widened out. Trees and stones seem more like me each day, and the paintings I see seem more seen into: with my senses, as with the birds, I climb into the windy heaven out of the oak, and in the ponds broken off from the blue sky my feeling sinks, as if standing on fishes.

—Rainer Maria Rilke

PART ONE

1

LONG AFTER my husband left me, I still thought about him. The funny thing is, I always remembered him in one spot. I have this one image of him that is stronger than all the rest. He's standing in a field. It's a day when we've been working since breakfast to get hay baled because it looks like it's going to rain, and if we don't get it done before the rain comes, we're going to lose a whole crop. Anyway, I look up and see Leon has wandered off. He's standing in the distance, at the edge of the field. His back is to me. Doves are cooing on the telephone wires above his head. Everything else is so still, as if before a storm, that the doves sound especially loud. Leon's shoulders are drawn up toward his ears, as if he's holding off a cold wind; but there isn't any wind, it's July, and real warm. The sky's got a lid of dark clouds, bending like a dome over the valley. In the distance, I can see my father-in-law's house. Things seem so quiet to me. I wonder what Leon is doing. It feels like a moment between things, still and full of anticipation, and I think, It's because of the rain. Any minute it's going to break from the sky like it's never broken before. I want to call out to Leon, "Let's get going!" But somehow I can't bring myself to say anything, to break the stillness. I look at him. Even from a distance I can see how his hat fits low on his ears and flattens them out. He looks strong, a big, square man. I'm looking at him and I'm thinking how good he looks out there. It seems to me that maybe he's stopped work in order to look over the land he grew up on. But then he turns slightly and I see what he's really doing. He's relieving himself on the silver weeds that grow along the ditch on the other side of the fence. He bows his legs slightly in order to rearrange himself and buttons up his Levi's. Well, that's it. That's the whole picture that keeps coming back to me when I think of Leon. I just don't know why I chose that one over all the others.

Actually, it seems like it chose me.

I was thirty-four when he actually left. It happened on a Thursday in the middle of January.

"I want out, Verna," Leon said when I walked into the apartment around noon. I'd just finished the early shift at the bowling alley. He didn't even give me a chance to get my coat off before telling me what he'd prepared to say. The room was damp and cold, and he stood against the light coming from a table lamp, which we needed on even during the day.

"You say you're quitting me? You want a divorce, is that it?" I stared at my husband, who shifted his weight from one foot to the other and nodded, his head bobbing on his short, thick neck.

"That's it," he said. "I want out."

"Well, there's the door, Leon."

"That's a helluva response."

"Leave the dry-cleaning ticket on the dresser, would you?"

He kicked the duffel bag at his feet. "Is that all you've got to say? 'Leave the dry-cleaning ticket'?"

"I've pretty much said everything else. I've talked myself out lately trying to make you feel better. No point in arguing now. You want to leave, Leon, you just go right ahead and do it. There's the door."

"That's what I figured on doing. I just thought you might have something to say besides 'There's the door,' cold as hell, like you were just waiting for it."

"You think I ought to be surprised? I truly am not, Leon. For months I've been hearing stories about you and Pinky. Jesus, the terrible part is losing your husband to somebody named Pinky."

"Leave her out of this."

I laughed at that. "I wish I could. If she'd stayed out, you might still be in."

"Oh, hell, Verna—there were problems before. You can't deny that."

"For you, maybe. Things pretty much suited me just fine."

He said, "You think you're easy to live with?"

I said nothing.

"You know what it's like being married to somebody who's so damned happy all the time? It gets on your nerves, that's what it does."

I said, "I used to wonder what the hell you expected, what you wanted to change." I slowly unbuttoned my coat, my fingers still stiff with the cold. "Beats me why you're so unhappy. I stuck with you for seventeen years, Leon, and most of those years were pretty good for both of us, I'd say. I don't know what turned it bad for you these last couple of years, but I stuck those out too, thinking you might get yourself straight."

"Oh, it's all me. Always me, isn't it?"

"The truth is," I said, "I'd stick with you now, but I don't think it would work . . . you, me, and Pinky. You got every right to walk out if that's what you've decided. I'm not going to give you any argument."

For a moment I thought, He's going to change his mind. Something showed itself, a look so involuntary it was like a tick or a spasm: the pouches beneath his eyes quivered. But the convulsion passed and he said, "I haven't finished packing."

"Fine," I said. "Take your time." It was over. That was that.

I dropped down into a chair, feeling very cold. Everything seemed fixed, rigid, permanently still. The apartment was in the basement of a fourplex, positioned so that it caught the harsh canyon winds and little of the southern light. It was windowless and damp in the winter, and this was January, the coldest month of the year in Utah. Silverfish crawled out of a crack beneath the baseboard and wriggled on the floor like tiny landed trout. We'd just had the place fumigated. A lot of good it did. In weather like this, the bugs came in anyway.

I pulled a cigarette out of Leon's pack of Lucky Strikes

sitting on the Formica coffee table and crossed my legs, assuming an attitude of waiting, as if I were in a dentist's office. What else was there to do? There was a good side to this; I could see it. Things had become clearer. I had figured it was coming and now it was here. Still, my breath was short, and I felt afraid of something. I could hear Leon in the bedroom going through the closet, the sound of wire hangers scraping along the metal rack. He moved to the hall closet, and there were thuds and bangs, and then the sound of glass breaking.

"What broke?" I asked nonchalantly.

"Coleman lantern," he said, retrieving the broom and dustpan from the kitchen. "You know when it started to go wrong as well as I do, Verna. It started when you stopped going to church." We were both Mormons, but we'd fallen into bad habits.

"Oh, hell, don't start up with that! I just got tired of pretending, Leon, that's all. Smoking in bathrooms, sneaking beers like we were. How are you supposed to be an adult and still hide in bathrooms to smoke? I told you why I quit going to church. I didn't believe it anymore."

"Well, maybe I did."

"I never expected you to stop just because I did. I think you're looking for something to blame me for. We'd both been pretending, right from the beginning. We pretended we didn't smoke, and we pretended we didn't drink, and we pretended we hadn't had sex so we could get a recommend from the bishop and get married in the temple like everybody expected us to. And then we kept right on going to church, because that was also expected, wasn't it? But I got tired of pretending."

"I think it might have been different if we'd kept going to church."

"I doubt it."

"We might have had faith in something other than ourselves."

I didn't agree, but there seemed no point in arguing. I

opened a copy of *The Horseman's Digest* to indicate I was
through discussing religion. My eyes fell on an advertisement
for a worming medicine. The complete life cycle of a worm,
from egg to adult, was present in colorful pictures.

Leon left the room and returned with a load of stuff from
the hall closet: two rifles, a pistol, fishing equipment, and his
snowmobile suit. He dumped them near the duffel bag.

I eyed the pile of his belongings. "You and Pinky must be
planning a sporting life."

He ignored my remark, tossing his waders and a canteen
through the doorway.

"I took half of what was in the checking account," he in-
formed me.

I shivered and hugged myself for warmth. A song came
into my head, and I began softly singing. It was a song I'd
picked up off the jukebox earlier that morning; I'd played it
over and over again until I knew the words.

"Sitting there singing," Leon said with disgust, and threw
his motorcycle helmet onto the pile.

"You know what this song is? 'You Can't Have Your Cake
and Eat It Too' by the Statler Brothers." I paused to puff on
the Lucky. "I figure that's a true thing if I ever heard one." To
my way of thinking, it applied directly to Leon's attitude about
religion. He wanted to have everybody think he was a good
Mormon, and at the same time he wanted to break all the
rules. What was the point of trying to live like that?

"You could spend your whole damned life singing,
couldn't you, Verna? Well, I'm sick of your singing."

"Oh, Leon, come on! You can't go getting jealous over my
singing when I'm being so good about Pinky. No man ever
lost his woman to a song or two."

He slammed the bedroom door.

"Besides," I called, "someday I might just get rich and
famous off my singing, and you can say, 'I knew that Verna
when she was still working in the bowling alley in Willard,
Utah.' " I knew he wasn't listening, just as I knew I'd never

become famous. This was a little joke that used to make him laugh. The truth was, I liked to sing because it was the one thing in the world guaranteed to make me feel good—it was the one thing I was pretty good at, too. But Leon had never appreciated it much.

I ran my fingernail underneath the Formica where it had begun to peel away from the tabletop. "No man ever lost his woman to a song or two"—I'd remember that and write it down; there was a song in there, a good beginning, anyway. Beginning of a good song and the end of . . . what? I couldn't really call it a bad marriage; it was just an *ordinary* marriage. We had hardly even fought. That was the funny part, thinking of somebody leaving when you never even fought with them, though things had gotten worse lately, since Pinky. I'd had my own one small affair, so brief it lasted only an afternoon, but it didn't send me packing. This was different. I saw now that I'd been a fool not to see earlier that Pinky was no small change.

I looked around the living room. Had it always been so drab? I saw that there wasn't enough color. The rug was a depressing brown, except where it was worn and the white thread showed through. The walls were covered in a dark paneling. The Barcalounger where I sat was a dirty orange tweed with grease stains on the arm rests and the seat. Leon never bothered to change his clothes when he finished at the garage. Nothing in the apartment had escaped picking up the grease, the oil, the smell of dirty old engines. Whoever invented tweed must have been trying to help women like me hide dirt. Still, this chair looked terrible. There was a stack of *Field and Stream* magazines holding up one corner of the coffee table where the leg had broken off. I couldn't stay here, that much was certain; and as I began to imagine myself in different places, an idea suddenly started taking shape in my head.

I got up and walked into the kitchen. It smelled of chili. Leon had warmed up last night's leftovers for his lunch. The pan sat in the sink, full of water turned a reddish brown with a few bloated beans floating on the surface. I leaned against the counter and folded my arms, staring down at the buckles on my shoes.

"How much was in the checking account?" I called out.

"Five hundred and fifty-four fifty." He picked up an armload of clothes off the floor and headed for the door. "I sold the horses but I'm leaving you the trailer."

"I don't want the trailer. What am I going to do with a horse trailer and no horses?"

"Sell it if you can't make the payments. You'll get as much out of it as I got out of the horses. Look, I want to be fair, Verna. It's not like I'm cleaning you out. You're getting all this," he added, nodding toward the living room.

" 'All this,' " I repeated. "A bunch of broken-down furniture."

I walked over to the pile of Leon's belongings and picked up a gun.

"What are you doing?"

"Getting ready to shoot you—what do you think?" The rifle rested on my hip for a moment, pointed at his stomach. "Oh, hell, Leon! Don't look so scared, I'm only joking. Come on, I'll help you with this stuff."

I led the way up the outside stairs and out onto the snow-covered driveway. We lived on the main highway, and trucks passed at all hours, going at a terrifying speed. The skinny dog that belonged to the Wimmers in upstairs B was nosing through an overturned garbage can. A storm had moved in during the night and was now in full force, and the air was thick with great white flakes.

When Leon started walking toward the pickup truck, I caught his arm. "Un-uh. You take the Rambler. I can't pull a trailer without a truck. I'm keeping the truck." I eyed the '62 Rambler. I wasn't keeping that piece of junk. The windshield wipers didn't even work. During the last big storm we'd had to tie Leon's shoelaces to the wipers, run them through the window wings, and pull them by hand all the way home from Salt Lake City.

He didn't argue with me. We carried load after load up the steps and to the car, filling up the trunk and backseat. Leon's belongings took on a beauty as they were assembled in the trunk of the Rambler. The green camp stove and flexible hip waders, a polished bamboo pole, red woolen shirts, a blue jacket—I felt as if he were going on vacation, escaping with his movable property, while I would be consigned to the brown rooms again and made responsible for their contents.

As we went up and down the steps, neither of us spoke. Every once in a while, I shook the flakes from my hair. The snow fell onto my face and stuck to tiny hairs on my cheeks before melting against my skin. Sometimes I felt the flakes just before they melted, clinging to my face like lint, whispery and tickling. Once I slipped on the ice, and Leon, quick and sure, grabbed me around my waist to keep me from falling. I stiffened and pulled away, but in that brief moment I caught sight of his eyes, and I thought, He's scared, he isn't the least bit sure of what he's doing.

"Slippery," I said to him quickly, straightening up and putting some distance between us.

When his things were all loaded into the Rambler, I returned to the house and took a fresh set of sheets and a few towels out of the bathroom cupboard.

"Here," I said. "You'll probably need these." Who knew where he'd be sleeping the first night, or the second? Even the third? He might not be running straight to Pinky. He might need to make his own bed. I handed them to him and closed the bathroom door and sat on the toilet for a while. The kids upstairs were jumping off their beds again. Every few seconds there was a heavy thud on the ceiling and the sound of shrieking laughter. The cold seeped through a gap around the window. One window in the whole apartment and it was next to the toilet. From the floor of the shower, a faint smell of mildew rose from a damp wash rag.

I stood up and looked at myself in the mirror. I brushed my damp hair with even strokes until it lay flat from the part.

Maybe he would leave if I didn't come out. Maybe I'd come out and the Rambler wouldn't be in the driveway. I took out my reddest lipstick and applied it thickly. If he was still there, I would come out looking good. I pursed my lips and blotted them with a piece of toilet paper.

And then I stood there looking at myself. I saw a tall, lanky woman—a woman with brown eyes and red hair. I saw my thinness, and the spattering of pale freckles I've never liked but which over the years I'd finally grown used to. I saw the small mounds my breasts made under my blouse, breasts no man would ever yearn for in any fantasy. I took in the full mouth and the straight, thin nose. The odd thing about looking at yourself in mirrors is how the longer you look, the more unfamiliar you become to yourself. I stared at myself until I became objective and I could say, truthfully, You're not exactly pretty. You're like a man in some ways. But there's something there that's okay, that might even be better than being pretty—something that could be attractive in either sex.

I stared until my eyes just couldn't look at themselves anymore, and then I turned my back on the mirror, leaned against the sink, and folded my arms. I stared down at the golden dots on the linoleum.

There were angry voices now coming from the Wimmers' upstairs, and the kids began to cry. Joy Wimmer was yelling at them, working them over with threats, telling them they'd better quit jumping off the bed or else they wouldn't get to go with her to get Daddy from work, they wouldn't get no cookies, and they wouldn't get to watch Princess Patty on "Ding Dong School." She meant it, she said. If they jumped off that bed one more time, she was going to smack their butts. Grandma wouldn't take them to the mall on Saturday. And they wouldn't get to go to Lagoon for the ward party. Her voice sailed down through the heat vent as if she were somebody on a dimly broadcast radio program. "You just try it and see what happens!" Joy Wimmer yelled. "One more jump and

you guys have had it. No dinner, no ice cream, no nothin'!"
What a hell of a lot of threats, I thought. Joy Wimmer was a
pretty nice woman except when she didn't think anybody was
listening, and then she could sound pretty bad.

Was that true of everybody? Suddenly, it seemed to me
that it was, that we only think we are the people we imagine
we are when we're pretty sure somebody's listening. Joy was
like a different person up there than the woman who always
fussed over her kids in public. All those threats. It seemed like
everything in those kid's lives for the next two weeks was
going to be wiped out if they made one more jump from the
mattress to the floor. And yet, I could imagine them just waiting for her to turn her back so they could test it a little. I could
imagine their defiance rising in them in irrepressible urges,
willfulness and life sparkling in them like a million little lights,
a natural resistance to all the meaningless restrictions in the
world. I could imagine them falling down softly on the mattress, landing on their butts, just to get one more illicit bounce
before they gave up. I liked kids. I thought I understood something about them. It was so easy to put myself inside them and
see how they worked. But it was just as well I'd never gotten
pregnant myself, I thought, because of the way things were
working out.

Things were quiet upstairs now. In order to busy myself, I
took the Comet and cleaned the sink. I cleaned the soap as
well, which Leon had left clotted with a gray film. Some hairs
had become embedded in the soap, and in trying to dig them
out with my fingernails I left little pockmarks all over the surface of the Dove.

There was a knock at the door. "Just a minute." I picked
out two yellow barrettes and clipped my hair away from my
face. I was not as pretty as Pinky, that was certainly true. Pinky
had been a runner-up to Miss Wyoming. There wasn't a person who met her who escaped learning that fact from the
mouth of the former beauty queen herself.

I opened the door and found Leon standing in the hallway,

hands in the pockets of his jeans. His short, damp hair looked electrified in the light that came from the bedroom behind him.

He handed me a slip of paper. It had an address on it in Evanston, Wyoming.

"This is where you can reach me if you need to."

I folded the paper and nodded.

"I got a job in a garage up in Evanston," he said. "I might be able to help out later, send some money or something."

"Oh, Leon, why don't you just go!" The thumping overhead started up again; apparently the kids had decided to risk everything. A smell of cleanser came to me from my hands, a smell that was familiar and suggested a certain industriousness.

"What are you going to do?" he asked.

"Set my hair and go to the laundromat."

"You know what I mean."

"With my life? Hell, who knows. Just what I've always done, I suppose. I'm going to have myself a good time. I figure I can do that with or without Leon Fields."

"Vern, I feel bad about this."

He always called me 'Vern' when he wanted something from me. What that would be now, I couldn't think, unless it was forgiveness.

"I wish it could have worked out differently. I really do. And I'm sorry—"

"You know what, Leon? I could forgive you for running off with Pinky. A man falls in love with another woman—I can understand that. He wants a new life—okay. You know what I can't forgive you for doing? I can't ever forgive you for telling my mother that I was the first one to take my garments off. I consider that to be about the cheapest thing you've ever done." I referred to the time when he'd been untrue to me at a depth I thought cruel. He had led my mother to believe (or so she later told me) that I had been the first to stop wearing the holy underwear, and by doing so, steered us on a wrong course—one he was powerless to abandon or alter, as though

the woman, as with Eve, were again to blame, responsible for
what in truth was a man's own complicity. He sold me out, just
a little, in order that he himself might look a little better.

I walked into the living room and put on a record. He
stood for a few moments, staring at my back. Then he walked
out. I heard the Rambler starting up, backing out of the drive
. . . fading away. I could have cried, but I didn't want to, so I
fought the impulse, setting something firm against it, and I
didn't. Instead, I began thinking about California.

In California, I thought, I'll get an apartment that's so
bright I'll never have to turn the lights on during the day. The
bedroom will have windows, so the sun will be the first thing I
see when I open my eyes in the morning. I'll look out at palm
trees. Oranges will grow right outside. I won't need a coat. I'll
go down to the beach. I'll walk right out into the waves.

I could see a bright blinding light around me and it was
California. I could see the waves, how they curled up and
folded over on top of themselves. I could see oranges hanging
on trees like Christmas bulbs.

In the time it took for me to listen to one side of *The Best of
Hank Williams,* I had worked out the details. When the record
was over, I dialed information for Los Angeles and got the
number. I called an old friend, somebody I hadn't seen for
years.

"Jolene?" I said when I had her on the line. "You aren't
going to believe this, but this is Verna Fields . . . you know,
formerly Verna Flake . . . ?"

The next morning I left everything, or almost everything,
just as it was, and closed the door on an apartment that still
looked as if somebody lived there.

Before leaving town, I wrote three notes. One I mailed to
Doreen, my boss at the bowling alley, informing her that I was
quitting and asking that my paycheck be forwarded to me in
care of Jolene Wenke and giving the address in Los Angeles. I

wrote my landlord and said I had moved; he was welcome to what I left behind; maybe he could rent the place furnished. The last note was for my parents. I intended to leave it in their mailbox so I wouldn't have to face their questioning. I said I would call them at the end of the week, that Leon had left me and I was going to Los Angeles for a while, to try my luck. That was the way I put it; that's how it felt.

It was dawn when I set out in the pickup with the horse trailer in tow. Inside the trailer were some things from the house I knew I'd need, a few boxes I'd packed the night before, some odds and ends. These belongings had none of the assembled beauty of Leon's possessions, which from the trunk of the Rambler had seemed to announce the life of fun in store for their owner. My own accumulation had the configuration of domestic habits—an ironing board, a vacuum, silver-plated serving trays kept tarnish-free in plastic bags, a mattress, blankets, a set of pans and dishes, boxes of clothes and old records. But this didn't trouble me. I was heading for promising, beguiling Los Angeles in order to get on with my life, and I was taking what I needed to do this. That Los Angeles was a beguiling place, I had no doubt, though it was an impression formed largely by television shows, and even earlier by a plastic necklace I'd had as a child, a luminescent oval showing an orange sunset, the black silhouette of a palm, and an iridescent turquoise sea made out of genuine butterfly wings, which gradually, even under plastic, began to decay and separate into powdery blue fragments.

My parents' car wasn't in the driveway. This seemed a good sign to me. I could leave the note on the kitchen table and add a line saying I was sorry to have missed them and it wouldn't look like I'd tried to avoid the whole business of explanations and goodbyes.

A cement driveway bridged the ditch in front of their small house. The water in the ditch wasn't flowing now but had frozen into opaque stillness. Snow mottled with car exhaust and dirt from the road lay in a ridge along the ditch. Pieces of petrified wood sat on the porch, and a branch of twisted oak that looked like a snake. Somebody had drawn eyes on it and attached a small piece of red felt for a tongue. That would be my dad's sense of humor. On top of the railing, a pair of cotton work gloves had frozen into stiff shapes, like arthritic, disembodied hands. The sign on the front door, which had been there as long as I could remember, was carved into a piece of yellow knotty pine and said KWITCHURBELLYACHIN.

I entered the house quietly. A plastic runner covered the carpet. The rows of plastic geraniums in the planter box in the entryway had faded so that the leaves were almost white, the blossoms only faintly rosy. So little changed here that sometimes it seemed like the effects of light, the fading of color, was the biggest alteration that ever occurred. The furniture was never rearranged; nothing was ever subtracted, nothing ever added.

I could hear someone in the back room. It was Aunt Fannie listening to records. Fannie was actually my mom's aunt; she had lived with my parents for many years. She was over ninety and partially blind.

She was lying on her back on the couch when I walked into her room. Her eyes were closed, but I could tell she wasn't sleeping; she was listening to the Book of Mormon being read aloud on Records for the Blind. The flat metal boxes in which the records were mailed from the church library in Salt Lake City were stacked up by the record player, and their khaki color and official stamps gave them a military look. The reader's voice, grave and sonorous, droned on in a tone portending both salvation and doom: "Let your light so shine before men that they may see your good works and glorify your Father who is in heaven . . ."

I touched Fannie's arm. The delicate, mottled skin slid loosely beneath my fingers.

"Oh," Fannie said, startled.

"Hey."

"Your mom and dad went to an early session at the temple."

"You look pretty today." I touched Fannie's blue dress. Beneath the many folds of skin, her eyes were a bright and watery blue, accentuated by the color of her dress. She had a serene look.

"I still got my hair in tissue!" She laughed and began undoing the twists of toilet paper that she used to set her hair in tight little bundles. She smelled of the Ponds cold cream which she used as a lotion for her hands.

"Turn that off," Fannie said, meaning the record player. Instead, I turned the volume down and explained that I couldn't stay.

"I'm taking a trip," I said.

"Oh?" There was an ineffable distance in her these days, a lack of attention that caused her to mull over every single thing that was said and then slowly form a studied reply, which was often simply the repetition of what had just been said. Age had taken her into its realm, drawing her closer and closer to its receding center, softening her senses. Remarkably, it was happening so gently.

"You're taking a trip," she said. "Where?"

"Los Angeles."

"Your uncle Heber and aunt LaRue live down there somewhere. You ought to visit them."

"I will—I got their address." I waited for a moment, and then I asked, "You don't still have an address for Inez, do you?" Inez had been married to my oldest brother, Carl. He had died many years ago.

"Who?"

"Inez," I said, louder this time.

"No," Fannie said sadly. "I wouldn't know how to reach her anymore. I don't think anyone has heard from her for a few years."

"I thought maybe I could contact her while I was in Los Angeles. Didn't she used to live in Hollywood?"

Fannie shook her head. "Someplace like that."

"She lived on a street with the name of a flower—Jasmine or Magnolia or something. I remember that."

"I wouldn't bother," Fannie said.

"You wouldn't bother what?"

"I wouldn't bother to look her up."

"Well," I said, and then let it pass.

"I should be going, I guess," I said.

"While you're here," Fannie said, "could you thread a few needles for me?"

I picked up the sewing basket and asked what color of thread she wanted. When I'd done five needles, she said she thought that was enough, and I said I'd be going; but rather than get up as I'd planned on doing, I just sat there. After a while, I said, "I'm getting a divorce."

"A new horse?" Fannie said slowly. "That'll be nice. You've always loved horses, haven't you?"

I couldn't see the point in correcting her. Really, the thing was said just to test it, to say it aloud, and it was perhaps better that Fannie didn't know.

"It will be nice," I said, and kissed her goodbye.

Outside, the magpies were racing above the power lines, and the day looked as if it were going to be drab and gray. I thought of my parents, who were in the temple doing work for the dead. Twice a week they dressed in white and assumed other people's names, maybe some Germans, say, or some Irish who'd lived in the seventeenth century. They took the names of these long-dead people so they could be baptized for them. The goal, I'd once been told, was to baptize the entire white race of the world since the dawn of time, so there was lots to do for people like my parents who traced their ancestors, birth by birth, gathering up the names. I thought of Doreen, who would just be arriving at work, and of her husband, Bud, who came in early and turned on the heat in the bowling alley, which was always so cold and still in the mornings, such a big place that it seemed a little spooky until the heaters warmed things up and the first women from the ladies bowling league arrived. I thought of the apartment I'd left, still full of furniture. I thought, I've forgotten something, I know I have; but I couldn't think what that thing was. I tried to imagine where Leon was at that moment, but I couldn't think of him anywhere definite, although suddenly I could picture him in the Rambler driving across some ugly, flat part of Wyoming.

I started the truck and shifted it into four-wheel drive and cut across the unplowed lane behind Wolthius Dairy, turned onto the highway and drove slowly toward the freeway, passing places that were familiar to me my whole life—Rogers Poultry Farm, Pettingill Orchards, RV Acres, Cindy's Sew 'N' Save, Smarties, the Best Cafe, all quiet at this hour. As I turned onto the freeway ramp, an Orange Crush bottle rolled across the top of the dashboard and clanked against the windshield. I thought, Does anybody ever get what they want or only what they think they want? Pulling over, I reached for the bottle and set it under the seat. I checked behind me for traffic. In the rearview mirror, the town was obscured by steam coming from the cherry cannery. This may be Zion, I thought, but I'm headed for a more promising land. Already I imagined myself shopping in new supermarkets, driving down different streets, strolling through unknown malls, and working at a new job, though at the moment I could not imagine what that would be.

2

I WAS BORN just after the war in a town at the edge of the Great Salt Lake. The waters fluctuated each year, so that sometimes the road that led to our house was dry and usable, and sometimes it ran right down into the lake and disappeared, like a joke. I used to look at the road running into the water and think, Here are two incompatible things, the road and the water. The sunsets over the lake were incomparable.

The Great Salt Lake is all that remains of a big sea that once rolled over most of western Utah and small areas of eastern Nevada and southern Idaho. Called Lake Bonneville by early explorers, who named it after one of their own, that prehistoric fresh-water lake was almost as big as Lake Michigan and far deeper. Dinosaurs lived on its shores. Lush tropical plants grew where now there's only desert and scrub. For a time, Lake Bonneville spilled over the rim of the Great Basin, north into the Snake River, but as the climate changed it shrank up on itself, breaking up into half a dozen smaller lakes. Through thousands of dry years, it receded, leaving higher and higher concentrations of mineral salts behind and creating, at the present site of the Nevada-Utah border, a vast, level, salt-strewn desert like nothing else under the American sun, a poisoned stretch of earth called the Salt Flats.

Almost nothing grows here on this land.

Eventually, people found a use for the vast salt plain that was formerly the bottom of Lake Bonneville. They discovered it worked well as an automobile speed course.

My brother Rodney used to lie in bed in the dark listening to radio broadcasts of car races from the Salt Flats. His hero was Ab Jenkins, a Mormon born in Utah in 1883, who was the first man to begin using the Salt Flats as an automobile race course. Holder of more world's unlimited records than anyone else in the history of sports, Ab Jenkins is the only man in his lifetime who ever drove an automobile continuously without relief for twenty-four hours. He once raced an excursion train across the Salt Flats, from Salt Lake City to Wendover, Nevada, and won. His car was called the Mormon Meteor. In 1950, at the age of sixty-seven, he made his fastest lap ever—thirteen miles at 199.19 mph. He attributed his accomplishments and stamina to the fact he never in his life tasted liquor or tobacco. I know all this because of Rodney's passion for the radio broadcasts from the Salt Flats. I can't forget the deep voice of Hot Rod Hundley, the radio sportscaster, floating around the room in the dark. Why I still remember this essentially useless information I don't know.

"Explain the Mormons to me," someone once said. But before I could answer, he added, "What I don't like about them is how they think they're so exceptional. They like to make exceptions of themselves. They think they're special." I wanted to tell him, no, it's not just that, it's not so simple. I had one image, of a small green satin apron in the shape of a fig leaf, stitched into smooth scalloped leaves and worn over perfectly white clothing; but it was nothing I could speak about. A fig leaf, decorated with a fine embroidery of veins. Worn by both men and women, green and shiny and pretty.

When we go to our temples—for washings and anointings, to do baptisms for the dead, to marry each other, and to take out endowments and prepare for missions—every single piece of clothing we will wear once we are inside is carried with us in small little suitcases. Every piece of clothing is white.

To get inside, we show our recommend from the bishop—a recommend we can get only by going through interviews every six months, in which we're asked, Are you clean? Have you kept yourself pure? abstained from liquor, cigarettes, coffee? attended your church meetings? paid your tithes? been faithful to your spouse?

Only then, when we have our recommends, can we pass through the checkpoint and enter the temple. Then the women go to one dressing area, the men to another. We take out the white clothes we've stowed in the suitcases. We wash and bathe. The men put on white shirts and pants, white socks and shoes, even white ties and belts, and the women wear white dresses, white nylons, white shoes. And of course, beneath these clothes, everyone will have on the white garments, thin and silky against the skin. White everything, head to toe. Like angels, really. White does that to people—makes them look pristine, ethereal, and ready for the Second Coming. After everyone has changed clothes, the rituals begin, the enactment of scenes from the Bible, the little plays performed in fantastically painted rooms, through which all the people in white move quietly, serenely going from room to room, until the last and final moment, when they pass through the veil. To see a whole group dressed like this is like glimpsing the hosts of heaven. More white than you can imagine in one place. It looks holy, it really does. People seem pure with all that white on. All white . . . except the aprons: the small green apron that each person will be wearing, the shiny satin fig leaf, which restores original innocence, I guess, and turns everyone into Adams and Eves.

How could you not feel exceptional?

The house I grew up in was wooden and small, and, like most houses in Utah, it had a basement which was cool in the summer and dank and cold in the winter, and that's where the kids slept, in the basement, stacked up on bunk beds like tiers of chickens in a coop. This house was surrounded by a big lawn and lots of fruit trees, chicken pens, rabbit hutches, and rows of raspberry and gooseberry bushes; a garden, and various sheds, as well as a large sandbox for play. There was a view, as I've said, of the Great Salt Lake, the deadest lake in America, and the roads and fields that occasionally disappeared under its waters. The kitchen window overlooked the lake. The living-room windows faced a highway called the Old Brigham Road, where farmers set up stands in the late summer and sold peaches and pears, tomatoes, bottled honey, plums and watermelons and apricots, to motorists who drove up there just for that reason, to buy fresh produce.

There were eight kids in our family. The kitchen was the center of our lives. White shoe polish was kept in the cupboard above the oven, with the Wheaties and Cheerios, the salad oil and potato chips, and the small bottle of olive oil— never used for cooking because it had been consecrated for anointing and healing the sick. I polished my own shoes on Sunday mornings, which were always rushed and chaotic. First the men got up and used the bathroom, dressed, and left for priesthood meeting at eight o'clock. With the men gone, my mother started washing the younger kids and helped them get dressed. The older ones she told what to do, and tried to get them to do it faster. Two of us took a bath at once. After our hair was washed, she poured a rinse made of vinegar and warm water over our heads, to condition our hair and make it shine. It gave us a faint smell of pickles. When it came time to polish my shoes, I spread newspaper out over the kitchen table and first wiped the shoes clean with a dishrag. The polish had a little wand attached to the cap, and at the end of the wand was a furry ball which absorbed the liquid polish. Polishing the shoes was like painting. I could never get the polish to really cover the black scuff marks, but each week I added another film of milky white to my shoes as the liquid, which went on shiny, dried to a dull finish. Then the men came home to get us for Sunday school. My mother, who always had a lot of last-minute things to do, was the last one out of the house. By that time my father would be sitting in the car in the driveway, impatiently honking the horn.

Mormons train for public speaking early. By the time you're five years old, you're ready to stand in front of a congregation and give a small speech, what's called a two-and-a-half-minute talk. Parents usually write these speeches out for their children and go over them repeatedly, helping the child to commit a story to memory. The stories are from either the Book of Mormon or the Bible—Joseph Smith discovering a box of buried gold plates or Jesus walking on the water or magically multiplying loaves and fishes or raising the dead— stories that naturally appealed to a child's sense of the fantastic. The first time I was asked to give a two-and-a-half-minute talk my mother taught me the story of Jesus driving the money changers from the temple and night after night we rehearsed it, until I could repeat her very short version of these events almost perfectly, word for word. But when I finally stood at the pulpit in front of the congregation, I remembered something else I'd been taught, and said:

> *I'm a cute little girl*
> *With a cute little figure*
> *Stay away, boys,*
> *Till I get a little bigger*

The eight children in my family were all born about two years apart from one another, six boys and two girls. My father used to tell people that he had six sons, and they each had two sisters, which made it sound like he had dozens of kids, and that was probably how it felt to him most of the time. Our neighbors, the Stringfellows and the Harlines, each had more children in their families than we did: the Stringfellows had eleven kids, the Harlines fourteen. But still, I thought eight was a lot; it *felt* like a lot.

It felt like a lot because of the impersonal lives we led, the way we were shaped and molded as a group: getting bathed in twos and threes when we were small; eating meals with a dozen people at the table; riding in cars where we sat on other people's laps, or else nestled on the floor near the center hump, or sometimes fit ourselves onto the shelf near the back window. It felt like a lot because of the bunk beds we slept in, the way we were stacked even in sleep, and because we each had the same kind of bedding—army-issue green wool blankets which my dad bought at the surplus store in Plain City. It felt like a lot because of the one bathroom we shared, and how you could never be in there for more than thirty seconds before somebody knocked on the door and said, "I've got to get in there." Years later, when I discovered that people actually *ran* baths, I was amazed, because nobody ran a bath in our house—nobody ever had the time or the luxury of allowing the water to fall in the tub before they did. I remember sitting down on the cold porcelain of an empty tub, turning on the taps, and splashing the dribble of warm water that came out onto my shoulders and chest, shivering and waiting for enough water to accumulate in the bottom of the tub to take the chill away, only to have the hot water run out altogether long before that ever happened. It felt like a lot because we were always getting hand-me-downs, clothes that had gone through someone else and still had their slight impression—a jacket that drooped in the front because someone else's fists had been shoved down into the pockets, a rump-sprung skirt, or a blouse with tiny sprigs of cotton bursting from the worn collar. It felt like a lot because there was no privacy. My parents were always dashing around in their garments, hoping to slip from the bathroom into the bedroom unnoticed. There was no mystery about what the other sex looked like in my house; we were always getting caught naked when we forgot to lock doors, and people sitting quietly on the john had doors suddenly opened on them and could only yell "I'm in here!" There were always, forever, these surprises, these interruptions, these reminders of the inescapable crowdedness in our house—the leveling influence of a lack of privacy. And then, of course, there was the religion, which strove to make us all the same, in thought as well as deed.

Mormons, as many people know, wear holy underwear called garments. They're one-piece items of clothing, with a round neck, sleeves, and legs, that cover the body from the knees to the elbows. Over the right breast, at the navel, and above the right knee are little marks that have secret meanings. The purpose of the garments is to serve as a sacred reminder of certain temple rituals and to promote the wearing of modest clothing. To buy them, you go to special stores, called Relief Society Distribution Centers—that used to be the case, anyway, when I was still wearing these things. It's a bad thing for a Mormon to stop wearing his or her garments. It's a fall from faith. At all times they are to be worn next to your skin, which means that if women wear other pieces of underwear, like brassieres or panties, they must be worn over the garments. Garments come in two different fabrics, nylon blend and cotton. Some people like the thicker cotton garments for winter and the thinner nylon ones for summer. You pull them on like a swimsuit, stepping through the neck. Women's garments come with lace around the neckline if you wish, an optional adornment. Garments make it impossible to wear sleeveless dresses or shorts. Men's garments have open crotches with buttons at the back, like old-fashioned long underwear. Women's garments are a little more intricate in these arrangements. In the winter, freshly washed garments used to hang from lines in the basement and looked as thin and milky as cocoons or second skins shed by snakes. In the summer, drying among the other family wash, the wind took them and twisted them on the lines; they were the thinnest of clothes, and therefore rose easily in any breeze.

All the children slept in one room until we were older and the boys were divided from the girls. The bedrooms were in the basement next to the furnace room, where a coal fire burned in a furnace nine months out of the year. A truck brought the coal. It came in large, heavy lumps. The truck backed into our driveway, lowered a chute to an open window in the basement, and the coal slid down the chute into a big bin. A beautiful, fine black dust arose as it rushed down the chute. From this bin, the coal was then shoveled into the furnace as needed. The fire never died in the winter months. You could open the door to the furnace and see the bright hot coals and flames of fire, a beautiful inferno which made you want to stare into it. When a mouse was caught in the traps kept in the laundry room, it was taken to the furnace and thrown into the blasting hot fire. Dead or alive, in it went, striking the coals with the tenderest of thuds. This seemed a very normal thing to do. I remember how Lyle Wangsgard, my brother's friend, gave me my first kiss on an afternoon when we were playing hide-and-seek in the darkened basement. We stood in front of the open furnace where a small mouse, freshly caught, was roasting over crimson coals, and Lyle put his large, wet mouth over mine.

Growing up, we all had jobs—delivering newspapers, picking fruit, baby-sitting, yard work, whatever brought in spending money. I cleaned Helen Tavetian's house. Mrs. Tavetian taught sewing and cooking at the girls' reform school. Her hair, when it was loose, fell below her knees, but in public she wore it parted in the middle and divided into two braids that she wound around her ears and pinned in place, like large, lumpy platters. She had been born in Armenia. Saturdays, while I vacuumed her floors and scrubbed her tub, she spent her time making pastries that had fifty layers of paper-thin dough. When I married Leon, she gave me *Joy of Cooking* and a subscription to *The Improvement Era,* the church magazine. She was a massive, tall woman, very competent and forthright—some said domineering. In another time, she might have led armies or promoted the passage of laws benefiting women, or even been an adventuress, dressing in men's clothes and crossing the Sahara. Such was her air of strength. Instead, she tried to make cooks and seamstresses out of delinquent girls and instructed me in the difference between a good wax job and a bad one. Her husband, Garth, was a forest ranger. Her children—a boy and a girl—had faint little mustaches and got straight A's in school. It was amazing how much I came to know about these people from cleaning their house week after week.

In order to make money, my younger brother James sold doughnuts. He took them door to door, walking the neighborhood after school, with a wooden box fastened by a long strap hanging around his neck. In the box were white paper bags, each containing a dozen doughnuts. Later on he used the same box to carry bottles of Watkins Vanilla which he also sold door to door, accompanied by his imaginary friend, Larry. He would knock on someone's door and say, "Larry wants to

know if you want to buy any vanilla." After a while he got
another job candling eggs at a small egg factory owned by a
man who was a friend of my father's. His job was to hold the
eggs in front of a candle flame and check for any dark spots in
the yolk. The dark spots were blood and meant the eggs had
been fertilized and they weren't good to sell. The eggs with
blood spots in the yolks were brought home and scrambled up
for our dogs, two brindled boxers who foamed at the mouth
and flipped spittle from side to side whenever they turned
their heads.

All the kids had jobs to do around the house, and you
couldn't complain, either. My mother said "Dust!" and we
dusted and didn't whine. We weeded, brought in eggs, picked
cherries, washed windows, raked leaves, and ironed big bags
of dampened clothes that had been sprinkled and then frozen
and stored in the big deep-freeze so they wouldn't mildew.
The one job I liked more than the others was polishing the
house plants with mayonnaise. I took a cotton ball and put a
little mayonnaise in a cup and then dipped the cotton in the
mayonnaise and rubbed all the leaves on every plant in the
house. They were all slick-leaved plants, and with a coating of
mayonnaise, they shined, pure and clean, as if they'd just been
pulled out of water.

There is no landscape like the landscape of childhood, terrain at once vivid and hauntingly vague. What remains for me
are dozens of images and names, faces and events, animals and
objects, a light I associate with dusk, fallen leaves, the smell
and feel of thick grass. My first memory is of throwing a stone
at a goose floating serenely on a small pond and seeing the
beautiful ripples in the water; my second is of having my hair
cut. Somewhere, a little later, the image of a kind man, Lawrence Bagley, arises. Mr. Bagley, who lived up the road from
us, owned a chinchilla farm. When he bought his first chinchillas and started his business, I remember my parents joked
about him. They thought he was nuts. Whoever heard of such

a thing? Raising animals for fur coats! Each pair cost thousands of dollars, and it took years to develop breeding stock and build up a profitable business. The whole idea of such a venture was viewed with skepticism. Nobody expected it to last long. They couldn't take it seriously. Lawrence Bagley and his chinchillas were sort of a humorous topic around town. But it was an idea that could, and did, make perfect sense to us, my younger brother James and myself, children who were fascinated with animals.

Chinchillas are bunchy little rodents, smaller than cottontails, and resembling rabbits more than squirrels. They have sweet little faces: whiskers stick out on each side of their mouths at least three inches. They sit humped up, they hop, and their fur is a kind of gray-blue, exquisite in color and also very soft to touch. About one hundred chinchilla pelts are needed to make just one ladies' coat. There were only seventeen such coats in existence the year Mr. Bagley began his business. His chinchillas were housed in wire cages with wooden floors and were carefully tended. The cages were contained within one large pen whose door was secured with a padlock. James and I sometimes walked along the river, avoiding the road and its traffic, to get to the Bagley place in order to look at the chinchillas. We stood in front of the rows of cages and gazed into their small, intelligent eyes. To us, they were fascinating, delicate creatures. But we didn't understand why chinchillas were such expensive animals. It didn't seem as if they should be worth so much more than our own rabbits at home. They liked carrots. If we pushed a carrot through the holes in the wire, they came and fastened their teeth on it and wiggled their whiskers as they chewed. Lawrence Bagley told us the pairs mate for life.

I know there are other animals that mate for life. I've since learned about snow geese, and certain cranes native to the north, as well as the penguins of the South Pole and some types of whales. Still, it amazes me there are animals that would rather die than live without their mates. What accounts for this? What configuration of genes, particularly as it would seem to work against survival? And what if in our own lives it were also possible not only to swear devotion, but to follow through on such a promise? Have things changed so much? Can we still hope to live a long and full life based on a vow, putting our hearts on a deep and unquestioned track of fidelity?

I remember one morning James and I walked up to the Bagleys' to visit the chinchillas. They weren't in their cages. The door to the pen was wide open; the padlock that normally held it closed was gone.

Mr. Bagley, who hadn't yet discovered his chinchillas were missing, came out and found us staring at the empty cages. He looked at us, startled, and then found the padlock lying on the ground nearby, picked it up, and shook his head. He assumed the worst and accused us of turning the chinchillas loose. No amount of denial on our part could convince him that this wasn't true. He was terribly upset and told us he was taking us home in his car.

When we got home, Mom was in the kitchen making a cake. He told her what had happened, that he had found us standing in front of the empty cages. Not an hour earlier, he said, he had seen the chinchillas, fed them, and locked the pen as he left. The only thing he could figure was that he had not fastened the padlock tightly, and we'd come along, taken it off, and turned the chinchillas loose. My brother and I listened to this explanation from the corner of the room, where we sat at the kitchen table, worrying about what was going to happen to us. We said we didn't do it. The chinchillas were gone when we arrived. We didn't know anything about it.

Then my brother spoke up and said, "Maybe Larry did it," and suddenly I knew we looked bad. Everyone in the neighborhood knew about James's imaginary friend, Larry, and how he often took the blame for things James did.

I looked at my mother, who appeared very worried. Mr. Bagley started talking again, saying how valuable the chinchillas were. He reminded us that each pair was worth thousands of dollars—thirty-two hundred dollars, to be exact, he said. If they weren't found, somebody was going to have to pay. Mr. Bagley wasn't normally a mean or severe man, and he had trouble putting forth this threatening news. The loss of his beloved chinchillas had made him uncustomarily tough. He seemed close to desperation.

I said, "We really didn't do it, Mom."

I could see my mother didn't know who to believe.

Finally, she said, "Perhaps we should start looking for them. The children and I will help."

She put on her large brown shoes, the ones she reserved for berry picking in Idaho and for the hikes with her class of Mia Maid girls from the church's youth program. It was fall, and we needed coats. She pulled an old plaid jacket on over her housedress. Mr. Bagley went on ahead in his car, and we headed for the river, planning to walk along through the willows. Maybe, my mother said, the chinchillas would be drawn to the water and to the tender grasses that grew on its banks. We followed the path through the orchard, heading toward the river. Windfall apples rotted on the ground around us. Mother walked slightly ahead of us.

At one point she stopped and turned and looked at us. "You really didn't let those chinchillas loose?" she said, staring us straight in the eye.

I made sure my eyes held hers. "We really didn't," I said. I thought she believed me. She smiled slightly and said, looking around us, "Where would you go if you were a chinchilla who'd just been turned loose?"

Neither James nor I tried to answer that question, but I walked along thinking about it. I could not think like a chinchilla, no matter how hard I tried, and I did try.

The poison ivy had turned a brilliant red and was easy to spot; but still, as we moved through a thicket of oak brush, my mother kept pointing it out to us, telling us to be careful of touching it.

"Where would chinchillas go?" my mother asked again,

looking around the woods. We passed Helen Tavetian's raspberry patch, which bordered the river, and my mother
stopped and pulled a few raspberries from their stems and
gave them to us to eat. "I hope Helen doesn't mind," she said,
taking a few more for herself. When we reached the river, we
stopped and looked at the water, breaking over the rocks,
splashing down toward the cannery and the rodeo grounds.

"Thirty-two hundred dollars," my mother said suddenly,
"for a pair of rodents! How can he keep anything so expensive? You'd be worrying about them all the time. Do you
think he's telling the truth? Do you think they're worth *that*
much?"

We walked upriver, toward Mr. Bagley's place. There was
no point in walking single file, mother said; we should fan out
a bit. She told my brother to move up the embankment, where
the weeds were like a golden carpet. I moved even farther
away from the river, and we began walking more slowly, looking down around our feet. I was amazed at the color of the
grasses and of the sticks and the willows around me. I seemed
to notice every growing thing, and also the small holes in the
ground made by rabbits or snakes or ground squirrels. I was
excited by looking at these ordinary things. There were
striped red sticks on the ground, and yellow leaves, and red
leaves with brown spots, and tapered leaves with a small crease
down the center. There was a bit of newspaper and a few
pages out of a book. Someone had left a tire; grass was growing in the center of it, contained and green. We passed by a
place where cars could drive down to the edge of the river.
Fire pits had been made and the blackened rocks left in circles.
There was a picnic bench and, beside it, a strange metal object.
I lifted the piece of metal, like a sword, and tapped James.

"Put that down," Mom said. "You'll get soot on his
pants."

We walked on and kept looking farther from the river.
The bank grew wider. Every once in a while, I looked over at
my mother, who appeared beautiful to me in the sunlight, her

long curly hair falling alongside her face as she looked down at
the ground. We made circles and retraced our steps. We
walked back and forth between the edge of Lawrence Bagley's
back lawn and the river bank, passing under the shade of cottonwood trees that grew tall. We spotted Mr. Bagley once,
walking around his property, searching the fields that lay just
next to his house.

We had gone back and forth to the river, through the
trees, maybe four times, changing our paths slightly each time,
when James called to us. He'd found the chinchillas!

They were huddled down in the grass. Four of them were
grouped together, another two were off by themselves, hidden by a bush. The last pair wasn't far from the others, sitting
bunched up at the base of a cottonwood. We formed a small
circle around them, one group at a time. My mother held out
her arms in a half-circle and knelt down. They had been tamed
by their lives in the pens and were no more difficult to catch
than our own rabbits when we let them loose on the lawn.
Mom made a kind of sack out of her coat and we carried them
like they were small apples we'd gathered, only they were
warm and they wiggled against the fabric.

"Thank heavens," Mr. Bagley said when we delivered
them, and watched as he put them back in the wire cages with
the wooden floors. He looked at all of us as if to say "Sorry for
all the trouble." I stared back at him. Did he know he'd been
wrong in accusing us?

Once a year, year after year, on or about the Fourth of July,
my family left our small world by the lake, populated by chinchillas, the Tavetians, the Harlines with their fourteen children, and abandoning all our normal routines, we took our
vacation. We loaded up our Buick and headed south for Arizona. The trips were more like pilgrimages than vacations
since our destination, which never varied, was my grandmother's house in Snowflake, a town in north-central Arizona
not far from the Painted Desert and the Petrified Forest,

where it was hot and dry in the summer and cold and dry in the winter. My great-grandfather Flake had settled the town. It was named after him and an apostle of the church, Erastus Snow.

Snowflake is still full of Flakes and Snows, Hatches and Shumways, Hunts, Turleys, and Crandalls, descendants of the families who settled there originally. For a while just after the war, the town seemed to be dying. People were moving away. Then a paper mill was built and boosted the economy. But it came too late for my father, who'd already left and made his way up to Utah. Still, duty called him home for a visit every Fourth of July.

The route we followed to get to Snowflake each year took us past the Big Rock Candy Mountain, through Bryce and Zion canyons, into Kanab, over the Kiabab Pass, and across the Colorado River to Flagstaff.

Each year when we came to the Colorado River, my father stopped the car just before the bridge. Everyone got out and began looking for a rock, the bigger the better. Then we walked single file out to the middle of the bridge and looked over the railing, down, down a terrifying distance to the canyon bottom where the river ran. Striations of sediment gave the river a multicolored look—red, brown, yellow, green, the colors lying one next to the other. The river seemed thick and sluggish with the burden of its colors. You could imagine it not moving at all.

There was always a wind on the bridge above the deep gorge, and no matter how hard I clung to the railing, safe behind the barrier, I felt precarious. What were we doing up here, on the brink of disaster? No manmade structure seemed safe enough to allow us to be standing where we were, up in the air, on a narrow bridge straddling the deep canyon. I felt dizzy when I looked down. I preferred looking straight out at the great yawning gorge carved by what looked from this angle like a puny sort of river.

As we stood there, the wind flapped my mother's dress

against her pale thin legs. My father's dark hair was lifted into ice-cream-cone curlicues. His glasses glinted in the sun. His shirt fluttered. We all peered down over the railing. Inevitably, each year one of my older brothers snuck up behind my mother and gave her a gentle, playful shove while she pretended to get angry and clung to the railing. "That's not funny," she'd yell. "Cut it out."

And then eventually we'd do the thing we'd come to do, and one by one we let our rocks drop and measured the time it took falling things to land.

My great-grandfather Flake was a polygamist. He had two wives, Lucy and Prudence, who lived with their children in adjoining houses, built of the same salmon-colored brick, and facing the main street of Snowflake. He was an outstanding man, the pillar of the community, patriarch, sheriff, church leader, and widely respected by saints and gentiles alike. He was reputed to be a peacemaker and was often called upon to settle differences. It was said that he didn't carry a gun, but he'd been known to stop criminals with a rock thrown with uncanny accuracy at a terrifying speed. When polygamy was outlawed in the 1890s, men like my grandfather were caught in a bind. What could they do? Choose between wives, abandoning parts of their families? Risk imprisonment and financial doom? Some polygamists in Snowflake took their wives and children and fled to Mexico, where apparently nobody cared too much what went on. Others were sentenced by courts to prison terms for refusing to give up wives. William Flake spent six months in the territorial prison in Yuma, Arizona, where he found the conditions so terrible that he set about petitioning for reforms. He was disgusted by the filth in which the men were expected to live and by the tainted meat they were served. The meat wasn't fit for animals to consume, he wrote to the governor, who happened to be a friend. Reforms were instituted in the prison as a result of his stay. When he was released, he went back to his two wives and his many children and the brick houses facing the wide main street of Snowflake. He opened a dry goods store, and he hauled freight, from Snowflake to Fort Apache and Flagstaff. Later, he served as a state legislator. While he preceded his two wives in death, it didn't come for him too early. There's a picture of him on a horse at the age of ninety-three. With him is his old white bulldog, who followed him everywhere.

Sometimes, on the road to Snowflake, when we were driving along steep mountain roads, my father would say, "Let's move over to the edge and have a closer look." Then he would take us to the brink. He brought the car so close to the edge of the road that, from where we sat, huddled in the backseat, it seemed possible we would go over the cliff.

"Stop it!" Mom would yell. "Stop being so foolish, Arlo."

"You think we're a little close? Naw, we've got plenty of room."

"Don't! Don't even pretend!"

"The trick is not to go too far. You've got to know just how close to that edge you can bring the tire. Of course, sometimes you miscalculate a little."

"Stop this right now!" she'd yell. "What do you think you're doing?"

"She gets kind of excited, doesn't she?" my father would say to us, looking over his shoulder. He grinned at us and raised his eyebrows. He expected us to be his co-conspirators.

What were we thinking of, the children in the backseat, when he drove to the edge like this? I try to remember. I know I was frightened, but in a thrilled sort of way. I remember us laughing, as though we were on the roller coaster at Lagoon, the amusement park back home. I remember feeling safe, sure that Dad wouldn't ever kill us. I gave him powers of control that, now that I think back on it, I know he didn't have. It occurs to me that we were simply lucky.

I know that once, at least, the tire caught the lip of the

road, and his face whitened because he had gone too far, played the game too rambunctiously, and he'd almost driven us over a cliff. But something enabled him to bring us back. Somehow, he corrected things in time. Afterwards, he and Mom didn't speak for miles, and when she finally said something, it was to curse him as a fool, a jackass, the stupidest man alive; and he was so frightened and sorry, he took it from her, let her say things to him we'd never heard her say before.

He was a strong father. He could be severe one moment, and the next he'd be taking you for ice cream and letting you ride down the road on the hood of the truck. There were parts to him I've never understood: how he could be so tender to people, the kindest man in the world when it came to helping somebody in need, a neighbor or even a stranger, and yet have a hardness, a resolute opacity, when he wished to affect it.

I remember once he had a money-making scheme. He decided to breed boxers for profit. When he learned that any pure white dogs born in a litter had to be destroyed or else none of the other pups could be registered with the Kennel Club, he seemed to have no difficulty drowning the albinos. In the first litter there were two white puppies. He let them live a few days, just long enough for them to have a presence in our lives, and then one day he filled up a metal tub with water, set it in the breezeway, took the pups from their mother, and held them under the water until they didn't move anymore.

My father once bought two and a half acres of land up on the bench in the foothills above the small town of Layton. His intention was to build a grand house there. It would have a swimming pool. The house would sit very high above the fertile valley. What a view we'd have! The sunsets over the Great Salt Lake would be ours. From big bay windows facing the lake, we would be able to see the open-pit copper mine gouged in the side of the Oquirrh Mountains opposite us, over a mile wide at the top. Animals previously ruled out by lack of space would now be kept—horses, sheep, and pigs. We would roam the canyons above our property as though we were pioneers and explorers. But the house was never built. For several years we made Saturday pilgrimages to our property in Layton, riding in a small homemade wooden trailer attached to the truck. We cleared rocks from the sloping land. We cut back oak brush and we leveled sage. We worked steadily and hard, following Dad's instructions. We imagined all this time what it would be like to live so much further from a town, to have new neighbors, to go to a new ward, to meet our bishop, to have a swimming pool, and to make friends with local kids and feel the whole vast landscape was ours. We worked on this land as if preparing the way for the future, but it never came that way. At some point, we knew we would never live there on that land, that we'd been preparing for something that would never happen. And quietly, without any fuss at all, we abandoned this plan. I have since learned that this is how most disappointment comes—gradually, very gradually, so you can stand it.

When Leon and I first married, I felt an incredible freedom. I was seventeen years old and suddenly had a house of my own! One that I could fill with things I liked. I had no one's schedule to meet but my own. I felt Leon and I were inventing life anew, from the furniture we chose to the food we ate to the TV programs we watched.

He proposed to me on a cold and clear day in the early part of winter, while we were horseback-riding in the hills above town. We had just come up a steep dirt road and broken out onto the bench, and the horses were heaving with the effort of the climb, when he said, "Let's rest a minute," and got down off his horse.

I got down, too, and sat beside him on a rock. We were high up in the foothills, with a view of the whole tilting valley and the lake below us. Suddenly he knelt in the thin crusty snow at my feet and, taking out a small velvet box, handed it to me with gloved hands and asked me to be his wife. I didn't even think. I just said, "Sure."

We went home and told my parents, who were sitting downstairs watching TV.

"What do you want to do this for so young?" Dad said. "You're not even out of high school."

Leon spoke up first. "We're in love," he said.

"Well, I think it's just great," Mom said.

Dad looked at her quizzically. "You do?"

"Yes, I do. I think they make a great couple."

"You couldn't hold off awhile?" Dad said.

"No," I said. "We couldn't."

"I'm not sure you've got both oars in the water, gal," he said. "Marriage isn't what you think."

I didn't know what he meant, because I certainly did have an idea about what it would be like—and what if I was wrong?

"Your dipstick might not quite reach the oil on this one," he added. "You get what I'm saying?"

Leon said, "We're sure about this, sir."

"No kidding?" my father said.

We got engaged at Christmastime during my senior year, and I remember showing off my ring in typing class, and the teacher staring at it with sort of an odd look of disapproval. I thought she was envious because she was young and unmarried, but she could have been thinking, What a fool. I felt so sure of things then. Leon was six years older than me. He'd already established himself, become a lot of what he was always going to be—a mechanic, a horsebreeder, a guy who looked for good times. So why shouldn't we get married? What was there to wait for? We weren't working toward anything. We didn't have anything to finish. We only saw ourselves together, having fun. The thing is, it didn't work out that way; and here I am, stuck with only this memory of Leon standing at a distance from me in a field of hay on a day when it's about to rain, looking at his back while he's pissing on pale silver weeds that have been blown flat by the wind.

Before Leon left me, we used to spend every Sunday with his parents, in their house across from the church in a town on the edge of the lake. We lived in Willard; his parents lived in Perry, just a little to the north of us. What makes Willard different from Perry is a big factory, located at the west edge of town, where they process pie cherries and ship them all over the world. His father was a welder who worked at the steel mill most of his life. His mother taught fourth grade for thirty-eight years, until her retirement. Leon's father and his two uncles lived in houses next to one another. These three brothers, although each quite different from the other, had a bond of closeness that seemed unshakable, unbreakable, eternal. When the youngest brother went to Libya to work the oil fields, his wife and their small twin boys were taken care of by the remaining brothers as if they were their own wife and children. Entering this family was like becoming part of a large compound, where brothers and their wives, and children who were cousins, and the cousins' children as generations were formed, continued to gather in ever-increasing numbers. Finally Leon's father retired from the steel mill. For a while, he worked in the soft water business, opening up a Culligan store, where, late into the night, Leon worked with him, regenerating softeners and repairing the broken ones. "Hey, Culligan man!" kids would yell at him when they'd see him delivering softeners around town.

Then his father, who had always longed for a farm, quit Culligan and bought eighty acres at the edge of the lake, where he planned to raise cattle and breed Arabian horses. But the snows were heavy that year, and the lake rose in the spring. The next year was even worse. After five years, the water had risen to record highs for the century. All but an acre and a half of his land was under water. Fortunately the house sat near the road, at the edge of the property farthest from the lake, and they were able to stay put, even during the worst of the flooding.

Still, some Sundays when we went down to the farm to visit them, the lake was so high it reached the back lawn. Salt crystals formed along the grass. The apple trees were killed by the briny water. Treetops rose from out of the lake, and the maroon tips of tamarack willows. The barn of a neighboring farm was soon swallowed by water so that it seemed to be a floating houseboat of some kind. A rowboat turned up from somewhere—it just seemed to be there one Sunday, caught in the salty mud at the edge of the lake, and no one knew where it came from.

Leon and I used boards for paddles and rowed out to the barn one day. It was isolated and spooky circling it, a thing completely out of place. We peered in the windows of the hayloft, which normally would be way above our heads. I can't tell you how quiet that barn was, sitting out in the lake. It was in ruins, yet there was something wonderful about it having succumbed to the unstoppable waters.

Years have passed since I worked at the bowling alley and visited my in-laws at the edge of the lake every Sunday. During those days, I was always trying to make something out of nothing. A good marriage out of a bad one. Meals out of whatever was in the cupboard. A pleasure-class horse out of a mare whose legs were too short, or a designer bathrobe out of three towels sewn together.

But mostly, I was just trying to make my husband stay with me. Did I love him so much? Or did we just acquire the habit of each other while I was still a teenager and ready to be set loose on the world with a man? I don't know. Once, when my friend Jolene asked me that question—"Did you love him"—I said, "I think so," and she said, "Listen, if you have to think about it, maybe you didn't."

The day he left is the day when the biggest change in my

life occurred. That much I know. Life fell into Before and
After. Before Leon left me, and after. Before I left the only
place I'd ever known in my life, and after. From that moment
it became clearer to me how things might work as opposed to
how they always had. I saw there were more choices in the
world than I had imagined. Everything opened up when I left
home; and yet, everything was at once lost. And it all started
with him saying, so simply it's ridiculous, "I want out."

3

THE MORNING AFTER Leon left, I took the main
road out of town, and with only one backward glance,
set out for Los Angeles. By nine o'clock I was already south of
Salt Lake City and making good time. The sun was trying to
shine through the dense clouds, and an eerie yellow light hung
over the Great Salt Lake. And then gradually the sky lowered
as clouds settled thickly over the lake; everything darkened,
and it began to snow just as I rounded the point of the mountain and passed the state prison.

It snowed heavily. Snow built up on the roads until they
were white paths stretching out in front of me. I worried about
the trailer, which wasn't tracking too well. In Nephi I pulled
over for some coffee, and as I drove slowly along the city
streets I saw something that saddened me. It was an old white
house that looked a lot like a place Leon and I once bought.

We had seen the house listed in the paper. It was advertised as the PERFECT STARTER HOME. It cost only nineteen thousand, so we got his father to co-sign a loan and managed to
paint a pretty financial picture for the two of us so the bank
would give us the money.

To somebody else, it might not have looked liked much, a
two-bedroom frame house that was built in the twenties. But it
had trees that were as old as the house, and I think we fell in

love with those trees as much as anything, and with the garden
that looked like only older gardens can, a place were secrets
had accumulated and were held in dusky and still suspension,
as if some person were going to come back to reveal them.
The more time I spent in that garden, the more I felt its en-
veloping calm, the more it seemed I could make anything
grow in that soil—rhubarb, sunflowers, rows of shiny chard.
There was a bit of junk around, old propane tanks and abandoned equipment, which we always planned on getting rid of.
But somehow we didn't before a fire caused by a faulty wire
on the TV set burned the place down. Looking at the house in
Nephi, I got to thinking about that freak fire, and other things,
good and bad, that had happened to us over all our years
together.

All morning and into the afternoon it snowed. Driving
through the storm, I could see only a small distance around
me. Sometimes black-and-white magpies flew down out of the
clouds and across the fields, where a golden stubble of winter
wheat pushed through the snow and illuminated the surface so
that from a little distance, it looked as if an aura of warm light
floated above the icy surface of the land, a hovering golden
glow. I couldn't see beyond the fields. A veil of gray mist and
falling snow surrounded me. I moved as if enveloped by a
small clear space in the weather, a hole of visibility in which I
was the central figure. As I moved, so did the area of visibility.
My seeing was what created the space in the storm, pushing
out the perimeter; and as I moved, the boundaries moved with
me, and new objects emerged out of the white edge of the
storm. A farmhouse came into sight and grew dark and definite in form. Then I passed by it and saw it sinking into the
storm again. Trees emerged and dissolved in the same way, as
did horses in the fields, and cows, and telephone lines. I began
to feel dreamy drifting through things this way, watching a
softly cocooned world of ever-changing boundaries. I started
to think, If I weren't here to see this, would these areas of

visibility exist at all, or would it all just be one big white storm, unbroken in its blanketing effect?

Sometimes, especially recently, it had seemed as if I had slipped through normal thinking into some kind of state of hyperawareness. For instance, an ordinary word suddenly would seem thoroughly strange to me—a word I used all the time, like "kind" or "bad" or "strong." Suddenly a word like this seemed like a completely foreign thing in my mind, and I wondered, Is this really a word, and can it mean what I think it does? I'd start to mull it over, turning it in my mind—kind kind kind—trying to make it an ordinary and meaningful thing again, trying to reattach it to something real in the world. It didn't happen often, this sort of thing, but occasionally a crack like this opened up. I didn't know what this was; I wouldn't know what to call it. But I felt it again, drifting through the snowstorm.

He was standing near the off ramp for Fillmore, a lone figure with his thumb stuck out. I saw him and tried to brake, but the tires locked on the snow-packed road and I felt the truck begin to slide. I took my foot off the brake and began to pump the pedal. I could feel the weight of the trailer, pushing from behind, and I thought, If it doesn't slow down soon, it's going to jackknife. But then I felt the trailer gently come into line, and I came to a stop very gradually.

The hitchhiker had to run down the road to catch up with me. He stood at the window, a plume of breath coming from his mouth. I must have looked scared because he was staring at me with an odd look on his face, and he didn't move. He just stood looking in the window at me. He wasn't dressed right for the weather. He looked half-frozen, a thin, wiry man, maybe a little older than me, blue from the cold. He had a black stubble of beard, and when his lips parted, I saw his teeth were bad—very bad.

"What's wrong?" he said.

"Trying to stop for you I almost blew it." I jerked my head

backwards, in the direction of the trailer. "The horse trailer. It almost jackknifed."

He grinned at me foolishly, as if I'd said something funny.

"I still feel a little shaky," I added. "That's all I needed was to wreck. Are you going to get in or what?" He looked a little frightened himself—or, I should say, startled.

He climbed into the truck. He carried a worn duffel bag, which he put down by his feet. His shoes looked like Sunday shoes to me, thin and fancy. They must have felt like blocks of ice on his feet. Snow was wedged around the soles and packed into the laces. I turned up the heat a little as I pulled back out into traffic. He wore a cap, which he took off and shook slightly, letting the wetness fall onto the floor.

"Where are you headed?" he asked.

"Los Angeles."

"Hey." He chuckled. "I can't believe my luck. That's where I'm going. If you could give me a ride all the way, I'd be glad to help with the driving."

"I don't think you'd better drive."

"Why not?"

"Unless you're used to pulling a trailer it can be tricky. You're not used to it, are you?"

"Well, no."

"That's what I mean. But don't worry about it. I'll give you a ride all the way. What's your name?"

"Duluth Wing."

"Duluth Wing? Now where do you get a name like that?"

"The same place where you get every other name. Somebody dreams it up in their head. In this case, it was my mother's idea. She named me after the town where she was born in Minnesota."

"Verna," I said, "Verna Fields," and I shook his hand.

"Damn," he said, "it's cold around here. I been lookin' for a ride for hours, standing out there in that shit."

"Well, it looks like you finally got one."

He laughed. "Nice. Very nice." He seemed nervous to

me, but he unzipped his jacket and took it off, as if he'd finally decided to make himself at home, although I couldn't imagine that he'd warmed up yet.

"Are you taking horses to Los Angeles?"

"No, I'm not."

"There aren't any horses in the trailer?"

"No."

"You're just taking the trailer?"

"Yes. I need it to haul my worldly goods," I said, and laughed, thinking of all the junk back there. "Really, there's just a bunch of stuff in there. I needed a way to get it all down to Los Angeles. I'll probably sell the trailer once I get settled there."

"It sounds like you're moving."

"I'm moving," I said. "That's for sure."

"I meant permanently," he said.

"That's what *I* meant, too."

We fell silent. I waited for the shape of a conversation to define itself, but nothing came out. I hadn't really meant to stop for him. I just did. I stopped before I thought about it. Now I was thinking about it, and I wondered if I should have. Strangers aren't the easiest company, although you can get lucky and run into somebody who helps you pass the time in a good way. I couldn't tell about him. I wasn't sure about Duluth Wing, whether I ought to have stopped for him or not.

Finally he said, "Funny how it gets dark so early here in the afternoon."

"I know. Winter light. It makes it seem like a very short day."

"It does."

"When it gets dark so early, it seems like it's time to eat, but I'm never very hungry that early, you know. Still, when it gets dark, I think, Time to eat. Right now, in fact, I'm thinking, Time to eat."

I lit a cigarette. "Where do you live?"

"L.A.," Duluth said.

The way he said it—"Elay"—made it sound foreign, like a very exotic location, a city in a distant land, some place where Arabs lived. Elay . . . Allayh . . . Hilayh. A biblical place.

"What are you doing here in Utah?"

He looked uncomfortable, as if I'd asked him something he didn't want to answer.

"My wife," he said. "I mean, my ex-wife . . . She got remarried and moved here. I came to see my daughter."

We didn't talk for a while after that. I went back to thinking my own thoughts. The conversation with Leon kept coming back to me. In particular, I remembered how he had said it might have made some difference if we'd kept going to church, as if we needed something to act as the glue in our lives, something other than ourselves to believe in. He was so afraid of being an outsider that he'd rather pretend he was something he wasn't than face up to his difference. There were good times when we were just together and simply who we were and we didn't need anything else—fishing and camping trips, times with the horses. Where was this religion he needed so much then? I saw all his sporting goods piled up on the floor and him preparing to leave and I thought, None of that is mine now.

"Are you planning on stopping somewhere for the night?" Duluth asked suddenly.

"No," I said. "I thought I'd just drive straight through to Los Angeles."

"That's good."

"Why?"

"Because I don't have enough money on me for a motel room." He looked away from me when he said this.

At Parowan, we pulled off the freeway and stopped at a Dairy Freeze. I ordered a cheeseburger and a malt. He had a hamburger and asked for water in a large cup. I saw him counting out change, coin by coin, to come up with the price of a burger. I ask him if he wanted something to drink besides water and held out a dollar bill.

"No, I don't want to borrow nothing."

"Take it," I said, and held it out again. He shoved my hand away—a little roughly, I thought.

It was dusk. While we ate, we sat in the truck. The storm had eased up, and I could see some brown cows standing in a field across from the Dairy Freeze.

"Have you ever been to L.A. before?" Duluth asked.

"No," I said, turning to look at him, "I haven't. I'm looking forward to it, though—especially thinking about the weather."

I looked back at the cows and the tips of some Mormon poplars swaying in the wind. "My parents went to L.A. once," I said.

"How'd they like it?"

"Well, not too good."

I told him about the time my aunt and uncle Heber and LaRue, who lived in Los Angeles, asked my parents to come visit them. They finally convinced them to do it one winter, when the weather in Utah was terrible and my mother was happy to get out of the cold, which froze up locks on car doors, made the sidewalks treacherous, and generally caused them to feel confined and worried. My father doesn't like to travel, and it took a lot of coaxing to get him on the plane. Until the last minute he kept trying to cancel. He'd flown only once before in his life; it was an uncertain experience at best. But eventually they boarded a plane in Salt Lake City. Heber and LaRue were there to meet them at Los Angeles International Airport—a terrifyingly large place, my father said, with confusing signs, wild drivers, and unimaginably large crowds. "I could never drive in that place," my mother said later. My father added, "You wouldn't have time to think on those freeways."

Apparently things went just fine during the first half of their visit. Heber and LaRue seemed happy to see them. They played cards, ate lots of good food, and simply sat out in the

California sunshine, which seemed like a blessing to them. In no time they'd met a few people at church, attended a couple of social events. All was going well. It was nice to just relax and be out of the cold weather for a few weeks. The difficulties began when my father decided Heber's trees in the backyard needed trimming. They would do much better, he said, if they were cut back. Heber told him he didn't want them cut back, but my father kept at him about it. Soon, it wasn't only the trees that needed trimming but a century plant and the rosebushes. "I like them the way they are," Heber said. "I don't want them pruned." Back and forth it went until one day, while Heber was out doing errands, my father took some clippers and cut back all the plants. When he saw what my father had done, Heber was furious. LaRue, who didn't mince words, was also upset and felt that my parents should leave, even though their original plans called for them to stay another week. Heber and LaRue's nerves were frayed by their visit.

Heber called them into the kitchen the following morning and said he and LaRue felt it was perhaps better if they left. My father felt embarrassed and more than a little hurt, but he and my mother, who had really begun to long for home anyway, said, "Fine, we'll see if we can't get a flight out tomorrow."

"How about this afternoon?" Heber said.

But there were no flights from Los Angeles to Salt Lake City available that afternoon, so my parents were obliged to stay until the following day, and to forget their problems they decided to go out for pizza. They tried to act normal, as though it didn't matter that Heber and LaRue had asked them to leave. It was their last evening in California, and my parents hoped to make it festive. They were still on vacation, and they wanted to have a good time. They sat on benches at the pizza parlor—my father next to Heber, my mom by LaRue. Perhaps as a way of raising his spirits by horsing around, my father bumped his brother slightly with his hips. When there wasn't any reaction, he moved sideways again and bumped Heber lightly once more. Heber suddenly turned on him, furious, and yelled, "What do you think I am—a queer?" It was too much. My father couldn't understand this coming from his eighty-year-old brother. In some way, Heber really seemed to think my father was making a pass at him!

I looked at Duluth, who was just finishing off his burger. "After that, whenever people mentioned California to him, my father shook his head, as if to say, 'You can have it!' He still feels that way."

Duluth laughed. "Can you imagine, thinking he was queer," he said.

"Well, you have to know my dad."

While I was talking, a man had come up behind the cows in the field, and he was driving them toward a gate near a tree-lined lane. On a crude sign at the entrance to the lane was written: RABBITS FOR FUN FOOD FUR PROFIT.

"How was your hamburger?" I asked Duluth.

"Fine," he said. "Just what I wanted. I'm a happy man," he added, and smiled, showing his dark teeth.

Parowan wasn't much of a place. I noticed that a lot of stores were closed up, failed business ventures. A yarn shop, a beauty parlor, even the Sears catalog store had gone bust. All afternoon we'd passed small towns and farms that were unkempt and shabby looking. Nothing appeared to be completed if it was new, or maintained if it was old. Fences were patched with different-colored boards and tied together with twine and wire. Cars looked old even if they were newer models, because they hadn't been washed for so long. The older houses needed work; the newer ones looked as if the owners had run out of money before they could complete their plans. These were usually new brick homes with treeless yards and dirt driveways and big picture windows with the manufacturer's stickers still attached to the glass. Small cement mixers stood abandoned near little pyramids of gravel. Things were broken all over the landscape. Old cars clung to weedy embankments. Tractors stood idle in fields.

"You never see anybody out working around these farms, do you?" Duluth said.

I said, "Well, it *is* winter, you know." But it was true; for miles we passed farm after farm without seeing a sign of life. Except once in a while, a baby in a diaper stood at a window, or a child riding his tricycle over frozen ground in the faltering light looked up to watch us pass.

When we finished eating, I decided to take a shortcut and turned onto a secondary road that ran west through hills made of red dirt. It was now almost dark. I began singing a Patsy Cline song, "Today, Tomorrow, and Forever". Then I sang my favorite song, "I Fall to Pieces."

When I finished, Duluth said, "You've got a real good voice."

"I like Patsy Cline. Those are her songs, you know. And nobody can sing them like she could."

"I don't know anybody who sings just for the pleasure of it."

"Maybe they're afraid they're not singing good enough," I said.

"Singing seems like one of the oldest, most natural activities of man," he said. "So, you know what that means?"

"No, what does that mean?"

"If we've become afraid of singing for fear of making fools of ourselves, we've become estranged creatures indeed, haven't we?"

I didn't know what to say to this. I was struck by the way he said "estranged creatures indeed."

"Do you sing?"

"No," he said. "I've become one of the estranged creatures myself."

We hadn't driven far on the two-lane road when deer began showing up in the headlights. Whole herds were on the move in the night. The snow must have forced them down into low-lying areas. Dozens of them stood by the roadside and bounded across the road ahead of us.

"Deer," I said, and slowed down.

Duluth Wing sat forward and peered out the windshield. "My God," he said, "there are dozens of them."

The headlights blinded the animals, and they froze into positions where they stared full-force at us, as if the light made them unable to move. Their eyes appeared red, or sometimes incandescent. Even though I had slowed to ten miles an hour, it felt dangerous to be moving at all, so fast did the deer dart out onto the road. Adding to the ghostliness of the deer, appearing as they did so suddenly in the lights of the truck, was the layer of snow on the ground, which made it seem as though the animals were emerging and disappearing out of nothingness, a pale, bottomless space.

I stopped the truck. "There's no point in going on tonight," I said. "It's too dangerous. If we keep going like this, we're going to kill one of these deer. I didn't know they'd be here. I didn't expect this. I should've just stayed on the freeway."

There was a little turnout, not too muddy, where I could park. I got out and went around to the trailer and returned in a few minutes with two thick blankets and a pillow, which I gave to Duluth. I told him I'd sleep in the trailer, where I had a down-filled bag to keep me warm. He looked at me, hesitant, as if he were worried he might freeze to death during the night; but I knew he wouldn't even feel the cold under those blankets, which included one my grandmother in Snowflake had made. It was so heavy it felt as if you were sleeping under one of those metal aprons they put on you in dentist offices to keep X rays from entering your body.

"See you in the morning," I said.

I had swept the horse trailer out before leaving home, so the wooden floor was clean, but the smell of hay and horses was still strong. I opened the side door near the feed boxes and looked out at the night. The stars were very beautiful and filled me with an intensity of feeling that was nearly religious. I moved all the boxes to one side so I would have a place on the floor to sleep. After a while I closed the door and got into my sleeping bag. I remembered there were candles in a box, found them, and lit one so I'd have light for a little while. The candlelight inside the trailer was as beautiful to me as the stars had been.

I thought of Leon.

I saw him standing in his parents' backyard, with the lake to his back. He was petting their dog, Clancy, a redbone hound that was always kept tethered by a long leash to a wire clothesline that ran overhead from one end of the yard to the other. He knelt over the dog and it licked his face. When he stood up and walked away, the hound ran after him, and the chain, attached to the clothesline, made a sound of metal singing against metal. Even though the dog belonged to his parents, it was devoted to Leon. He was good with animals. He seemed effortlessly to gain their affection and trust. As he walked, he raised his hand and the dog leaped happily into the air after it. He continued raising his hand like that, walking along, causing the dog to jump beautifully, happily into the air.

Gradually I felt sleepy and blew the candle out. Outside, the deer were still moving, picking their way across the snow-encrusted earth, passing through the landscape of cedar and sage. I could hear them stepping quietly, like people stirring in another room.

I wasn't the first person in my family to fall in love with Leon. He was my sister's boyfriend first. I was thirteen years old when Janice and Leon began dating. The first car I ever drove was Leon's black Mercury. He took me on a ride one day and let me sit on the seat between his legs and steer the car down a deserted road that ran out past Thiokol and the Golden Spike monument.

"Keep her goin' straight," he said, and then he took his hands off the wheel and I knew I was in control. I knew I had the power to steer that thing anywhere. I drove halfway to the turnoff for Promontory Point and back again. I felt as if I controlled the world. That was my first driving lesson, sitting between Leon's legs, riding in that Mercury down a straight road with nothing but salt brush and cows around us, and I thought, This has got to be one of the best things in life, going this fast and controlling it.

"That's enough," Janice finally said, meaning she was getting bored with me at the wheel. "She's had enough time now. Make her stop."

In those days, I shared a room with Janice, who didn't like my sloppiness. She made a line down the center of our room, dividing it with a string tied to a bureau drawer and the knob on the closet door, and told me not to cross it. Just to get to my side of the room I had to duck under the string.

"You're a slob," she said. "Just stay on your side."

Even when I tried to make improvements, I couldn't ever satisfy Janice. We were so different. I think I was an embarrassment to her. She didn't like horses or the smell I brought to the room when I'd been out riding. She thought I might try to develop more refinements, take better care of myself, like she herself did. She was a good student, four years ahead of me, popular, a success in every way, whereas I was always getting into trouble for something. I never wanted to be the center of church youth activities like she did. Also, there was the simple fact of our ages that separated us, four years that were difficult to cross.

However, I think her shunning me built up a resentment that surprised even me by its outcome.

One day I found her yearbook in the closet. Leon, who was almost as popular as she was, was listed in the index as appearing on eleven different pages—as a member of sports teams, the student council, the ski club, Junior Boosters, the debate squad—and he was also pictured in his cap and gown, clean-cut and square looking. There was even a picture of him and Janice in the back of the yearbook, in the section reserved for paid advertisements from local merchants. They were sitting in a booth at Uncle Leo's Noodle Parlor, smiling and looking up at Uncle Leo, who was handing them plates of jumbo fried shrimp.

Looking at the pictures of Leon, I got an idea. I put on red lipstick and I kissed every picture of him in the yearbook. Eleven perfect crimson lip prints covered his face. Then I took a pen and wrote on the bottom of every pair of Janice's shoes, "I love Leon."

I got into a lot of trouble for it. Janice claimed her year-book was ruined—"totally ruined," she said. "A complete mess. How am I ever going to show it to anybody again? And where am I ever going to get all those signatures again? How can I replace what people wrote to me?"

A little while after that, Janice met a returned missionary named Stan Henderson, and she and Leon broke up. Stan Henderson and Janice got married at Christmastime, with me as one of the thirteen attendants, all of whom wore red velvet dresses with white marabou trim. They moved to Provo, where Stan was going to school. Leon just faded away. I didn't see him again for almost four years, until one night when I went to a Mutual dance for church youth in Farr West and he came up to me and started talking, telling me things he'd been doing, which included working at Marler Tire Company, driving a truck for a while, and roping with some guys from Plain City.

Not long after that, he came to visit me at the house. It was the summer between my junior and senior years. I was the same age then that he'd been when he and Janice were going together. My mother said, "I don't believe it," when I told her Leon was coming over. My dad said, "Just like a bad penny, keeps turning up."

The day he came to visit me I waited for him outside. It was a hot day, and I was wearing shorts. We sat on the porch, looking out toward the lake. Seagulls were wheeling around in the sky like pieces of blowing paper. He talked about his mom and dad, and his brother, Norville, who was fighting forest fires in Idaho. He smelled like cigarettes, and I said, "Have you started smoking?" and he grinned and answered, "On occasion." After a while I got up to go into the house to get us some Cokes and he stopped me and said, "This is the part on a girl I like. Right here." And he put his hand on me to show what he meant. The part he liked was where my shorts let a little of my rear show, where it curved over and met the back of my thighs. He kept his hand there for a moment, looking up at me, and then he traced a finger along that crease, and I shuddered from wanting what I thought he was offering me.

I was seventeen. He was twenty-three, and from then on we went together. My dad said, "You're a fool to take your sister's hand-me-downs in boyfriends." But that's exactly what I did.

Years later, I thought about what I'd done to Janice's yearbook, and how I'd kissed all those pictures of his face with lipstick and written "I love Leon" in blue ink on the bottom of her shoes. I wondered, Does life prefigure itself like that? Is the future, in some shape or another, already in us, leaking out in unreadable script, long before it arrives?

In the morning I awoke and stayed in the sleeping bag awhile because it was too cold to get up. A little light came in through the crack between the doors of the trailer. I folded my hands behind my head and looked up at the shaft of light. I remembered what had happened with Leon, how he had simply walked out, and I felt empty, as if he had just then—at that particular moment—left me all over again. I remembered closing the door on the apartment where we'd lived, how the broken screen had fallen closed with a thwwack. This morning I had the sense that I had closed the door on something else. I had set myself on a course now, which made me feel both excited and nervous, lost and free, happy and sad, as if things were going to come in pairs of opposites from now on.

I got out of the sleeping bag and put my boots on. They were cold and took the warmth out of me quickly. It was still very early. A low mist, like vaporous clouds, had descended, but it wasn't snowing. All around the trailer were the small cloven prints of deer hooves. I followed them into the brush and squatted down to relieve myself. The warm urine burned a hole in the snow.

Sometimes in the morning when Leon awakened before me I heard him in the living room, grunting through a series of sit-ups. "Whew," he'd say later, standing at the foot of the bed. "Seventy-eight," he'd say, or "Ninety-three"—always some number just short of what you'd think would be a logical goal, as if he'd given up just before he'd reached it. He'd pat his stomach proudly, and yet the flesh would jiggle. He was a high-school athlete who never outgrew that role in his mind, although his body kept getting larger and larger, until he groaned when he leaned over to pull on his boots. He was never really fat, just large and soft with a roll above his belt. Still, he'd do those sit-ups, pat his stomach, and announce an impressive number, as if he were counting something very important.

I looked up at the ridges, which were pink in the morning light. Damned how things worked out, I thought, and I meant Pinky—how could he go for someone like that, so obvious, so false, with an answer for everything, unable to resist a mirror, a window, any reflective surface? I studied the small bluish berries on a juniper bush next to me, picked one, and crushed it between my fingers just to smell its pungent pulp. Then I went to wake up Duluth, whose foot I could plainly see, sticking out of the blankets and hooked up on the dashboard, his sock touching the windshield.

Duluth Wing wasn't an easy person to fathom, so I hadn't really formed an opinion of him. Still, I felt that for some reason I was taking care of him, seeing that he got delivered where he was going. Sometimes he made me nervous, however. I sensed he was a man with a lot of problems. When I reached the truck, I saw he was still sleeping. I looked through the window at his face. He had deep lines around his mouth and eyes, and even in sleep he looked tired. His hair was thinning. I saw how he'd drooled on the blanket, just like a baby, and when I opened the door of the truck, the noise it made woke him with a start, as if somebody had popped a cap gun next to his ear.

"Hell," he said, sitting up fast. "You scared me!"

"If you have to do anything, you should do it now," I said, "so we can get going. It's miles before we get to a town."

We made good time driving that morning. There wasn't anybody on the road that early, and you could easily have felt you had the world to yourself. Duluth protested when I bought him breakfast in Orderville, but not too loudly or for too long. I decided I liked him better the more I knew him. Over breakfast we talked about our travels, where we had and hadn't been in the world. Duluth had been a lot more places than I had. I'd never been outside a few western states, while he'd visited Hawaii and had lived in Toronto, Canada, once. As we sat and talked, I studied him. There was a sadness in his face. He looked like he needed a break or had had too many bad ones; again I had a sense of him needing someone to help him, and I was glad I'd given him a ride.

Still, there was something about his look that was unpleasant, and I couldn't decide whether this was just a look of defeat or something worse, such as cruelty.

We drove on and came to St. George. The white spire on top of the temple rose up above everything else in town and looked nice against the backdrop of deep red hills. On the very top of the spire, the golden angel Moroni glinted in the sun. On the outskirts of town we saw a big billboard advertising the St. George Hilton. A shapely girl in skimpy clothes was pictured on the billboard.

Duluth looked up at it. "That looks like an ad for women," he said. "Like they got a woman who looks just like that waiting in every room for everybody who checks in."

I laughed. "Don't everybody wish."

"Do you suppose they've got women like that in every room?" he asked. "Just waitin' for you?"

"No, I don't suppose they do."

"Too bad. They sure make it look good."

We drove down the Virgin River Canyon, and then cut through a little corner of Arizona, the Grand Canyon State, and ten minutes later saw the sign that said we were entering Nevada, the Silver State, so that within the space of a half-hour, we'd been in three states. That's the kind of thing kids take notice of, and it delights them.

As soon as we crossed the Nevada state line, we saw a new development, some modern buildings that hardly looked finished, called the Peppermill Casino.

"That's a stupid name for a casino," he said. "It sounds like a loaf of bread. They ought to call it the Silver Slipper or Lucky Jim's—something like that."

"Or Lucky Duluth's," I said. He frowned at me.

"You're probably a whole lot luckier than I am," he said.

"Well, I don't know about that. I sort of figure luck comes in two halves. You've got one half of it inside you, you know, carrying it around like a wish you haven't gotten yet, and the other half is out there, waiting for you to make a match. You know what I mean?"

"No, I don't," he said.

He had no idea what I was talking about, I knew that, and I didn't feel like explaining right then about Bob More, the pilot. So I just said, "It's an idea, that's all, just an idea," and I looked out at the desert, and thought about how I met Bob More, and about how nice it would be if there were some way to see him again one day. I was pretty sure that wouldn't ever happen. I'd never see him again. Bob More was always going to be nothing more than a memory.

4

THIS IS HOW I met Bob More. In the spring of 1972, a plane crashed into the Great Salt Lake. The pilot managed to survive the plunge into the water and somehow freed himself of the wreckage before the plane sank beneath the surface. I know what happened next because I met that pilot later and he told me everything in lasting detail.

It was night when he crashed. The sky was clear, and the pilot could see stars. He was trained in celestial navigation, and from the stars he figured out which direction was east. There wasn't any point in swimming in any other direction. He knew there weren't any farms or ranches or towns, except to the east. To the west, there was only the beginning of the Salt Flats, miles of empty, poisonous earth, and barren hills dotted with ancient caves. To the north lay the Golden Spike, where the railroads met in 1867, and the mini-town of Thiokol, a defense contract installation that came alive only during the day, when hundreds of workers arrived by bus and left the same way, a dry saltpan country surrounded by fences which were monitored electronically. To the south, there was nothing but salt marsh and a sewage facility. But to the east, there were all the small communities that hugged the shores of the lake and which often fell victim to the fluctuating waters— Farr West, Plain City, Pleasant View, Slaterville, Hooper, Clinton, and Willard, where Leon and I lived. It was in this direction that the pilot began swimming.

He was a strong man, just thirty-five years old, but his back had been injured in the crash, and he found it painful to move his arms. After a while he turned on his back and, floating, kicked his legs slowly. It's not hard to float in the Great Salt Lake. In fact, it's impossible to sink, though you can still drown. He thought of his wife and his children, who might even then be waiting for him at the small airport in Elko, where they lived. By now, perhaps, she would realize he was overdue and begin to worry, sensing that something was wrong. The water was cold, and the salt stung his skin. He felt faint and was afraid of losing consciousness, and in order to stay alert he kept trying to picture his wife, forcing himself to focus his thoughts on her.

She often wore a green dress with yellow butterflies on it. In the place where it buttoned in the front, it sometimes dipped between her breasts just enough for him to catch a glimpse of the lacy edge of her undergarments. He never told her this—how when she bent over or turned a certain way, the curve of her white breasts showed far down toward the nipple, how those breasts were cupped in lace, because she was modest and he didn't want her to correct it and she would have, had she known. She would have put a pin there or added another button. Instead, he waited for her to bend over to some task while wearing that dress so he could catch a look of what seemed like the only illicit sight his wife would ever unconsciously afford him—just this edge of lace curving over the tops of her breasts. Now, floating effortlessly in the water whose salt content was almost seven times that of the ocean, he kept his mind on his wife, on the green dress with the yellow butterflies, on the sight of the lace and the dark edge of her nipples, on a colorless mole at her throat, on the thought of her bending to some task.

The pain in his arms increased. It became harder to move his legs. Still, the water bore him up, refused to let him sink. But the salt got into his eyes and his nose, and several times he accidently swallowed a mouthful of the nasty-tasting water. Once he gagged, and a tiny little island of pumpkin-colored vomit appeared, floating beside his head. He found it harder and harder to move his limbs. The water was colder than he'd first thought. He had injured something, somewhere in his lower back, in his spine. Occasionally, he would lift his head and look across the flat black surface of the lake at the tiny lights of Hooper, Farr West, Clinton, Pleasant View, and Willard and think, I'm not getting any closer. The distance never seemed to change. But he knew that the natural movement of the lake was toward the edges, toward shore, and he tried to believe. He tried to have faith that he would make it.

The pain got worse. He was afraid of losing consciousness. He kept trying to call up the image of his wife, to catch her bending to some task and glimpse the white swells of her breasts, to see her in the green dress with yellow butterflies. Above him, the stars held their steady course. Orion had changed position over a peak in the distance, and he noted this small heavenly alteration as a passing of time. And then, miraculously, a shape appeared on the surface of the lake. It was only a log, a thick piece of telephone poling, saturated with creosote and floating high in the water. The pilot managed to lift his injured body onto the log. His cheek rested against its oily surface, his arms fell on either side of it, and he suddenly felt as if he were safe, that it would be all right now to rest.

That night, the night the pilot from Elko crashed into the lake, Leon and I were playing cards with his parents in the room they'd converted into a den, which was at the rear of their farmhouse, facing the lake. The TV was on, as it always was, in the background. We were playing hearts. Leon's mother was winning, and, as usual, she couldn't conceal her happiness. But then, during my deal, Leon's father got up to go to the bathroom and left two of his cards in there near the toilet, so that when we got to the end of that hand, he was short of cards.

"I guess we play it over," I said, laughing at the thought of those cards sitting in the bathroom.

Leon's mom objected. "I can see why you'd want a redeal," she said. "Who wouldn't if they'd taken as many penalty points as you just did?"

"Now, Mary," Leon's father said. "I don't think we have to get upset."

"Well, I don't know how we can count our points up the way it is," Mary snapped.

"It certainly doesn't matter to me," I said.

Sometimes I felt that when Leon's mom played cards, she found an outlet for emotions that were otherwise unacceptable to display. Her aggression could come out, all in the name of fun, and she could make hard, uncompromising drives toward victory for herself, something denied her in a community where being a good woman meant being nice to everybody all the time even when you didn't feel that way.

Leon's dad said, "Let's just let it stand."

"Okay with me," I said.

"I'm sure I don't care," Mrs. Fields sniffed. "I'm sure it doesn't matter." She tried to laugh, but it was a pitiful sort of laughter, the kind no one else can join.

I felt dulled and unhappy. I just wanted to give in to her now, let her have her own way; but I knew there was no chance to do that.

"She takes her cards kind of seriously," Leon's dad said to us.

"Don't make me mad," she answered. Soon they were arguing, in a kidding kind of way. Leon yawned and put down his cards and turned up the sound on the TV. Sports news was on, and he was soon lost to me. I think we were all tired of cards anyway and this was an excuse to quit. The game just fell apart then.

Mrs. Fields got up and left the room. Mr. Fields yelled out, "Sore winner! You were ahead of me, you know," and laughed.

I sat at the card table and stared sideways at the TV. I thought, I'm never playing cards here again.

"How about a Pepsi?" Leon's dad said. "A Dr Pepper? A Sprite? Some ice cream?"

I accepted a Dr Pepper to show my goodwill.

When he left the room, I whispered to Leon, "Let's go home, pleeease."

"I want to see what the the Celtics did," he said.

After he saw what the Celtics did, he wanted to see who Johnny Carson had on. Mrs. Fields marched in like a martyr and set down four glass boats filled with banana splits.

"Banana splits," she announced. "Banana splits for everyone, anybody who feels like it." She was red in the face, and perspiring slightly. I accepted out of politeness, the principle that governed so much of our lives.

What misery there was in small circumstance. Mr. and Mrs. Fields weren't bad people; usually we all got along. I felt sorry for everybody right then, sorry for all the smallness and meanness in the world. What terribly stupid things end up hurting us, I thought. I felt my own life eaten up by smallness right then, without my wanting it to go that way.

I ate my banana split, and then I said I was going outside for a while.

The dead apple trees looked stark at night. It was spring, and spring was my favorite season for the memories of childhood it carried, when snow had melted from the mountains and places opened up to me again, places in the foothills where I liked to ride my horse.

I walked to the back of the house and looked out across the lake. The lawn had turned white. It was already dead from underground water laden with salt, but it was still springy to the step. The neighbor's barn was an odd shape rising up out of the water in the distance. I smelled the sour stench of the surrounding marshland, a kind of eggy, pukey smell which, remarkably, you can get used to and then it isn't so bad, only the first few whiffs.

Out of the darkness, another form beside the barn took shape on the surface of the lake. It was long and it was moving gently, rocking in the water—a canoe? I wondered. But who would be out at night? Maybe it was a dead animal, a cow or a

horse that had been washed into the water and was now floating toward shore, floating easily and riding high in the salty
water. I stood watching the thing get closer to me, and not
until the end of the log touched the dead grass at my feet did I
see that a man was attached to it, draped over its surface like a
big clump of weeds.

The paper the next day ran the headline: WILLARD WOMAN
RESCUES PILOT FROM THE GREAT SALT LAKE. There was a picture of the pilot taken before the accident, and a picture of
myself, standing near the spot where I'd been the night
before. Suddenly I got a lot of attention. I was in the news.
People were calling me up. But I hadn't rescued him; the
paper was wrong, and I kept pointing this out to people. He
had just floated in to me, arriving on his own, like baby Moses
in his bulrush basket.

His name was Bob More and he lived in Elko, Nevada,
with his wife, Ida, and their children, Sam and Susan. His back
was injured in the crash; he also had broken ribs, and a damaged kidney and spleen. I never expected to hear from him.
But I did—several times. He phoned from the hospital while
he was still recuperating to thank me. Our conversation was
stiff, as if we were people who were supposed to have a lot of
important things to say to each other and actually had none. I
thought that was the end of it, the last I'd hear from Bob
More. But a letter came one day, and this is part of what it said.

I used to think there was luck in the world, and I still
do, but now I know it's luck with two halves. This is
what my accident taught me. Another way to think of it
is timing, I guess. You're in the right place at the right
time, and that's luck. But you're only half of it. Whatever, or whoever's waiting for you has to be there, too.
So you only ever carry half of the combination of luck
around with you, waiting for that meeting. And you've
got to be ready, and by that I mean both determined
and receptive. I wanted to live so badly after my crash,

but if you hadn't been there at the lake shore to meet me, I might not have survived. Let's face it, I was pretty far gone, unconscious by then, coming in on a wing and a prayer. I could have slipped off and drowned, face down in the mud. That meeting was the most important in my life, and isn't it funny, we never even spoke a word, let alone a greeting. What I want to tell you is, I think you must have had a will to live as strong as mine was just then so we could make that match.

Leon was jealous of that letter from Bob More. I let him read it so he would see there was nothing in it, but it didn't help. He read it and dropped it on the kitchen counter and said, "What's all this stuff about luck with the two halves? Is he on the make? When he talks about making a match with you, it sounds like he's on the goddamned 'Dating Game.' "

"I think he's just grateful, that's all."

"Maybe he had some kind of religious conversion out there on the lake. Maybe he's gotten wigged out." He went to the fridge and got a beer.

He turned to look at me and lifted his beer can, in what looked like a kind of toast but turned out to be a warning. He shook the can at me. "Just don't be writing him back," he said. "You don't need any pen pals. Let it drop, OK?"

I couldn't tell him how close to the truth Bob More had come, how I had felt my life slipping away from me that night, plummeting fast, and how I had gone outdoors to try and keep it from going by with such a feeling of waste. It seemed I *did* want to live as badly as he did, just in a different way. Maybe there was something to what he said.

I didn't think too much more about Bob More until I got a call one day, about six weeks after the letter came. It was him. He was out at Zito's Supper Club on Highway 89. He wanted to buy me lunch.

I went without telling Leon, not that he was home to tell. I just dressed and left the house without thinking, as if I'd been summoned. I was curious. There was something else as well.

I suppose I did feel that something connected Bob More and myself, some turn of fate that had placed us at the same point on the shore of a lake one night when it mattered; but I might not have thought this way if I hadn't been influenced by his letter. There are possibilities in every circumstance, I saw that. Everything can have an outcome you don't expect and in which you might be involved. Every moment spent passing through life you're putting yourself in the traffic of luck.

He was waiting for me at Zito's, already seated at a table. I thought he looked completely recovered, robust and healthy. He was very polite to me. He stood up and held the chair.

"Would you like a salad? A shrimp cocktail? Something to start?" he said immediately. He caught my sweater and straightened it when it started to slip from the back of the chair. I don't think I've ever met a man who was more polite.

"What would you like to eat?"

"Well, I need a little time," I said. "It takes me a minute to make up my mind."

"Please feel like you can order anything. The steaks are good here, especially the T-bone."

I studied the menu for a moment. "I'll have a shrimp cocktail, a salad with ranch dressing, and a T-bone." I like it when you can order freely, when you don't have to worry about money; but I guess everybody does.

"Did you fly over from Elko or drive?"

"Flew," he said. "In my own plane. I'm flying again. I bought shares in another Cessna. It's like getting back on a horse once you've been thrown, I guess." He smiled shyly at me. "I didn't want to be scared of flying. So I forced myself to climb in the cockpit again."

He was a man who looked like a lot of men I knew, hair combed neatly around his ears, framing a round face and tanned skin and a hat line from the sun. He had nice green eyes, gentle looking. Sometimes I think there are only two kinds of men in the world, the gentle ones and the aggressive ones. He was gentle. If anybody ever pinned me down and made me say which Leon was, I'm afraid I'd have to say aggressive.

"I'm so glad you came, Verna," he said. "It's important to me that you'd come."

"I don't know why."

"It just is," he said, and he looked down at his big brown hands, clasped in front of him on the table.

It was over lunch, while we were eating our steaks, that he told me the story of what happened during the time between when his plane crashed and when I found him. He spoke softly about his first moments when he realized he'd lived and how he managed to climb out of the plane before it sank. He talked about his pain, his fear, his wife, the green dress with the butterflies and the illicit sight it sometimes afforded him, his sickness, his awareness of the position of stars, his despair and his faith. When people tell you so many details of things, you don't forget them, and I was sure I would remember everything Bob More was telling me. I ate while he talked, although I noticed he let his steak sit on his plate until the fat turned cold and white. Not too far away from us, at another table, a man was eating alone. A salesman, probably. A traveler. Everything he did seemed so self-conscious and deliberate, from taking a drink of water to lifting a forkful of food, and I thought, That's what loneliness does to you—you never forget that there's nobody but yourself for entertainment, and so everything you do has a mental echo around it, a small reflection of itself in your brain.

He was right, the steak was good, and I was happy sitting at Zito's, a place where the Toastmasters' Club met and people charged things to accounts, expensive enough to have an air of serious dining. There's a difference between eating and dining, and what we were doing was dining.

"The last thing I remember," he said, "before I blacked out was seeing the branch of a tamarack bush rising up out of the water. I knew then that I was close to shore. I never thought a single stick would look so good."

"You should eat your steak."

He laughed. "Is that what you've been thinking all the time I've been talking?"

"No," I said. "I've been listening. Honestly, I have."

"I don't have to be anywhere for the next hour," he said. "I'd like to take a drive with you."

"Where to?"

"Someplace where there's water."

It gave me the creeps that he said that, "Someplace where there's water," considering what had happened to him.

"Not the lake. Somewhere else," he added. "I'm not looking to relive anything."

"I guess we could drive up to the dam. That's only about ten minutes away."

He paid the bill. We took Harrison Boulevard to Twelfth Street, which turned into the canyon road near the golf course. People were out on the greens, pulling small carts down the fairways. A woman made a swing with her club and everyone stood frozen, looking off for a long while in the same direction. I passed the tree where Bugs Mansfield had been killed in high school. I never passed that tree without thinking of Bugs. I told Bob More the story about Bugs Mansfield, how he'd died one night, smashing his car against a tree.

"Do you think his spirit is there?" he asked.

"Where?"

"Right in this spot—maybe fused with all that's around us?"

"Well, I never thought of that," I said.

"I often think the place where you die is where your spirit lives for a while. Then maybe you return to the most important place in your life—the house you liked best, or the place where you were born."

"This happened a long time ago. I don't know where his spirit is now. I wouldn't know about something like that."

Maybe Leon was right about Bob More being weird. It occurred to me this wasn't normal talk. We passed a bar called the Hermitage, and then we came up the rise at the end of the canyon and saw the reservoir stretching out before us, a big irregular basin of water in the bottom of a high mountain valley.

"Are there fish in the dam?" he asked.

"Yes. Plenty of them."

"Do you fish, Verna?"

"Occasionally. Why?"

"Because I like to fish. I like to stand near the water and look at reflections. I like to be outdoors. I almost don't care if I catch any fish or not."

"That's a good attitude," I said. "That way you can't be disappointed if they're not biting."

"I like you," he said. "I really do."

I couldn't think of anything to say to that.

"Don't think I'm too odd," he said quietly. "I'm really not that weird."

I knew he was somebody to trust, and I think I knew right then, at that instant, what was going to happen that afternoon.

It seemed to me that something probably had happened to change him during that night of the plane crash, although I couldn't have said what it was. I didn't know what he was like before. But now he seemed kind of religious in a way that didn't have any connection to the sort of religion people all around me believed in. His featured a subtle connectedness, which seemed to include everything around him, stars, trees, all of nature. He had sweetness about him, as if he just couldn't appreciate things enough.

When we got to the dam, he asked me to drive to the other side, where there were places to park and you could walk right down to the water. We left the car and made our way toward a large cottonwood tree that threw a long strip of shade onto the beach. The sand was damp. He had on cowboy boots, and he left prints that were very pointed at the toe. We were both dressed all wrong for the beach, me in a dress, him in a shirt and dark pants, and it felt funny to be wearing dressy clothes, walking along the edge of the dam.

We sat down beneath the tree. I looked out over Pine View Reservoir. The water curved, and where it met the beach there was a strip of green moss and algae growing in the shallows, and then the sand, and then a bank of weeds and a few cottonwoods, each standing separate from the others, making dark patches of shadow which, due to the angle of the sun, sloped down toward the water. The hills were splotchy with dark spots, too, shadows from clouds.

"I don't know how I can thank you, Verna," he said.

"You don't need to."

Down toward the valley floor, the mountains were brown. Higher up, trees, greenish blue from this distance, grew thick on ridges and down into ravines. The clouds were densely white and billowy, very beautiful and shaped like atomic explosions. I heard a sound I recognized, a killdeer, which must have been trying to draw us away from her nest because we'd gotten too close. The wind around us was warm, and once in a while it came up in a strong gust and rustled the cottonwood leaves above above our heads. I had to keep flicking ants off my legs, but at least they weren't red ants and they didn't bite. Still, I thought, it would have been nicer without the ants. I was aware of everything around me, the wind, the water, the sky. I felt peaceful, and I thought this came in part from Bob More and his peculiar calm.

After a while, he lay back against the sand. "Verna," he said.

"What?" I said, although I thought I knew.

"Did it make any sense to you?"

"Did what make any sense to me?"

"What I said in my letter? About luck having two halves?"

"It made perfect sense to me," I said.

"Sometimes those meetings never happen."

"You don't find the other half of your luck."

"That's right," he said. "You don't find it."

"What were you doing out there that night?" he asked.

"Escaping a pitiful argument," I said.

"You were trying to find peace."

"How do you know that?"

"Because that's what we all look for."

"I felt life slipping away from me. I saw the way things get balled up for the stupidest of reasons. I felt like it was all going to be the same forever. I'd just had an argument with my mother-in-law. Well, not really an argument."

"There are things we just don't understand that are always working in our lives."

"What do you mean?"

"Opportunities," he said. He turned on his side and faced me, propped up on his elbow, and continued. "I'm fascinated by coincidences. Lately I've been keeping a list of them. When things happen that seem coincidental, I write them down. I want to see just how often things like that happen, whether there isn't a pattern."

"What kind of things have you recorded?"

"Well, the other day I was reading a magazine article on Ayers Rock, that place in the middle of Australia. Later that same day I walked into a restaurant, and sitting at the counter were some people who were wearing T-shirts, and printed on the back of one were the words 'Ayers Rock.' "

I expected a better coincidence than this, something that would have more personal meaning for him than a rock in the middle of Australia. But I nodded and smiled as if I understood exactly what he meant. For a long while we didn't say anything, then I asked what he did. "Farming," he said. "Twelve hundred acres of hay."

I felt his hand on my back. "It probably won't be the same for you forever," he said. "Life isn't like that. There's a level of tolerance inside each of us. When it isn't going right, things change almost without us working for it."

He stood up and took my hand and helped me to my feet and starting walking purposefully toward a barn at the edge of the dam, as if he'd known the barn was going to be there all along and we were going to end up in this spot and that nobody would be in the barn and no one would see us go in and there would be a bed of hay, a perfect place for us.

It didn't take so long; I think we were both expecting that it would be over quickly—not the sort of loving where you're fooling around, having fun, but something more urgent. I was surprised he wore garments. I would never have thought he was a strict Mormon; I thought he was something entirely different. And he didn't seem to care that he had to step out of them in front of me, awkwardly pulling them down around his feet, standing before me and revealing all his failed religiosity, his fall from his faith, because, in fact, he was calm and purposeful and serene. He didn't act as if what we were doing were wrong. He even said, very gently, in a kind way, "Are you protected?" and I said, "Yeah, I got an IUD."

All during the time we were making love, and for a time afterward, he stroked my forehead. Then we dressed and I took him back down to his car at Zito's and we said goodbye, unemotionally, like two people who had been to a school board meeting or something like that, and who were going to see each other the next day, only I never saw him again. He drove away in a car that said BUCK MUELLER FORD on the bumper.

It was the only time in seventeen years that I was unfaithful to Leon; and when I heard about his affair with Pinky from Doreen, who had seen them together one night at the Trocadero, I thought, What can you say? I knew I couldn't act righteous, that it would have to work itself out, and that I would play a part so incidental it wouldn't matter much what I did or said. I don't think I would have felt much differently if I hadn't done what I did with Bob More in the barn near Pine View; but because I had, I understood how something can catch you up like that and make you act in ways you never would have planned. That's just the way things are; nobody sees the future, or their part in it. You just go on, discovering yourself in the grip of feelings you never knew you owned.

5

THE ROAD ran straight into the desert, down one side of a wide valley and up the other side. We passed two big factories of some sort, set out in the middle of nowhere with nothing but sand around them. I couldn't decide what kind of factories they were. Cement plants? Chemical? Some kind of mineral processing. Maybe bauxite or gypsum? Boxcars stood idle on a rail line next to the buildings. Whatever was produced there was taken away by train. We were miles from any houses, climbing a long slow hill, way on the other side of Las Vegas. There were cars parked near some low buildings out by the factories. Did people drive out there every day? Where did they live?

I pointed out the factory or plant or whatever it was to Duluth. "What do people do out there, do you think?"

Duluth said, "Masturbate a lot, probably."

I didn't like it that he'd said this. It seemed coarse and dirty to me. I was quiet for a while.

"It smells like rain," he said suddenly. "Either that or the radiator is starting to boil over onto your engine."

It wasn't rain. I looked down at the temperature gauge and realized we were in the red.

"That's no good," I said. I pulled over and stopped on the shoulder of the road. "We'll have to wait for it to cool down."

Duluth brushed the front of his shirt, as if there were crumbs there. "At least it's not too hot out here this time of year," he said. "We could dry up like dog turds out here if it was hot."

"I hate this wind," I said.

"Wind can make you crazier faster than anything else."

"I think I'll take a little walk."

"I'll be here." He leaned his head back and closed his eyes.

I got out and began walking between the sparse, brittle brush into the sandy desert, toward the base of some mountains. The land formed sloping bowls, so the earth tilted up toward the mountains in all directions. The mountains out here were the color of dried mud, and it didn't look like one thing grew on them. The wind blew hard against my face as I climbed.

Sometimes as a child I'd be driving with my parents toward Snowflake, crossing through one of those endless desert valleys that crisscross the West, and I'd look out at the unbelievably dry and hot-looking earth and think, We'll die out here if this car breaks down. Of course, there were other cars on the road. We wouldn't have been left unattended. Someone would have stopped to offer us help. But still, I had these fantasies. I saw us taking a little side trip; it wasn't beyond my father to suggest something like this. I saw us turning off the highway onto one of those little dusty roads that were used by ranchers to check on sheep or cattle in the distant hills, just two tire tracks, pale and hardly worn. I imagined us driving out into the desert, sagebrush scraping our car, dust rising behind us, the whole family bouncing on our seats.

Hours later, in this fantasy of mine, we break down, the car refuses to go. I imagine us marooned in the incredible stillness of the desert, the sun beating down. At first we're optimistic. We settle ourselves in the shade of the car. Mom gets out the green metal jug with the little silver spigot and runs lemonade into paper cups. She sings to us:

> There's a long, long trail a-winding
> Into the land of my dreams
> Where the nightingale is singing
> And the white moon beams. . . .

Dad tinkers with the engine. We hunt for horned toads. But the heat starts to really get to us. Hours pass and we begin to see there's really very little hope we'll be rescued that day. Buzzards begin circling. Night comes and the temperature drops. The coyotes howl, a few feet away. We hear rattle-snakes where there really aren't any. Day breaks. The sun comes up and becomes increasingly merciless. Another day passes, and we're weak, all of us. Our water runs out, and there's nothing to do but face the end. Naturally we pray, and we think about the relatives that are waiting for us on the Other Side. Luckily we belong to a religion that promises this won't be THE END, so we face death with courage, saying family prayers. Later, a rancher finds the bones—two adults, male and female, and eight little skeletons of ascending size.

It had always seemed to me that my family was close to such perilous situations. How could we have been so fool-hardy as to stand on a bridge above the Colorado River, where a sudden gust of wind might have pitched us over the railing? Why did my father let us ride in a rickety, homemade trailer when we went out to work on our property in Layton? Or stand on the running board of the truck while he backed up? Did he really mean to endanger us when he drove close to the edge of a cliff, or was he just kidding, the way he pretended? And how could we have trusted a mere automobile to carry us across the vast and unpopulated deserts? Now that I thought about it, our lives were so awfully ordinary, so cushioned and plain and secure, without any real threat encroaching on our daily rounds, that I must have longed for the danger and excitement a real accident might bring.

Once, on the road to Snowflake, we did have an accident, a real crash, while my mother was at the wheel. She hit a couple from Wisconsin broadside. They were driving a Lincoln Continental, towing a little Airstream trailer, and without looking they pulled out onto the highway right in front of our car. I was lying on the backseat with my father. When my mother hit the brakes, Dad and I slid from the seat and landed on James and Farley, who were sitting on the floor. There was so much damage to both cars that they had to be towed away from the site of the accident; but, amazingly, no one was hurt.

It meant, however, that we had to stay in a motel in Tuba City for three nights until our car was fixed. It was one of those motels in a U-shape that had a little carport for each room. Years later I drove through Tuba City and noticed the motel was still there, only now badly rundown, the carports clogged with weeds.

The couple from Wisconsin, Midge and Art Whipple, stayed in the same motel, waiting for their own car to be repaired. They weren't members of the church, and my mother saw an opportunity. It gave her a chance to demonstrate the good qualities of Mormons to some outsiders—qualities like friendliness, for instance, and forgiveness. Even though the accident had been the Whipples' fault, Mom went out of her way to reassure them it could happen to anybody. The important thing was that we were all okay. Furthermore, she demonstrated her tolerance by telling Midge Whipple that it was okay to smoke in my parents' motel room when the Whipples visited. My mother had never allowed anybody to smoke in a room where she was. I'd seen her ask people to go out onto the porch to have their cigarettes. And finally, as if to prove that Mormons weren't as straightlaced as people thought, Mom told one of her jokes.

My mom's jokes were always about the same thing. They were harmless little off-color stories that she told with verve. When she told the Whipples one of her jokes, we were sitting outside our motel rooms, in the faltering desert light. The rest of the kids were exploring the streets of Tuba City; I was left with the adults, who seemed somehow to forget I was there, or to regard me as one of them because I was so tall for a kid. They sat on metal patio chairs with backs that were fluted, like seashells. I sat on the grass, which was full, I remember, of clover.

Mom started out by saying she heard a story the other day. She really shouldn't tell it, but, well . . .

"Go on," Midge Whipple said.

Mom leaned forward slightly in her chair.

"This couple gets married, you see, and goes on their honeymoon." It was amazing to me how many of my mother's jokes started this way.

"Marge," my father said, "you're not going to tell *that* one! Good hell!"

"Oh, it's not so bad! I've got worse," Mom said.

"Go on," Midge Whipple said again. She and Mom had begun some female complicity in this thing now.

"So it's their wedding night," she said, "and the fellow begins to undress. First he takes off his shoes, and his wife sees that he has the worst-looking feet, especially his toes. They're all misshapen and deformed, and she says, 'Good heavens, what happened to your toes?' "

"This one kind of drags on," Dad said to the Whipples. "Don't crap out—she'll get to the punch line before long."

"The fellow says to his wife, 'Oh, my toes look like this because I had toelio when I was a kid.' The wife says, 'Don't you mean polio?' 'No, no,' he says, 'it was toelio.' She thinks it's kind of funny, but she doesn't say anything. Then the fellow takes off his trousers and she looks at his knees."

"We're working our way up here," Dad said in another aside to the Whipples. "You can kinda guess where we're headed."

"This fellow's got terribly deformed knees, all scarred and ugly. She says, 'Well, what happened to your knees?' He says, 'Oh, I had kneesles when I was young.' 'Kneesles? Don't you mean measles?' she says. 'No, no,' he said, 'it was kneesles.' She doesn't quite know what to think. Then he takes off his— you know, all his clothes, and she takes one look at him and says, 'Don't tell me, let me guess—you had smallcox, too, right?' "

The Whipples really laughed at Mom's joke, but nobody ever laughed harder at a joke, her own or somebody else's, than my mom. She laughed till she made little buck-snorts and sometimes opened her mouth so wide she showed her gold teeth. My mom can put anybody in a good mood. Her good

humor is unstoppable. She could convince anybody that the
Mormons aren't straightlaced. And yet she never fails to think
of herself as a representative of her people, first of all and
above everything else a Latter-day Saint.

I could tell it was coming, what happened next. They sat
there a while longer, out in front of the Bide-A-While Motel,
looking down the main street of Tuba City, commenting on
small things. And then she said to the Whipples, "Do you have
any interest in investigating the church?"

"Why? What did they do?" Art Whipple said.

My dad laughed.

"No, I mean in learning more about it."

The Whipples looked suddenly uncomfortable. Midge
said, "Sure, although we're Catholic, you know."

"Oh," my mother said, undeterred, "well, that's interesting," although it was not that interesting to her; it was just
some kind of misconception that needed to be dislodged. And
then she simply began by saying that Mormons believe that
their church is the true church of Jesus Christ, restored here
upon the earth in these latter days, and started telling them the
story of the boy Joseph Smith, who was visited by angels when
he was twelve years old and directed to the hill Cumorah,
where he found golden tablets buried in a box. . . .

I left at this point, because I'd certainly heard that story,
and walked to the rear of the motel, where the desert seemed
to start exactly at the edge of the blacktop, and large tanks
marked PROPANE were lying in rows and appeared peculiarly
white in the sun, and I looked out toward a row of purple and
red hills, wondering if there were any wild horses out there,
wishing I could get one for free.

Duluth hadn't moved. I could see his head was motionless,
resting against the doorjamb. He looked pretty small, sitting
in the blue truck with the copper-colored trailer attached to it.
I thought he was sleeping, he was so still. Then suddenly he
put a hand out the window and waved at me and I waved back,

and I realized he'd been watching me all this time.

I started walking back toward the truck and trailer. The desert had a thin, dry crust over it that broke with each step. A little rabbit turd looked like pure silver in the light. I had walked quite a ways, all uphill, and now it felt nice to be swinging my arms and coming down fast, stretching out my limbs.

"How's it going?" Duluth said as I came toward him.

"Okay." I got in and turned the key. The engine was still too hot to drive away, so we sat there.

"I've been thinking about my little girl," he said.

"How old is she?"

"Three. Yup, just three. She's a tiger."

"You don't have a picture?"

"No, I don't. I guess I should. That's what I'll do—I'll write her mother and ask her for a picture."

"Where does her mother live?"

"Orem," he said. "Boy, is that a depressing place. I kept saying to Melanie—that's my ex-wife—'What are you *doing* here?' Her husband is a muffler salesman for Midas. He got her to move with him to Utah, back to his hometown."

"I bet you miss your daughter."

"You can say that. I miss her mother, too. I miss everything about the life we had and we're not ever going to have again and I can't see making with anybody else." He looked out the window. "I don't see much of a future for myself anymore, to tell you the truth."

You can't say anything to anybody when they tell you something like that. You can't say "I'm sorry" or "That's too bad" or "I'm sure everything will be okay."

"I can tell you the precise moment when things went wrong, when I knew that we were in trouble," he said. "It happened at a party in Los Angeles. Some people she worked with at the phone company had asked us over. I didn't really know them. There was this guy there named Stu. Melanie, my wife, started flirting with him from the moment we arrived.

She was being pretty outrageous—you know, I mean really laying it on thick—and he was the kind of guy who can get a woman to do that very easily, a southerner with a big-time drawl. Ham Jowls, I called him. But that was later when I gave him that name. That night I didn't know anything about him, except he was coming on to my wife, looking her up and down.

"They were drinking, we all were, getting loose fast, and some people were doing drugs, too. There was a lot of dancin' around. I looked over one time and noticed Stu sitting close to her, holding a cigarette up in his hand. She had on a blouse that dipped in the front, giving him something to look at. And then something happened. He began undoing her blouse, one button at a time, when a piece of ash dropped from his cigarette and fell down her blouse. She didn't even try to get it out, she just started screaming, 'Duluth! Duluth!' and in a second I was across the room. I took hold of him from behind, putting my hands around his neck. I said to him, 'I always come when I'm called.' Then I turned him loose. And that was that—he left pretty quickly. Later, when we were in the car on the way home, I said to Melanie, 'Do you have to make every man in the room get a hard-on?' 'Well, it does cheer them up,' she said. And I knew that was what she would be doing from then on—cheering men up."

He rested his head back against the window. "Don't you think it's cooled down enough for us to be on our way?"

"Probably."

"It's not that I'm rushing you," he said. "I'd just like to be home before dark."

Everything around us was was still, except the wind outside occasionally made the dry plants tremble. It was awfully empty out here—empty and dry, with that wind, which made you want some Chapstick or something for your lips.

"Explain the Mormons to me, would you?" he suddenly said.

"What do you want to know?"

"I come all the way up here to Utah to visit them—you know, Melanie and my daughter, Tiffany—hitchhiking in the cold. They knew I was coming. I arrived last Monday and called her from a phone booth in a service station. I was about froze to death, and all I wanted was directions to their house so I could sit down and get warm. I was even hoping she might say she'd come over to the station and pick me up. But she didn't. It was supper time, and I thought maybe they'd offer me something to eat. I was hungry. I had all these hopes, you know, all these ideas about what it'd be like when I finally got to Orem. I'd been hitchhiking for two days, so I had plenty of time to imagine the nice reception I was going to get, this nice reunion with my daughter, who I haven't seen for months. But instead, she said, 'We can't see you tonight because it's family home evening. You'll have to wait until tomorrow to come by.' I said to her, 'Melanie, I don't got anyplace to stay tonight. I was hoping you might let me sleep on your couch so I can spend some time with Tiffany.' 'Oh,' she said, 'well, I have to ask Walter about that.' "

"Walter is her husband?"

"Yeah, the muffler pusher. He got them to convert to the church. So Walter decided it was okay for me to come over. I walked there in that damn cold because your good-hearted Mormons didn't offer to pick me up. I arrived at seven. Their family home evening was just starting. First we all prayed together, kneeling around their couch for so long that my knees started to burn. Then Melanie stood up, went to the piano, and sang a song. After that Walter read a poem, and finally Tiffany told a story about a pioneer giving food to Indians and finished up by singing 'Jesus Wants Me for a Sunbeam.' I thought to myself, What is this? Then we played a game called Book of Mormon Trivia, where we drew cards from a deck that ask questions like, 'What was the name of the spectacles Joseph Smith used to translate the golden plates?' You can imagine how good I was at that. Hell, I bet you don't even know that, do you?"

"Urim and Thummim."

"Well, there you go . . . I couldn't even *say* that. We ate some lousy brownies, the only food they offered me, Walter said another prayer, and everybody went to bed. I couldn't even sleep. All I could think about was these weird people.

"The next day Melanie had a church meeting and she took Tiffany with her, so I couldn't spend any time with her. I passed the time at a local bar that had some of the worst drunks in there I've ever seen. That night there was a ward bazaar, so I didn't see Tiffany then, either, and the next day she had to go to something called primary, another church meeting."

He shook his head. "Anyway, I didn't get to see her much. It ended badly—you know, I got upset and said some things. Walter said I didn't need to come up no more, I wouldn't be welcome. I think she's lost to me. I think I might as well start admitting that she is."

He sighed. "I don't think I got a kid anymore. I think they're going to make her into someone I wouldn't ever recognize."

"Well, don't give up," I said. "She *is* your daughter."

"Hell, I already gave up on a lot of things—so many things I don't know what I got anymore. I don't know why I'm going back to L.A., I got nothing there. Four months ago I lost my job. Not that it was that great a job—you know, assembly-line stuff. Still, it meant I couldn't keep my apartment. I moved into my brother's garage. That's as close as his wife's going to let me come to living with them. Things got worse. Now, I'm livin' in a goddamned garage, I don't have a car, I can't get a job without one, I couldn't afford insurance anyway, I have four DWIs."

"What's a DWI?"

"Driving while intoxicated. Three or four of those and they take your license."

"I see."

"I just don't see it—I don't see no future. Why do things go so wrong? Tell me that?"

"I couldn't say."

"I couldn't either."

"I guess you got to keep trying."

"Who says?" He stared out into the desert. "Just tell me who says?"

"Well, I don't know," I said.

"This wind . . ." he said. "I think it's getting hotter. I hate this kind of wind."

I started the truck. The temperature was okay. So I pulled out, with the truck straining a little as we started up the hill. I wondered if we could make Los Angeles before dark. I tried to think of something to say to Duluth, but I didn't know what to tell him. All I could think of was Frank, because that's who Duluth reminded me of now . . . Frank Wolanski. I don't know why I didn't see it before.

6

THE SUMMER I started working in the snack bar at the bowling alley, a man came in one day.

"What is goot here?" he asked me. He had an accent of some sort.

"You want to know what's good here?"

"Yes. I would like to know this before I order."

"You want my honest opinion?"

"This is what I am asking you, yes."

I leaned over the counter so I could speak low to him. "Nothing," I said.

"Notink?" He raised his eyebrows.

I shrugged. Doreen, my boss, was sitting at the other end of the counter, working a crossword. She looked over at us and I smiled. My customer smiled, too, and then we looked at each other again.

"My goodness," he said, widening his eyes. "Notink. Imagine this."

"However," I said, "if you were to put it another way, if you were to say to me, 'What's passable in this place?'—well, I'd say the hot roast beef sandwich."

"This is what I will have."

"Good choice."

"Thank you," he replied.

"Comin' right up, then. The house specialty. One hot roast beef sandwich."

This was the beginning.

That first day, he began talking to me, telling me about his life, and I learned a lot about him. He was originally from Poland, he said, but he'd been dislocated by the Second World War. His dream was to come to America, but work had been found for him elsewhere, in Norway, during a postwar resettlement program, and that's where he ended up, in Oslo, living in a tiny room he rented from a butcher and his family. Although he hated the food there (the people, he said, ate so much fish that they smelled of fish oil) and found the northern light depressing, he was happy to be alive and receiving help, just to have survived the war. Still, he thought a lot about America, which is where he really wanted to be.

Finally, after a few years in Norway, where he worked in a glass-bottle factory, he was able to immigrate to Chicago, and he found a job in a Hotpoint plant assembling refrigerators. Many other Poles worked in the plant, so he didn't feel so alone. In fact, he didn't even have to learn English right away. Where he lived in Chicago, everybody was Polish. He bought a red convertible with his earnings, having little else to spend his money on; and in the summer, when it was hot, he went north to the Canadian woods for his vacation, driving his convertible. In the winters, he went south, to the Ozarks, and once drove as far as New Orleans. The car made him feel free, as though he had truly arrived in America.

On a lark, he decided to drive cross-country one summer; and, breaking his usual vacation pattern, he headed west, intending to visit Los Angeles. But instead he stopped in southern Utah, where he met a woman in a cafe. She was friendly.

They began talking. When she learned he was headed for Los Angeles, she warned him, "Don't try to drive across the California desert in the daytime. You'll cook out there." She suggested he wait and start out in the evening.

She was part Indian, and very beautiful to him. It seemed natural that they'd spend the day together, waiting for the sun to set so he could start out across the desert. They drank cup after cup of coffee, and then, in the early afternoon, they moved down the street, to the VFW bar, where she knew somebody who would let them in, even though they weren't card members. After a few drinks, they got into his red convertible and drove to a place outside town, near a river, where they could be alone. They stayed out there a long time, parked where they could hear the water gurgling over the rocks in the river right next to them. He said this spot reminded him of the forests in his native Poland. He liked it very much. He was grateful to her for bringing him to such a place. Later, they made love. "You're a good loverboy," she said afterwards. He couldn't think of anything to say in English that would begin to express his feelings, so he just smiled at her, and nodded.

They really fell for each other, and suddenly he wasn't so anxious to get to Los Angeles anymore.

For several days, they drove around together, stopping in motels at night, buying a bottle of Scotch when they felt like it, and eating steaks in roadside cafes. She took him to Zion National Park, and to Bryce Canyon, which he found extraordinary—otherworldly, in fact. "Fantastic!" he kept saying, looking at the landscape. His English by then was a little better, but still he kept using the same word over and over, trying to describe his reaction to this incredible terrain. "Fantastic!" he'd cry, at the red rocks, the pillars, the arches of stone. This was the landscape he'd dreamed of as a child. It was all he'd imagined, and much more.

He left her in a motel one night to go to a store for some beer. When he came back, she was gone. For two days he stayed around the motel, asking questions in town, hoping she would return. He even contacted the police. Nothing happened. It was as though she had disappeared into the air. He couldn't give the police any details about her because he didn't know anything, except her name. They sized him up—a foreigner, a flashy car, a half-Indian woman he'd just met. The case didn't interest them much.

Then one morning, a man knocked on the door of his motel room. He'd heard that the Pole had been asking questions. He said he was able to help him find the woman he was looking for; he knew where she was.

"You know where Dolores is?" the Pole asked.

"Her name isn't Dolores, first off," he replied.

It would cost money—fifty dollars. The Pole had never seen the man before and was suspicious. Nevertheless, his feelings for the woman were so strong that he paid the money and followed him to a town, miles to the south, just over the Utah-Arizona border, on reservation property. They parked in back of a rundown hotel. All around the hotel there were trailers, parked higgledy-piggledy, where people were living in filth, surrounded by all kinds of trash. Wires ran everywhere. Garbage was piled in overflowing cans. The Pole had never seen such a depressing place. The man told him to go inside the hotel and ask for Flora.

Flora, it turned out, wasn't there. But the Pole saw that all the women in the hotel were prostitutes, that it wasn't a hotel at all, and he left without waiting for Flora to return. He went back to the motel room and got drunk. Should I go back to see her? was the question he kept asking himself that night; but he wasn't thinking too clearly, especially as his drinking continued well into the morning, and he couldn't find the answer.

In many ways he was an old-fashioned man, from a family that had once had money, and although he'd seen a lot in the war and had been changed by it, he knew well enough there'd be no future with Flora-Dolores, no matter what he did. He decided he would forget her.

He didn't return immediately to Chicago, however; nor did he go on to L.A. He stayed on in southern Utah and each day went out driving and gazed at the extraordinary landscape. He thought deeply about Flora-Dolores, for as a refugee he knew that in the long process of forgetting and remembering, one had to first set things very clearly in mind. He thought about her during his day trips to Moab and Monument Valley, and the longer journeys he made to Arches and Canyonlands and the Hovenweep ruins, which sat on a high mesa overlooking valleys with springs and patches of green grass. He thought about her until she was positioned properly in memory so that he might go on.

Later that week, he got a job with an oil company, and he never returned to Chicago. He settled among strangers in Utah and developed an interest in rock hunting, which eventually preoccupied him and took him to remote places and made him seem eccentric and lonely. Imagine, he said, a woman changing your life like that, all in a few days. And then you never see her again.

He told me this story while sitting at the counter in the snack bar. There were no other customers. It was a slow morning; I didn't have anything to do. We'd been talking for half an hour, without interruption. Behind us, we could hear people bowling. Sometimes they yelled when a person got a spare or a strike, and it sounded like a party the way the noise suddenly erupted, a party where everybody was forgetting all their troubles and just having fun.

I was bothered by one thing in his story. Why did he trust the man who told him where to find Flora-Dolores? Why didn't he stay and talk to her and find out if she really did work in that place? It could have been a trick, just to get his money. He should have found out if she really was a prostitute.

"Yes, but you forget," he said. "The point is, she left me while I went out to buy beer. Doesn't that suggest to you that she wished to be rid of me? That she had something to hide?"

"I still would've stuck around and talked to her," I said. "I'd want to know for sure."

The Polish man looked at me as if he were thinking this over; then he paid his bill and left.

He kept coming back to the snack bar after that first day, until it was his routine to come in pretty regularly. Doreen kidded me about it; she said he had a crush on me. Did I care? Not at all, especially since he was a nice old man. I saw him watching me sometimes, but I didn't mind. He seemed to have his reasons.

One day he said, "Never mention this to me again, or to anyone else, but I have a daughter who would be about your age, if she's alive. You will never mention this again, now?"

So I thought I'd figured it out. It wasn't romance that drew him to me, not the lust of an old man for a young woman. No, it was because of his daughter; that was his interest in me. I reminded him of her. And because I'd agreed never to mention it again, I couldn't ask him, "Did she get lost in the war?" "How were you separated?" "Was she sent to a camp?" No, I just had to leave it. I didn't tell anyone else. I never mentioned his daughter to him, just as he'd asked. But I did wonder.

His name was Frank—Frank Wolanski. I liked the way he talked. When he said a word that ended in "ed," such as "walked" or "worked" or "liked," he made the "ed" sound like a whole separate word, pronouncing it like the name of the TV horse Mister Ed: "I like-Ed that dress you wear." "I work-Ed till noon." "I walk-Ed today because the car is broke-Ed."

He once told me that when he was a child growing up in Poland, he and all his friends read some books about the American West. These books had been written by a man named Karl May, a German, who had never even visited America. Nevertheless, they were so vivid in their descriptions of the West—its frontier towns and the horses and buffalo and the Indians and their ways of life, the big red rocks and wide open spaces—that Frank had no difficulty picturing these places. Frank and his friends spent hours pretending they were in Utah, Wyoming, and Nevada. These words—"Utah," "Wyoming," "Nevada"—held within them the notion of a wonderful, fantastic world, where things would be like they were in the books, wild, dangerous, and adventuresome. "You can't imagine," he said, "what these words mean-ed to us, these places. We love-ed your West." In Frank's mouth, Utah became Ootah—more ancient, more primitive sounding, a place of prehistoric men and roving dinosaurs.

Frank was one of those really nice people who exist in the world—kind, bright, intelligent. I came to see that. There was something else, too: he possessed a gracefulness and something like charm. Sometimes I thought he came from such an old world that I couldn't believe he was still alive, as though people who behaved like him died out long ago; he was so polite and elegant. He had the bright, black, intelligent eyes of some animal, like a chinchilla. He was also sharp and quick, extremely alert. I saw him assessing every situation, bringing to it some superior experience and wisdom. Things often went unsaid, but I saw the assessment in his eyes. He may not have shaved, his clothes might be worn, but he had a presence, a certain air, that seemed to overcome these things.

We kept telling each other stories, Frank and myself, and all the time I had in the back of my mind that I reminded Frank of this daughter, who was lost, I was sure, in some terrible circumstance caused by the war. Doreen and Bud, everybody at the bowling alley gave me a hard time, because Frank stopped in every day now, for either breakfast or lunch. They called him my boyfriend, and I thought it was stupid of them. I liked him. I'd never known anyone like him.

When we talked, we described things that had happened to us, and things that were still happening. After a while, it seemed there wasn't anyone else I could talk to quite like I could to Frank. It was as though we loosened something in each other, both feeling and memory.

I told him how when I was small, every night before I went

to bed, I used to go into my father's room to kiss him good night. I did this on instructions from my mom. "Kiss your dad before you go to bed," she'd say. "It would make him feel so good." He'd always be in bed, lying there in a dark room, flat on his back, his body under the covers, which were folded back neatly over his chest. On a bedside table, his small portable radio was tuned to some station that played instrumental numbers like "Danny Boy" and "Smoke Gets in Your Eyes." The room was so dark it was like entering a cave. Only the light of the radio guided me to his side. His eyes were closed, but I knew he was never sleeping. He'd hear my approach and stir slightly. "Good night, honey," he'd say, sometimes not even opening his eyes as I bent to kiss him. Then I'd leave the room. It would be eight-thirty, no later. He retired early, retreating after dinner to his bedroom, in order to be lulled by the radio into a place quite different from the one where he'd spent his day, working in the copper mine. The next night, my mother would say the same thing to me—"Kiss your father good night before you go to bed; it would mean so much to him"—and again I would enter the dark and tinkly realm and approach the bier of his making.

Frank said that during the First World War, he was was so malnourished that he was hospitalized for rickets. The family was starving, like so many other people. They lost their money. His mother opened a shop and repaired umbrellas, bags, and shoes. Then he saw his first movie from America, where people were driving cars. His first thought was, If they have cars, they must have food. His mother died. He went to live with aunts in an apartment in Warsaw and attended a school run by nuns. Eventually he became an apprentice to a glass worker. And then the next war came.

He asked about my husband, and I tried to tell him something about Leon.

Leon loved to hunt, especially in the early years of our marriage. Sometimes I'd go out with him, but usually I didn't carry a gun. I went along for the exercise, to drink beer and horse around, just to be out in the woods. One time when we were deer hunting up by Soda Springs in Idaho with his friend Jack Buffet, I remember, a weird thing happened. We had been hunting all day, with no luck. There were too many hunters out that day—more hunters, it seemed, than deer. The narrow roads were jammed with trucks carrying hunters. We kept driving further and further into the mountains to try and escape them. There's a rule that you can't hunt from a car; you're not supposed to just drive along roads looking for deer to shoot. But everybody does it anyway.

We were car hunting ourselves that day. Suddenly Leon saw a buck scrambling up the face of a hill. A hunter in another car ahead of us saw the deer at the same time. They both jumped out, sighted the deer, and started shooting. I could see dirt kicking up all around the buck from where the bullets were hitting. The deer was now frantic; you could see his muscles, very powerful, bunching as he struggled to escape, running straight up the steep hill. The volleys were coming from both Leon and this other guy. They were blasting away. Finally, the deer was hit, and stopped so suddenly it seemed like he lifted off his feet and dropped sideways, unmoving. Both Leon and the other hunter rushed up the hill. They both claimed to have shot the deer. Jack Buffet backed Leon up, of course. A big argument started. They screamed at each other. Their voices echoed through the canyons. I looked around me. The leaves on the aspens were quivering, they were almost never still; whole hillsides seemed active just because of these leaves, it took so little wind to move them. Mountains were visible, and beyond those mountains, more mountains. We were so alone. There weren't any towns for miles. We were specks of nothing in this landscape. It seemed so incredible that Leon and this guy were screaming at each other, getting ready for the actual fist fight that came later, all over this dead deer. In the end, Leon got the deer, but only because Jack Buffet, who is a pretty big guy, was with him, and together they pinned the guy when he started hitting out at them, and smacked him, and then just walked away with the buck—or, rather, dragged it down the hill behind them, its antlers catching and furrowing the earth.

Frank always listened to every word I said, just as I did with him. Often he didn't say anything. He'd just shake his head, those beady eyes shining, alert and knowing.

"Okay, Toots," he'd say when it was time to go. Then he'd take my chin in his hand and squeeze it a little. "See you later."

He started drinking one winter, and it got to be heavy drinking, though I know he tried to hide it from me by coming in early each day, before he went to the bars. But I'd see him occasionally when I passed the Trocadero, a popular bar on Highway 89 where a lot of people from Thiokol went after work and in between their swing shifts. I could also see it in his face, which grew puffy, and in the way he stopped keeping himself up, so that sometimes when he sat down at the counter a certain ripe odor came from his clothes.

Usually the first thing I did when I came in to work each morning was fill the plastic ketchup and mustard bottles. Doreen left all the ones that needed washing soaking in a detergent solution in one of the sinks. That way the ketchup that had hardened around the tops worked itself loose and all I had to do was rinse them good under the faucet and fill each bottle again. Ketchup came in ten-pound cans, and each time I opened a new can, thin little slivers of aluminum filament would come loose and drop down into the catsup and disappear before I could fish them out. I sometimes wondered, Did anybody ever find those little aluminum slivers in their burgers?

I was cleaning the squeeze bottles one morning, getting ready to refill them with ketchup, when I looked out the back door of the kitchen and saw Frank on the other side of the parking lot. I was alone in the kitchen, and I stopped what I was doing to watch him. He didn't see me; in fact, he seemed quite oblivious to everything. As he walked, he looked at the ground, his head down. He was weaving unsteadily, and he stopped by a dumpster and put his hand on it for support. It was the middle of the hunting season. The Ben Franklin store had a sign out that said OCTOBER BLAST SALE to attract the hunters. Frank had gotten a hunter's Day-Glo orange vest from somewhere, and he was wearing it over an old sweater. His baggy pants were so rump-sprung they bowed out like a bubble in back. The vest was so bright it almost hurt to look at it, and it made Frank's sallow complexion look even worse. Without even bothering to turn away or to hide himself between the dumpsters, Frank undid his pants and started urinating on the blacktop. I turned away. I thought, I've got to do something for him. I really do. But as it happened, I got caught up with things in my own life and forgot my resolve to help Frank. Instead, I just pitied him now, whenever I saw him; and that was a terrible feeling for me, as I'm sure it was for him.

He still came in to see me once in a while. But he seemed embarrassed by his condition, and we no longer talked the way we had. Gradually, I had become aware of Pinky and the threat to my marriage, and a long, slow unraveling began, which I admit took up a lot of my attention. I no longer felt sorry for Frank. I started feeling sorry for myself.

One day, walking to my truck after work, I passed by the Trocadero and saw Frank's familiar shape sitting at the bar, about two or three stools inside the door, and on a whim, I walked in and sat down next to him.

"Hello, Toots," he said. His glass was empty, but it didn't seem like he was drunk.

"Hi, Frank. Can I buy you something?"

"Sure." He named what beer he was drinking.

I didn't notice her right away—not until I paid for the drinks and looked up in the mirror behind the bar. She was sitting with Jack Buffet and Eddie Stringfellow, at a table just behind me.

Suddenly Frank spoke up. "You ever need protection," Frank said, "you call on me."

"Why would I need protection, Frank?" I asked. Maybe he was drunker than I'd thought. It was certainly a comment out of the blue. I tried not to look in the mirror, to pretend I hadn't seen her yet.

"That I don't know. I'm just telling you, I would help you. I am a Hussar. You know Hussar? These were the finest troops, the very best."

He lifted his glass and we toasted.

"To the Hussars," I said, and looking in the mirror, I added, "and the hussies."

I said it loud enough for her to hear, and I saw her look up at me. Jack and Eddie looked up, too, and they seemed kind of embarrassed that I had caught them having a drink with Pinky. They were Leon's best friends, and my friends, too, and I figured they owed me loyalty. By then, I figured everybody knew she was Leon's girlfriend. I'd been about the last person to find out.

I felt hotness rising in me that I was powerless to stop. I felt like hurting her, at least insulting her. There were things that needed to be said. You don't just take up with another woman's husband and then imagine you can sit calmly in the same room with her.

"Hey, Verna," Eddie said.

"Hi, Eddie."

Jack didn't say anything; he just grinned foolishly at me. I felt like pushing things a little.

"What are you guys doing, trawling bars like this?"

"Eddie wanted to go hunting after work," Jack said, "but this is as far as we got."

"Looks like you bagged something, though." I looked at Pinky. She appeared helplessly frail to me. She had the kind of shape where her thin legs were set so wide apart at the crotch that even when she was standing normally, there was a gap between her thighs. I'd heard men say that you could drive a semi through that kind of gap. She always wore skin-tight Levis, a wide tooled belt, and some kind of shirt with a frill on it. She looked up at me, smart and unrepentant.

"To tell you the truth," Pinky said, "I ought to be going."

"That's a good idea," I said. "Why don't you hop in that car of yours and drive yourself all the way back to Evanston?"

"I have no intention of doing that," she said coolly.

"She has no intention of doing that," I said to Frank, who looked at me, perplexed by what was going on. I felt drunk, even though I hadn't really had one full beer. I wanted to be drunk, however—to be so far gone I could blame anything I said on the beer, and I pretended a little that I was already tipsy.

"Don't go," I said to Pinky. "We could shoot some pool. Play pairs. Me and Eddie, you and Jack. Frank could be the referee and call the shots in case one of us was cheating—you know, not playing fair?"

She started to say something, then hesitated, as if she didn't know whether I meant what she suspected I did.

"Do you ever get any discount on stuff?" Jack asked Pinky suddenly. Pinky worked at the Sprouse-Reitz variety store. I guessed Jack wanted something.

"No," she said. "They don't give employees no discounts like that. I think they should—everybody does. But they don't care nothin' about what we think. They're real tight in that store."

"Too bad. I need some gardening hose."

"What do you need gardening hose this time of year for?" Eddie said. "You're a little late to start the tomatoes."

"My automatic waters broke again. I tell you, I got gypped on that system. I need some hose to run water to a couple of troughs," Buffet said. "I was just going to jerry-rig this thing."

"What is 'jerry-rig'?" Frank asked.

"It means make something work temporarily," I said. "You know, it's not the real thing but it's next best."

"I still don't get this."

"It's like something breaks and you don't have the right part to fix it, but you patch it up with other things so that it'll work for a while."

"Ah," Frank said.

I felt like all three of them, Pinky, Buffet, and Eddie, were watching me as I explained "jerry-rig" to Frank. They probably thought he was a pathetic case and wondered why I'd come in to join him at the bar. I guess everybody looked at Frank now and just saw a sad old man, a bad drunk. All I was thinking was, I've just described the state of my marriage—it's jerry-rigged, okay?

"Try K-Mart," Pinky said. "Everything's cheaper over there."

"Have you ever wondered what would happen if there really was a nuclear blast?" Eddie said.

"Bring up a depressing subject, why don't you?" Pinky said in her drawl. She was wearing a western shirt with lots of pearlized button snaps. She had large breasts that strained at the snaps.

"I mean, why would you do that?"

"I don't know," Eddie said. "I really don't. It just came into my mind. I mean, you try to imagine it, and you can't begin to."

"How long would we last?" Jack added. "Probably not very long. Even if you made it, you're not going to have telephones, and they'll probably stop delivering gas to stations so you can't drive."

"I thought of getting a couple of burros," Eddie said.

Pinky laughed at this—a high, shrill laugh. I thought, Isn't it incredible that we're talking here like normal people, covering up the fact that she sleeps with my husband?

"Burros?" Pinky said.

"Hell, the Bureau of Land Management can't give 'em away. Nobody wants burros. You sure wouldn't have any trouble getting a couple," Jack said.

"But I was thinking," Eddie said, "that if you had to get around and there wasn't any cars, you could have a few burros and pack stuff. Keep a riding horse for yourself, you know. But use the burros to carry your water and stuff."

"Where would you be going, Eddie?" Jack asked. "Where the hell would you be headed with your burros?"

"Well, I might want to get over to my parents' place in Malad to see how they're doing. That's fifty or sixty miles away. Hell, that's a long ways to walk, and if you didn't have a car to drive because there wasn't any gas, those burros would come in handy. I could pack stuff over to my parents, take them some food, make sure they're okay."

"Burros are hardy, that's for sure," Pinky said. "They're cute, too." I was disliking her then, very much, but I was also disliking that she was getting bolder here, talking now as if everything was going to be just fine, that she didn't have anything to worry about from me, and we were just going to sit there drinking beer and gabbing about the chances of surviving nuclear war. I had to fix this, set her straight, but I wasn't sure how.

"They'd have to be pretty hardy to survive a nuclear blast," I said. It seemed ridiculous to me, the whole idea of keeping burros to get around after the blast.

"I don't know what's going to happen," Pinky said. "I just go day by day."

I looked at her when she said this, and she looked up at me. I saw that she was harder than I'd thought—I mean by that stronger—and that she wouldn't give up easily. "Excuse me," she said. She got up and headed for the bathroom. I gave her a few seconds, then I got up and followed her.

She was already in a stall when I walked in, but I knew she must have heard me and known who it was. I looked around, wondering what I was going to do next, knowing that it wouldn't be good but uncertain just what course I was taking. And then I saw it, the tin bucket in the corner with a damp mop sticking up in it, and I removed the mop and took that bucket to the deep metal sink and filled the bucket with water. I carried it into the stall next to Pinky and stood on the toilet. I started to lose my balance and wondered if I was going to fall down off the toilet seat; but I didn't and I looked over the top of the partition that separated the two stalls and saw Pinky squatting there, her pants lowered. I dumped the whole bucket on her, fast, so that the water hit her hard and flattened out her hair. She yelled. The water was cold, and the coldness must have shocked her, plus a bucket of water weighs a lot and it must have hit her hard. She looked up, her face wet and shiny and water dripping from her hair, and seemed surprised to see me, though I wondered how she could have been. Who else did she think would do that to her? I grinned and said, "I hear it's much drier up in Evanston. You ought to reconsider my suggestion about going back there."

"You bitch!" she yelled.

We both came out of the stalls at the same time—she hadn't even had time to do up her pants—and she lunged at me and caught me by my hair. I grabbed her neck and yanked her backwards, so that she lost hold of me, and then I just squeezed her neck for all I was worth, letting loose with all the anger that was in me, and I heard a small, delicate little *pop*.

Something in her neck had cracked. She slid down onto the floor, moaning, and I let go of her. And then I was out of there fast, hurrying back toward the bar.

"Well, Frank," I said, "do you want to have some dinner? We could go up to Maddock's and get some fried schicken and scones." (I said "schicken" because that's the way Frank said it.) I realized my knees were wobbly.

"Sure, Toots," he said. "That's a pretty good idea."

I had to help Frank up from his stool and steady him until he found his legs.

"Keep your nose clean," Eddie said.

"Tap it light," I said back.

"See you," Jack said.

"See you," I said to him.

Tiny flakes were whirling out of the sky when we walked outside the bar. I had to support Frank to get him to my truck. He wasn't staggering drunk. He just seemed weak and unsteady, like old men do. We drove out Harrison Boulevard to

Five Points, where the road veers off toward home. The snow starting coming down a little thicker, and I turned on the windshield wipers. I thought of calling Leon from a phone booth to tell him I wouldn't be home for a while, then decided I wouldn't. It was late in the day. The light was gray and dim. Ben Lomond was a ghostly big mountain in front of us.

We passed the Thirteenth Ward church. Teenagers were walking along the sidewalk, on their way to Mutual. All the girls wore their hair the same way—long, and flipped away from their faces, like Farrah Fawcett-Majors.

Frank said, "I have to go to the bathroom."

"Can you hold it till we get to Maddox?"

"No," he said.

I waited till we'd passed the Sheriff's posse grounds and the golf course and then pulled over. He got out of the truck by himself and walked off into a little thicket of trees. I heard the urine falling and knew he hadn't gone far and hoped he wasn't pissing on his shoes or, even worse, his pants. I saw Frank coming back toward the car. His zipper was still undone.

"Do your zipper up, Frank," I said. "You don't want to be letting the cows out of the barn."

"That's right," Frank said. His thin hair, which hung down in a fringe from a mostly bald crown, was greasy and had been swept behind his ears. He hadn't shaved in several days at least. Still, he had on a sports coat made out of a shiny blue material, and his shirt, although not pressed, was buttoned to the top, and this made him look together, sort of. I guessed it would be all right to take him to Maddox.

Maddox Restaurant had a big revolving gold crown on top of the roof and a sign that said, WORLD'S FINEST HOMEGROWN BEEF. The restaurant was out in the middle of farm country. It overlooked Willard Bay and the lake. They did raise their own beef; it was a big cattle operation as well as a restaurant, and you sat at windows that faced the barns and watched the cattle, all white-faced Herefords, munching hay in the feed cribs or ambling slowly through the green fields, which were fenced in white picket. It was like a picture-perfect farm, and Maddox was a restaurant where people went when they had something to celebrate—a birthday, a missionary's return, a visit from out-of-town friends. "Real food for real people" was the motto on the menu.

It was always crowded, and Frank and I were told we had to wait, which we did, in the foyer, where a woman who looked a lot like my mother's friend June Wadman played popular tunes on an organ.

"This is very nice," Frank said. "I like the organ music."

"Oh, you've never been here before, huh?" I asked, trying to sound normal, as if Frank and I were ordinary people who fit right in. But we didn't, and I noticed people were looking at us. I still had on my waitress uniform with its short skirt and my badge that said HELLO! I'M VERNA; and Frank—well, he looked like Frank, somebody on the way down or already there. Other people were dressed as if it were Sunday and they were going to church.

I heard someone say, "Delmore received his call. He's going to Argentina."

"You must be thrilled."

"We are, and he's so happy—he wanted to go to a Spanish-speaking country."

"Look at those rings," Frank said. He was admiring the rings on the organist's hands. She had one on every finger, and each one was large, glittering, and showy. "My goodness. Beautiful."

He stood up, and before I could stop him he was walking over to the organist.

"Where you going, Frank?"

"Just to have a look at these rings."

The organist looked up, alarmed to see him standing so close to her, and maybe, I don't know, maybe she also smelled his particular odor, the one that had been accumulating on his clothes for weeks, and she did not smile. She frowned at him.

"My goodness," he said to her, "so much jewelry! Where did you get so many rings like this?"

"Ha," the organist said. Ha. Just one sound, which came out of her mouth like a little doggie bark.

"Do you know Bach's fugues?" he asked.

"No, I don't believe I do," she said. Frank sat down on the bench next to her, and I thought, This isn't going well.

The organist stopped playing.

"Do I interrupt you? I'm sorry," Frank said. Then he put his hands on the keyboard and started to play. I was waiting for someone from the Maddox family to come in and tell us we'd have to leave, or at least that Frank would have to stop bothering the organist. But no one came, and the organist just kept looking at Frank, smiling, frozen, as if too embarrassed to move. Surprisingly, Frank played something very short and very nice, and I could tell that people were surprised he could play so well, and everyone was listening to him then, because he seemed to make that organ come alive, and afterwards there was a polite little round of applause. I myself was surprised that he could play the organ like that. But when he stood up, I saw that he'd wet himself, and again I thought, We're going to have to leave, this is going all wrong.

I said, "Frank, come here a minute."

I led him over to the window, where we could look out at the cows lit up by big spotlights out in the feed yards, and turned him so that our backs were to the room.

"You've wet yourself," I said.

He looked down. He began to get agitated, and I thought I saw tears forming in his eyes. "Oh, no," he kept repeating, and he tried to brush the front of himself off, as though he'd accidently spilt something there.

I thought, It's going to get even worse here. Frank's going to freak out, he's getting so upset, and I'm going to have to take him to the truck. He won't like that and neither will I. It seemed like everything was going from bad to worse, and I felt like I was on the run, still escaping from the scene in the ladies' room at the Trocadero. Had I really hurt her? I wondered.

"Calm down," I said. "Look here, we'll cover it with your coat. It'll be okay. We'll just go have dinner and it'll be fine." As I said this I buttoned his sport coat, so it hid the front of his pants. "It hardly shows," I said.

The hostess called us then, and seated us in the dining room.

We ate a lot of food that night. It was as if neither of us had eaten for a long time. We had their special country fried chicken, two baskets of it, and lots of homemade scones, split and stuffed with butter and honey, and we didn't spare the sour cream on our baked potatoes, either. We each ordered a big dessert. Afterwards, we had coffee, and we stayed a long time, just talking.

We were like our old selves, the way we'd been when we first met each other. We were just ordinary people then, not somebody who'd just thrown a bucket of water on her husband's girlfriend and wrestled her to the floor, not somebody who'd lost control of his bladder completely and was fated to suffer more and more indignities in life.

At one point Frank said to me, "People think Poland is just some lost place, somewhere with lines for food and strikes, that sort of thing, a Russian puppet. But you know, it was the very heart of European civilization. You say Europe now, you think of France. But no, it was Poland and Czechoslovakia that was what we mean-ed by Europe. The cradle of civilization, no?"

"Eastern Europe?" I said.

"No!" Frank pounded the table. "Not eastern—middle! What I am sayink is, only now is it eastern. Once it was central. The heart of Europe."

I didn't know why this was important to him, but it seemed

to be, so I nodded and said, "Yes, sure." What did I know about geography? But I did understand this: he had lost his heart, his home, his Europe.

"Guess what was the first thing that was rebuild-ed in Warsaw when the war was finally over."

"What?"

"The statue of Copernicus!"

"No kidding."

"That tells you something about these Poles, eh?"

Later he brought up Flora-Dolores. The day he met her, he said, when they went to the VFW bar and then drove out of town and ended up at a river, which was swift and broke over big rocks, splashing the banks so that everything was damp, there was a smell that he had never forgotten.

"What do you think-ed this smell was?"

"I don't know, what?"

"Cottonwood trees."

"Cottonwood trees?"

"The most beautiful smell. It makes the nose tingle!"

Frank laughed, and I looked into his glittering dark eyes and could see the happiness this memory brought him. At that moment, memory was so powerfully activated that Flora-Dolores was still with him after all these years: he was parked with her in the red convertible, he was younger, he was in Ootah, he was holding a woman in the land of his dreams, he was in the damp and odoriferous forest with Flora-Dolores and there was no limit, yet, to this thing but only heartfelt love and many, many possibilities.

It was pretty late when we left Maddox; the busboys were beginning to straighten the chairs at the tables and roll out tin buckets and mops that smelled of cleaning solution. Frank lived at the Golden Spike Motel, across from the feedlots that were part of the coliseum, and I smelled the cows when I pulled up out front and saw them milling about in the darkened pens.

When I dropped him off that night, he was happy. We both

were. We sang as we drove from Maddox back toward town. Frank had so many more troubles than I did. I saw that. I saw that his troubles were of a deeper kind, while mine were so ordinary they hardly seemed worthy of my grief right then. But I was starting to feel that grief anyway; and the closer we came to the motel where I'd leave Frank, the more I began thinking about going home to Leon, who was probably waiting up for me, an idea that filled me with dread, though for no specific reason, since I was not afraid of him. I wondered, had Pinky already somehow reached him and told him what had happened? It didn't matter, really. I no longer hoped for things the way I once did. I had become weary, I think, of the dishonest life we led.

I said good night to Frank. I knew Frank was ill, ill from alcohol, and that he lived day to day in a state of clouded consciousness now. I didn't think, however, that Frank's troubles would take him from me that night, especially that night, which had ended with singing and high spirits. But they did, all because he didn't go home and stay there, didn't go inside the Golden Spike Motel, where I left him, but decided to go out to the bars again; and then later, much later, he came out and headed home, walking along the railroad tracks that cut west of town. A line of boxcars had been shunted over to onto the rails behind the Pillsbury mill, and he must have gotten sleepy or felt like he was going to pass out, because he lay down in one, just climbed up into one of those boxcars and lay down and he never got up again, because you just don't go to sleep outdoors on winter nights in Utah and expect ever to wake.

All of this I found out later, when his body was discovered in Tonapah, Nevada, by a brakeman who saw a hand through the slats in the boxcar. Frank had gone all the way to Tonapah before somebody found him, and then it took people a long time to figure out who he was, to trace him back to Utah and the Golden Spike Motel. There wasn't a single relative that could be located for him.

"Can you imagine dying like that?" Doreen said, when we heard about it. "Just dying, without leaving chick nor child?"

That night I went home to Leon, and found him still up, sitting in the kitchen, tying flies. It didn't seem to me that he knew I'd had a fight with Pinky in the Trocadero.

"Hi, hon," he said when I came in. He had a patch of rabbit fur in his hands, and he was pulling out little hairs and twisting them at the roots. His tackle box was on the table. In the various compartments were the things he made his flies out of, bits of silver and gold thread, tiny iridescent objects, small barbed hooks, pretty little feathers. His empty beer cans were lined up on the table. Music was playing—some music, I remember, that I didn't like; it was loud and harsh, ricocheting music, just some horrible noise.

"This here is going to be a fly that no fish in the world is going to be able to resist."

"How about that."

"When this fly flies, the fish dies." He looked up at me and smiled and drew a finger across his throat in a sign of death.

His big hands worked slowly with their tiny materials. You had to have patience to tie flies, and I was always surprised to see how much patience he had for this, because in other ways he wasn't a man to wait for things. He wore a brown western shirt with a different-colored yoke. The yoke was blue, like his eyes. On opposite sides of his chest, two brown horse heads had been embroidered, and the horses faced each other, like they were talking across his buttons. I wondered where he'd been that evening, if he'd been out somewhere himself, and I wondered why he didn't ask me where I'd been, how come I'd come home so late, but these were like the unspoken things that had begun to happen. I sat across from him for a while, and then he got up and turned off the music and put the TV on and opened another beer. I went to bed, leaving him to watch the late-night movie.

While I slept, I had no knowledge of the other thing that

had happened: that Frank had stopped in the boxcar, not too far from the motel and his own bed, that he had laid down and gone to sleep by himself, had frozen to death, and then had been taken for a ride, beginning in the early light. He crossed the Salt Flats, and wound down toward Tonapah, arriving there in the afternoon when the setting sun lit the twin hills above the cemetery, making it look like the city of gold, and he lay in the boxcar, undisturbed for another night, having died, as Doreen said, without chick nor child—unless in some far-flung corner of Europe there lives a woman, about my age, who herself has managed to survive, and who has within her those genes of Frank's, perhaps some of his gentleness and his intelligence, maybe a part of his looks—the bright black eyes, for instance. But this, whether or not this woman exists, is something I don't suppose I'll ever know.

Sometime during the next week I saw Pinky. She was sitting in her Buick at the Frosty King. Around her neck was one of those white padded collars. She looked uncomfortable in it. She tried to turn her head, once, and look out the window in my direction, as if she knew I was sitting there in my truck at the stoplight, just watching her; but she couldn't manage to turn around completely, and gave up. I guessed I hadn't broken her neck after all, only wrenched it.

I wanted her to see me, to see how fine I was, how uninjured. I thought of driving right past her and maybe even honking and waving, and then suddenly it didn't seem worth it anymore. The thing was done and over. With that little *pop* in the ladies' room, something had opened up, and both anger and hope had escaped from me. Or was it just Frank's death that made certain things seem so stupid and meaningless? When the light changed, I headed in the other direction, turning west, just in time to see the last little slip of the orange sun disappear behind a row of tall cottonwood trees.

PART TWO

LOS ANGELES

7

FAR OFF in the distance, something golden shone like
fire. Square monoliths, like blocks of bullion, fresh from
the mint.

"What's that?"

"The city," he said.

"What's this, then?"

"The city."

"This is the city, too?"

"It's all the city. It's a big place."

"This is all Los Angeles?"

"You could say that. It's all part of it."

"But it's so flat. What about the buildings?"

"What buildings?"

"The big buildings."

"There aren't any," he said. "Not in this part."

"Where are they?"

"Downtown. That's what you can see, off in the distance."

"How long before we get there?"

"Soon," he said. "It's not far now."

"Do we just stay on this freeway?"

"Yes," he said, "just keep on going." He closed his eyes
and his head rolled back against the door frame.

I drove on, with the "city" surrounding us, consuming and
gray and unimpressive, but now there were big shopping
malls bordering the freeway. I wondered, How do you know
when you've arrived when everything goes on this way?
Where does one thing end and another begin?

Tall signposts rose up above everything, above the palm
trees and the light poles, making a little forest of their own,
announcing SHIRL'S FITNESS CENTER. . . . THE CARPET BARN . . .

ICESKATING . . . WATERBED GALLERY . . . LAMPS PLUS . . . IN 'N
OUT BURGER.

He opened his eyes and sat up straighter and looked
around.

"It's so gray," I said. "It must be overcast today."

"No," he said, "it's just L.A. One of those bad days."

A yellowish cloud covered the land. Buildings were indistinct, also trees. In fact, nothing was clear. The power lines and
rooftops disappeared into grayness. There were many lanes of
cars going in each direction, but the land itself was lost to me; I
couldn't see it. When the roadbed did rise up suddenly, giving
a feeling of being above things, there was still nothing beyond
the freeway to look at, because of the flatness to the land and
because nothing was visible in the clouded light. At one point,
far off in the distance, it looked like there might be a range of
mountains, bluish shapes, faint and cloudy. Ghost mountains.
The houses and buildings, the shopping malls and businesses,
went on forever in every direction, surrounded as if by smoke.
The cars moved together steadily in flowing unified streams,
and they were driven fast. Sometimes brown cement walls
bordered the freeways and there was nothing to see except
cars, rushing in opposite directions.

I thought, This is California. I've arrived.

Again the fire flamed up. It was close now.

"The sunset," Duluth said. "It makes the glass buildings
look gold and orange."

"It's beautiful," I said.

"You're going to see some nice sunsets down here, because of all the smog, you know. It makes them pretty."

It was still light when we finally reached downtown and the
orange glass towers. We stopped at a building, where Duluth
Wing's brother worked, and I sat at the curb while he went
inside to borrow money, although I told him it didn't matter,
he didn't need to pay me back the money he'd borrowed during the drive. But he was insistent, as if it were a matter of
pride, so I said "Okay" and double-parked because there

weren't any spaces big enough for the truck and trailer.

While I waited for Duluth, I looked around and felt astonished by what I saw. Everybody looked foreign. The signs on the stores were in Spanish. Spanish films were advertised at a movie theater. A store marked DISCOTECA played music so loud you could hear it all up and down the street. There were so many people on the sidewalk it was hard for those going in one direction to get past those moving in another. Even the billboards were in Spanish. PURA VIDA, one said, an ad for beer. It seemed like I was in a foreign city. I was used to seeing people who reflected my own likeness, and these people certainly did not. Everything seemed suddenly odd, as if I'd been dropped down abruptly in a new land. I felt I had traveled a distance much further than you could go in two days' worth of driving.

I waited, but Duluth didn't come out. Ten minutes went by. I began thinking, He's ditched me, he's just gone and run out.

"You have to move," somebody suddenly said, and I turned around to see that a policeman had stopped his motorcycle next to the truck. "You can't just stop here," he said.

I could see there was no pleading with him, so I pulled out into traffic, thinking I would circle the block; but once I was in that lane of cars, there wasn't any possibility of doing anything but staying with the traffic, which was carrying me forward faster than I could think. The trailer didn't make it any easier to maneuver. Ahead of me the street divided. There were signs that said HARBOR FREEWAY NORTH and HARBOR FREEWAY SOUTH, and I took the exit south because I couldn't do otherwise. Once on the freeway, I moved as part of a flow of cars heading right into the setting sun, which was so bright I could hardly see. Then I was on something called the Santa Monica Freeway, and I saw there wasn't any possibility of returning to the spot where I'd left Duluth Wing.

So who left whom? Maybe he'd intended to come back out of that building and give me the money, or maybe he hadn't;

but if he did, he'd find me gone and think I'd just driven off without him. I didn't like it when things were left so unfinished. Did cities always make you feel so helpless? Later, when I looked at the directions Jolene had given me, I found that, miraculously, I was on the right freeway, heading in the right direction, the exit I wanted was coming up shortly; and just as quickly as I'd seen how anonymous forces in the city could make you feel separate and confused, I realized that at the next moment you could feel fortuitously placed, as if the elements had conspired to give you a break.

I took the exit for Beverly Hills, and after driving for miles along a wide street lined with one-story buildings, totally different from what I'd seen downtown, I made several turns and came to an area of large houses, surrounded by the biggest lawns I'd ever seen. Everywhere were large apartment buildings that looked like castles with perfectly kept gardens. Sprinklers were turned on, and all around me things were being watered and there was a nice grassy smell. I slowed down, looking for Jolene's address, and it struck me how green and perfect everything was.

Jolene Butterfield had once been my best friend, a friendship that ended when her father, a railroad brakeman named Dick, was transferred to Great Falls in the winter of 1955. We were nine years old when her father announced they were moving to Montana, and we took the news with a mixture of feelings, sorry that we were not going to see each other but also sure that we would never stop being friends, that this separation might be an adventure, somehow, for both of us. I guess this is the kind of unreal thinking common to children, who have a hard time imagining that anything they've ever known might end. It did end, however; and I never saw her again until three or four years ago, when I got a call from her one night. She was passing through town, and I met her at the Trocadero for a beer.

"What are you doing?" she asked me right away.

I told her I was working in the bowling alley, married to
Leon, and then I asked about her.

"I'm an artist. I live in Los Angeles. I'm married to a wonderful man named Vincent. He's from the east . . . a musician.
I'm very happy."

She looked happy. She looked like someone who was sure
of herself and could be comfortable in any situation. "Sophis-
ticated" was the word I thought of later to describe her to
Leon. But she really didn't seem like anybody I'd ever known.
That was the thing—she was a total stranger to me.

She was an only child. Her mother and father, Dick and
Ada, were young, much younger than my parents, although I
don't know now how many years difference there really was
between Ada Butterfield and my mother, whether or not my
mother had just had so many more kids than Ada Butterfield
and this had made her seem older, more settled and wise. Ada
Butterfield was none of those things. She was a wild one.

I remember I use to see her, stretched out on her chaise
lounge, wearing a blue terry-cloth outfit that was little more
than a bra and panties, with a matching terry-cloth band
around her head, sporting dark glasses and smoking cigarettes
and reading magazines on Sunday mornings when my family
left the house for church.

"Look at that doll," my dad would say. "The bathing
beauty of Orchard Avenue."

Dick, her husband, was usually sitting near her or else
working in some other part of the garden. A dragon tattoo
curled around one of his biceps. He always had a cigarette
stuck between his lips, which he could smoke entirely from
start to finish without using his hands. They weren't Mormons;
they weren't even from Utah originally but had moved there
from some place like Detroit, or perhaps Cincinnati. They
were extraordinarily exotic people to me.

Sometimes, when I'd be over to the Butterfields', Ada
would say, "Honey, let's just kick up our heels," and she'd
grab my hands and start dancing me around to some music that

was on the radio. I remember them standing at the sink in the kitchen, Dick and Ada, making dinner together while Jolene and I watched some program on TV, and how Dick, when he didn't think anybody was looking, would put his arms around her and grab her by the rear end and lift her up off the ground, or kiss her on the neck. My parents never did this.

I felt there was something wild, something that I wanted, always there at their house when I entered it, something that said, "Any minute you're going to dance, any minute you're going to do something that you never thought of doing before." The smell of smoke and beer and coffee—forbidden and dangerous substances—filled their house and clung to their clothes.

Sometimes my mother said to me, "I don't understand why you can't pick a member of the church for a friend," and I knew she didn't approve of the Butterfields, the way my clothes smelled of smoke when I came home from visiting them. But she didn't try to force me to give them up.

Occasionally, Jolene would come with me to visit the chinchillas at the Bagley place, but she didn't really like them, she said, because they smelled. Even then I could see our differences, how she had a daintiness I didn't, a certain fastidiousness that I wouldn't ever acquire and which seemed fussy and whiney to me even at the time. She seemed to have no feeling for animals at all, not even dogs or cats.

Over at my house it was the usual free-for-all, always a bunch of kids trying to get what they wanted and making a lot of noise in the process. Things had their predictable patterns, and everything—*everything*—was tied to the church, it was our life, so there was this strange order to the chaos, a sober uniformity lacking altogether in the Butterfields' house.

The morning Jolene moved to Montana, we stood outside her house and waited for the real-estate people to finish some business with her parents. The kids who lived next door, whose father was in the Air Force and had recently returned from a tour in Japan, yelled over the fence at us, a word that sounded like "Bakatadi!"

"Bakatadi" meant "shit" in Japanese; by then every kid in the neighborhood knew that. We didn't like these kids.

"Bakatadi on you!" Jolene yelled back. "And on your mother!" It was a wintery day, I remember, and a chilly wind was blowing against my legs, and I looked down to see that my skin had tiny cracks in it which formed little segments on my legs, like the lines in dried mud. We were shy with each other, not knowing how to say goodbye, and we focused all our attention on the kids we didn't like, on reassuring each other how perfectly stupid we thought they were.

Ada squeezed me when it was time to go. "Honey," she said, "you were one of the best things about this neighborhood, and we're going to miss you a heap. You come on up and visit us in Great Falls."

And I thought I would; I could see myself getting on one of those trains that Dick Butterfield worked on and riding it all the way to Montana. I figured I would do it as soon as I was old enough to make a trip by myself. But then I was only nine, and all I could say to Ada Butterfield was "I will—I'll come visit pretty soon."

I did not go to Great Falls. I never saw Jolene again until I met her that night at the Trocadero. And yet, when I called her and said I was moving to Los Angeles and needed a place to stay for a few days, she said of course. "Of course we'll help you," she added. "Plan on staying as long as you need to."

And now I was here. I looked up to see lights on in the windows. I put on fresh lipstick, straightened my hair, and climbed out of the truck.

"My God!" she said, hugging me as soon as I was through the front door. We turned around a few times, holding on to each other.

"I brought you some chili sauce," I said. "I've got some jars of pears for you in the truck." I hadn't known what to bring to her, and I thought a homemade gift would be nice.

"Chili sauce? I remember this stuff from meals at your house years ago!"

Jolene turned toward the other people sitting in the room, a man in a chair and a couple on the couch.

"Let me introduce you to my husband, Vincent, and our friends Leonard and Sandra Hockman. Verna . . ." she said, then hesitated and asked, "Are you going by Flake or—"

"Fields," I said. There was a mirror in which I caught sight of myself. I noticed I'd split the arm of my coat where it joined at the shoulder, and when I reached out to shake hands with the Hockmans, a gap opened in the stiff material, like a little bow-shaped mouth forming a hello.

"We just finished dinner, but there are some leftovers," Jolene said. "Do you want something?"

"No thanks." The people on the couch were grinning at me. Jolene's husband looked more serious. He sat there, studying me, his face expressionless, and I felt a little awkward. Everybody was dressed very nicely, as if for a party. The woman on the couch sat sideways, facing her husband, with her feet on his lap. I felt like I'd interrupted something.

"Well, sit down," Jolene said, and dropped into a chair abruptly, as if to show me how it was done. Everyone was still looking at me.

"I think I'll get my bags out of the truck first."

"Vincent can help you with that, can't you, Vincent?"

"There's not much," I said. "I can get it."

"Oh, well. Why don't you help her, Vincent?"

Vincent started to get up and stumbled slightly. Was he drunk?

"I can get my own suitcase," I said.

"No, no," Jolene said. "Let him help."

Vincent followed me outside without speaking. "I can't believe how green everything is," I said, turning toward him. He was just a little taller than me, and very thin. He had straight black hair, and a thick lock flopped over his forehead and swung in front of his eyes when he walked.

"I mean, I'm not used to seeing everything look so green like this."

"Oh?" he said.

"Especially in the middle of the winter. I picked up this hitchhiker on the way down, so I had company most of the way."

"Oh?" he said again.

"Isn't that dangerous?" he added after a moment.

"I don't know—is it?"

"Apparently not. You're here."

"How long have you lived here?" I stopped and looked up at the building. It looked like something out of a movie, a castle. It was made of stone and built around a courtyard filled with flower beds with all the flowers in bloom.

"Two years."

"It must cost a lot."

"It's fairly expensive," he said.

"It's very nice. Can you pick these flowers, or don't they like you to?" I asked, looking at the blossoms.

It took him a moment to answer. "I don't think they'd like you to."

"Oh," I said. "Well, it'd be nice if you could—then you'd always have fresh flowers in the house."

I walked to the back of the trailer and opened the doors. He stopped at the curb and said, "What's *this?*"

At first I didn't know what he meant, and then I saw what he was looking at. "A horse trailer," I said. I took out a big brown suitcase and a smaller plastic tote. He picked up the suitcase, and I took the smaller bag and followed him up the walk. I thought, He doesn't like me. I felt his coolness and I wondered why.

Suddenly I stopped and inhaled deeply. "Do you smell that?" I asked. "I don't know what it is, but I could die smelling that."

He didn't respond.

"Do you know what I'm talking about? Can you smell that?"

"Yes," he answered, looking at me curiously. "Yes, I can."

"Well, what is it?"

"Jasmine," he said. "Night-blooming jasmine."

"It only blooms at night?"

"I think so," he said.

"How odd!" I stood still in the warm, perfumed darkness, savoring this remarkable smell.

He turned away abruptly and hurried up the path, and I followed.

"Leonard doesn't like the idea, but I do," Sandra was saying when we returned.

"Just put your things down right there, dear, and I'll show you where you'll be staying later," Jolene said to me.

It comforted me to be called "dear" by someone my own age, although it seemed a little odd, too. She certainly had changed. She had maroon hair.

"Leonard and Vincent and Sandra all play in the same community orchestra," Jolene said to me as I sat down in a chair near a fireplace. "Leonard and Sandra have just moved here from Toronto, and we're discussing whether they ought to buy a house right away or just stay in their apartment and look around some more before they make such a big investment."

"Oh," I said.

"Big deal, huh?" Sandra said, and giggled.

There was a fire in the fireplace, and it surprised me, because the windows were open and I couldn't understand having a fire when it was warm enough to have the windows open.

"More drinks?" Jolene asked.

"I never say no," Leonard said.

"I think that's a yes," Vincent said dryly.

"I haven't asked you, Vincent, which musicians are you particularly fond of?" Leonard said as Jolene handed him another glass of wine. She also gave me one.

Vincent frowned. "No favorites, really," he said.

"None? There must be someone you like."

"John Philip Sousa."

"Tell him the truth, Vincent," Jolene said.

"Wayne Newton," Vincent said.

Sandra gave a big laugh.

"Donka shane," Vincent said.

"You *are* funny," Sandra said, wiggling her bare feet and taking another sip of wine.

Jolene, who looked annoyed, said, "Tell him who you like, Vincent. He likes Schubert. He's doing his dissertation on Schubert."

"Ah, Schubert!" Leonard said. "Very interesting. A rather complex man, wouldn't you agree? He stands between worlds, doesn't he?"

"What worlds are you speaking of?"

"The worlds of classical and romantic music."

"I suppose you could say that."

Leonard went on. "His music was emotional in the romantic manner, poetically conceived, but nevertheless cast in the formal molds of the classical school. A very interesting composer, Schubert. What aspect of his work does your dissertation deal with?"

"Really," Vincent said, "I'd rather not discuss it. I'm just beginning to formulate my ideas. It would be premature to talk about them."

It was clear Vincent was uncomfortable. But Leonard persisted. "Have you ever heard 'The Devil's Palace of Desire'?"

"Yes, of course."

"Charming example of his lyricism and high spirits."

Vincent said nothing.

"Tell me," Leonard said, "we know so little about you, except Jolene says you work at home. What do you do for a living? Obviously you can't live on the salary the orchestra pays, none of us can. Do you have some side business? Stocks? Teaching . . . ?"

"I have a small income," Vincent said quietly, "so I don't have to work at the moment."

"Ah, a remittance man!" Leonard chirped.

"What's that?" Jolene asked.

"It's English, I suppose," Leonard said. "It used to refer to the sort of chap who went out to the colonies—Burma, say, or perhaps Africa—and didn't really do anything but managed to live quite nicely—not lavishly, but with style, because each month he received a remittance, a small check from home."

"That's rather odious," Vincent said. "Implying that I fit the description of a man who does nothing but sit around waiting for checks from home." He frowned and looked down at his hands, as if cross with Leonard; but Leonard quickly assured him that he meant it as a compliment, after all—wasn't the world made better by all those people with time on their hands who could afford to make contributions to culture?

"Vincent never sits around. He's always busy," Jolene said. "There's his music, his dissertation . . . and his hobbies . . ."

"Why do I feel like a child whose mother is extolling his virtues?" Vincent asked. He looked at me. I smiled and shrugged. Then he did something that surprised me. He crossed his eyes and then let them go back to normal. I laughed and looked down at my drink.

"Leonard doesn't mean to be rude," Sandra said, giggling again. "He'd like nothing more than to be a remittance man himself."

"I don't doubt it," Vincent said.

"Don't be so touchy, Vincent. God, musicians are so temperamental!" Jolene said, turning toward me. "If I had known that . . ."

"If you'd know *what?*"

"Oh, Vincent, lighten up."

There was a bad feeling in the room at that moment, and I wondered, What do these people feel for each other?

After a moment of silence, Leonard suddenly turned toward me and said, "And what brings you to Los Angeles?"

"My husband left me," I said. "I wanted to start over in a new place."

"Oh." There was a silence.

"What do you do?" Sandra asked.

"My last job was in a bowling alley." There was another long silence. The Hockmans, I noticed, exchanged quick glances.

"And who is your favorite musician?" Vincent asked abruptly. "That seems to be the number-one question on everyone's mind this evening."

"Vincent . . ." Jolene said.

"Oh, that's easy to answer," I said, smiling. "That would be Patsy Cline, no question about it."

"Interesting," Leonard said, smiling, and yet looking at me in a way that made me think that maybe he didn't think too much of my choice.

The Hockmans stayed a little longer, discussing real estate and the difference between one part of town and another, and then finally, around eleven o'clock, they left. After they'd gone, Jolene took me upstairs and showed me the room where I'd be staying. It was across from their bedroom, with a bathroom in between us. The room had a view of the courtyard. Jolene opened the windows and showed me how the couch made into a bed and where to put my clothes in the closet. She pointed out a small pitcher of water next to the couch and a bowl of fruit sitting on a table. "In case you get hungry or thirsty in the night," she said.

She told me how to use the various lights in the room and pointed out where extra blankets and pillows were. Then she said she was exhausted and she'd see me in the morning; we'd have breakfast together. She kissed me lightly, first on one cheek, then, surprisingly, on the other, and I waited, hesitant, uncertain whether there were more kisses coming and where they would land. Vincent stood in the doorway, watching us.

"Good night," he said, and raised his hand in a small, feeble wave.

Later, I heard them murmuring in the next room. They talked for a while, and then it grew quiet.

I stood at the window looking out. The sky was milky, and I realized it probably never got completely dark here in L.A. It must be the perfect city to see from outer space, with its billions of lights spreading out in symmetrical grids over the flat land.

Well, here I was.

The room was large. Every wall was a bookcase, and every shelf was full of books. There was a desk facing the window. The desktop had been cleared off. There was a feeling of neatness, of everything in its place. A small white statue of a man, just his head and shoulders, sat on one of the shelves: FRANZ SCHUBERT was written across the base. But the most interesting thing about the room was all the lights. There were a dozen lights, all different kinds: floor lamps and lights affixed to bookcases, lights shining upward and downward or attached to walls so that the light diffused and spread out, making beautiful shapes. There were little lights and big lights, lights that had covers perforated with tiny holes that threw a pattern of pinpointed light on walls. There were cones of light and beams of light. Crazy! So many lights. I was used to one light in the middle of the ceiling, which you turned off and on with a switch near a door. Why did they need all these lights? When I was finally ready for bed, it took me a little while to figure out how to turn each one off.

I lay in bed on that first night in the city and thought of Leon. When I tried to picture him, I saw him in his father's fields again.

Only this time, I saw myself, too, as if from a great distance up in the sky. I saw how in my old clothes I made a rather sad figure.

Could I have tried harder?

There was only this, a man and a woman in the fields. The man didn't even see the woman. The woman saw nothing else but the man. And then the rain began; the first drops fell, unbelievably large, and splattered like small wet bombs on the dusty surface of the tractor.

8

IN THE MORNING, I sat in the kitchen while Jolene fixed breakfast.

"Have you ever had lox?" she asked me.

"Locks?"

"This stuff." She tipped a plate of something melon-colored toward me. "It's a special kind of salmon."

"No, I've never had that," I said.

"It's delicious. We're having it with eggs this morning."

"Sounds good," I said, though I didn't much like fish, especially for breakfast.

"Tell me, did all this just happen suddenly?"

"All what?"

"With your husband."

"Well," I sighed. I didn't know how to begin to tell all that had happened, how it was and wasn't sudden . . . how I'd known about Pinky but didn't think it was going to lead to what it did.

I was thinking this over, how to begin, when Jolene said, "If it's too painful, just don't talk about it."

"Well . . ." I said, and then I didn't know where to go. "It isn't that. . . . It's just hard to know where to begin."

"Don't answer this if you don't want to, but I'm wondering—did you love him?"

"I think so."

"Listen, if you have to think about it, maybe you didn't."

"I don't know about that," I said. "What I meant was, I'm

pretty sure I did. I was happy for a lot of years with him." I could hear Vincent in the next room. He was reading the newspaper. The paper rattled and he cleared his throat. I was sure he was listening to us.

"I don't believe in divorce," Jolene said.

I didn't know it was something you could or couldn't believe in. It seemed like something that happened to people, who sometimes wanted it and sometimes didn't.

She broke some eggs into a bowl and began beating them. She was wearing a sweater with big sleeves, and I kept worrying that the sleeves were going to dip into the eggs.

"But I suppose it's inevitable," she went on. "Because it's just so easy. That's what bothers me. It's so easy to get divorced. Everybody does it. And for what? To meet somebody else who it's not going to be any different with. We live in bizarre times, don't we? Nobody knows whether something will work anymore, whether the person they're with today will be the person they're with tomorrow. How do we behave? Everybody thinks they can invent themselves anew, that another person will make it different. Divorce is the big answer to everything. Everyone I know has gone through a divorce— some twice, or even three times. It's a mess."

"It wasn't my idea to get divorced," I said.

"Oh, I'm not saying anything about you, don't get me wrong."

"It happened to me."

"Of course. It can just happen, I guess."

Like birth or death, I thought.

She sighed. "If the other person doesn't want to stop it, I suppose it's very difficult."

"All I know is I wouldn't have left Leon if it was up to me. I was hoping things would work out. But they didn't."

"Of course," she said again. Then she called out, "Vincent, come to the table, please," and began carrying food into the next room.

After breakfast, Jolene said, "Are you okay for the day? You have things to do? I've got to get to my studio."

"I'll be fine," I said.

"Oh, good," Jolene replied. "I'm off, then."

When she'd gone, Vincent and I were left alone. He sat across the table from me. I had set my bangs with a pink roller, just one, and as I turned to look at him, I felt it swing loose and almost fall off, so I took it out.

He said, "What are your plans for the day?"

I shrugged and was about to say something, but he spoke up first. "You know, I work here at home," he said.

"What do you do?"

"I'm studying for a degree in music. At the moment, I'm writing a paper on Schubert."

"Who's he? I saw that little statue of him up in the room."

"Well, he's a composer, but that's not really the point." He looked away, as if he were trying to say something that was difficult for him.

"I need a very quiet place to work," he said. "I don't know what your plans are, but if you stay here for very long, it would help if you understand that I need to work undisturbed."

I nodded and smiled at him. "No problem," I said.

He said, "Oh, good, because I work in the room where you're staying. If you wouldn't mind letting me get in there early in the morning, I could keep to my routine. It's very important to me."

"Okay," I said.

"If you need anything now, could you get it from the room? Because I'd like to start work soon, and I'd rather not be disturbed."

He got up and began clearing the dishes. I looked down at my hands for a moment, and when I looked up, I said, "It's a funny coincidence, but I love music, too. My father's a musician." I thought of him playing his drums at the Golden Hours Center with Gene Moffatt and Rubio and his friends. "I guess

I got my interest in music from him," I added.

"Oh, really?" He scraped the dirty plates and then care-fully stacked them. "Excuse me," he said, and headed for the kitchen.

He was just finishing the dishes when I came downstairs with my things. He wore big yellow rubber gloves, and when he turned to face me, he held his hands up in front of him, like a surgeon who is about to operate and doesn't want to touch anything for fear of contamination. A lock of straight black hair fell over one eye. His face was so skinny his bones stuck out. His cheeks, nose, and chin made sharp angles out of his pale skin.

"Can I ask you something?"

"Yes," he said.

"Why do you have all those lights in that room?"

"Well," he said, "light is very important to me, I suppose. All the different and subtle effects of light. It has a great effect on one's mood, light. It seems nice to have a number of possi-bilities."

"Oh. I was just wondering." I still didn't get it.

"Well, I'll be off," I said.

"Do you know what you're going to do today?"

"I might visit relatives. Or I might go to the beach and look at the ocean."

"The easiest way to get to the beach," he said, "is to take Santa Monica Boulevard all the way to the ocean. This street takes you to Santa Monica Boulevard, the one right out here." He pointed out the window.

"I'll probably visit my relatives," I said.

"Well, that's up to you," he said.

"Is it all right if I just drop the horse trailer at the curb?"

"Drop it?" he said rather worriedly.

"Unhitch it."

"I guess so," he said, "though I don't know how long you can leave it there. There might be a city ordinance or something." After a moment he added, "Can I ask why you brought a horse trailer with you?"

"I brought it because it's valuable and I didn't have time to sell it. I figured I'd sell it here."

"Oh. Well, yes, I guess that makes sense."

"Seen you later, then," I said, backing away.

Outside, there was so much light on everything it was like an overexposed picture. I stood at the curb for a moment, letting the sun soak into me. Suddenly I looked up and saw Vincent standing in the window, watching me, but he moved away quickly when he saw me looking up at him, stepping out of sight, before I could wave goodbye. Why did he do that? I wondered.

It took a few minutes to unhitch the trailer, and then I drove away, thinking how everything was so strange, so completely and utterly unknown, and I wondered, what was I doing here anyway, with no better plan than I had?

I followed Santa Monica until I came to the beach, then turned south and came to Mar Vista. A man at a gas station gave me directions. The house wasn't hard to find. It was a little white frame house with a long porch and two rockers—just what I would have expected from Heber and LaRue.

"This is a surprise," LaRue said, in a voice that didn't seem surprised but was flat and sounded blasé. She held the screen door open with one hand, and with the other she clasped a carrot, holding it as if it were a flashlight or the end of a garden hose.

"I was looking at you through the screen thinking, Now who is that? I thought you was the neighbor girl for a moment. She comes over and borrows the *TV Guide.* Heber! Heber!"

Into the dark rooms of the aging house she called for her husband, who only moments before, she said, had been right there. Now he didn't seem to be anywhere. The house was a dark, cool place. Trees and foliage had grown up around the windows and blocked out the light.

"Heber!" she yelled. Her voice lacked substance, but it was the only part of her that seemed frail. LaRue was thick in the middle, shaped like an egg, with a flat rear end and legs that looked too spindly for her bulk. She wore a lot of heavy turquoise jewelry.

"Where'd he get himself to?" she asked, genuinely perplexed.

LaRue came from New Mexico, where she had been born and raised in the small town of Thoreau, just north of Albuquerque. When she married Heber, my father's oldest brother, she moved from Thoreau to Snowflake, where Heber worked as a livestock inspector. Then they moved to Chinle, in the middle of the Navajo reservation. Heber worked for the government motor pool, operating an agency garage. During that period, in the 1930s and '40s, they amassed a collection of Indian rugs, kachina dolls, pottery, and jewelry by taking in these objects as collateral on tires, car repairs, and small cash advances for booze. The Indians, who rarely had the means to reclaim their belongings, left one object after another with Heber and LaRue, until their house was crammed with stuff. Once LaRue showed me some things from their collection, which was kept in dozens of shoe boxes under the bed and on the upper shelves of their clothes closet. "This here's a nice piece," she'd say, laying out an old necklace on the bed. There were boxes of these things everywhere. In the sixties they moved to California to be near their son, who was an agronomist at a university. LaRue was now eighty-seven; Heber was ninety-one. The Flakes lived a long time.

I followed her into the living room, which smelled musty, and sat down on a couch that was slightly damp. I assumed these things were due to the house being so near the ocean, although I couldn't be sure. Even the air felt wet.

"What are you doing down here?" LaRue asked. She sat

down opposite me and looked at me levelly. LaRue was a
no-nonsense person. Some relatives described her as crabby.

"A vacation," I said. I didn't feel like getting into the details of the truth.

"Where's Leon?"

"He's home."

"Oh." She looked a little bored.

"Well, it's a surprise to see you," she said. "What we used
to say," she said, pointing her carrot at me, "was that if you
dropped a knife, your visitor that day would be a man. If it was
a spoon, it was going to be a woman. And if you dropped a
fork, a child would be coming. I was trying to think if I
dropped anything this morning."

"What'd it mean if you dropped a spatula?"

"That I don't know."

"People must have been hard up for company in those
days."

"We were," LaRue said. "You don't know what it's like
living miles from the next house. You get so lonely you start
aching for people to visit."

"It's a funny idea, silverware being used to foretell the
future."

"Your grandmother believed in it."

"Mom used to say, if one magpie flies across the field, it's
good luck coming to you. If two magpies fly across a field,
though, that's bad luck coming your way."

"We don't have magpies here in the city," LaRue said.

"I wonder what that means."

"Maybe it means there's no luck around."

LaRue said, "Something else. Your grandmother used to
say that if a rooster come up on the back porch, wherever his
tail pointed would be the direction that the company would be
coming from."

"That's funny," I said. "I'll have to keep a rooster sometime just to try that out."

"I don't remember when the last time I saw you was," LaRue said.

"Neither do I."

"Probably before your folks visited us here. We didn't have such a good time. Your dad cut back all Heber's trees and made him mad as hell."

"I know. I heard."

"It doesn't make any difference now, of course. Trees grow. In fact, they've all grown back."

"People forget, too," I added.

"Oh sure," she said.

"Do you want a Pepsi?" LaRue asked.

"Sure."

"I don't know where Heber went to. I'll look for him." LaRue got up slowly out of her chair, still holding her unpeeled carrot, and tottered off to the kitchen.

I looked around the room. There was a framed picture of the prophet Joseph Smith hanging over the piano. He looked like Napoleon Bonaparte. I remember once reading that near the place where he was born in upstate New York, the church erected a monument, and just before you reach the site there's a marker pointing the way that says: VISIT THE JOSEPH SMITH MONUMENT, WORLD'S LARGEST POLISHED SHAFT. On top of the piano were a few smaller pictures, including one of a goofy-looking kid holding a clarinet.

I walked to a window. Because of the way the house sat on the cusp of a hill, I could see the ocean over the rooftops. It was still a little ways off. There were many houses in between myself and the ocean, but the streets sloped down toward the sea, and the water seemed to rise up, as if it, too, sloped, only upwards, toward a horizon that was higher than I was. The water looked rippled and velvety, like the skin on a boxer dog—only, of course, the water was blue-gray, not brown, and it turned charcoal-black where it met the sky.

"Sometimes you can see Catalina Island," LaRue said when she returned. "I guess it's too smoggy today." As she handed me my Pepsi, the ice tinkled in the glass. LaRue had slight palsy and her hands weren't steady. I wondered if LaRue would have the information I wanted.

"Heber's sleeping," she said. "He'll get up later."

We sat down.

"I wanted to ask you something."

"What's that?"

"About Inez."

"What do you want to know?"

"Does she still live in Los Angeles?"

"Yes."

"Do you have an address?"

"Yes. I've also got a phone number. If it's still good. Inez moves around a lot. You never know where to find her."

"When was the last time you saw her?"

"Quite a while ago. We don't actually see each other. I'm too old to go out much. Heber and I are kind of scared of driving. We go to church, the grocery store, that's about it."

LaRue's head wiggled slightly—the palsy. She sighed and looked sad. "The last time I visited her, she was still married to a fellow named Jim, who didn't treat her well. He was quite a bit older. He has something wrong with him—some kind of cancer, I think. Can you imagine that? Another husband with a sickness? I don't know why some people have as many troubles as they do, but I don't know anybody who's had worse luck in life than Inez. And she doesn't deserve it, although I don't suppose anybody does."

"Is she still living with this guy?"

"I don't know. They were living here for a time, then they moved down to El Segundo, and I think she may have left him now. The last time I spoke to her, she was living in East L.A. She didn't mention her husband. He wasn't good for Christobel. That's why Inez sent her away to live in the home. Christobel has emotional problems—I'm sure you know about that. Your mother must know it. She's like a little girl, and here she is a grown woman."

"I thought I'd try to see Inez while I'm down here."

"I'll give you her number. Don't be surprised if you don't recognize her. Life hasn't been good to her. I think this husband drank, and I think she got to drinking there pretty good, too."

I looked up at the picture of the goofy-looking kid on the piano. "Is that your grandson?"

"Yes, that's Marlin," LaRue said. 'That picture's pretty old. He's on a mission now in Honduras. When he found out where he was going on his mission, he called me up and told me, and I said, 'Where's Honduras?' "

"Central America," I said.

"Yes, he told me that, but until then I'd never heard of it."

"It's down there by the Panama Canal, isn't it?"

"Yes, right there where the map gets skinny," LaRue said. "I send him letters addressed to 'Hermano Flake, care of Los Mormones.' "

"What does 'hermano' mean?"

"Brother."

"Oh." Hermano Marlin Flake. It sounded terrible.

"Let me see if I can find that number," LaRue said, and after several rocking starts she propelled herself from her chair. When she came back, she brought the telephone number for Inez, and also an address, which she said might not be good anymore. She brought a more recent picture of Marlin as well, who still looked goofy. Then she showed me another photograph, and when I looked at it, my heart ached a little. It was a picture of my brother Carl, and Inez, and their little baby, Christobel, taken out of doors, on a day when the sun was shining brightly. Carl stood beside Inez, and just slightly behind her. His hands were clasped on her shoulders, as if he were holding her up and at the same time presenting her to the world. Inez looked trim, and her shiny black hair was styled in a sleek pageboy. In her arms, baby Christobel was being cradled for the camera. Inez smiled. She looked so young. Carl, who was very thin, looked straight into the camera. He appeared serene, as though he were a man with a future, in spite of the fact that his neck was bandaged and behind him stood a wheelchair. Farther in the distance, hardly in focus, was the soft, amorphous shape of a white building with many windows—the Alameda Naval Hospital, which would be his last, lengthy residence on earth.

When I left LaRue's house, I took the picture of Carl and Inez with me. I drove down to the beach and took my shoes off and walked in the water for a while. Then I sat on the sand and looked at the waves. The ocean was beautiful, but it frightened me. I saw a seagull, standing on the sand, struggling to free itself from the plastic rings that join a six-pack of soda. One of the rings had become caught on its beak and now circled the seagull's head just below its eyes. The bird shook its head and opened its beak over and over but it couldn't get rid of the plastic stuck on its head. Suddenly it lifted into the air and flew out over the sea, the plastic rings still trailing from its beak.

I drove home in beautiful light. It was the winter light of California, pastel, reflected from hundreds of windows and filling the sky just above the horizon with an icy pink. No one was home when I arrived. I let myself in. There was a note from Jolene: "We've gone out with friends. Make yourself at home. Chicken in fridge."

I made a sandwich and watched TV for a while. Later, alone in my room, I took out the picture of Carl and Inez and propped it up next to the statue of Schubert, where I could see it from the bed, and I left it there until the next morning, when I knew Vincent would be coming up to work. After that night, it became a ritual: each night I took the picture out, putting it in the same place, and each morning I removed it, slipping it into the pocket in my suitcase. In this way, I began living with the image of Carl and Inez and little Christobel, and I thought of them more and more each day.

9

I DON'T KNOW HOW Inez and my brother met. I doubt anybody asked him that before he died. I know that she came from Mexico to the United States when she was a child. Her parents were farm workers. She met Carl in San Francisco in 1953. He was in the Navy. She was working in a beauty parlor and living in the Mission District, in an apartment she shared with her mother.

Sometimes I wonder, How could this have happened? How did they ever get together, a Mormon and a Mexican? But all I know is the year, 1953, and the place, San Francisco, and that he was a sailor and she a beautician.

I don't know how long they'd known each other before she became pregnant. I know that Carl wasn't yet eighteen, and Inez was twenty-three, and that when my father found out his son intended to marry a Mexican woman who was pregnant as well as six years older than him, he contacted my uncle Raymond, a lawyer who lived just outside San Francisco, and learned that legally, not only did Carl not have to marry Inez, but she could have charges brought against her for corrupting a minor.

Armed with this information, my father tried to talk Carl out of marrying her, but it didn't work. It was too late. Carl sent word that they'd already married, and he was bringing his bride home to Utah for a visit, just as soon as he could get a leave from the Navy. He confessed he didn't know her very well. But he knew the child was his, he said, and he felt honor- and duty-bound. That was Carl.

For weeks before they arrived, the talk was of their visit— of the spic, the wetback, the son who had been hoodwinked. I figured listening to all this that she was a monster who had attached herself to my brother and from whom he could now never escape.

I was nine years old the summer they visited. It was the time of the Korean War, which meant nothing to me except that Carl was sometimes on ships in the Pacific and this, I knew, caused my parents to worry for his safety.

Carl had dropped out of high school, or, rather, flunked out for lack of interest. He just never bothered to graduate. I suppose he'd seen the Navy as some kind of future, a way to leave Willard and see some of the world, a chance for a more adventuresome life. I remember the morning he left home to report for service. My father and mother said goodbye to him in the living room, while it was still dark outside. I was there, too. Everyone else was asleep.

"Never do anything to bring shame on the family name," my father said to Carl that morning just as he was leaving. This was something that had been said by his father, and by his father's father, who had lived during a frontier time when a man's name meant a lot in a territory. But where Carl would be going, family reputations wouldn't mean much.

It seemed funny to me that Carl was leaving us when it was still dark outside, as if his call to military duty required that he slip away under cover of night. He was the most handsome of all my parents' children, although that didn't really mean anything to him; he wasn't vain. He was just perfectly formed, a beautiful young man who, I realized much later, looked a lot like James Dean. He was the oldest, and he'd borne the hard edge of my father's personality, the first to plough the tough emotional landscape. Now he was coming home with his bride, Inez Mendoza, and we were all curious. But none of us was prepared for what he brought.

They arrived in the afternoon and walked to the house from where the bus had left them on the highway. They held a suitcase between them. We saw them coming up the road and formed a half-circle just inside the door, waiting to greet them. My father, who was prepared not to like Inez and to punish his son by maintaining a disapproving and detached attitude, stood behind us. Inez, however, was like a whirlwind of energy that, once set loose in our midst, couldn't be controlled.

She called my father "Dad" and hugged him and then, to everyone's surprise, rubbed his balding head and said at least she wouldn't have to give him a haircut. She called my mother "Mom." "Dad and Mom," she said. Her teeth were extraordinarily white next to her deep brown skin. Her eyes and hair were black and they carried light. She wore a beautiful dress made out of a shiny red material, which fit her curves closely. She was sleek and well groomed. Her pregnancy didn't yet show. More than anything else, she was so confident as to appear sort of brash. With all her warmth, however, this brashness was turned into something wonderful—a confidence and a natural ebullience. She was irresistible, and at the same time intimidating.

I was instantly terrified of her, and when—during the introductions, working her way down the line of kids—she finally came to me, I turned and fled. I ran downstairs and hid underneath the stairs, in a closet near the laundry room.

In a while she came down to find me. Calling my name, she coaxed me out of the closet. She held my hands and knelt down in front of me and said she was going to give me a haircut, would I like that? She laughed and talked so fast, in a kind of language that I could understand but which was still somehow foreign, and all her warmth and vivacity pulled at me, and I felt that I was in the presence of an extraordinary person, so different from us.

She said, *"Tu eres mi hermana."*

I tried to pull away.

"Do you know what that means?"

I shook my head.

"You are my sister." She laughed. She told me I was pretty. *Muy bonita,* she said.

Later, I found myself trying to be near her as much as possible. I wanted to touch her clothes, to stand next to her, to feel the force of her burning attention on me. Sometimes I saw Carl standing in the background, watching her, mute but pleased, as if he'd brought us some remarkable discovery and was now letting us examine it. My father remained aloof. My mother, who was herself pregnant with her eighth child, was cordial to Carl, but she withheld her approval. Inez seemed hardly to notice their coolness.

Carl and Inez left the following Thursday, on a bus, boarding it late at night. My parents didn't speak about her afterward, at least not in our presence. It was a subject they preferred not to discuss, although I couldn't help feeling that she had charmed them a little, too. It was simply a touchy topic.

A short while later my mother received an official-looking letter from the Navy. It was signed by a doctor. She didn't understand its contents, and since she had an appointment with her obstetrician, she took it along, hoping he would explain it to her. The letter said that her son had sarcoma, discovered during a physical examination while Carl was at sea. He had complained of a pain in his collarbone, which he thought came from an old basketball injury suffered in high school. But tests showed that it was sarcoma, already quite advanced, and he was being sent to the naval hospital at Alameda, near San Francisco, for further examination.

"What's sarcoma?" my mother asked.

The doctor told her the truth. Carl had bone cancer, which was invariably fatal. He didn't have long to live.

In fact, it took him a little over a year to die. He was nineteen. Most of that time was spent in the hospital; but twice, for very brief periods, he was allowed to return to the apartment in the Mission District, with the outside staircase leading up to the two rooms. There he briefly shared the ordinary things of life with his wife and mother-in-law. These visits were always short, but Carl was happy just to be home, with his pregnant wife and his mother-in-law, in their little apartment, like other couples, other families. He was content with small daily events such as meals, radio programs, records, the newspaper, and a night's sleep curled against his wife. "Fate deals you a hand," he said to Inez, and he tried to play his out with dignity, though they never forgot he was dying.

Most of the time, however, Carl was in the hospital, and Inez slept on a cot near his bed and, during the day, continued to work at her job in a beauty shop right up to the time when the baby was born. It was a girl, and they named her Christobel. Carl, drugged on morphine, gazed at the baby girl from his hospital bed and smiled at his accomplishment. People who visited him—aunts, uncles, my parents—found him remarkably peaceful. He lost weight rapidly. Toward the end, he weighed only eighty pounds, and he was taking doses of morphine, having built up a resistance to it, that would have killed a normal man.

There had never been any question that Inez loved him. She had known he was her true husband, as some people do know these things, the first time she met him. But now her love took on a fierceness, a passion that seemed like religious fervor.

Only once did I make the trip with my parents to visit him in the hospital. I remember sitting beside a window where I could see the bay.

Inez hardly let go of him during the whole visit. She smiled a lot. You could see how much she loved him. He was quiet—drugged, I suppose, now that I think back on it. Still, he seemed peaceful. If she got up to move something or fetch a glass of water, he followed her with his eyes. Then he would reach out for her, and instantly she was there by his side again, taking his hand. She kidded; she sat on his bed, stroked his head, and made jokes for visitors.

Once, she held him in her arms and tried to get him to drink. You could see with how much love she was trying to coax him back from the edges of his terrible sickness, trying to keep him with her. All that energy inside her poured out and broke over him! There were times when it seemed she could do it. Sometimes, she said, both she and the baby spent the night in the hospital room with him. Nurses bent rules for her. But normally, the baby stayed with Inez's mother, in the apartment with the outside staircase, so that Inez might be alone with him. The end, the doctors kept saying, was not far away.

The summer Carl finally died was a very long one for us back in Willard, Utah. My mother gave birth to a son in June, bringing one child into the world as she was losing another. Almost weekly my parents would get a call from the doctors saying, "You'd better come, it doesn't seem like he'll make it through the night."

Three times that summer my parents went to Carl's bedside and neighbors cared for us. But Carl wouldn't die that night, or the next; and eventually they'd have to return to Willard to take up their responsibilities again, leaving him in the care of the doctors at the naval hospital, and of his dark-eyed wife.

That summer my brother Farley broke both arms in a fall from a slippery slide, and it was my job to feed him at mealtimes. Then my sister broke her leg jumping off a picket fence in a long nightgown, and accidently I threw a ski pole through James's cheek. Every time my parents left, something else happened. Pinkeye ran through the house. We slipped the car out of gear and drove it through a neighbor's fence. I think they began to feel that if they left us one more time, they'd come home to find their children invalids, their house wrecked, and themselves unable to cope.

Then one morning, at the end of the summer, before school had started, Carl died in the arms of Inez, with my aunt nearby in the room, holding the baby, Christobel. In his last hours, according to my aunt, he told Inez that he had not loved her when he married her, but that he had grown to love her very much. He said he wished he could be with her longer, and he was sorry he wouldn't see Christobel grow up. Then he let go of all these things. As each of us children awoke that morning and came upstairs one by one, my mother was waiting for us in the kitchen, standing at the point where the linoleum was broken and the stairs met the small entryway, near the back door. She looked at us and said, "Your brother died last night," and kissed us. To the next child that came upstairs, she said the same thing: "Your brother died last night." She gave us this news in a room so small that we could hardly pass each other without bumping. I think she needed that small space, that closeness, to make her announcement manageable, to contain the sorrow, confining it so it wouldn't spread too far too fast.

The funeral was held the next week. Inez came to Utah, and my parents treated her as kindly as their own grief permitted. My father, however, was furious to discover that she'd ordered a cross put on Carl's tombstone—natural for a Catholic, perhaps, but a blasphemous thing to Mormons, who don't believe in crosses. So the cross put a distance between them; but since there was already distance there, it simply had the effect of giving my father something to focus on, some further proof of Inez's incomprehensible ways, evidence of the inevitability of her remaining a foreigner, forever unable to be assimilated into our family.

"What did she think she was doing?" he demanded of my mother, referring to the cross.

"He was her husband. She has rights, too."

"But she didn't ask us if she could put a cross on the tombstone. She should have asked."

"Let her have her way, Arlo."

"I'll let her have the insurance money, I'll tell you that. All of it. She can have all the money and go off and make a new life for herself."

"I'm sure she intended to do that anyway," my mother said wearily.

He didn't want his son to lie under a slab of marble with a cross on it. But it was too late. The cross was carved. And it seemed to him that Inez had gotten the last word, had sealed his son in death with a graven symbol.

The funeral was held at Lindquist and Sons and attended by the whole ward. Inez requested that my cousins sing "Vaya

con Dios"—my father didn't like that either, but he couldn't
do anything about it; the arrangements had already been
made. And so my two prim cousins Bidge and Adlee Fuller
sang a Spanish song in a tremulous and uncertain duet: *Vaya
con Dios.* . . . Go with God, Carl.

When it came time to close the casket, a curtain was drawn,
separating the family from the rest of the mourners, so we
could have a final moment with the body. I remember Inez
wailed, making a sound I couldn't have imagined a human
making before I heard it that day. She laid her body over
Carl's and refused to allow them to shut the casket. She took
off a ring and picked up his lifeless hand and tried to force it
onto his finger, but it wouldn't go on. I stood at eye level with
the body, watching all this, and looking at Carl's thin young
face. Wasn't he going to wake up any moment and say, "Stop
fussing over me?" My father finally coaxed her away, and they
closed the lid.

My parents saw that she received all the insurance money,
the pensions, everything that was due from the government.
They were uncertain how to regard their grandchild, but
clearer about their feelings for Inez. She had always seemed
foreign to them, someone who had existed outside their lives.
She would go back to a distant city. They didn't anticipate any
closeness with her. However, as it turned out, they didn't lose
touch with her completely, mostly because of their grandchild,
Christobel, and over the years they learned these things:

She married again, a few years after Carl's death. Her husband, a middle-aged Irishman named Joe, was a policeman.
They had two children, quite close in age. Then they learned
her husband had a kidney disease, fatal unless he received a
transplant, then a very new procedure performed in just a few
hospitals, one of them located in Denver. Inez and Joe traveled to Denver, stopping in Willard en route to visit our family. We met the new children, Joey and Dolores—or Lola, as
she was called. Christobel, then five, was a quiet and sweet
child, who resembled Carl in a certain distinct way—namely,

her blue eyes. In Denver, Inez donated a kidney to her husband, but the transplant didn't work and he died, leaving her with three children now and only one kidney. She was not yet thirty, and had watched two husbands die long, slow deaths.

I remember walking down to the lake with Inez during their visit, strolling with Christobel between us, holding on to her tiny hands. "It stinks like hell, huh?" Inez said of the lake. We stood there looking out over the water, not speaking to each other. She did not seem quite so high-spirited to me anymore.

The next time we heard of Inez was in the 1960s. A cousin who saw Inez in San Francisco said she was living with the three children in a basement apartment which was unfinished and had dirt floors. Pictures of saints and the Virgin decorated the walls. Inez had seemed terribly religious. She talked a lot about Carl. The children were shy and hid from my cousin. Her health didn't seem good. But she was still working, she said, as a beautician.

Later, my parents received word that Inez was in Los Angeles. They received a letter from her. Christobel had been diagnosed as having learning difficulties. She was twelve years old but she had the skills and aptitudes of a six-year-old. She was large for her age. My parents were sent a picture of her. She wasn't a pretty girl, but her face still had a sweetness about it, although in the photograph her eyes looked dull and faraway. Inez needed money for special teachers and asked my parents to help, which they did.

"I'd like to have Christobel come visit us," my mother told my father.

"No," he said.

At last we heard from Inez that she'd married again, but things had gone from bad to worse. Christobel had been sent to live in a special home for the retarded. Inez wrote that she feared her new husband had molested her. Christobel was nearly eighteen years old. Inez didn't say anything more about her new husband, whether she was still living with him or not, and the thing we were all asking, the thing we couldn't understand, was, How can she stay with him if she suspects he's done that to Christobel?

In this special home for the retarded, Inez went on to say in her letter, Christobel was being taught skills that might help her make a living and one day be more independent. Each day the girls were taken to motels, where they worked as cleaning women. Christobel made enough money to pay for her room and board in the home, a big house on a wide boulevard near downtown Los Angeles. Inez saw her several times a week. She was doing pretty well. Inez didn't think that Christobel was mentally retarded, not really. "She's a slow girl," she wrote, "but she's no dummy." Christobel wanted to come visit her grandparents for a few weeks. Would they consider this possibility?

After much discussion, my parents finally agreed to let Christobel come. By now Christobel was a young woman, not the child they'd last seen. They didn't know what to expect, but when she arrived, they discovered an immature and troubled girl. She was overweight and slow-moving, reticent and shy. Sometimes she was sweet and inquisitive, however, in a childlike way. "What's this?" she would ask about different things she saw in the house, or when they were out driving. Other times she seemed coarse and wild, like a trouble maker and she told them stories about her life in Los Angeles, about the things she did there, about stealing and the boys she'd known, and my parents turned away and tried to change the conversation, embarrassed by things they didn't want to hear. At night they would ask each other, "Do you think what she says is true, or is she making it all up?"

Sometimes my mother went further and at chosen moments gave Christobel moral lessons based on simple teachings from the Book of Mormon. She'd say things like "Your body is the temple of the Lord, and you should keep it clean" when Christobel talked about drinking and smoking. Or she'd say, "You should wait until after you're married before you let a boy have sex with you. Otherwise, he won't respect you and he won't want you for his wife." She bore her testimony to Christobel. She said, "Knock and it shall be opened, ask and ye shall receive," urging her to read the Book of Mormon and in private prayer to ask the Lord if it wasn't true.

But the only thing Christobel really seemed to listen to were stories about her father. "Tell me about Carl when he was a little boy," she said. She carried a picture of him, a hand-tinted photograph of Carl in a sailor's uniform. He was to her the embodiment of everything lost and everything desired, sentiments she'd inherited from her mother. His death had robbed her of a different, and better, life. "What was he like when he was a baby?" she asked. "Do I look like him?" "Do you have any more pictures?"

One day, when Christobel had been there a week, my father took her along with him to the senior center where he played drums. He left her in the card room while he went into the auditorium, just next door, to entertain with his combo. While he played, elderly couples danced, moving slowly around the wooden floor.

Suddenly, someone came rushing in to get him. "You'd better come quickly," the man said. "It's your granddaughter."

Christobel was standing quietly by the door when he walked into the card room, her hands limp at her sides and slightly turned out, as if displaying their emptiness. There was broken glass everywhere, little frosted shards. He discovered she'd gone into a supply closet and taken a box of light bulbs out and begun throwing them, one by one, against the wall near where some seniors were playing cards. They had exploded like small bombs. The seniors were very disturbed. They were huddled together in small groups, staring at my father. Some were frightened, some were perplexed, and some looked on as if they were bringing all the wisdom of their years, and of their own family entanglements, to this present situation in order to try to understand it. Hadn't they seen something like it in their own lives, an instant when the

unthinkable happens and people in their own families
behaved worse than could be imagined? And wasn't it always,
in some way, violent?

My father listened as someone explained what had happened. Christobel stared at the floor. She looked up at him
sheepishly when he finally approached her. He asked someone
to sweep up the mess for him. Quietly he said, "Come on,
Christobel, let's go home."

Dad called James when he got home, and James came to
get Christobel that afternoon, and she spent the rest of her
vacation with him and his family on their farm in Clinton.
James had a kind, calm nature. Nothing bothered him. He'd
seen a lot, too, because he'd worked in rest homes and prisons
and for a while in an alcoholic treatment center. He knew how
these things happened, how easily the surface broke up, revealing the darkness below. He had no trouble with Christobel; he'd known worse cases. When it came time for her to
leave, he took her to the airport and gave her a big squeeze
before she got on the plane. "You stay in touch, you hear?" he
said to her.

Occasionally since then, I've asked my mother, "Have you
heard from Inez lately?" She's received a couple of letters
since Christobel's visit, but they are just ordinary letters from
Inez saying how fine everything is, and my mother writes back
and says how fine everything is with her, too. My father has
maintained silence on the subject since that day.

"I'm going to teach you some new words," Inez had said
to me during that first visit, when I thought I would never
meet anyone so beautiful again. "These are words in my language, Spanish."

"I know a Spanish word," I said.

"What?"

"Savvy," I said.

"Savvy?" she said. "What's this savvy?"

"That's what my dad says," I told her. It was, I thought, a
foreign word. A Spanish word.

I remember once how Jeannie Wangsgard, one of the Wangsgard sisters, who lived across the road from us, said, "What does your dad mean when he says 'savvy'?"

She asked this when we were killing chickens one day. Pots of boiling water were sending up steam. I remember we weren't actually killing the chickens yet. We were standing under the clothesline in the Wangsgards' backyard. Garments floated around us, so airy and thin that they actually seemed like angel chaps, which is what they were jokingly called. The chickens were squawking. Mom and Mrs. Wangsgard were sitting at a picnic table, newspapers spread before them. Dad was sharpening an ax. Mr. Wangsgard was in the chicken coop, and shortly he came out carrying two chickens by their feet, dangling them upside down. The chickens squirmed and twisted, craning their necks, just like kids do when they're being carried upside down and trying to right themselves. It was autumn, and there was a smell of burning weeds that people were clearing from their ditches. Dad took the first chicken, laid its head on a big round stump, and chopped it off.

"He's always saying, 'Savvy, savvy, you savvy?'" Jeannie Wangsgard said. "I don't get what he means."

Dad shook the headless chicken by its feet, holding it away from him so the blood wouldn't splash on his clothes. Then he laid it on the grass, but it didn't stay put—it twitched to its feet and ran around and finally dropped in the dust.

"Get that chicken out of the dirt," Dad said to James. "And wash it off good with the hose before you put it in the pot, savvy?" Brother Wangsgard handed him another chicken. When the first chicken was dunked in the pot of boiling water and pulled out, the smell of hot, wet feathers came to me.

"Verna," Mom called, "here's a chicken to start on."

"It means 'understand,'" I said to Jeannie Wangsgard. "Understand?"

"What a weird word! I never heard that from my dad."

More chickens had their heads cut off. Soon everybody at the table had a carcass, and we were busy pulling out soggy feathers, and all the kids, led by Jeannie Wangsgard, were acting like smart alecks, and saying "savvy, savvy, savvy," over and over chanting it in sing-song voices, "savvy, savvy, savvy," and still my father swung the ax, and one after another the chickens fell.

Inez said, "This word 'savvy'—that's no Spanish word. I'll teach you something else . . . something much better."

And then she said the words, and I repeated them after her: *"Tu eres mi hermana. . . ."*

"That's it. That's all you gotta remember."

"Yes," I said. "Okay."

"And don't you never forget it," she added.

10

ON MY SECOND DAY in the city, I began looking for a job, and also an apartment.

I started by checking the classifieds in the newspaper, both the Help Wanted and the Apartments for Lease ads. Then I called and began making appointments, full of blind hope and a feeling of promise that the city itself held for me. I'd come this far—how could it not work out?

Vincent lent me a thick book of maps, and I started to learn my way around the city.

During the first week, the days varied little. Each morning I ate breakfast with Jolene and Vincent, who both went immediately to work, leaving me with the paper and the feeling I ought to get lost. Breakfast might be the only time I saw them during the day. Many evenings Jolene worked late, making her paintings in her studio, which was in another part of the city. Other nights they went out or spent the evenings alone in their bedroom.

Sometimes they asked me to go places with them, but more often than not they went off by themselves. I had a key and let myself in and out of their apartment. Jolene acted like a person I'd never known—a civil stranger—and Vincent, though he was always polite to me, was cool and distant. They were not much warmer with each other. I thought they were an odd couple. From the first I felt something was wrong between them. I sensed this tension and I wondered, What is it?

One night they were going out to dinner and invited me to come. Just as we were leaving Jolene said, "Why don't you wear one of my jackets?"

I saw that she was embarrassed by my outfit, so I accepted her offer. As I stood in front of a mirror, looking at the way her jacket fit, she stood behind me, her maroon hair sticking up all over her head, and frowned slightly.

I said, "That's nice," looking at myself in the mirror. Vincent waited by the door, and when I glanced at him, he looked away.

Jolene said, "Yes, but . . . something's wrong."

"What?"

"Do you know one of your shoulders is higher than the other?"

"No," I said. "I've never noticed that before."

"Well, look," she said. "Look how your left shoulder is so much higher than your right."

"I guess it is."

"Try and relax." She pushed down on my shoulder, though that certainly didn't help me relax.

"Isn't that better?" she said.

"I suppose it is," I said.

Sometimes I heard them at night, watching TV. They had a TV on a little stand, and they rolled it around the apartment from room to room, closing doors behind them. It seemed odd to me; we all could have been watching TV together. But instead, they'd take the TV into their bedroom, and I could hear the sounds of TV voices through the wall that separated our rooms.

Often they complained they were tired. Jolene was preparing for a show. Vincent closed himself in his room all day to
work on his paper. It wasn't much fun being there with them.
More and more I felt I was intruding and wished I were settled
in a place of my own or that I knew some other people with
whom I could stay, or at least visit; but there were only Heber
and LaRue, shut up in their musty house in Mar Vista.

I tried to call Inez, but her telephone had been disconnected. One morning I drove to the address that LaRue had
given me for her. It seemed to take forever to get there. As on
the first day I arrived in the city, I found myself in a neighborhood where all the signs were in Spanish. The buildings were
old and rundown, and everyone looked Mexican to me.

I knocked on the door of the apartment. A man answered.
I asked for Inez. He frowned at me and shook his head.

"Does she still live here?"

He said something in Spanish and closed the door in my
face.

I stood there for a moment, feeling offended, and then I
left.

The second week in the city I began to feel scared. What
was I doing here? Every apartment I called about or looked at
cost too much money. Every job was wrong for me, or me for
it. I went to look at places knowing I couldn't afford them but
thinking that things would come together, the right job, the
right situation, which would allow me to settle in a place of my
own.

Occasionally, especially at night, I had thoughts of returning to Utah; it seemed too difficult to make this new life, which
wasn't like anything I had imagined, anyway. I was too far
from where I was from, and I had no idea people needed so
much money to live, or that to live alone was so much more
costly than having a husband.

I thought about Leon all the time. Sometimes it seemed

we'd been temporarily interrupted, as if I was vacationing or he'd been sent to a different city to work a temporary job, and that, inevitably, the day would come when we'd be back under the same roof, living out our marriage. Other times it seemed like it had already been years since I'd seen him; he was an indistinct memory, a husband lost to me as surely as if he'd died in a war or an automobile accident.

I drove to the ocean one day, but the beach was lonely and barren, and out on the horizon a band of brown smog lay above the water and made even the sky in this place look used and spoiled. A yellow foam, carried in by the surf, was deposited in clumps on the sand, where it scudded along, borne by the wind like hordes of small, scurrying animals.

I interviewed at a bank and also a mortgage and loan, but my stenographic skills weren't current, and I didn't know anything about computers. Restaurant jobs paid too little; I knew I couldn't live on that. I didn't seem to present myself right for a job as a clerk in a clothing store. "You don't have the look," one woman said to me. "You just wouldn't fit in."

And then something happened. I read about a position as a receptionist in a dental office, and I decided to apply. The office was near downtown, right in the neighborhood where I'd gone looking for Inez. There were two dentists, Dr. Marvin Lovestedt and Dr. Emilio Ruiz. They shared a building with a martial-arts school and a donut shop. The sign on the front of the building said DENTISTA FAMILIAR, UPSTAIRS and also advertised TWILIGHT SLEEP FOR DENTISTRY.

Dr. Marvin Lovestedt met me in his office.

"I could use a girl like you," he said at the end of my interview. "We'll be in touch."

I came away hopeful. But two more days went by, and I heard nothing from Dr. Marvin Lovestedt.

I waited, driving around the city during the day, looking at apartments, and lying at night in the room with the floor lamps, the wall fixtures, the lights that shone in all directions, wondering about Leon.

Where was he? In Evanston? It wasn't much of a place to
be. Evanston was an oil boomtown that had been overrun by
workers who couldn't spend their money in bars fast enough.
There was a wild feeling in that town, too many single men
making too much money, too many bars with not enough
women to go around. A pari-mutuel track just outside town
drew a crowd. Once we drove up there to go to the horse
races. In the afternoon we went into town and bought a bottle
at the liquor store. I waited outside for Leon, looking at a
collection of dusty decanters in the window. Then we drove
back to the racetrack and drank the bottle in the parking lot.
We lost forty dollars. That seemed like a long time ago.

Three days went by and I didn't hear anything from Dr.
Lovestedt. I began to think I wouldn't get the job, and it worried me because I had very little money left now. I could
hardly afford the gas to drive anywhere.

One morning, I decided to stay in the apartment instead of
going out into the city. Maybe something would come to
me—the other half of my luck, as Bob More would say—if I
just stayed put in one place.

As usual, that morning we all had breakfast together, and
after Jolene had left, Vincent asked me what my plans were for
the day.

"I'm waiting for a call," I said. "I think I'll just stick
around here today."

"I see."

"I'm pretty close to getting a job, I think."

"What kind of job?"

"Working for dentists."

"Oh."

"I'll do the dishes today," I said. He didn't object, but
thanked me, and went upstairs to his room.

When I finished cleaning up the kitchen, I went out into
the garden in the courtyard. The weeds had begun to take
over an area, choking out some flowers. I knelt over a bed of

snapdragons and petunias, lifting the flowers to look closely at them. Out of the corner of my eye, I saw him watching me, standing slightly back from the window, half hidden by the drapes. It seemed a little silly that he caught me studying the flowers. But then I thought, Why is he watching me, hidden that way? I did not look up at him, but pretended I hadn't notice him there. I began weeding the flower beds. After a while, I'd built up a dozen piles of weeds on the sidewalk. I put the weeds into several large stacks and then made a couple of trips carrying them to the garbage cans in the alley. He was still watching me.

Once, when I went inside for a glass of water, I met him in the kitchen. He was making himself a cup of coffee.

"You don't have to pull weeds," he said. "We've got a gardener who comes around for that." The lank piece of hair that flopped over his eye was partly obscuring his vision of me, and I had an urge to brush it out of the way. How could he stand it? Every time he blinked, his eyelashes stirred the fringe of hair.

I said, "I don't mind. I don't have anything else to do. I'm just waiting for that call."

He looked at me curiously, but then he smiled, something he didn't do too often. I thought, Perhaps he doesn't believe me about the job.

"Okay," he said, then added, "I made a little extra coffee. There's some there for you if you'd like it."

I took my coffee outside and drank it sitting on the steps. I wore a blouse that was embroidered at the yoke with a drawstring at the neck. I noticed the strings were frayed, and I tied little knots near the ends so they wouldn't unravel more.

Later, I got the hose out and washed the dirt from where the weeds had lain on the sidewalk. I sang as I worked. It felt good to be doing something simple and absorbing. As soon as I started singing, he came to the window again. I kept singing and tried to ignore him watching me. Then I heard the phone ring, and I knew, I just knew, that it was for me.

Dr. Lovestedt wanted me to come in for another interview. He and Dr. Ruiz were still undecided, he said, but they were very interested in talking to me again.

The interview took place the next day. It lasted only ten minutes.

"I knew a Mormon in the service," Dr. Lovestedt said when he found out I was from Utah. "He was nice. But there was something a little unreal about him. I never figured it out."

After a little while he said, "Well, that's fine, just fine. Frankly, it's between you and another girl." He was sitting behind his desk in a windowless office. He smiled and rubbed his small hands together. I thought, It must be helpful having small hands if you're a dentist. He was a little man, just over five feet tall. His head appeared slightly oversized for his body; he reminded me of one of those mad scientists in old late-night horror movies. The worst part about him was his teeth. They were dark and uneven, like Duluth Wing's—bad teeth for a dentist.

"Frankly, we're divided over this thing," Dr. Lovestedt said. "The other girl we've been talking to probably has better office skills. But I think you'd fit in better here. I really do." He smiled at me. "You're a pip," he added.

"What's a pip?"

"Oh, you know." He laughed.

"Oh, yeah," I said, not knowing what the hell he meant.

"Give us another day or two to make up our minds."

On the way out, a tall woman with blue eye shadow motioned to me. She took hold of my arm and led me to the door. The reception area was rather shabby looking. Magazines with torn covers lay on a soiled couch. The walls were dirty.

"I'm Marilyn," she said, "Marilyn Tooner. I'm the hygienist here. I just wanted to tell you I think you've got the job. I didn't want you to walk out of here worrying. I'm pretty sure Marvin will hire you."

"Really?"

"Dr. Ruiz is concerned because you've never worked in a dental office before," Marilyn Tooner said. "But Marvin wants you. He thinks you're right, and he'll convince Dr. Ruiz. I'm sure it's going to work out."

I wondered why Marilyn Tooner called Dr. Lovestedt "Marvin" and Dr. Ruiz "Dr. Ruiz."

"I hope so," I said. "I could use this job, I really could."

"Well, I'd better get back to my patient," she said. "But I'm sure I'll be seeing you again."

A young girl was leading a smaller boy around by his hair. She opened the door and led him into the hallway, still guiding him by his hair. I followed them out.

"Don't worry," Marilyn Tooner called after me. I waved goodbye to her and called "Thanks!"

Outside, the sunlight was very bright, glaring off the pale sidewalk. I looked around me. All the store signs were in Spanish: COMIDA SALVADOREÑA . . . CARNICERÍA LATINA . . . EL PAVITO . . . TIENDAS DE DESCUENTO . . . ROPA DE NIÑOS . . . ZAPATERIA. There was a large park across the street. Some men were playing soccer on the grass. There were pretty trees and little benches and a band shell. A street divided the park. On the other side of the street, in the middle of a grassy area, was a lake, big enough for paddleboats to circle on its surface. In the center of the lake, a fountain shot water high in the air. The plume of water dispersed, and, even as far away as I was, I could feel the mist on my skin. The lake smelled funny, as if it were stagnant, and, in fact, the water was murky. As I walked down the hill, I could see thick ropes of moss lying beneath the surface.

I decided to walk through the park. Suddenly, as I came to a small area where there were benches overlooking the lake, I saw her.

She was sitting beside a man in a blue coat. She had changed so little that it was startling. Still the same pageboy hairstyle, the same red lipstick, the close-fitting dress. I hurried up to her and said, "Inez."

She looked up at me.

"It's me," I said, "Verna. . . ."

She didn't smile. She stared at me and said nothing; the man next to her stared, too, and then I realized it wasn't her. Of course it wasn't! She was much too young. Inez would be much older than this woman.

But the resemblance was startling, and I continued to stare for a moment, and then I said, "Sorry," and turned quickly away.

Of course she would be older. The woman I had spoken to looked like Inez the last time I had seen her. That was years ago. She would have changed. I hurried away, walking fast with my head down, unsettled by my mistake, until I came to the street where I had parked the truck.

As soon as I turned the corner, I saw a sign, nailed to a post, that said APARTMENT FOR RENT. The sign was in front of a pumpkin-colored building which sat high above the sidewalk on a small hill that rose steeply. A wild, untended garden surrounded the apartment building. There were artichoke bushes with purplish-blue thistles in bloom. Steep stairs led to the entrance, and as I climbed them, I passed mailboxes with the names of the tenants: Perdue, Pulido, Edgington, Beal, Boggs, Kihm-Maurer.

I reached the entrance, out of breath, and rang the bell of the door marked MANAGER. Instantly it set off the loud barking of dogs.

"Shut up, Pookie!" someone yelled, and then a small gray-haired man opened the door and said, "Can I help you?"

"MacArthur Park?" Jolene said that night over dinner. "That's not such a good neighborhood."

Vincent frowned at me and nodded. "She's right," he said. "It isn't exactly safe."

Jolene said, "I don't know how I'd feel as a single woman living in that kind of neighborhood."

"You should think about this," Vincent added. "You'll have to be very careful."

"There are gangs in that area," she said.

"It's very rough," he added.

"It seemed okay to me."

"Yes, but you saw it in daylight. And you really can't tell just by looking at a place once."

"It was the first place I saw that I thought I could afford."

"Well, that is a factor," Vincent said.

Factor? What did they mean? That was the whole ball of wax.

"And the job? What happened with the dentists?"

"I think I might get it," I said. "And I'll only be a block away from work."

"That's a plus."

"Well, you'll just have to be careful. Very careful." Jolene looked at me. I looked at Vincent. Vincent looked out the window. And suddenly I didn't feel so good.

The next day Marilyn Tooner called. She was phoning for Dr. Lovestedt, who wanted me to start the following Monday.

"Well, that's it," I said to Vincent when he came downstairs. Jolene wasn't home when the call came.

Vincent said, "We should celebrate, don't you think?" He opened a bottle of wine. I was touched by his kindness. Then it occurred to me, Maybe he's just happy I'll be out of his hair now.

"Funny how things work out," he said, lifting his glass.

"Cheers," I said weakly, thinking of the small colorless apartment, gangs, Dr. Lovestedt's shabby office.

"Yes, cheers," he replied.

Early the next morning, I awoke and began packing up my things. It was still dark outside, and I worked by the light of the lamps, which I'd finally gotten used to. By six o'clock I was packed. Then I sat at the window and watched the sky above the next apartment change from dark to light and waited for Jolene and Vincent to wake up.

At eight I opened my door and set a suitcase in the hall. Vincent came out of his room, dressed in a robe. He was so thin it hung loosely on him. It was the first time I'd seen him in a bathrobe, and it seemed oddly intimate.

"I heard you get up," he said.

"I couldn't sleep anymore."

I looked down at my belongings: a leopard-print jacket, the brown suitcase, a plastic tote bag.

"Well," I said, "I guess it'll be all right," and I was really thinking to myself, although I'd spoken out loud.

"What?"

"Everything's working out," I said.

"You're certain this is the right apartment for you? I mean, you don't want to spend a little more time looking?"

"No. It feels okay."

"Because you could always stay here, you know."

"I think I'll like it where I'm moving."

He hesitated for a moment, then gave me a serious look. "Would you do a favor for me sometime?" he asked.

"What?"

"Would you sing again?"

"Again?"

"Yes," he said. "I heard you singing the other day. When you were out in the courtyard."

I pretended I hadn't known he'd been watching me from the window. "Oh," I said, "I didn't know you were listening."

"I like your voice. In fact, you have a wonderful voice. I don't know whether you know that."

"Oh. Thank you."

"It sounded as if you were singing some sort of hymn. Could it have been a hymn?"

"Was it this one?" I began singing: "When the soft sun down the far west is gliding. . . .' "

He just stood there, looking at me, a little smile on his lips. "Yes," he said, "that's it."

Suddenly Jolene came out of her bedroom.

"You're up early," she said. "Singing with the birds."

"Yes," I said. Vincent looked annoyed, and again I

thought, There's something wrong here. Something wrong
between them.

"Well, I need coffee," she said. "I can't move in the morning until I get my coffee. Let's all go downstairs and I'll fix
breakfast."

"You go ahead," Vincent said. "I have some work to do,"
and he turned and closed the door on us.

It was mid-morning before I left them. They both stood at
the curb to say goodbye to me. They promised they'd come
see my new apartment soon. Vincent shook my hand; Jolene
hugged me. I realized I'd spent more time with him than I had
with her, and I really had hardly come to know either of them.

"Just a minute," Jolene said as I turned to go. She ran into
the house and came back out with an armload of clothes.
"Take these," she said. "Just a few things I don't wear anymore."

I thanked her, and they stood at the curb while I jockeyed
the truck and trailer out of the parking space. We waved to
each other. And then I drove away, with the load of her hand-
me-downs piled on the seat next to me.

11

WHAT ABOUT LONELINESS? You're edgy, too
aware of yourself, you hang suspended, like a self-
enclosed bat, dark wings folded over yourself, in a quiet cave
of your own making; and in the heavy air in the room around
you—heavy with stillness and your own stale living—you find
too much time for your mind to think only of itself. You wait.
Something, someone should be there, and they're not, and the
question is, When will it change, and how? There is, above all,
the sense of loss, of something *gone,* and you know what
you've heard isn't true, that absence doesn't make the heart
grow fonder; it makes it anxious and and full of a dull, unspeci-

fied aching which is very difficult to banish.

As long as I was in the room at Jolene and Vincent's, surrounded by cones and slats and flat planes of light, sleeping on the foldout couch in the room overlooking the courtyard filled with flowers, I felt safe. I floated slightly above reality, like a saint in a religious picture. I was neither here nor there. I could pretend I was visiting the city, a vacationer who might or might not stay. But now I was expected to show up for work each morning; I had taken an apartment; my own name had been added to the list of tenants. For the first time in my life, I lived alone. Free time hung heavy.

In the evenings, I sat by a window in the living room where I had a view of a palm tree in a neighboring yard. It wasn't exactly the view I had envisioned when I imagined myself living in L.A., nor was it the kind of palm tree—it seemed burdened with dead fronds hanging from the trunk in thick and rattling layers. But it *was* a palm, and it was a view of sorts, although what I saw when I looked out the largest of my windows was an alley that ran behind the apartment building. I faced garages and dumpsters and the backsides of aging buildings. There were no trees with oranges hanging on them like Christmas bulbs but, rather, strings of power lines and concrete walls covered with graffiti. But a nice breeze seemed to come from the ocean, moving eastward down the corridor created by the tall buildings along Wilshire Boulevard, and there was always this feeling of sea air, traveling down the artificial canyon.

The feeling of the city, I discovered, is first of all sound. The freeway was a faint, constant hum, like air conditioning in a neighboring room. Each morning, bells rang in a nearby church. And there were the produce trucks, which pulled up in the alley behind my apartment throughout the day and sounded their musical horns—harsh, grating versions of "La Cucaracha" and "Around the World in Eighty Days." From these trucks, all kinds of fruits and vegetables were sold, as well as rice, pinto beans, tortillas, and lard, small toys in plastic bags, and even candles adorned with colorful stick-on pictures of the Virgin. It seemed natural that in Los Angeles, the city of the automobile, people would do their grocery shopping from trucks.

People used the alley as a shortcut to the market on the corner. They roamed through it day and night. Some were aluminum-can collectors and carried bent hangers for hooking cans from garbage bins. They rifled through dumpsters; I saw them day after day and I thought, That's become their work, their daily job. When I wasn't at work, I sat in my window and watched these activities. Kids hung out in the alley, too, and also the homeless, and sometimes I noticed teenagers spray-painting walls. Once I even saw them spray the legs of a drunk sleeping in a doorway, so that when they were finished with him, one pant leg was red and one was blue, and still, through-out all of it, he did not move.

All this I watched from my window, where no one saw me.

In the mornings I was often awakened by someone yelling, "Get your fucking car out of the way!" and horns would begin blasting. People double-parked, blocking other cars, and there were always arguments. There were domestic fights, too, bickering and sometimes worse things.

One evening I heard screams and lifted the blinds to see a man kicking a woman who was lying on the pavement in the middle of the alley, clutching two bags of groceries.

"Leave her alone!" I yelled, "or I'm calling the cops."

He looked up at me and said, "I know where you live. You better stay out of it!" and while, preoccupied with me, he wasn't looking, the woman on the ground got up and began swinging at him, landing one alongside his head that put him on the ground.

And always there were the sirens, and the police helicopters at night, shining their searchlights down in conical patterns which were broken into irregular shapes by the buildings. The blades beat overhead throughout the night, going *whhhummmffffph whhhummffffph whhhummffffph,* and even the air inside the bedroom seem to vibrate a little.

Each day I walked to work. The job wasn't difficult, but it was boring, and increasingly I thought about home, about Leon and the sort of life we'd had, where everything was familiar and the days had been full with things I'd taken for granted, family, friends, community, all now gone, and I wondered, How did you make friends in a city where you didn't know anyone? What did you do?

I didn't hear from Jolene and Vincent, and they didn't return the messages I left on their machine. I even drove over to their apartment one day and put a note on their door, but that wasn't answered either. They were the only people I knew in the city, aside from Heber and LaRue and the people at work. Weeks went by, and I began to think, I don't know Jolene and Vincent at all, not well enough to know what's happening. Why don't I hear from them? Are they just busy, or are they avoiding me?

I didn't know whether it was my mood, just feeling lonely, or what, but I began to wonder whether I'd ever been close to anyone. The question was, Could you ever really know another human being?

I remembered how I discovered that I hardly knew my brother Arnold at all. I'd always thought we were pretty close. We were only eighteen months apart and had always confided in each other; and yet, years after I left home to get married, I learned something about him I never would have guessed. He told me that during his senior year in high school, while working at the Orpheum Theater as an usher, he had made extra spending money by selling marijuana hidden in the bottoms of popcorn boxes at the refreshment stand. I never would have suspected this. All those years I had looked at him and seen only this slightly awkward kid who liked science and the sight of sliced vegetables under a microscope.

Beneath the lives we see are the lives that are really lived, complete and utterly unknown. It might take years of acquaintance, friendship, or love to fathom even a small portion of these hidden selves. Suddenly I had queer feelings, like I might never have known anyone.

I realized I didn't know anything about Jolene or Vincent. I hadn't even really known Arnold. This led me to wonder, Had I ever known Leon?

I sat alone in my apartment at night and thought about him. He had a thick layer of something over him, I decided, and I thought it had to do with being a man, and also a Mormon. He did everything men were supposed to do and practically nothing that women did. He hunted deer, elk, and moose, shot an assortment of birds out of the sky, and he fixed cars, understood engines, took things apart and put them back together again. He won roping contests. He wrestled, threw footballs, played basketball. He could lift heavy things because he was strong. He stepped so heavily when he walked that the floors shook. He wasn't afraid of getting on any horse, no matter how mean or unpredictable it was. He simply forced it to do his will by gathering it up under him, letting it feel his weight and the pressure of his heels, taking its head in his hands by shortening the reins and not giving it an inch, pushing it forward and containing it at the same moment, so that the animal was instantly put on alert and bunched up tight beneath him, as if pent up by an invisible force. Then he simply conquered it through sheer domination, as men have been doing with animals forever.

No, I don't think I knew him very well. These qualities I have described, they're only the visible things, outward manifestations of a person who remains quietly unexposed, growing more distant now, with time.

One day, returning from work, I was walking through the park when I saw a man lying face down near a fountain. His belongings were stuffed into plastic bags that surrounded him on the grass. From somewhere came the sound of a baby bird,

the unmistakably frantic chirpings of distress, like the protests
of a small chick separated from its mother. In a metal crate,
like those used to haul milk bottles, I saw the bird, which had
been confined and was running from one end of its makeshift
cage to the other, apparently unable to fly. It was very young. I
assumed it had been injured or orphaned, and rescued by the
man lying face down on the grass, his belongings forming a
protective ring around him, like buoys floating on the sea. The
bird was only inches from his head. How could he sleep, I
wondered, with the constant sounds of distress filling his ears?

Suddenly he opened his eyes and looked at me.

"What are you looking at?"

"I'm looking at the bird."

He frightened me, but I decided to stay to talk to him like I
would anyone else, as if he were a normal person rather than
someone dirty, in rags, with all his plastic bags surrounding
him on the grass.

"What do you think this is, a show?"

"No, I think it's a baby bird."

"What's it to you?"

"Nothing, really."

He stared at me for a few moments, and then he put his
head back down on the grass, and I moved on.

The first news came from home. I received a letter from
my parents. My mom had filled up one side of a sheet of paper,
my dad the other. They mentioned Leon. My mom said she
was sorry. My dad said he'd like to make a suggestion: "You'd
be a smart gal," he wrote at the end of his portion of the letter,
"if you get Leon to keep up your health insurance. This should
include dental work, savvy?"

I read the letter sitting in front of the window in my bedroom. In the alley below me, a man was leaning against a
garage, drinking out of a bottle wrapped in a paper bag.

"See that he doesn't let your policy lapse, that's all

I'm saying. Take my advice. You don't want to be stuck with a lot of dental work or medical bills if anything should happen."

My mother added:

I got up at 5:30 this morning and went through two sessions at the Temple before going over to the Japs to pick up some pearl onions. Your father's helping me do some mustard pickles. Janice is supposed to pick me up for lunch. She'll be here any minute. We were very sorry to hear about you and Leon. I'm sure it's been rough on you. It's your life, though, we know this, and you must do what you think is right. However, if there's anything we can do for you, honey, just ask. Are you planning on staying down in California? Have you seen Heber and LaRue yet?

The man with the bottle looked up at me. I looked down at him. I thought, I'm getting a divorce and my father says, get him to keep up the policy on your teeth. My mother says she's sorry but it's my life.

My parents had reached that point where their capacity for nostalgia was what sustained them. The *idea* of family had taken over. When they were younger, they thought their children were always *becoming,* and their job was to help them; then they *became,* and there was nothing for my parents to do except watch the events that occasionally transformed their children's lives. Some of them had already tried life in another city or state, or switched jobs, or husbands or wives. From this new distance we all pretended to be grateful for this freedom: children whose parents no longer told them what to do or had such great expectations; parents who couldn't be held responsible for their children's failures anymore. Their advice was now quite watery and pale, colored by thoughts of their own failing health. So this is what it now came to: Try to guard against rotting teeth.

At work I became friendlier with Marilyn Tooner, who was divorced, the mother of three boys, and a member of the Self-Realization Fellowship, which held its meetings on Sunset Boulevard in a building with golden onion-shaped domes. Marilyn invited me to a meeting once and I went, but I had no desire to go back. It seemed like just another kind of church to me, no better or worse than most, just the same sort of business, an attempt to get you on a particular track. But Marilyn felt it was more than this. It was new age thinking, she said. "It's the *future.*"

"All time is happening at the same time," she said to me one day. "Do you understand that?"

"No."

"Well, think about it."

"Okay."

"Think about how it could be one time in Tokyo and another in San Francisco. What does that tell you about time?"

"That there are time zones?"

"Think some more about it," she said.

We took our smoking breaks together, and since Dr. Lovestedt didn't allow cigarettes in the office, we had to go outside and sit in Marilyn's car in the parking lot across the street from the park. MTOONER had been painted on the little concrete ridge in front of her parking space. We had a view of the lake. The mist from the fountain collected in fine little droplets on the windshield. One cigarette lasted seven minutes. We usually sat out there for the time it took to have two cigarettes, smoked one right after the other. Occasionally, a couple rented a paddleboat and circled the lake slowly, and we could see the thick green moss clinging to the blades of the paddles as they turned in the water. People in the boats often looked bored, disappointed in their boat rides. Several boats were broken and had been left in the middle of the lake, half-sunken. Marilyn wore blue eye shadow, laid on so thickly that it creased by the end of the day into little parallel bands of color. At the corners of her eyes were many flowing wrinkles, formed by years of smiling. We talked about where we came from, about our families and hometowns, and the men we'd known in our lives, compressing all this information into our short smoking breaks—sessions that seemed almost confessional in nature, filled with bursts of self-revelation. And then we just went back to our jobs and forgot everything.

A letter from Leon arrived. He was still in Evanston, he said. Everything was expensive there, inflated by the oil boom. His job was working out okay. He'd bought two horses. He was surprised to hear I was in Los Angeles. He'd like to start the divorce proceedings. Did I want to get a lawyer, or should he?

I thought I understood why he was in such a hurry to get divorced. He could marry Pinky then. Otherwise, why the rush?

I could imagine their eagerness to become husband and wife. It was already a tangible thing to me. I saw myself as the only remaining impediment. I could already picture the children Leon and Pinky would produce, kids who should have been better looking than they were but would end up being ordinary and rather colorless instead. I saw them all at home, imagining a small house miles from town, surrounded by horse corrals and cars needing mechanical work, I saw the way they would go shopping together at the local supermarket, Leon pushing the cart with one kid stuck in the basket, sitting on the little shelf near the handle, his legs poking through the holes. I could see Pinky all manicured for public consumption—coiffed, sprayed, powdered, and packed into tight jeans—choosing items off the grocery shelves, going over the meat packages carefully and grabbing baby food in a reckless, definite way, snatching up toilet paper, Pampers, and canned soup, reaching for a loaf of bread so aggressively that it collapsed under her grip. I could see the two of them putting the grocery bags in the back of their truck, hefting the kids into the cab, and I could see them driving out of town, out where the buildings ended and the nothingness finally took over and all around them the sagebrush was the tallest thing and nothing was so colorful that it drew attention to itself but everything, all around them, simply blended in its mutedness and scale—brush to earth, earth to road, horizon to sky—naturally subtle shades bleeding into a pale purple distance, as they rode toward home.

I did not answer his letter. I saw no need to open the door for that future.

One afternoon when the sky was gray and the weatherman predicted rain, I walked to the address LaRue had given me for Inez and knocked on the door of the apartment once more, as I had weeks ago. Would Inez open the door this time? No one answered. I knocked again. Though I felt timid, I grew bolder in my knocking. I was no longer sure why I had come to Los Angeles, and I felt I needed to find Inez, that tiny, unclaimed piece of family that had been cast off years before. I knocked again and again, not wanting to give up. Later, after standing there a long time, I realized that no one was going to answer the door and I left.

The rain came down hard that day. The alley curved slightly, like a wide gutter. Down the center ran a path of red bricks. The rain slid down the bricks, making an instant stream. Rain moistened the stucco buildings and deepened their color. Across the alley, water gushed steadily from a pipe, falling onto a tin roof, as if someone had turned on a hose. It rained all afternoon and into the night.

> Dear Mr._____ :
> This is to remind you of your appointment
> with Dr. Marvin Lovestedt, on the_____ of
> _____ .

There were dozens of these cards to be filled out. It was important that the reminders went out on time. I was always behind, because there were so many things to do—answer the phones, act as receptionist and see that everyone signed in, filled out the proper forms, and paid before they left. There was filing to do and future appointments to schedule. Patients were late— nobody was ever early—and as the day wore on, the dentists fell increasingly behind schedule until the last patients some- times arrived an hour before the doctors saw them.

And always there were the kids of patients, who should have been at home but instead were brought along and left with older brothers and sisters to care for them in the waiting area. At times things became impossibly chaotic. I watched children tear the covers off magazines, draw on chairs, scream for things, and hang on doorknobs pleading to be let into where their mothers were. I'd forgotten how awful children could be, how drawn to bullying and whining, and how they stared at you with cold, keen eyes and then ignored you.

One day, when two brothers had been left alone in the waiting room and were fighting, rolling around on the floor, punching each other, I stood up and said, "Knock that off or I'm going to bang some heads together." The boys looked up, startled.

"I mean it," I said. "You stop that fighting or . . ." I brought my fists together and said "Pow" to show them what I meant.

They grew quiet, and I sat back down in my chair and went back to filling out the appointment cards. Suddenly, I looked up to see a man had entered the office. It took me a moment to realize it was Vincent. He looked around him, uncertain, until he finally saw me.

"Hello," he said quietly. The small boys looked up and watched him cross the room.

"Hello," I said. He looked at me and smiled. "How are you?"

He shrugged.

"I've called and left messages," I said. "I even drove by

your place once and left a note on the door. Where have you been? Where's Jolene?"

"We've been preoccupied," he said. "Things haven't been going so well."

"What's wrong?"

"It's complicated," he said. In fact, he didn't look well. He had a pinched and hard look, drained of what little color he naturally had.

"What happened?"

"Jolene left," he said.

The phone rang, and I had to answer it.

"Do you give twilight sleep?" a man asked.

"Yes."

"How much to pull a tooth?"

"Twenty dollars if there are no complications."

"Twenty dollars?"

"That's a special. It's regularly fifty."

"But what if there are complications?"

"Then the doctor charges according to how much time it takes to treat you."

"Is that the price with the coupon? I'm calling you because I found this flyer on my car."

"That's the price with the coupon. You have to bring it with you."

"Right. Okay. I'm coming in. When can you take me?"

I checked the appointment book. All the while I could feel Vincent watching me. "I have an opening tomorrow at two. I'll put you down. Name, please?"

"Mohammed Satter."

"Tomorrow, Mr. Satter. We'll see you at two."

As soon as I hung up, a patient walked in. Vincent interrupted and said, "What time do you get off work? I'll come back."

I told him five o'clock, and he left, saying he would see me then.

He was waiting for me outside, sitting on a ledge beneath the DENTISTA FAMILIAR sign. We walked toward the park.

"How do you like this neighborhood?" Vincent said.

"It's like being in a foreign country," I replied.

"Does that mean you like it or not?"

"Yes, I do." How to tell him that I felt lonely without making it sound like I was feeling sorry for myself?

"Do you know," I said, "that they sell single cigarettes at that store?" I pointed to a store on the corner. "Five cents for one cigarette. There's a little container by the cash register. Some people only buy one at a time."

"Maybe they're trying to quit."

"No, they're just poor."

"That's different," he said.

"Yesterday I saw a young couple with a baby in a stroller. The man was pushing the stroller. The woman suddenly stopped, bent over, and started looking at the dirt around a tree. She stood up and smiled at him. She had picked up something. At first I couldn't see what she'd found, but then I could tell what it was . . . two cigarettes—not butts but whole cigarettes. You should have seen the way she smiled at her husband, as if this was a very lucky thing. They stopped right there, each took one and lit up."

"You must be getting quite a view of life here."

"How's your paper on Schubert going? Are you almost finished with it?"

"At the moment, I'm stuck. But I'm sure something will come to me."

"I'm sorry about Jolene."

"Yes, well . . ."

"What happened?"

"It's complicated."

"Where is she?"

"I believe," Vincent said slowly, "that she and Leonard are living in Toronto. Jolene's pregnant. She thinks Leonard's the father, although she's not quite sure, unfortunately. To me

it doesn't make any difference who the father is. We had an
agreement—no children, not ever, no exceptions. So yes,
that's where she is, Toronto, I think, with Leonard, Leonard
Hockman."

He turned his face toward the sunset.

"Beautiful light," he said.

When we reached my building, he followed me up the
outside stairs, past the rows of tall artichoke bushes and the
plaques bearing the names of the tenants. Once inside, I invited him to have a drink.

He sat in the only chair I had. I brought a stool from the
kitchen for myself. While I poured drinks, he came into the
kitchen and stood behind me, looking over my shoulder. I was
nervous because I couldn't get some ice to separate so it would
fit into the glass. Finally, I took a chunk of ice in my hand and
cracked it against the side of the sink. It broke and slid down
into the bottom, where I'd left a few dishes, and now it wasn't
too clean, but I had to save it, it was the only ice I had. He
watched me rinse the ice off and put it in the glasses, then he
walked away and I heard him wandering around the apartment. I looked out the window. In the alley, a man was standing next to the dumpster, eating something. It was a piece of
squash. He was scraping it out, using his fingers to bring the
pulp to his mouth. He wore a sky-blue cap and tennis shoes.
Bits of what he was eating fell onto the ground by his feet,
pieces of bright orange squash.

Vincent was standing in the living room. I handed him his
drink. The brown suitcase stood in the corner, beneath my
radio, and he was looking there, off in that direction.

"The interesting thing about this room is that it has the
feeling of imminent occupation or departure."

"I'm not going anywhere."

He turned around and picked up a book I'd left on the
table. "What's this?"

"A library book."

"Oh? On whose advice have you begun reading?"

"Nobody's."

"Really?"

"It's a book I got at the library near the park."

"Which library?"

"The local branch library." I could have said, *It's filled with bums. You should smell it in there. You can hardly breathe for the smell. Still, it's a place to go. You see how people are still trying, still reading and studying, even when they're down. The librarian's a short, fat man whose pants droop so you see the band of his shorts in back. The books are sometimes sticky. Nobody ever cleans the floors. Still, it's a place to go.*

He went to the window and stared at the stucco wall of the next building, and then he moved around, so he looked out past the building, at the palm in the next yard that was never still, and the tall building beyond it, St. Vincent's Hospital.

"It's cool here, isn't it?"

"There's always a breeze," I said.

In the apartment opposite us, separated only by a sidewalk, Mrs. Beal flushed her toilet, a suddenly intimate sound. She turned on the water in the sink, then turned it off, and I saw her come into view in the window frame, step up to a towel rack, and dry her hands, a shadowy figure, like an out-of-focus snapshot. "Come, Pookie," she said. "Come, Teddy Bear, my little darlings."

"Do you have a stereo?"

"No, it's broken. I just have a radio." I pointed to the shelf in the corner above the brown suitcase.

"Let's have some music," he said. He turned on the radio. A man was speaking: ". . . so there is the possibility then that we are not in a system which is merely mechanical and in which we are merely flukes . . ."

"Ah . . . Alan Watts." He switched the station. "He means well," Vincent said. "He wants us all to be so much smarter than we are, so much better. But I can only take so much of him. Besides, we want music today, don't we?" He moved the dial from station to station until he found his kind of music, the sort I heard him play often in his room, what I would call serious violins. He sat down again, where he had been before, in the chair by the window, and bowed his head. With his forefinger and thumb held together, he marked out a little pattern for the music in the air.

"I used to have to guess the names of compositions for my mother," he said, looking up at me. "She would play a record for me and I would have to guess what it was."

"Did you get them right?"

"After a while. Anyone can be taught, you know."

"What's the name of this?"

He smiled. "Haydn."

"Haydn? Aren't you supposed to be able to name whether it's Symphony Such-and-Such, or Concerto Number Something?"

"First you learn to guess the man behind the music, listening for his personality and features. That's the key. You look for the signature in the composition."

A helicopter flew low over the apartment, beating the air noisily with its blades and making it hard to hear anything. But suddenly the violins got livelier, and the music grew and built into a louder sound, a faster tempo, as if in competition with the helicopter, and a hedge of white flowers began moving violently, as if in time with the music; but it was only the wind from the chopper blades, stirring them into a frenzy.

"Mmmmmm," Vincent hummed to this part of the music. "Mmmmm-mmmm." He shook his head and his limp hair parted and flopped around.

When the piece finished, he said, "Symphony Number Twenty-three in D."

I smiled. "Very good."

"You only suppose it's correct," he said. "I could be bluffing."

"I guess."

"Have you been to the beach yet?" he asked.

"Not really," I said, thinking of my brief visits to the ocean and how I'd been disappointed.

"We'll go on Sunday," he said. He didn't ask me if I wanted to go; he simply said "We'll go."

He stayed long enough to finish his drink and then got up, buttoning his sweater, preparing to leave.

"Sunday," he said at the door. "We'll start early. Be ready by nine."

12

HE ARRIVED at exactly nine o'clock. I stood outside and watched him walk up the steps. It was a clear day. The doves that nested in the tall trees next door were cooing.

"We're going up the coast," he said. "Do you have your swimming suit?"

"Isn't the water too cold to go swimming?"

"We'll see. Bring it along anyway."

I went back inside and got my suit. His car was parked at the bottom of the steps. I'd never seen his car before. It was a convertible, the color of celery. The top was up, and I thought, I wish he'd take the top down so I could have a convertible ride; but I didn't suggest it, because I figured he'd have it down if he wanted it that way.

I said, "What kind of car is this?"

"Mercedes-Benz," he said.

"It's pretty nice."

He smiled at me. "Anybody can have a car like this, do you realize that? All it takes is money—no brains, no talent, no taste, nothing but cash."

We drove down Hoover until we reached the freeway. The freeway ran straight toward the ocean. As we neared the coast, we entered a dark, curving tunnel, and when we came out, there it was, the sea, like a sudden surprise, blue and festive looking. The beach was dotted with people who looked like colorful little spots on the sand, and then I realized the spots weren't people at all but trash barrels, painted different colors. Suddenly Vincent pulled over to the side of the road, got out, and took down the convertible top. "Put these on," he said, and handed me a scarf, and a cap made out of red wool. The air was misty and fresh, and the sun was warm, and I said I didn't think I'd need them.

"You will when we get moving. It gets quite cool. Take these too," he added, and gave me a pair of sunglasses. He looked at me. "That's good," he said. "You look fine. You'll be warm now too."

The road curved along the water on our left. On our right, brown, sandy cliffs rose up steeply. They had been worn into scalloped ridges and looked crumbly and soft. Occasionally I glimpsed a figure walking along the top of the cliff next to a white fence.

"It's a shame," he said, looking out at the water. "I used to come to this beach, but now it's too polluted. Even the lifeguards are getting hepatitis. You have to go further north now to swim."

"Too bad," I said. The beach he pointed out was right next to us. It was a pretty place. A stretch of smooth sand started at the road and made a flat surface until it reached the water, and then it dropped down a few feet to the ocean. The sand was so perfectly flat it looked like it had been swept clean. The waves curled up, pale turquoise and almost transparent, and dropped back down into a darker sea. The moment before they broke, I could sometimes see murky objects trapped in the curl. Seaweed? A fish? Driftwood? We drove by houses built on top of the the cliffs. In places the cliff had eroded and the houses were hanging over the edge slightly. Part of their cement foundations were visible. After a while, the houses thinned out and we were surrounded by ocean on one side and on the other, open land, fields of yellow weeds and little purple flowers. We passed Malibu, a famous name, but it didn't look like much of a place to me. When we stopped at a light, I noticed that the flowers in front of the shopping center were made out of plastic, stuck in ground covered with little painted rocks.

I looked over at Vincent and studied his profile. He was somebody I would not have ever seen myself with, a different kind of man.

"It's a funny place, L.A., isn't it? Don't you find it an odd place?" he asked.

"I guess," I said. "I don't really know it well enough to say."

"But you've looked at it now. How does it strike you?"

"Big," I said.

"It's very ugly, isn't it? I mean, the buildings, the cheap architecture, the awful sprawl. And yet, the place itself is like a garden."

"Yes," I said. "All the flowers. It's like that. Like a big garden."

"Did you know that Los Angeles is now referred to as 'the Capital of the Pacific Rim'?"

"The Capital of the Pacific Rim," I repeated. I didn't really know what this meant.

"It's hard not to think of Troy or Carthage and the Phoenicians, or some place like Constantinople. L.A. is like one of those major places in history, the great shipping ports. I get that feeling, don't you? Already I can see how we'll have our moment and then we'll pass, just like those other races and their cultures, those ancient trading centers, the once-flourishing hubs of the world. Do you see that?"

"I don't think so," I said. "I'm not good at history."

"Think of it," he said. "You've got a big ocean, the Pacific. The Pacific Ocean is sort of a circle—about half the world, roughly. The Indian and the Atlantic oceans are little oceans compared to this ocean. It's fathomless."

It certainly looked fathomless to me as I gazed out at it, but I thought, Well, everything's got to have a bottom. Then I said that. "Everything's got to have a bottom."

"Right!" he cried. "And do you know what's at the bottom of the Pacific? Massive ranges of mountains, some of which have popped up and formed islands—Hawaii, Samoa, the Solomons and the Marquesas . . . Fiji, Tonga, Tahiti . . . islands with wonderful names, places that are just the tips of those unseen mountains, rising on pedestals of lava. They're surrounded by the vastness of the great Pacific. And at the edge of this ocean, on the rim of the great basin that cups all this water, you have Asia, Australia, Japan and Russia, North and South America, all hugging the edges—sitting on the rim. And reigning over all of this, there's Los Angeles, the capital. Think of it . . . I mean, as history—the history of one half of the globe."

It seemed to me I had never seen anyone behave so oddly, get himself so worked up about something that as far as I could see didn't have anything to do with anything. I didn't know what to make of it.

"You aren't thinking of it, are you?"

"I don't know," I said. "I'm not sure what you're talking about."

"I'm talking about looking back at Los Angeles, the Capital of the Pacific Rim, a thousand years from now. Seeing it as a place in time. It won't last, of course. Those who dominate are destined to turn up on the bottom again one day. Who'll be next? Or are we beyond that now?"

"I don't know," I said again. "I don't know about any of that." I looked out at the ocean. Now I saw it as a circle of water, and I imagined mountains on its bottom. I pictured islands surrounded by little reefs. I tried to imagine Japan on the other side of the water, but it was too difficult to picture just how far away that was. I tried to imagine I was at the center of something, as he suggested, tried to see myself in the Capital of the Pacific Rim. I tried to think of it as an important place; but it already seemed that way to me, so I didn't get his point.

"What do you think cities are for?" he asked me.

"I don't think I've ever thought of that," I answered.

"Think of it now," he said.

"I guess they're for people who want to be where there's a lot of activity. They want to be around different kinds of people who are doing different kinds of things rather than just staying with what they know. I guess people go to cities for adventure, and maybe to get jobs. Or to get away from where they're from because they don't like it anymore."

"Keep going," he said.

I looked at at the ocean. What was this, a test of some kind? I felt a little annoyed.

"You're kind of putting me on the spot," I said. "I don't really know what cities are for. I never thought of that. I think maybe you and I think of different things, you know? I don't find this talk all that interesting. I'd rather just look at the scenery. I like that, just looking around."

I glanced over at him. He'd lit a cigarette and now he was smoking it. He turned and smiled at me, but I couldn't see his eyes because he was wearing dark glasses, and I knew he couldn't see mine.

We slowed down for a signal, and when the light changed, he made a left turn.

"Where are we?"

"Point Dume," he said.

On our left was a gas station and a shopping center. We turned down a residential street. The houses were large, partially hidden by trees or set back on lots that were deep and covered by manicured lawns bordered by flower beds. These lawns were so perfect it was hard to imagine they were made of real grass. We were on top of a bluff. I could see the ocean, but only at the horizon and in the middle distance. I couldn't see the beach. The beach seemed to be far below us, and I couldn't tell where it began. He parked the car and put the top up.

"We'll have to walk a bit," he said. "I hope you don't mind. But you'll see—it's worth it."

We walked along the paved road for quite a ways until it dead-ended at an open field. At the edge of the field, we crawled through a fence and started down a dirt path. He walked in front of me, carrying a bag over his shoulder. He had on dark shorts and a pair of heavy black lace-up shoes that looked entirely wrong for the beach. There were no houses near us now, except a big white one that sat up on a hill above us and looked like a palace of some kind. We were almost to the edge of the bluff. Earlier, when we were on the paved road, I had been able to see up and down the coast, where the land made a horseshoe, but now I couldn't see anything except the gently sloping bluff, covered with grasses and a few trees, and the deep blue ocean ahead of me. The path was taking us to what seemed from this height like the edge of the world.

"We're up so high," I said.

"All the better to see."

"But how do we get down to the beach?"

"Follow me."

He led the way to the edge of the cliff, where I looked down and suddenly saw how everything dropped away. The cliff was very steep. One step and I would have been over the edge, and suddenly I felt his hand on my arm, as if he were preventing me from falling.

I saw a beautiful beach below us. It curved gently. There were rock outcroppings at either end of the beach, which made it seem sheltered and contained. The cliff formed a backdrop. It had a private and protected feeling. There were no people on the beach; it was an entirely empty place, as if remote from civilization. The water rolled toward the shore, gentler than before; there were no crashing waves here. I could see clusters of something green floating just below the surface of the pale turquoise water, so that the sea looked mottled, like the skin of a frog.

"I've never seen anything like this before."

"Greece looks like this," he said. "Come on."

We climbed down a wooden stairway. As soon as we'd settled ourselves on the sand, Vincent stripped down to his bathing suit and tested the water.

He was thin, so very thin, so different from any man I'd known. Pale, fragile, serious. Almost feminine in his movements.

"It's cold," he said, turning toward me, still standing in the water. He came back and spread a blanket on the sand and laid down. He was incredibly white, all over the same color of white, as though he'd never seen the sun, and his ribs were little ridges under his flesh. I sat down on the blanket beside him, still wearing my clothes. He closed his eyes and seemed to fall asleep immediately.

The wind sent grains of sand scudding across the surface of the beach. Quietly, so as not to disturb him, I got up and went back to some rocks and took off my clothes. I put my bathing suit on. Little goosebumps rose up all over me. I returned to the blanket and stretched out next to him. I found that if I lay down, it was warmer; it was cool only if you sat up where the wind could chill you.

Later, he awoke and said, "Should we swim?"

"I don't know about that. I'm not much of a swimmer."

He walked down to the water again.

"Isn't it cold?"

"You have to get used to it first," he said. "You can't jump right in."

I tested the water. It was freezing. "I don't know," I said, and again added, "I'm not a good swimmer." I looked at the ocean. It frightened me.

"It's all right. I won't let anything happen," he said. "Come on. At least walk along the surf with me."

We walked for ten or fifteen minutes in the surf, from one end of the beach to the other, until the water didn't feel so cold anymore.

He began talking again. He said that every family seemed

to have its central story that dominated the mythology of that
group, and to which every family member finally contributed.
There was always one event, maybe two or even three, something that had happened to the family, around which things
begin to collect—emotions and a sense of common identity.
He'd been thinking about this for some time.

"What would it be for your family?" he asked. I didn't
know and said so, and he fell quiet again. We simply walked
along, looking at the sky, the rocks, the sea. I thought he was
odd. I'd never met anyone like him before. Again, I caught his
profile. I kept staring at it, in brief snatches, because I was
trying to see us together as we were, walking on a beach, just
the two of us. He turned abruptly and said, "Let's go in."
Then I followed him into the ocean, stepping out into the
water, until it swirled around my waist and splashed on my
breasts.

"Now," he said, and dove in. I followed him. It was shock-
ingly cold, and I felt a pain in my ears.

Beneath the surface, sea grasses moved gracefully, swirling
and floating in a solid carpeting. I could see the sandy bottom
only occasionally, when the grasses parted and a hole opened
up. Small fish were swimming around us. Vincent stayed close
to me, and I kept looking at his body, moving underwater,
pale and unreal in the bright green sea. We came up for breath
and dove down again. I felt safe with him there; I never would
have gone into the ocean on my own, I was there only because
of him, and I stayed right next to him. He reached out every
once in a while and touched my arm when he wanted to point
something out to me.

After a while we floated on our backs, looking up at the sky
streaked with thin clouds. Then I began to feel chilled; goosebumps rose up all over me, and my fingertips were numb, and
Vincent said it was time to get out.

We lay in the sun, warming ourselves, until I felt my suit
become dry. I felt wonderful after the swim, and I was glad I'd
gone in.

"How old are you?"

"Thirty," he said.

"Where were you born?" I asked him.

"I was born in New York," he said, "but we moved away from there. We traveled a lot."

"Why?"

"Because that's what rich people do. They travel a lot. It comforts them. It makes them feel that they know the world. But of course they only know the nice parts." He smiled and looked out at the sea.

"Oh."

"When I was small," Vincent said, "my father used to call me into his study to talk to him. I never knew what he wanted from me, exactly. He'd talk to me like I was his peer or something. He'd say, 'I really don't know whether so-and-so can be trusted,' someone in his firm who he had doubts about. I'd sit there listening to him. He never expected me to say anything, I don't think. After a while he'd say, 'Okay, Vinnie, we won't solve this one today, will we? Go out and play,' and I'd be dismissed. That was it. He never talked to me about normal things that I might be interested in. I suppose he thought he was developing my business sense. In truth, I hate the very idea of the business world. I always have."

"What kind of business was he in?"

"He owned a mine in West Virginia, where his family was from. We lived there for a while, in the town near the mine. We lived in a big house, completely cut off from everyone. I was sent away to school, so I never knew a single kid in that town. I had a sister and a brother. My father didn't think we needed anyone else; he discouraged us from having playmates. He felt the family should be enough. He didn't think we needed friends. Each night, he and my mother ate alone. My sister and brother and myself ate separately, in a long dining room, waited on by three servants—a servant for each of us. They were also gone a lot. My parents would suddenly go off on a vacation—to London or France or Italy. For a while, before I understood what it meant to travel, I thought they had the remarkable power of simply being able to disappear and then later materialize again. Really, I was raised by servants. I don't know what it's like to have a mother and father, a so-called normal life."

"I can't imagine that."

"What always surprises me," he said, "is how no one in my life has ever been curious about how I was raised. I think people are embarrassed to ask, and of course I understand that. It could also just be deadly boring. I'm not saying I think anybody should be that curious. But it's made me feel lonely, as though my past was beyond explaining."

"Well, how were you raised?" I asked.

He smiled. "Once my mother insisted I go to this party. We were staying in Switzerland, where we often went for at least part of the winter. I didn't want to go. It was some kid's birthday party. I was just a teenager—maybe thirteen, and very shy and insecure. Just before I left for the party, she stopped me and said, 'You look so pale, Vincent.' She opened her purse and took out some rouge. She put a little on my cheeks. I was horrified, but I would never have thought of stopping her. I just stood there and let her do it. 'Better,' she said. She put a little more rouge on my lips. I wanted to die, thinking of going out with rouge on my cheeks and my lips, but I was spineless and dominated by my mother, so of course there was no question that I would go to the party this way.

"When I got to the party, some kids noticed the rouge. This kid named Stewart said, 'You've got makeup on, haven't you, Vincent?' I denied it, but he kept up with it, until some other kids joined in. 'You're wearing makeup! Vincent's got makeup on!' they yelled. I just kept denying it, over and over, but it was terrible, because I knew they knew I was lying, and I couldn't be convincing, no matter how hard I tried. Now I was not only wearing makeup and suffering that humiliation but I was lying, and that made me look terribly weak. Everyone knew the truth. Just knowing the truth makes you very strong, especially if it forces your victim to lie. Finally I left the party, I just left, and I began walking back to the village instead of waiting for the chauffeur to pick me up. It was terribly cold and I wasn't dressed right, but I didn't care. When the car came to get me, I wasn't there. And then later, when I finally got home, I was punished, so everything, went wrong from the beginning, I was set up to fall, and all this so I wouldn't look pale. She never saw her mistake.''

"That sounds pretty bad.''

"It was awful.''

"Where did you meet Jolene?'' I asked.

"That's another story,'' he said, and closed his eyes and seemed to doze off. I thought he wasn't really sleeping but didn't want to talk anymore. We stayed a little while longer, lying quietly in the sun, and then he suddenly got up very abruptly and began putting his clothes on.

"It's late,'' he said. "I've got to be somewhere.''

We climbed the stairs leading up the bluff and walked back to the car. He drove me home and dropped me off, just as the sun was setting. During the ride, we hardly spoke. "I'll see you soon,'' he said. "I hope you don't mind me not walking you to the door, but I'm in a rush.''

After that day at the beach, he began coming by my apartment.

At first his visits were irregular, and then he started stopping by every few days. He'd call me at work and ask what I was doing that night. I never had anything planned in the evenings.

He'd say, "Could I come by later?'' I'd always say, "Sure.'' Pretty soon he didn't even bother calling. He just showed up.

He'd arrive with a bottle of wine, stay an hour, perhaps two, just long enough to finish the wine, and then he'd leave. About seven o'clock, I would hear Mrs. Beal's dogs, Pookie and Teddy Bear, begin their loud barking, announcing the arrival of a stranger, and I knew it was him. Then I would hear his shoes coming up the sidewalk, a sandpapery sound against the cement. Finally, I would hear his tap on the glass, open the door, and let him in. I'd take his bottle of wine, open it, and pour us each a glass while he turned on the radio and searched until he found the music he liked, the serious violins or tinkling piano, the big orchestra sound, the boring symphonies. Then we'd just listen to music. Or I'd tell him about my day, what I'd seen on the way to work, where I'd gone for lunch, what happened with patients, or repeat some of my conversations with Marilyn. He seemed to have nothing to report, and little of anything to say.

I can't explain how nice these evenings were, how I began to look forward to them, for reasons not easy to understand, because nothing ever happened. Vincent simply arrived. We listened to music. I talked. He listened. We drank some wine. He left. I think it was simply that I did not feel so alone anymore.

Each day I walked to and from work, passing through the park. Marilyn said, "You're crazy to walk through that park. Don't you know that's where all the drug deals are made? There are muggers and bums. It's not safe."

But I didn't feel threatened. I don't know why, but I never worried, although it did seem to me that the park was a place for men. You hardly ever saw couples or families there, except on weekends. Almost everyone was Hispanic. It was a man's park, a place for old men's games of chess or cards. Younger men played basketball and soccer. It was a place for the unemployed and the newly arrived immigrants—men who sat on the backs of benches and talked in low voices, looking listless and anxious, or who just lay on the grass, staring, expressionless, as I passed by them. These men seemed very sad. It was a place for homeless people who sat up on benches, slumped over in the shade, or huddled beneath the eaves of a maintenance building. No one ever bothered me. It seemed to me that the people in the park were not so different from the other people on the street, ordinary and sometimes alone, poorer people trying to make things work out okay and just looking for places to pass time until that happened. These people would be surprised if you ever spoke to them, they were so used to their isolation. What I came to understand was how badly they needed a place to rest, how exhausting it was to be forever on the move.

In spite of the run-down atmosphere, the park was still a lovely place with beautiful trees. You can't imagine the graceful way the palms moved in the slightest wind, a wind that wouldn't be apparent to someone walking on the ground; but higher up, in the treetops, it sent the leafy canopies to rippling—like *slow* motion, undulating and mesmerizing. It was nice to look up and see that; it was good to have such a place to walk. And so I ignored Marilyn's warnings.

One day I was walking through the park, coming home from work, and I saw a man sitting on the grass. He was drinking from a bottle in a sack. I thought I recognized him. The man with the bird, I thought—the man who'd been lying on the grass next to the baby bird in the metal crate. But then, as I got closer to him, he looked up, and I saw it wasn't the man with the bird at all. It was Duluth Wing.

"Duluth," I said.

He looked at me, his face blank.

"Don't you remember me?"

"Oh, sure," he said, "I remember you." But he appeared puzzled.

"I gave you a ride from Utah."

"That's right." Now he nodded knowingly and smiled. "The woman with the trailer."

"Verna."

"Verna. Right. Now I got it."

"How are you?" I asked, although it was pretty clear. He was drunk and dirty. He smelled of booze. He sniffed as if he had a cold. From the shabbiness of his appearance, it seemed as if things had really changed.

"I wondered about you," he said. "You just disappeared when I went in to borrow money from my brother. What happened? Why didn't you wait for me?"

"A cop hassled me for double parking. I had to move, and then I got lost."

"I thought you wanted to ditch me."

"No, that wasn't it."

"It wouldn't be the first time someone tried to shake me off."

"Do you live near here?"

"Not exactly," he said, and looked away.

Suddenly I realized the truth. He was homeless. That was his cart parked next to the bench. He stood up and picked up a coat from the top of the cart, found some tissue in the pocket, blew his nose, and sat down again, on a blanket spread over the grass.

"I'm still out of work," he said. He pointed to the cart. "As you can see. I don't live anywhere right now. A few days ago I came over to this park because somebody told me you can use the bathrooms here and nobody bothers you. You can also get out of the weather. There's the library here."

"But what happened? I thought you were living with your brother?"

"It's easier to sleep out here."

"It can't be easier!"

"They asked me to leave."

"Oh. I see."

"Well, that's the way it is, anyway. I don't have any money and I don't have a job. I don't even have a car." He adjusted the blanket under his hips. It was made out of some shiny material and it looked almost new. "You don't have a cigarette, do you?"

I gave him one and watched him light it. He leaned back on the blanket. "What are you doing around here?" he asked. I told him about the job with the dentists and my apartment nearby.

"How do you get by?" I asked.

"Ask people for money. Collect cans once in a while. Pick up what food I can. It hasn't been so bad. Until the rain last week. And now, just the last two days, it's been cold at night. I have this cold I can't get rid of." He looked to his left, where in the distance some Mexican men were playing with a dog on the grass. The dog had a ball in its mouth, which it refused to give up, and the men were chasing it across the grass. But the dog stayed just out of reach, running in circles around them.

"I can usually get enough money to buy something to eat and drink just by asking people for change. That's about all I need. Something to eat and drink."

The dog ran out across a patch of dirt which had been freshly seeded and protected by a barrier of stakes and string, but now the dog was tangled in the string, bounding across the pale thin shoots of grass, pulling up stakes, and barking wildly.

"What about going to a shelter? Can't you do that?"

"No thanks," he said. "They treat you like felons in those places. Curfews. Rules. Crazy people."

The man called his dog: Farabundo! *Farabundo!*

"Besides, how much worse can it get?"

I didn't respond. I watched the dog, the men, the basketball players on the court in the distance. I could see people sitting under the trees behind the library. A cop car pulled up at the curb. Two boys started to walk away quickly, but the police called to them and made them stop, and then led them back to the police car and made them roll up their sleeves so they could see the insides of their arms. After a few minutes, the boys walked away, and the policemen drove off.

"Well," I said, "I should go." On impulse, I added, "Maybe we'll get something to eat sometime."

"Sure," he said.

I looked down at him. "I walk through this park all the time."

"We'll see you then."

"Bye."

I started to walk away and heard him say my name.

"Could you give me a dollar?"

"Oh, sure," I said, and gave him the dollar.

On the way home I passed the vegetable trucks. I looked at the apples and oranges, and the bananas. There was nothing at home for dinner except a part of a loaf of bread, and a little cheese. I wanted some cantaloupe, and bananas and apples. For seventy-five cents, I could have gotten a bag full of fruit. But I'd given the dollar to Duluth and I didn't have any more money. I walked home thinking about the fruit, craving the taste of it.

Later, when Vincent came over, I told him about Duluth. I even told him about the fruit, wanting it, and not having the money left to buy it.

"He's going to keep asking you for money," Vincent said.

"I suppose."

"Every time he sees you. And you'll give it to him."

"I suppose," I said again.

When Vincent left that night, he put two twenty-dollar bills in my hand. "That's for Duluth," he said. "Parcel it out slowly."

I looked for Duluth after that, but I didn't see him until the next week. It was sunny, warmer than the week before. Duluth was lying back on his blanket above a level area in the park where some boys were playing soccer. I talked to him for a few minutes and gave him a dollar.

"You're an angel," he said. "Now I know what an angel looks like. Looks just like you." His eyes were almost unbearable to look at, they had become so red and weepy—not from crying, just oozing some fluid. "I can't thank you enough. God bless you . . ." He tried to kiss the back of my hand but I pulled it away.

"Go on, Duluth—give me a break. It's just a buck." He seemed so overly emotional, even less in control than before. He had a paper bag, and in it was a bottle of beer. He took a drink and handed me the bag. I shook my head.

"Are you afraid of my germs?"

"No, I'm not afraid of your germs. I'm on my lunch hour. I don't think I'd like to go back to work after I'd been drinking."

"Why not?" He smiled and shoved the bag at me again.

"Because."

He slapped his knee. "Now that's a damned good answer! That's the answer I used to give for everything when I was a kid. *Because!*"

"Where *did* you grow up, Duluth?"

He face became serious, as if I'd suddenly sobered him up with one question. "Oh, hell, Verna, don't ask me any of that stuff. I don't want to get into it. Where I came from doesn't matter. Where I'm going doesn't matter. I'm here, that's all I know. Let it drop at that." He sounded angry.

"Fine." I didn't say anything. He had become upset very quickly.

"Sorry. I didn't mean to snap at you."

"It's all right."

"No offense?"

"No." I turned to leave.

"You're a good woman," he said, and let out a deep burp.

I went home that night to find another letter from Leon had arrived. He asked why I hadn't answered the first one. "Get in touch with me," he said, "as soon as possible." His address hadn't changed; he was still in Evanston. I put the letter in the trash and didn't bother to answer it. I felt like delaying the future that I sensed was already shaping itself up in Wyoming. I was in no hurry to ease the arrival of those children with their uninspiring looks. I figured wedding bells could wait.

Something else happened. I started running very low on money. I just couldn't get by on what Dr. Lovestedt was paying me; I realized that after a while. I was always short. There were hidden expenses. My phone bill went past due. I had so little left over after rent. It seemed like it was time to put an ad in the paper and sell the trailer.

I'd parked it in the alley behind the apartment, where I thought it would be safe. But when I went to look at it, I discovered it was covered with graffiti. Words were scrawled on the side of it in different colored paint: CHAVEZ LOCO . . . PURA . . . RAMIREZ . . . FEDS. The window above the feed bin was broken out. I found a blanket inside. There was an odor, and I knew someone was sleeping in there. How could I sell it in its present condition?

The next day I checked it again. Overnight a tire had gone flat, and then I noticed it had been slit. Where would I get the money to fix *this*?

My debts increased. I fell further behind. Then the phone was cut off. It didn't seem to matter so much. Why did I need a phone? Who called, anyway?

I rarely saw my neighbors, but gradually I formed a picture of them. Mr. Pulido, my landlord, kept his blinds drawn all day. He left his apartment each evening and walked to the Filipino Cultural Center, where he ate supper. At night he sat in a darkened room, watching TV.

Mr. and Mrs. Beal, though rarely seen, could frequently be heard, talking to their dogs, Pookie and Teddy Bear; and when they left their windows open, I caught other sounds, private and domestic, coming from their rooms, which were separated from mine by a narrow walkway. The slightest noise carried: Mrs. Beal clearing her throat in the night, any small noise, like a spoon scraping a bowl. (What did she eat? Ice cream? Cereal?) The Beals were retired and rarely left their apartment except to buy groceries, and then I saw them slipping out the back way, holding hands and looking furtively around, as if they feared an attack was imminent.

Mrs. Edgington, an elderly woman, was a complete shut-in, and also more disheveled than most people I saw who were living on the street. She was very overweight and could hardly walk; she never went farther than her door. Once or twice I'd

seen her standing on the porch, in unwashed clothes. Her gray
hair hung straight down in long stringy strands except on the
top of her head, where it formed a rat's nest of a dome, a pile
of matted tangles the size of a knit cap. All around her mouth
and on her chin, gray hairs had grown into a sparse, long
beard. She could no longer fit shoes onto her feet and so went
barefoot. Because she couldn't lean over or bathe herself anymore, her feet and ankles were mottled, smudged black. Once
a week her groceries were delivered by a boy from Lucky's
Market, who stood at her door and read off the items on her
shopping list one by one. She ordered ice cream, cookies, pies,
doughnuts, bananas, candy, potato chips, quarts of milk, and
boxes of cereal, food that would be ready to eat the moment
she opened a container.

I had never seen Mr. Kihm-Maurer, but I heard him playing the flute, and saw underwear on the line that I thought
belonged to him, grayish-white shorts and T-shirts so small
they looked like they'd fit a child. I knew these people by the
trail of clues: the newspapers piled up by Mrs. Beal for the
junkman who came up the alley; Mr. Pulido's magazines
stacked in a wire basket by the mail boxes; the Boggs' neat
bundles of trash set out by the steps. My neighbors were elderly, reclusive people. No one spoke to anyone. When you
saw them on the sidewalk or in the alley, they looked the other
way, as if trying to imagine you didn't exist.

I looked forward more and more to Vincent's visits. They
became increasingly frequent. One day he called me at the
office. He wouldn't be able to come to see me for a few weeks;
he was going out of town. When he got back, he'd call. Also,
something was being delivered—a present. I should expect a
delivery from a store.

"What is it?" I asked.

"Something for you" is all he would say.

Two boxes containing stereo equipment were delivered
while he was away, and after he returned from his trip—about

which he'd say nothing—he began bringing records over with him. Now, after the arrival of the stereo, he came nearly every evening.

I no longer questioned these visits. I just assumed he'd arrive now, each night, and gradually I began to see what was happening. I was falling for him, I saw that, and I thought he must be feeling that way, too, or why else did he come, night after night?

One evening he arrived a little later than usual. He began playing a record, filling the apartment with the sort of music he loved. It was strange, but I was beginning to like this music; I found myself giving into it more and more. I could even recognize a few pieces now, and name the composers. But tonight he was playing the stereo so loud that I felt the vibrations coming through the floor in the kitchen, where I was fixing dinner, and I felt slightly anxious, as if the music were working on me in a bad way, and the noise was too much, all wrong for my mood.

I opened a jar of home-canned pears. The pears were spotted with a soft layer of mold.

"Come in here," he called.

"I'm busy."

"I want you to hear this."

"I don't have time right now."

I looked at the pears. It was fruit I'd brought with me from Utah. Little islands of pale blue mold had established themselves on the surface of a sea of pear juice. I scooped the mold off the top and tasted the pears to see if they were still okay.

The music suddenly stopped and Vincent came into the kitchen. "I'm not going to play the next record until you come in and listen. What are you doing?"

"Trying to take the mold off these pears," I said.

"Won't they taste funny?"

"I don't know. I'll have to try them. Usually, you can take

it off and it won't matter. They still taste fine."

He was leaning over me, peering into the jar. His face was close to my own.

"I don't know whether I want any," he said.

Suddenly, turning my own face toward his, I kissed him. I hadn't meant to do this; I gave it no forethought or planning. (Later I thought, Why did I do it, how did it begin? But then, at that point, it was over, and I don't think it really mattered.) It had something to do with his closeness to me, and even the pears, which established a certain domestic feeling, so that for a moment we were a man and a woman, in a kitchen, preparing our evening meal, which would be like other meals that had come before and ones that would come after, a string of such meals connecting us as a couple, just like other people whose lives were threaded by such ordinary events. It was natural and spontaneous, it seemed right to turn toward him and find him, and I didn't hesitate afterward, when I'd kissed him once, to want more, so I turned more fully toward him and offered myself wholly then. I slipped my arms around him and prepared myself for the embrace I thought was certain to follow. He lifted his hands, I felt them briefly on my back, and then they were gone. I turned my face and pressed my cheek against his. I found that we were almost the same height, and this thought went through my head, We're the same size. It seemed to make us suitable, even more of a couple. My shoulders were even with his. I felt as if our arms began at the same point, our ears, our waists. And in our thinness we were alike, too. I had my hands on his back and could feel the small knobs on his spine, and I knew them to be similar to those on my own back. The bones of his shoulders were also sharp and hard, curving slightly forward, like my own. I noted all these things, feeling myself well matched to him. Although my thoughts were coming swiftly, these individual things were not so important as the overall feeling of my body moving not just toward him but into him, dissolving any separateness. I think I was already imagining how we would be together, how we were going to be, and thinking we would make love soon, when I suddenly realized that he was growing stiffer, that his arms were just hanging there and his hands weren't touching me. I was enclosing someone who was rigid and unyielding in my arms, and I don't know why it took me so long to realize that, or even if it was so long.

There wasn't any response from him. He hadn't moved. I had laid myself against him and I was holding on to him, but it was as if I was hugging a mannequin and I pulled back.

He didn't avoid looking at me; he stared right at me and said, "I'm sorry, but it wouldn't be right. It just isn't possible."

"Why?" I asked.

"I don't have those feelings," he said.

"Oh."

This was difficult to understand. What did he want from me? Why did he always come to see me? What were we moving toward if it wasn't something like this?

He read in me the disappointment, the confusion, and I guess he felt he couldn't do anything more, so he just left, and I heard Pookie and Teddy Bear barking as he passed the Beals' window, and Mr. Beal said, "Hush up, you little buggers!"

After he was gone, I sat for a long time thinking about things, about the way my life had gone up to that point and what was happening to me now. A horn sounded in the alley, and somewhere in a nearby apartment a baby cried. Mrs. Beal said, "Pookie, darling, come here." It was not what I had expected. Nothing was working out the way I had thought it would. It was not such a promising land, El-ay.

I remembered when once just after I arrived I went to the May Company department store on Wilshire and Fairfax and the saleslady was rude and I couldn't get change for the phone, then finally I did and called Jolene, but no one was there, and then I went out into the light on the sidewalk, but the air was bad, it smelled terrible and was hard to even breathe it, and I turned and looked at some people waiting for a bus, seeing in their faces all the hatred and boredom and futility of life, and a bus came, leaving off people who also looked tired and defeated, and nobody looked back at me but they all stared dully ahead, maybe because it was hot and there wasn't any shade and many of the people were very old, and then I looked over to where I'd parked my truck to see a ticket stuck on the windshield and a meter maid closing up her book, and I thought to myself, I'll never stand it here.

"These potatoes don't look too fresh. Are you sure you want to use them?" Mr. Beal's voice drifted in the window. "They've got eyes already. Look, they're sprouting."

It isn't just the loneliness, I thought, it's something else. Maybe despair, because you don't believe anymore, and you've got to wonder, How do people do it? How do you go on *without anything to connect you to it all?*

And then there it was, that picture again.

He's a lone figure in the fields. The doves coo on the telephone wires above his head. I see what he's doing. He turns. He rearranges himself, bowing his legs slightly so he can button up his Levis, and I see him look around, his eyes searching for me, and then he finds me and he sees that I've been watching him relieve himself and he smiles, I smile back at him and shake my head—and these looks we exchange contain all the intimacy of our days, and we are then, more than ever, husband and wife, immutable, connected not only to each other but to this land, his father's fields of newly mown hay which stretch in every direction and seem to hold us contained in their pattern.

I wondered, How long will this image haunt me?

Vincent simply stopped coming by. I waited for him, but he never called, he never arrived, he never climbed the steps in the evening anymore, setting Pookie and Teddy Bear to barking. He no longer knocked on the glass, though I waited at night, and listened. I even managed to get the phone bill paid, and service restored, just in case he happened to call. But he never phoned, nor did anyone else.

Weeks passed. And then one night the phone rang, and I thought—because the phone never rang—I thought, It's him, it's going to be him on the line. But it wasn't; it was someone else entirely.

It was Inez calling. She'd just talked to Heber and LaRue and heard I was in town and gotten my number from them, and she was phoning, she said, because she wanted to get together. She wanted to see me right away.

She said, "Why don't you come over here for dinner tomorrow night?"

13

IN MEMORY, I realize she was always exotic to me but never more so than the first time I saw her, when she and Carl arrived at our house a few weeks after their marriage, walking along the edge of the highway toward us, carrying a suitcase between them, holding on to the same handle as if this were evidence of their commitment to help each other out and link their burdens in life.

By the time Carl died and she returned to Utah for his funeral, arriving by plane this time instead of bus and bringing her small baby with her, something had muted in her. The person she had linked herself to was dead, and I think now, How did she stand that loss? Because to anybody, anybody who had eyes at all, she had been crazy about him.

When Carl died, she was still young and very beautiful, but the months of his long, slow death had taken their toll, and when she arrived for the funeral she was a different person from the vibrant, laughing woman who had drawn me out from under the stairway next to the laundry room and given me a haircut. Now she cried a lot. She would cry and then, as if unable to suppress her old personality, she would laugh at something and become animated again; these states alternated, and it seemed to me something like muted hysteria.

Carl's funeral took place one day early in September. At that time of year, breezes blew out of the canyons and mountains to the east, or sometimes, more rarely, the wind came from the west, across the lake, traveling across the Salt Flats. Fall was in the air. You could smell it on the wind. The long summer, the time of waiting, had ended, and relatives gathered for the funeral, driving in from Idaho and Arizona, gathering at our house early in the morning, bearing burdens of grief.

For the ride from the mortuary to the graveyard, Lindquist and Sons had provided a limousine, but only one, which couldn't begin to contain all our family. Mom and Dad rode in the limousine, with Inez, the new babies, and Heber and LaRue, who had flown in for the funeral. The rest of us rode in ordinary cars, Buicks and Pontiacs, standard family vehicles, washed for the occasion. We passed down Washington Boulevard, through a corridor of vacuum-repair shops, tailors, dry cleaners, and cafes. Policemen held up their hands at intersections and everyone stopped for our procession.

As we climbed up the hill at the south end of town, the lake came into view. Here and there, bald brown islands rose up. Some of these islands were subject to the fluctuating waters; they were there one year and disappeared the next. But the largest of these, Antelope Island, never disappeared; it was like a great brown boulder, always there, creating the illusion of a western shore.

The road curved past the armory and the Browning Arms Company. There was an empty field next to Browning Arms where the Hill and Gully Riders junior posse met for drill practice every Saturday morning during the summer. Patterns were worn into the earth, a cloverleaf shape where kids had barrel-raced their horses, and a string of linked figure-eights from pole bending. A dust devil whirled through the field, bringing up a funnel of earth and dissolving it again. The whole sloping valley and much of the northern half of the lake could be seen from this spot. This was where we were going to leave Carl; this would be his resting place, this cemetery on the hill across from the posse field. What you got up here was a feeling of the land falling away and of a great distance opening up before you.

It was a new cemetery. Most of the graves were marked by flat plaques set in the ground rather than the upright tombstones found in other, older cemeteries. It was inexpensive. That's why my parents had chosen it; it fit their burial budget. But I also heard my mother remark on the fact that it had a lovely view, as if this were the real reason Carl was being buried here. "It's high up," she said. "It has a lovely view. You can see everything from here." Why anybody who was dead would care whether he was high up or not, I didn't understand.

Trees had been planted at the cemetery, but they were still saplings. Some of them looked like they wouldn't make it; they showed no sign of leafing or recovering from the winter. They looked like markers shoved in the ground, sticks to guide snow plows.

The funeral cars snaked up the gravel driveway, between the yellow-and-brown lawn, half-dead from winter, half-alive with spring. There was no character to this gravesite yet, and it was possible that there never would be. It looked like a new golf course or driving range, a place to hit a bucket of balls after work.

When the limousine came to a stop, Inez climbed out first. She was holding her baby in her arms. My mother got out next, and she was holding her baby. Their babies were almost exactly the same age. Many people had remarked on the fact that my mother gave birth to one son just as another was dying. They also found it fateful in some way that my mother and Inez had been pregnant at the same time and delivered their babies within weeks of each other. It seemed like this should have connected them in some way, as if the genes had been intertwined, twice threaded into the future. But everyone knew it hadn't, that it brought up, instead, some unacknowledged conflict concerning who was more entitled to view the birth of the child as solace or compensation for such a terrible loss, the mother or the wife. The babies didn't look anything alike. Christobel was brown-skinned with blue eyes, thick lashes, and black hair that naturally rose to a festive little point on her head. Willie, my little brother, was the color of uncooked veal. He had a square face and no hair.

The coffin was carried to the grave and placed on the canvas straps, suspended on poles, which stretched across the rectangular hole in the ground. There it remained, hanging above the darkness, during the bishop's short speech and prayer.

Standing by the grave, I noticed that Inez had put on fresh lipstick during the limousine ride. I noticed her hands, how pretty her fingers were, how her nails looked like they were made of thick red plastic. Someone had taken the baby from her. My father was standing between Inez and my mother, supporting them both. Uncle Heber was on the other side of Inez. She wore a hat with a veil that hid her eyes but not her mouth. I could see her mouth curl and uncurl in a series of suppressed sobs; it almost looked as if she was silently singing, mouthing the words to some song. The coffin was covered with an American flag. Taps were played. Men from the Navy wearing sailor's uniforms folded the flag. It was beautiful watching them handle the cloth. They were so efficient, so sure of their role; they folded the flag precisely, and when they were finished, the result was a perfect, hard little triangle that looked weighty, and which they presented to Inez. She held it to her chest. The wind blew across the lake, stirring our dresses, causing the gladiola in the flower arrangements to tremble. The bishop prayed, and I was surprised at what an ordinary prayer it was, how it seemed almost boring because I felt I had heard everything before. I thought he should have said something special, although I don't know what that might have been.

But it was just some kind of regular church prayer he said, and I felt cheated. Then it was over, and I felt everyone around me dispersing, the larger, sturdier people turning away, the women stepping carefully across the grass in their high heels and the men walking slowly beside them, attending to them because they were frailer and weakened by their grief. Inez stayed by the grave for a moment and then my father led her away.

I stood looking at the casket, which had not been lowered but was still suspended above the hole. It felt as if we were leaving something unfinished, leaving his coffin hanging in the air like that. Who except the gravediggers would be there when he finally was put in the ground?

At the edges of the hole, green carpeting had been draped over the sides. I looked for a stone and found a small rock nestled in the grass. I wanted to see how deep the hole was, and I threw the rock in to see. It wasn't very deep. It seemed the stone had hardly left my hand when I heard it land in the bottom of the grave. Someone smacked me at the side of my head. It was Rodney, my older brother. "What are you doing?" he hissed. "Throwing rocks at the coffin?" I yelled, "I was throwing the rock in the hole, not at the coffin!" He hit me again. I tried to hit him back, but he held me away from him, his hand on my forehead, and I swung wildly at the space beneath his arm. Then he shoved me down, and I reeled and landed on my back on the grass. He walked away from me. I stayed on my back, looking out toward the lake. I felt my dress becoming wet at the spot where I'd landed on the soggy grass, but I didn't try to get up. I could see beneath the coffin. I looked between the posts, beneath the straps that held it above the ground, and I saw the blue sky and the top of the Oquirrh Mountains on the other side of the lake. I realized that I was lower than Carl, closer to the ground, and just for that moment felt that I had come to the place where I'd wanted to be in order to say goodbye, and I said it then, I told him goodbye, as if I had been looking at his face and not at the side of a fancy box that held him.

After Carl's funeral, my mother and father stood in the bathroom late at night, when everyone had finally left or gone to bed, thinking, I suppose, that they were finally alone. I had come upstairs for a glass of water, and I stood in the darkness of the front room, listening to them. There were large white flowers—lilies, I think—stenciled on the wallpaper in the living room; and in the dim light coming from a street lamp out near the highway, these flowers looked like boats, a flotilla bobbing on an endless gray sea. They had never appeared that way to me before.

The door to the bathroom was open. My father was wearing his garments, nothing else; and in the back, where they closed with a button, the material drooped and made him seem flat there, as if he had no rear end. My mother wore a robe made of the same blue material as her nightgown.

"I don't know why Merle and Effie didn't come," he said. "I expected to see them."

"It's a long way to drive. Merle's not well."

"We made it to their son's wedding. You'd think they'd have tried to come."

"It's over, Arlo. It's done with."

"I wonder if she plans on going back tomorrow."

"I don't know."

"It doesn't matter to me. She might as well stay a few days if she'd like, but I think she'll want to go home now, and get on with life. Don't you think she'll want to get back to San Francisco?"

"I suppose."

"I would think so."

"I feel like having a glass of milk," my mother said.

"You go to bed and I'll bring you one."

She put her hand on his shoulder. "It was a nice service, wasn't it?"

"It was fine."

"All those beautiful flowers." She sighed.

I saw my mother's face look older than ever before. She

was forty-three. She'd just had a baby. She'd worried it would
be a mongoloid, but everything had turned out all right, Willie was normal. Still, she looked as if the birth and the death of
her sons had been too much for her. In later years, I would
remember this moment as the time when she began to seem
much older to me.

"If they don't leave tomorrow, I wonder how long they
plan on staying?"

"What I don't know," she said, "is what we can do for that
baby. That's Carl's baby, and we've got to remember that."

"I know," he said.

"I know you know," she said.

Boyle Heights lay across the Los Angeles River, on the
other side of downtown, beyond Little Tokyo. The river was
really a concrete channel with hardly any water in it, running
through an area of railroad tracks and dilapidated warehouses.
The bridge arching over the river, however, was graceful,
with little lights topping cement posts which had been
sculpted into pretty shapes. It looked older than most things in
L.A. did.

Her house was at the end of a street that turned into a
cul-de-sac against a bare hillside. All the houses were crammed
together and painted different colors, some bright and festive
shades, like pink or yellow; others were drab and run-down,
with barred windows and cluttered yards. Her place wasn't
pretty, it was run-down, and in need of paint. A car was parked
on the grass. I pulled up out front and turned off the engine
and got out.

When I looked up, I saw her. She stood at the door wearing a gray housecoat. I would not have known her if I'd met
her on the street. The thing I was trying to ignore, the thing I
could not ignore as I came closer to her, was the bruise surrounding her eye, the red mark on her cheek.

"Hello, Inez," I said. I felt suddenly shy.

"So," she said. "You look about twelve. You look great,

kiddo, exactly that same, you know? What is it about you Flakes—you just don't grow old, huh?" She still wore the same color of red lipstick. She was thin; her dress hung on her bones loosely, and her face was gaunt. I glanced down, looking away from her face, away from that red mark and the bruise, and I saw that she wasn't wearing any shoes. Her feet were broad and brown, tapering to slim pretty ankles. A small gold chain encircled one ankle.

She took my hand and said, "Oh, boy." Just two words.

I looked at her and said, "I know." Then we laughed as if neither of us knew what to say.

We went inside the house, where a man was sitting on the sofa, watching TV.

"Jim," she said. "We got company."

I was startled first of all by his age. He was an old man in relation to Inez. She was in her forties; he looked over seventy. But it wasn't just that: he was also ugly. When he turned and looked at me, he scared me. In his face I saw meanness.

"Verna, meet Jim. Jim, Verna."

"Hello, Verna," he said. His voice was surprisingly soft and gentle sounding. He was heavy and had trouble getting up from his chair. His nose was purple and disfigured. It was hard to look at any other part of his face, his nose was so prominent and freakish, large-pored and marred by veins.

He stood up and smiled. "Jim Greenberg," he said, and extended a big hand for me to shake.

Inez said, "Jim, get her something to drink. What'll you have, kiddo?"

"Anything," I said.

"Anything?" he repeated. "The young lady will have anything, anything at all."

"A beer," I said.

Inez sat across from me. She lit a cigarette. "Tell me this, Verna honey. Just how many years since I seen you?"

I shook my head. "Mmmm . . . maybe fifteen or twenty years."

"Twenty, Jim—you hear that? Twenty years! I didn't think I seen you since Joe died." Joe was the policeman Inez had married after Carl's death, the one who had died of kidney problems.

"You know Lola's down in Tustin, going to beauty school, and Joey's in the Marine Corps."

"Oh . . . they're that old, huh?" Lola and Joey were Inez's children by Joe. I could remember them only as tiny, dark kids, pretty and quiet.

"I hardly see them anymore."

"I guess that happens."

"You see that picture there? That's Lola and Joey."

"They've grown up."

"They got their own life," she said.

Jim reached up and adjusted the picture of them, which was hanging crooked. Then he went into the kitchen to get our beers.

She asked what I was doing in L.A. and I told her. I told her about Leon leaving. I said I was trying life in a new place.

"That's too bad about your husband, kid. That's a bad break."

"There wasn't anything I could do about it."

"What you going to do, hon?"

"Just get on with things. I got a job down here, I got a nice apartment. So it's okay." I took a deep breath. "It's working out."

"In what part of town are you living?"

"Near MacArthur Park."

"Sure, you bet, I know that area. I used to live in an apartment near there before I met Jim. I wasn't sorry to leave it. Twice I got ripped off in that apartment. Once I came home and this guy had my stereo and TV and some other stuff and he was standing outside with it. He'd called a taxi to come get him—he had so much of my stuff he couldn't walk away with it, and he was waiting out back for a taxi to arrive. The taxi came just as I got home, and I looked at him putting all my stuff into the taxi and I said, 'What are you, crazy?' I started yellin' at him to give me back my things or I was calling the police, and he just turned to the taxi driver and said, 'Don't mind my wife, she's crazy.' The driver thought it was some domestic fight and he just drove away with this guy and all my stuff in the taxi. Jim, put on some music, huh? Put on that Lydia Mendoza, okay?"

Jim limped badly as he crossed the room to put on a record. I wondered why he limped. The music started, a woman singing sweetly in Spanish, accompanied by strumming guitars.

"Can you imagine that? A thief so stupid he calls a taxi? Well, that's L.A. for you. You don't do nothing here without a car."

He brought us our drinks and stood nearby, his bulky body looming over us.

Inez smiled at me. "Cheers, Verna honey. Here's to seeing you again. You look great, honey. It's so nice you come to visit me." We toasted and drank, and then Jim sat down in front of the television set. For a few moments we just sat there, all looking at the TV. Inez started to say something, but Jim interupted her.

"Look at that," he said. He was pointing to the TV. "Jeopardy" was on. The clock was ticking and a contestant looked very worried. She was trying to guess the name of the thirty-third president of the United States, and time was running out.

"Who do you think it is?" Jim asked me.

I took a wild stab. "I don't know. Calhoun?"

"Calhoun?" Jim snorted. "There wasn't even a president named Calhoun."

"There wasn't?"

Jim yelled, "Harry S. Truman! I bet anything it's Truman."

The bell rang and the woman, who hadn't gotten the answer yet, lost her chance to win more money. The host of the show said, "Oh, too bad," and told the contestant the answer.

The answer was "Who was Harry S. Truman?"

"I was right!" Jim said. "Was I right?" He looked at us.

"You were right, hon," Inez said.

"You bet I was right. How many people in the world know who the thirty-third president of the United States is, huh?"

"Well, I don't for sure, you can bet on that," Inez said.

"That's because you never studied anything except how to put curlers in hair. Now, I'm an autodidact. You know what an autodidact is?" he asked me.

"No, I don't."

"That's a self-taught person, that's what that is, and I am just that, a person who likes to read and who educates themselves."

"Funny, sounds like somebody who drives cars good," Inez said.

"Don't show your ignorance."

"Ha!" Inez said.

"Well, you gotta admit, I was pretty right about that one. Old Give-'em-Hell Harry."

Inez stood up. "Come on in the kitchen with me, Verna honey, while I check on the beans."

Jim laughed. "Too bad for her," he said, shaking his head at the television screen. "I ought to be on that program." As we left the room, I heard him switching channels.

Inez melted some lard in a heavy black skillet and stirred in a little flour. She took a cupful of beans from another pot on the stove and dumped them into the skillet, where they sizzled and spattered.

"Are you still working?" I asked.

"Only two days a week."

"In a beauty shop?"

"I take customers at home. We fixed the garage so I could work here."

"How's Christobel?"

"Oh, she's doin' so good," Inez said. "This place is so

good for her. We were lucky."

"Which place?"

"This home for girls who have problems. It's over on Rampart. She's been there over a year now." She put another cup of beans in the skillet and mashed them up.

"She makes three dollars an hour," Inez said, "and they give her a place to live, so it's pretty good. She gets trained for work. I tell you, Christobel may be slow, but she's no dummy. You'll see her. I want you to see her." She lowered her voice. "It's just not good for her to be here. She don't get on with Jim. He's been sick. He's got cancer, but the treatments have been so good, he's in remission."

The beans sizzled and thickened while she stirred.

"What kind of work do they give Christobel?" I asked.

"She cleans motels."

"And how old is she now?"

Inez smiled at me. "You should know," she said. "Twenty-six! Just like Willie, huh? How is little Willie?"

I looked down into the skillet of beans and then up at Inez's face. "Oh, he's fine," I said. "He's a parole officer up in Washington. He's got three kids now."

Maybe, I thought, he didn't do that to her. Maybe she fell and bruised her face. She stirred the beans, mashing them into a pulp, and then she poured the contents of the skillet back into the other pot.

"You look like Carl," she said.

"Do I?"

"I got some pictures of Carl," she said. "Maybe you've never seen them. Stay here. I'll go get them."

There was a picture of the apartment with the outside staircase leading up to the white wooden landing. Carl stands there with his arms around Inez. She is pregnant. Her stomach swells out in front of them. They look very young and very happy. They're a nice-looking couple. Inez showed me more pictures. There are wedding pictures. Pictures of Carl in a T-shirt and jeans, looking healthy. A picture of them taken in a

photo booth where Carl looks as dark as Inez. Carl with the
baby. Carl in front of a take-away seafood place. Carl and Inez.
Here and there. In a car. At the seashore.

Oh, Carl . . .

The last one was a photograph of him in his Navy uniform.
It had been hand-colored. His eyes are way too blue, falsely
shaded. Unreal. His lips are too pink, like a woman's mouth.

"Where did you meet Carl?" I asked, but before I could
get an answer, Inez spoke up suddenly.

"Not in the house, Jim. I don't want loaded guns in the
house."

I turned around to see Jim standing in the doorway, pushing bullets into the barrel of a pistol. He looked over my
shoulder, gazing down at the pictures on the kitchen table.
"Just strolling down memory lane, huh?"

He pointed the gun at the floor. Behind him I saw that the
program on the TV had changed and a rerun of "The Beverly
Hillbillies" had just begun. Jethro and Ellie May were playing
golf in the backyard of their mansion. One of their balls flew
through a window and plopped into Granny's soup. Jim continued to push bullets into the barrel of the gun. He did this
slowly and carefully, taking his time.

The gun scared me, but Inez seemed calm when she spoke
to him again. "C'mon," she said. "Put that thing away. We're
going to eat soon. I'm just waiting for the rice to finish."

Jim laughed. He finished loading the bullets and began
fitting a silencer over the end of the pistol. "Okay," he said.
"I'll go outside."

"That's his hobby," Inez said. "He's crazy for guns."

He opened a sliding glass door and said, "Come on. Come
on out here. I want to show you something." He meant for
both of us to come. Inez shrugged and dried her hands on a
dish towel, and we walked out onto the patio. A little plaster
Mexican was taking a siesta under a bush. The lawn was dry,
almost dead, it didn't look like anything you'd want to walk on
in bare feet. Some trash cans nearby smelled. The back of the

house faced the crumbling hillside. Jim looked around the yard and then limped over to the edge of the patio, where it met the dry lawn. I tried to imagine where the cancer was, how far it had progressed. Was it in his lungs? his lymph system? his liver? Or somewhere less deadly, like his prostate? He raised the gun and aimed carefully at a tree and pulled the trigger. *Pffftt,* it went. A lemon exploded, then another. He was shooting lemons off a tree.

Inez yelled, "Jim!"

He turned slowly toward her. "What is it, honeycake?"

"You're going to get us into more trouble."

"Look back there," he said. He pointed to the tree, the fence, a hillside covered with scrub just beyond the fence.

"There ain't a damned thing back there I can hurt. Nothing. You don't need to worry." He aimed at another lemon, but nothing happened, although I heard the little *Pffftt.* He must have missed, I thought in about as short a space of time as it can take you to think anything, but at the same instant I heard the bullet strike the fence, and a bright little spot of new wood opened up in the gray boards.

"Damn!" he said.

Each time he fired, the gun made the soft noise. No bang— just a small, seemingly harmless rush of air. He shot off all six rounds and began reloading.

Inez sat down on a picnic bench and sipped her drink, staring straight ahead. She had small, puffy bags under her eyes, and in this light they looked purple.

I thought of Leon, how he used to drive up to the American Falls reservoir with Jack Buffet and shoot pelicans. The pelicans flew along the Snake River, following its winding course until they reached the man-made dam, where, in the marshy areas that surrounded it, they nested, laying their eggs among the reeds. Leon and Jack Buffet would stand up on a bridge that spanned a gorge. The pelicans flew beneath them. They shot downward, toward the rushing water. When the big

birds fell, their corpses were carried away by the river. If the
Fish and Game Department had ever caught them shooting at
pelicans, they would have gotten stiff fines. But they were
never caught. The water took the dead birds away. I don't
know how many pelicans the two of them killed. Once,
though, they only stunned a pelican, and later they retrieved it
from a field where it had fallen. They brought it back to town
and took it to the sporting-goods store where Eddie Stringfellow worked and let it loose in Eddie's office while he was out
to lunch. They closed the door, so that when Eddie came back
and opened his door he found this pelican, injured and scared,
flapping around his office. How easily a man could shoot up
anything in the world—pelicans, lemons, deer, an old wood
fence . . .

Jim set the gun down on the redwood picnic table.

"Let's eat outside tonight," he said. "Let's have a picnic."

"Oh, Jim . . . the mosquitoes!"

"No, no, let's do it. Wouldn't you like that, Verna?"

"That'd be okay."

"See, she'd like that."

Inez looked away.

"I think people should take every opportunity to eat outside," he said. "People just don't think of this, of how nice it is
to sit outside and eat. Don't you agree?"

"Sure, that sounds fine."

"You bet it does. It keeps us in touch with things."

Over dinner he said, "You know, my father used to take
me hunting. One day he said to me, 'You can shoot a black-
bird, you can shoot a crow, you can shoot a magpie, but don't
ever let me catch you shooting a dove.' That was the worst
thing he could think of, shooting a dove."

Inez said, "And I bet you been killing doves ever since."

Jim became serious. "I have not. I have never shot a dove,
I want you to know that."

"Okay," she said.

"I want you to believe me."

"Okay," she said again.

"You've got to have limits in life. I mean, just because I like guns and enjoy shooting doesn't mean I don't have limits."

He reached out and touched her face. He touched the bruised part.

"What kind of meat is this?" I asked, looking down at my plate. Anything to avoid looking at them. "It's good. I like it."

"*Carne asada,*" Inez said.

"That's beef," Jim said. "*Carnitas* . . . that's pork. Little pieces of fried pork. *Lengua* is tongue, *cabeza* is head. We eat it all, don't we, honey? We don't waste anything."

"Get me another beer, would you, Jim?"

"*Cordero,*" Jim said, "that's lamb." He stood up, swaying, and got more beer. "I love lamb."

I saw that Inez drank a lot, that they both did; and by the time I left them that night, it seemed that they were receding from me, already numb to their surroundings. And yet when Inez said goodbye to me at the door, I saw that there was something left in her that was sharp and urgent. She pushed me forward and left Jim standing behind us in the doorway. We walked down the steps and she put her arms around me. Her arms were light, they weighed nothing, she was so small and thin. I thought she was just going to say goodbye. But she whispered in my ear, so low that Jim couldn't hear, "Meet me tomorrow night at a bar called Linda's Place on the corner of Rampart and Beverly."

I nodded slightly so she would know I'd heard her, and then I said softly, "What time?"

"Seven o'clock," she whispered.

"Good night, kiddo," she said, louder.

"Good night," I said.

"You just be careful driving home," Jim called. "You be careful on that freeway."

I backed out of the drive, and when I looked back at the house, I saw that they were still standing in the doorway. He had caught her up and was holding her from behind, his arm around her neck, in a gesture that could have been tender, like an embrace, but instead looked like a hammerlock. They both smiled at me and waved, over and over, as if I were leaving them to go on a long voyage and they were my well-wishers. As I drove away, I noticed they were still standing there, waving at me, and it didn't seem like anybody had ever given me such a long goodbye.

14

LATE IN THE DAY, when all the patients had gone and I'd finished my work, instead of going home I walked to the park and lay down on a grassy bank that sloped down toward the little lake. I didn't have to meet Inez until seven. There was no reason to hurry home.

The lake in the park had begun to smell worse as the weather turned warmer. It was April. Hardly anybody took the boats out anymore, and when they did, the paddles thrashed through the moss, pulling up thick, slimy ropes, turning sluggishly in the bottle-green water.

People were sitting on the grass or strolling along the walkway that circled the lake. I saw a man who looked so much like my father I was startled, only he was Mexican. I thought about how westerners can look alike, how in certain parts of this country the whites and Indians and Mexicans dress and move so similarly that they can be mistaken for each other. That was what I was seeing: a man in a Stetson and bola tie with Levi's riding high on his waist, whose mustache had grown white; from a certain distance, he could have been any race or nationality, just a man raised out in the West, where cultures had mixed for a few hundred years and the sun weathered everyone to the same brown color. That was how my father had looked for as long as I could remember.

The first job I recall my father having was driving a truck for P.I.E.—Pacific Intermountain Express. He hauled freight between cities in northern Utah and southern Idaho. At nights he parked the truck in front of our house, between the ditch and the highway. It was such a big vehicle that it blocked the view of the hills and part of the orchard across the road, and it sometimes seemed like we were living behind a billboard— the initials PIE were painted on the side in big red letters. Some people, usually kids, thought he delivered pies. Then, for a few years, he was a bartender, although he was a man who did not drink himself; and for a while he sold Thom McAn shoes in Salt Lake City, a job that left him with a lifelong interest in people's feet and the type of shoes they wore.

Sometimes, when he met somebody for the first time, he'd look down at their feet and say, "What size shoes have you got on there?" And they would say "What?" as if they hadn't heard him right. "Your shoes," he'd repeat. "They look to me like they might be the wrong size for you."

His feeling was that by and large, people wore shoes that were too wide for them. This could result in fallen arches, he'd say, or flat, sprawling feet. It was not uncommon for him to kneel down near someone's feet and start feeling his shoes, kneading the leather and pressing down where he imagined he'd find a big toe, and then give him some free advice: "Get longer, narrower shoes," he'd say.

I remember as a kid wearing shoes that were so big for me I could go a long while before I outgrew them; later I understood how much money was saved this way. But he would always make it seem this was the *wise* thing to do: wear longer shoes for the good of your feet.

After Thom McAn, he worked at Kennecott Copper Company, commuting twenty-five miles to the mine headquarters on the east side of the Oquirrhs. He oversaw employee relations, processed worker complaints, and fired workers for poor performance or drinking or when there were other problems on the job. It was not a job he liked. Disciplining and

firing people wasn't easy, and he had no respect for the bosses
at the mining company.

Later he quit Kennecott and went to work for the Air
Force as a civilian, and now my mother often took him to work
at Hill Air Force Base and picked him up at night so she could
keep the car. He was a purchasing agent—he bought paper
clips and pens and pencils to keep the Air Force going. The
military base sat on a bluff above the Weber River, near the
mouth of the canyon, between the towns of Uintah and Layton. It overlooked farming country. A tall 7-Up sign marked
the turnoff for the base. There was a bar there at that intersec-
tion called the Hill Top Club, and my father said men who had
drinking problems stopped in there after work. The bar was
decorated with a pink neon cocktail glass with two swizzle
sticks. First one swizzle stick lit up, and then the other one, so
there was the illusion of motion, of something being stirred as
the light flashed back and forth. I remember going with Mom
to pick him up from work, riding in a yellow-and-green Buick.
Each time we came to the guardhouse at the entrance to the
base we had to identify ourselves. Each time my mother would
point to the parking pass on the dashboard and say, "Arlo
Flake, purchasing."

"Why don't they ever get used to us?" I asked her once.

"Because they don't think," she said. "They've lost that
ability. They're robots in uniforms."

As soon as we were on base, we drove directly to the rows
of buildings, each one exactly like the next. My father worked
in a quonset hut. Usually he was waiting for us out front,
holding his black lunch bucket and a rolled-up newspaper, his
face expectant and serious, while in the background planes
took off and landed on unseen airstrips.

When all the children left home, my parents seemed sort of
lost. They just kept buying bigger and bigger TVs. I worried
about them. They seemed listless. When I'd stop to see them,
they'd be sitting in a room with the television on. The first
thing they'd do was turn the sound down on the TV, but

during our conversation their eyes kept wandering to the screen—sometimes nervously or sneakily, as if they couldn't leave it alone. Occasionally we didn't even try to talk at all but just looked at the television and kind of guessed what was going on without hearing any sound. Most of the time this was pretty easy to do, especially since they watched a lot of quiz programs or game shows, but other times we became mesmerized by actions that had no context, which we couldn't fit into any sort of story. Then my mother might say "What the heck?" at some bizarre image or occurrence. And my father would add, "I don't know what this is." I'd say, "Well, why don't you turn the sound up?" And they'd say, "Oh, we don't need to watch that darned thing right now—we see enough of it." Then we'd go on watching it, trying to understand something but sometimes just being lulled into a narcoticlike, communal stupor, happily seduced by the faces and the colors and the quick-changing pictures flashing soundlessly before us, which kept us from each other.

My mother came from Magna, a mining town near Bingham Canyon, where people were poor and lived in houses that had been built on hillsides so steep it looked like they sat on top of each other. Her first job was at Woolworth's in Salt Lake City, and she progressed fast from clerk to head of the notions department before she quit to go on a mission. She met my father in 1928 in the hill country of Kentucky, where they had both been sent on missions for the church. Trusting in each other, they married soon after their release from their missions, forming their pact, imagining even then that they would always be together, assuming their union would contain happiness, good possibilities, financial opportunity, and, of course, many children. But they were like those buildings they saw in the South, stately brick textile mills whose windows, at some date much later than the original construction, had been bricked over, leaving a shape outlined, faintly different in color, where glass had once been. There were rows and rows of windows filled in with brick, a shade different from the rest. My parents were like that now, late in their lives. You could still see the traces of where the windows had been, the penumbras of their hopes, their high-spirited youth, their physical beauty, and the love that they must have had for each other.

They were always frugal, watching their money carefully. They had to be, with eight children to provide for. Everything counted to them. There was nothing to spare. Management was forever necessary, and that was my mother's job, budgeting family income to cover all the hidden, creeping costs of day-to-day living.

I remember I once had a boyfriend named Gary, who came to the house one night while my mother was sorting dry pinto beans on the kitchen table, picking out the bits of dirt, the tiny rocks, the debris that came with the beans when you bought them in hundred-pound sacks. Her fingers worked quickly, flicking the good beans, one by one, into one pile and sorting out the rocks and twigs and dirt clumps into another pile. Gary watched her and later said to me, "Does your mother always count her beans?" and I thought it must have looked like that, like things were so tight that Mom had to measure out our portions, bean by bean, each night.

My father had a wood room. It was really a closet, with an ordinary door, next to the rumpus room in the basement. He gathered surplus wood from construction sites to burn in the fireplace in the winter. He found short ends of two-by-fours, strips of beams and slabs of heavy upright posts and cut these up into lengths that would fit into his fireplace. He collected pieces of four-by-fours and even one-by-twos. He foraged for scrap wood and stacked it neatly in the small closet—so neatly, in fact, that it looked like a mosaic, as if a pattern had been intended and fashioned by a sculptor.

When Carl brought Inez to meet us, my father took her on a tour of the house, as he did with every new visitor. When he opened the door to the wood room, she said, "So what's this? All you got in here is a bunch of junk wood, huh?" It did not please him that she spoke about his wood room like this.

"Junk wood, hell!" he said. "This is my winter fuel."

"Hmm! A nice room for just wood to live in," she added. "Nice to be a stick in this place! You take good care of your boards, Dad." Every time she said *"Dad"* I felt she was according us a privilege, that someone so wonderful could share a father with us, but I could tell that he did not feel any such honor. He pulled the cord that turned off the light in his wood room and went on to the laundry room, and then to the fruit room, with its two-year supply of food, the rows of preserved fruit, the shelves of ketchup and tuna and toilet paper, and the sacks of onions and beans and boxes of apples, food which the church advised us to stockpile in case of disaster.

"What we got here, Dad, a small grocery store?" Inez asked.

There were fewer people in the park now. The light was changing; people headed home to fix dinners, watch TV, gather together in their apartments. I got up and began walking toward Rampart, still thinking about home. I missed them, my parents and my family.

Just out of curiosity, I decided to check the parking lot behind the teachers' union to see if Duluth was there. That's where I saw him sometimes now, in a little area between buildings where there was shade and a few benches were placed in a small courtyard strewn with litter. I didn't even get to the alley before I saw him, sitting against a wall, around the corner from the liquor store. He was wearing an old blue suit, just the jacket and pants. He didn't have a shirt on, or any socks, and his ankles looked thin and fragile stuck into his big shoes. His skin was the color of brown leather, and where the jacket opened at his chest, I could see how thin he was; there didn't seem to be any fat on him. I realized he was getting thinner and thinner. Lately, his eyes also looked worse. I didn't know what was wrong with them, but they were rimmed with pale mucus. He was sitting on an orange blanket. Once again the blanket looked brand-new. The light on him was also very orange, the last light of day.

"Hi, Verna," he said.

"Hi, Duluth."

"It's warming up." He turned his face toward the sun.

"Warmer today than yesterday."

He coughed.

"Still have your cold?"

"Yeah. Can't shake it."

"Aren't you afraid you'll get stuck in this life and never get out of it?"

He looked at me and laughed, and then looked away without answering. I felt foolish, although I didn't know exactly why.

"Would you like to get some food?"

"What kind of food?"

"I don't know, Duluth. Does it matter?"

"Do you think I don't care what I eat anymore?"

"I'm only asking if you're hungry. If you are, maybe you'd like to walk up to Tommy's and get a hamburger."

"I don't want to go right now. If you have a couple of dollars to spare, I might get something later."

"Something to eat?"

"I don't feel that hungry."

"How long has it been since you've eaten?"

"Do you want to know the truth?"

"Yes."

"Two days." He coughed again.

"You're never going to get rid of that cold sleeping out in this weather."

"I'm not sleeping outdoors anymore. I found a place."

"Where?"

"I hope you don't mind. The trailer."

"My horse trailer?"

He nodded.

"I knew somebody was sleeping in there."

"I saw it parked in the alley."

"I might as well give up on ever getting any money out of that trailer. That was my investment, you know. That trailer is about the only thing I got out of my husband that was worth anything. I could have made money on that trailer if I'd sold it when it was still in good shape."

"You might still get something for it."

I shook my head. "I doubt it."

"Well, hell, I can move out—"

"No, forget it." I took two dollar bills out of my wallet. "Have a hamburger or something," I said.

"Thanks."

I started to walk away.

"Wait for me," he said. "I'm coming."

He got to his feet. We walked up Rampart Boulevard toward Beverly. An old woman I often saw at this time of day was selling food from a homemade cart. During the day, she cooked the food in her own kitchen, and then at dusk she put her pots in the cart and pushed it down the sidewalk and stood in the same spot, beneath some tall trees, and sold paper plates full of food. She was a small brown woman with a sweet face and she always had customers. She made tamales wrapped in corn husks, and *pupusas*—little fried cornmeal cakes filled with meat and spices. The napkins she gave out said "Orange Julius." I supposed she'd gotten them for free.

We walked slowly. People passed us on the sidewalk and stared. They must have thought we were an odd couple. Duluth had no socks and the backs of his shoes were broken down so he shuffled as he walked. His jacket was dirty, his pants torn at the knee. Every once in a while, he turned aside and coughed hard.

I realized it was spring, although you hardly knew it in this country, where spring wasn't that different from winter, and flowers perpetually bloomed. When we got to the corner, I told Duluth I had to meet someone and we parted. He said goodbye and crossed the street to Tommy's. When I looked back at him, I saw him standing in line for a hamburger. People had backed away from him, leaving a circle of nothing around him.

Ivy grew across the front of Linda's Place. The doorway was draped with a red curtain. I pulled it back and stepped inside, looking around for Inez.

She was sitting at the bar in the farthest corner of the room. She had settled in and was watching the TV mounted on the wall above the shelves of bottles, her chin in her hand. Her cigarettes were on the counter, and an open purse. An ashtray, already filled with butts, sat in front of her. She was finishing one drink; another, fresh drink sat in a glass next to her. She was dressed in nice clothes, but they were so old-fashioned looking that they reminded me of the way my mother dressed when I was little. She had that kind of 1950s look.

"How long have you been here?" I asked.

"Hey! A little while," she said. "I take buses, you know, and I never know how long it's going to take me, Verna honey, to get from one place to the other."

"Vurnahawney." It was one word, smooth and haunting, like "Valhalla."

"Did it take you long?"

"I work just around the corner," I said. "I walked over here. I haven't even been home yet."

"You know where he thinks I am tonight?" she asked, shaking her head. "Bingo. He thinks I'm playing bingo." All the years in the States hadn't taken away her accent.

I smiled. She looked at me.

"I need you to help me, Verna. You know, I don't have a car. Even if I did, I don't have a license, because I never learned to drive. I should have, but I didn't, and now do I wish I could drive! I mean, I'd give a lot for a car right now, you know, and to be able to drive it. But I don't have that, and so—well, I need you. I'm going to leave him, Verna, soon as I can, but I need a little help. I got it all worked out, though. I already got a plan."

She brought the cigarette to her lips and inhaled and blew the smoke out fast, letting her cheeks puff up as she did.

"And Christobel is coming with me, you can bet. We're getting out of this."

I just listened as she talked.

A long time ago, she had thought it would work out okay with him; but there were things she didn't know, and when she found out, it was too late. She'd tried to leave before, but he had come after her. He made scenes. He scared her friends. He threatened them. No one would let her stay with them for long, the way he came around, threatening to hurt somebody. So she didn't have anywhere to go anymore; none of her friends would help her. But now she had a plan, and she knew it would work.

He always promised it would be different, better, if she came back, and for a while it always was. But he was jealous of Christobel. Her other children, Lola and Joey, he didn't ever have any trouble with them. Of course, they both left home right after high school; they didn't like Jim much either, but he didn't bother them. Only Christobel—that's who he gave the hard time to, ridiculing her, teasing her, and then worse. And you know why? It was Carl, really. Because Christobel was Carl's; he wouldn't forgive her for that. He knew what Carl meant to her; he knew what she felt for him, and Jim couldn't take that he wouldn't ever replace Carl, that nobody could, that she wouldn't ever love anybody else like that.

He said he didn't touch her, that Christobel made the stories up; but Christobel wasn't like that, it wasn't like her to lie. He hadn't laid a finger on her, so he claimed; but after that Christobel was worse, much worse. He said she was a damaged child, she was retarded, and that you couldn't believe what she said, she was crazy. The thing was, the hatred between them grew until it was so bad, who could tell anymore what had really happened? So Inez sent Christobel to the home to live, and now she saw her only once a week when she took the number 14 bus over to the house on Alvarado run by the Sisters of Mercy and spent an afternoon with her. "She's no dummy," Inez said. "She might be slow, but she's not stupid—you can ask anybody about that. Ask anybody at the home, anybody who knows her."

I could not help thinking of the light bulbs exploding against the walls of the Golden Hours Center like small bombs. What about that? What did that say about Christobel? But I didn't bring it up, although I thought that someday I would like to ask about it.

Inez sighed. "Sometimes he's okay. And then I think, We can work this out—you know, like other couples do. We can make it, you know? We don't have to fight. Nothing's perfect. So I start thinking this way, but it still gets bad, he goes back to being mean—you know, he's jealous, and that's what sets him off. Even if he thinks I might be talking to somebody too much he goes crazy. Finally, I'd had enough and I got ready to leave for good. Then he got so sick with cancer, and I couldn't go then, not during all those months when he was in the hospital, and afterward—him needing help, you know—I had to stay. If I left him, he had nobody, and I couldn't see leaving him when he was so sick."

"Did he hit you? Is that where you got the black eye?"

She nodded. "That's pretty bad, Verna honey, huh?"

"You can't take that," I said.

"Not too easy you can't."

"Where will you go if you leave?"

"Mexico," she said, and she lit up when she said this. Some of the old Inez was there—mischievous, vibrant, excited. "Baja, Mexico."

"Mexico?"

"My brother Lorenzo lives outside a town called San Ignacio. It isn't too far down the Baja, Verna. We could make it in two days. Two days. You, me, and Christobel—if you take us, and I don't know whether you're gonna feel like doing it, I don't know." She looked at me. "I don't know," she said again, and I couldn't stand the sight of it, the way one eye looked out at me from a darkened circle of flesh.

"Are you kidding?" I said. "It sounds good to me. I'd like a vacation. I'll go with you. Sure, I'll take you."

"Damn," she said, and took hold of my hand. "You're not going to believe this place of Lorenzo's, although, you know, I haven't seen it myself, I only heard about it, but he says this town is like an oasis in the middle of the desert and he's got a farm there and he grows dates and oranges—you know, all kinds of things.

"It's gonna be different for me and Christobel," she added.

"I know it."

"I had enough of this other life."

We decided to leave in a couple of weeks, around the first part of May. We would drive to San Ignacio, where Lorenzo would be waiting for us. She would write him and tell him we were coming. Everything would have to be planned in secret, to keep Jim from knowing. We would meet again in Linda's Place the next week, her regular bingo night, and work out the details.

"I always liked you," she said as we left each other.

"I always liked you, too," I replied.

During the next meeting we set the date to leave, and I arranged for time off work. And then something happened.

I can't say exactly when I began noticing things—noises, a shadow, a movement in the night that told me somebody was there, outside the window, in the area between the Beals' apartment and my own, a distance of not more than twenty feet, half of it sidewalk and the other half a strip of earth that had been covered in wood chips.

Right next to the Beals' windows were some tall, thick bushes. I saw him standing in the shadows near those bushes one night. A breeze was blowing. It was cold outside; the weather had suddenly changed. I was sitting near the stereo, where I had a sideways view of things. I stood up and turned off the lights, thinking I would go to bed, and that's when I noticed him, when the lights were off in the room and I could see outside.

The moon was full. It was lighter outside than it was in the room. The blinds were open. He was standing against the building, flattened by the shadows so that he looked like he was part of the black bushes. It was too dark to see him clearly. He was only a silhouette. If he hadn't shifted slightly, I never would have noticed him. And then quickly he became absolutely motionless again, part of the night.

I wanted to go over to the window and look out, just to make sure somebody was really there, to be certain that it wasn't just my imagination; but I couldn't do that, because I didn't want him to think I'd seen him, so I stood still, my heart racing. Who was out there?

After a while I closed the blinds and stepped close to the wall, where I could see through a crack between the blinds and the window. There he was. He turned to the side and parted the bushes, and I saw him step away from the wall and steal quietly away, but I couldn't see him clearly. Who was it? Why was he watching me?

I didn't raise the blinds anymore at night. I couldn't be sure if he was still out there or not, because there was no way of knowing. It might be a Peeping Tom, I told myself, some weirdo who would go away; but I was really afraid it was *him,* and when I thought of him, I saw the bright new spot of wood open up in the fence, saw the perfect yellow lemon explode, leaving absolutely nothing behind but a smell on the air, and heard him say, "Let's eat outside tonight, let's have a picnic," and I was worried.

The only person I told was Marilyn Tooner. "You should call the police," she said. I didn't tell her about Jim. I just said, one day while we were on a smoking break, "I think I have a

Peeping Tom hanging around my apartment." "How perverted can somebody get?" she said.

But I knew that if I called the police and it was Jim they found out there, things could get worse. I didn't think they put Peeping Toms in jail. And there was no telling what he might do to me or Inez if we got the cops on him. Finally, there were only few days to go before we left for Baja. I figured we might be lucky and get away unharmed.

At night I sang, and sometimes I played the stereo loud just to calm my fears and fill up the place with sounds. After a while—I don't know why, exactly—I began to feel that he wasn't there anymore, and I got braver, and sometimes opened the windows at night, just a little, to see if I could hear anything.

Then, one night, I thought I saw him again, and I went back to keeping the blinds closed and the windows locked.

The days rolled by . . . the nights. And then, the evening before we were to leave for Baja, I heard the dogs bark, I heard the familiar sandpapery sound of the footsteps coming up the sidewalk, and the lightness of the steps on the porch, and even before he knocked I knew who it was.

15

"**L**OOK WHAT the cat dragged in," I said.

Vincent smiled, a small, faint little smile, and handed me a bottle of wine.

"Hello, Verna," he said, stepping inside. He started to take off his coat. I felt flustered, upset by the very sight of him.

"How have you been?"

"Fine." He smiled again, his thin, tight-lipped little smile, and said, "Thank you."

"It's gotten cold," he said, "hasn't it?"

"Give me your coat." He handed it to me. He was wearing

a tie and a knitted vest and he looked very nice. His hair was shorter, cut a little differently.

"Jolene's returned," he said. He put his hands out, like somebody giving up. And then he shook his head.

"She came back to L.A. a couple of weeks ago."

"Are you back together?"

"No," he said.

"Where is she?"

"She's living in her studio."

"Is she still with Leonard?"

"No."

He took a seat in his usual chair. I sat on the stool. We looked at each other. I thought I heard something outside and wondered if it was the Peeping Tom. A little early: it was still light out.

I stood up and went over to the window. Mr. Beal walked past outside carrying a small bundle of damp laundry. He stopped at the clotheslines and set his basket down and then began hanging up his wash. He pinned things up carelessly, hanging clothes every which way. Sometimes he didn't bother to use clothespins at all; he draped socks and shorts and towels over the lines, and then, when the wind came up, they blew off and landed in the dirt among the stones and broken flower-pots.

I put a record on, wondering why he'd come back now, after all this time. I chose music I liked this time, not his.

> *I'm on a honky-tonk merry-go-round*
> *Acting like the foolish clown . . .*

"What is this music?" he asked.

"Guess."

"I don't know," he said. "How would I know?"

"I just thought I'd make you guess—you know, like your mother used to make you do."

"My mother didn't ordinarily play hickabilly music."

"It's Patsy Cline," I said.

"Oh. Patsy Cline."

"Do you like it?"

"I'm afraid I don't much care for it."

"Well, to each his own."

After a moment I asked, "Don't you want to go back with her?"

"I can't."

"Why?"

"I just can't."

"Don't you want to?"

"No, I don't."

"I thought you loved her. You told me you loved her once."

"I did once. Would you mind if I put on some other music?"

"Yes," I said. "I would mind."

"I see."

I folded my arms. "I'd think you'd get sick of all those serious violins. Yayayayaya all the time, sawing away, you know, like it was the end of the world. At least this is a little upbeat—something with a little swing to it."

He looked around, as if searching for something to help him change the subject. He saw a book sitting on the stool.

"What have you been getting from the library lately? Are you still reading?"

"I haven't had time for reading. I've been doing other things."

"What?"

"Planning a vacation."

"Where?"

"I'm going to Mexico with a friend of mine."

"Oh." He hesitated, and I could see him wanting to ask something and also not wanting to ask it, and I let him decide what he was going to do; I just waited. It had been weeks since he'd come by. Let him think I'd met someone else.

"Where in Mexico are you going?"

"Baja," I said. "That's all I can tell you. It's sort of a private matter."

"Oh. I see."

He looked out the window for a moment, and then he looked at me, his face bland and passive. "You haven't opened the wine."

"Oh, the wine."

He looked down at his hands. "I have some things I'd like to say to you. Would you get me a glass of wine?"

I went into the kitchen. Why was I trying to be rude to him? Why had he come? There were times when I had felt he really didn't like me much, so what was I to think now, what was the deal here? Why had he come around again?

I handed him the glass of wine. "I'm going to Mexico with Inez and Christobel. They're my relatives—my sister-in-law and niece."

"Oh," he said, and he seemed remorseful or sad. He drank his wine. We listened to the music. After a while he said, "I didn't really want you to stay with us when you came to L.A., you know. I tried to talk Jolene out of it. I was very upset that she'd agreed to let someone come visit without asking me. I was afraid of losing my privacy. I'm very sorry for the way I've treated you. I'm afraid it was rather rude. I suppose you felt that."

"Why didn't you say so? Why didn't you just say it wasn't convenient for me to stay with you? I'd have understood."

He smiled. "I didn't want to appear stingy."

The wind lifted the blinds, and bars of light wavered on the ceiling, rippling like wind on shallow water.

"I'm trying to get at something. The question I've been asking myself is this. Is it possible to love someone if your first interest is always yourself? You've got to wonder. Does it mean you're just using them? Because, you know, you can't face the idea of being alone."

I looked at him.

"Does it?"

"I don't know what you're talking about."

"I don't know how to say this."

"Say what?"

"Something happened to change my feelings."

The dogs ran by, Pookie and Teddy Bear, followed by Mrs. Beal, wearing a purple muumuu. She stepped so heavily: *clomp, clomp, clomp. . . .*

"When I met Jolene," he said, "I was twenty-five. I had never had a girlfriend. She was my first. I was twenty-five and I'd never been with anyone. What does that tell you? Do you get an idea of how protected I was? We met in a park on a day when money was being raised for some cause and musicians were performing in an outdoor bandstand. I remember she wore these black ankle boots with sharp toes and high heels and buckles everywhere. They looked so terribly dangerous. It's funny—now that she's gone, I keep thinking of that day and those crazy boots. I mean, she seemed so wild to me, and so worldly, you know. I thought she knew so much more than I did."

I was very aware of the music as he talked. The words seemed to go with what he was saying:

> *I've loved and lost again*
> *Oh what a crazy world we're livin' in*
> *Love has no chance to win . . .*

"I think she thought I was as eccentric as she was—you know, an artist with radical ideas. It wasn't until much later that she realized how conservative I am, how really very normal—a little dull, in fact. In the beginning, I think, she saw me as some sort of case that needed help, you know. A shy musician who'd never had a girlfriend. She was going to help me come out of it. I don't think she understood how hard it is to change, to become something other than what you are."

He scratched his head and looked away, and when he spoke again, he was still staring out the window, as if addressing an audience that lay somewhere out there, beyond the screen, between the palms and the *Pittasporum*.

"After she left, things were pretty unbearable. That's when I first came to visit you. I thought that I just wanted your company, someone to talk to.

"You were very different. The surprising thing to me was that I found you very easy to be with. You calmed me down, just knowing that you were here and that I could always come see you. Suddenly I found I was writing music again—not just writing boring papers on musicians but actually *composing*— and I felt it had something to do with you, with your presence in my life.

"And then, that day in the kitchen, when you kissed me, I thought, What am I doing here? I don't want to get hurt again, I don't want this. I simply got scared and had to leave. It suddenly seemed like it would end badly again. But that was before it even started. Wasn't it?"

"I guess it was."

"I didn't want to mislead you."

"I figured you weren't interested in me."

"But I was," he said, still staring out the windows. And then he turned and smiled at me. "I am," he said.

"What?"

"I am attracted to you."

"You didn't act like it."

"I know."

"I didn't know what to think."

"Please don't think me too odd for saying this, but you're like a muse to me."

"A muse?"

"A guiding presence. A source of inspiration."

"Inspiration? For what?"

"I've written something." He reached into his pocket and took out some papers which had been rolled up and fastened with an elastic band. "It's for you." It was pages of musical notations, some sort of composition with the title "Silvia."

"Who is Silvia?" I asked.

He laughed, and sort of half-sang some words:

> *Who is Silvia? What is she,*
> *That all our swains commend her?*
> *Holy, fair, and wise is she. . . .*

"Oh, it's a song," I said.

"Yes," he said. "A sort of song."

"I'll play it for you sometime. Perhaps you'll sing."

There was a long period after that when neither of us said anything. Sometimes, I remembered now, it was like that with him. He simply grew quiet. It had always seemed okay with us, these times, as though neither of us was bothered by it.

It was the time I had come to like best, when, late in the day, a silence settled in these rooms and the light coming in through the windows was particularly beautiful. At such times I felt the purifying power of stillness, just sitting silent; it didn't matter what I did or didn't think. I felt better.

After a while he said, "I'm going to go now." But he didn't get up.

"You don't want more wine?"

"No, thank you. . . . When will you be back from Mexico?"

I said, "I think in about a week."

"Can I see you?"

"I guess so."

He stood up. "Goodbye, then."

"Goodbye."

"There's this," he said. "I wanted to give it to you."

He opened up a bag he'd brought and handed me a book—*Faust,* by someone named Goethe, with illustrations by someone named Delacroix. It was a beautiful book, weighty and solid. It had a brown cover with gold letters.

"Thanks," I said. It was a nice-looking book.

"There's something else, too." He handed me another

book, smaller, an inexpensive paperback. *Two Gentleman of Verona*. Shakespeare. A play. I had never read a play. Or a book of poems.

"Two of my favorite songs of Schubert's are based on Shakespeare's and Goethe's poetry."

"Thank you."

"When are you leaving for Mexico?"

"Tomorrow," I said.

"Tomorrow?"

"In fact," I said, "I've got to get up pretty early."

At the door, he turned and faced me. Then he put his arms around me and buried his face in my neck. He kissed my ear. He kissed my forehead.

He looked at me. He drew me close again, holding me under the arms, and he held me against him and buried his face in my hair. He held the back of my head and pushed it against the side of his face firmly, and I felt his chest going up and down, up and down, as if he were having a hard time breathing. His mouth opened, and warm breath came out onto my ear, and he made a little sound like sucking in air. Then he kissed me lightly on my hair and said, "Okay now," and he pulled himself away from me and left. Abruptly, he was gone.

PART THREE

MEXICO

16

"**C**AN I PAINT your toenails?"

I looked up to see Christobel, kneeling in the sand. She held two bottles of fingernail polish in her hand. One was red, the other a funny color of pink, like bubble gum.

"It's awfully windy out here," I said. "Won't you get sand in the polish?" Behind her, the surf rolled toward us, inching closer and closer.

"I'll be careful," she said.

I put my foot in her lap. She rubbed my toes, cleaning the sand off my nails.

"What's that you're reading?" she asked.

"*Faust.*"

"How many pages is it?"

I checked to see. "A hundred and eighty three," I said.

"Dang," she said. "That's a long book."

"It is." My eyes fell on the page before me.

> O the dice swiftly throw,
> Rich let me grow,
> Let me rake in my gains.
> Things are most unfair;
> If I'd gold, I declare,
> I'd also have brains.

"Do you have a boyfriend?"

I found I couldn't answer her. Did I? I looked at the brown book, and then at Christobel, and finally settled my eyes on the horizon. She was so absorbed in what she was doing, she didn't seem to notice that I hadn't answered her question.

We were on a beach in Mexico, between Ensenada and Tijuana, where the cliffs dropped steeply to the ocean. It was beautiful, the way the cliffs made a wall right up against the water, and we were the only people in sight.

I felt tired. Half the night I'd lain awake, worrying whether we'd make it back up the steep dirt road we'd had to come down in order to reach this beach. The engine wasn't running so well, and I wondered if the truck could pull the trailer up that hill. Far out in the surf, a fat concrete pillar stuck up above the water, and when the waves rolled in, they split, crashing violently around the post. I watched the water and wondered if anybody would dare to go swimming in such wild waves.

"Do you want pink or red?"

"Red, I think."

"Red is good," she said. "More mature."

Christobel liked to pretend she was a beautician. Twice now since leaving Los Angeles she'd asked to style my hair. Perhaps it was because of her mother, who had spent her life working in beauty parlors. Christobel had long red nails, and she liked to wear a lot of eye makeup; even now, when we were supposed to be relaxing at the beach, she was all made up, with bright blue eyelids and pink lips.

"I'd paint your fingernails, too, but they're not long enough."

I looked at my hands. "No, they aren't."

"I used to clean rooms at the Humpty-Dumpty Inn," she said. "Mr. Sesachari's so nice. He's the man who owns the motel. He gave us all the free cheese he got through the government program. He donated it to our center for Thanksgiving, so we sent him a card of thanks."

I nodded. Conversations here seemed out of context, out of tune with the feeling of the water, the sky, the waves. Mr. Sesachari. Free cheese. Thanksgiving.

Suddenly I remembered sitting on another beach. With him. I remembered his whiteness. How the wind had lifted little sections of his hair and ruffled them. How we had floated together in the pale green sea.

Christobel touched my toenail with the brush and I could

feel the coolness of the polish being stroked on. Far down the beach I saw Inez and Duluth Wing, walking away from me toward a rocky point that jutted out into the surf.

I hadn't intended to take Duluth with us to Mexico. I hadn't intended that at all. But this is the way it worked out.

Inez wanted me to take my horse trailer to Mexico to haul some stuff she wanted to take with her. She had a lifetime accumulation of goods, three husbands' worth of belongings, things that were valuable to her, and she didn't want to leave them behind.

When I told Duluth I was taking the trailer to Mexico and he'd have to find another place to sleep, he pleaded with me to take him along, too.

"I don't think there's enough room. I'm taking my sister-in-law and her daughter. That's all the people that can fit in the cab of the truck."

"I'll ride in the trailer," he said. "Or in the back of the truck, even."

"I don't know. I'm going to have all my sister-in-law's things in the trailer." To tell the truth, I couldn't see sharing close quarters with him. He had slipped down pretty far, especially in his drinking. I didn't know about taking him to Mexico, where I could see him causing trouble. On the other hand, how could I just leave him behind, to slip even further? It seemed urgent to him. He wanted badly to go. He pleaded with me. "It's just that I feel if I had a change, you know . . . " He didn't finish the sentence to tell me what that kind of change might mean to him.

"There's the money, Duluth. I can't just pay your way to Mexico."

"I can make some money!"

"Duluth, you ought to take a look at yourself."

"I don't need to. Don't you think I know what's happening? I just need a change. I can get myself together, if that's what it takes."

So after a while I just said, "Okay." I agreed to let him

come along, if he promised to help me fix up the trailer and to get himself straightened out a little.

It's amazing how the prospect of the trip affected Duluth. He came over and took a shower one night, and the next day I noticed he'd cut his hair. He started hanging out in the Safeway parking lot, where they put in a new system for basket retrieval, and he would con people into letting him take their shopping baskets back to the return area in order to collect the twenty-five-cent deposit. He walked around with a lot of coins in his pockets so that his pants drooped and he constantly pulled at the waist to keep them up. He was making money for Mexico, he said. Then one day he hitchhiked up to Triple A on Sunset and got an auto club member to get him some free maps of Mexico, along with a booklet that listed all the campgrounds; and I saw him sitting on the steps by the liquor store, studying these, when I came home from work. He worked out our route to San Ignacio. He even started learning some Spanish from a borrowed library book. I'd never seen him so happy. We fixed the tires on the trailer. Duluth cleaned it out. Finally we were ready to go.

The morning we were to leave, he came along to Inez's house, and honestly, if he hadn't been there, I don't know what we would have done.

Inez told us that Jim would be gone two hours. We had to haul all her stuff out of the house and pack it up in the trailer and get away before he came home and found her gone.

"Are you sure he won't come home early?" I asked.

"He never gets home before noon. We've got until noon."

I kept looking at my watch. The idea of him coming back from the shooting range, which is where'd he'd gone, with all his weapons in the car, made me very jumpy.

"Are you sure he can't follow us?"

"He won't know where I've gone or even how I got away."

Still, I was nervous, and we worked as fast as we could, carrying out chairs, a daybed, piles of clothes, and the contents of drawers dumped into boxes. This is where Duluth came in very handy. He worked like a dog. So did I. At one point I thought to myself, I've done this before, and I saw myself hauling Leon's belongings up to the trunk of the Rambler and then, the next day, filling up the trailer with my own things.

Once, I asked Inez, "What kind of work does Jim do?"

"Nothin' no more," she said. "But before he'd retired he was a meter reader for the gas company. He came from Detroit originally. Like everybody else, he wanted to be in California 'cause it's so nice here. You know, easy living."

He'd found that here, I suppose, in this little house with its backyard and his wife to care for him. All that was about to end, and I could imagine his anger when he came back and found her gone.

Inez hadn't been able to pack anything beforehand, because she didn't want to arouse Jim's suspicions; so we were throwing things loose into the back of the trailer, kitchen stuff, furniture, towels and sheets, anything she saw that she wanted, until I had to tell her there wasn't any more room. But she wouldn't leave a pink chair that she said she had to take, and finally Duluth just hefted it into the back of the truck, placing it on top of some other things, tied it down, and said, "That's where I'm going to ride," and he did—he sat up there lounging and putting his feet up on the matching hassock like a man sitting in his living room, only there he was with nothing but air around him.

"It's time to go, Inez," I said, thinking that at any minute Jim was going to show up. I hadn't thought that she would want to take so much with her. It felt a little like we were stealing. The rooms looked as if they'd been stripped of furnishings.

She left the house hardly looking back; but when we were a few blocks away, she put her head in her hands and let out a sob. Her back shook, and then after a few moments she wiped her eyes and sat back quietly.

Christobel was waiting for us, her things packed and sitting in a small suitcase by her feet, on the steps of the home where she lived. The house was surrounded by a tall fence with spikes on top. A woman came out of the house and said, "Oh, Christobel, isn't this exciting that you're taking a trip with your mother?" Christobel looked confused. The woman said, "Smile, Christobel—it's going to be fun!" and Christobel smiled. I tried not to stare at her, but it had been so long since I'd seen this niece, and she looked so different. She was a great, soft, overgrown child, slow and quiet, wearing heavy, garish makeup.

By seven o'clock that same night we were at the border, trying to buy car insurance, which Duluth, our guide and navigator and expert on travel in Mexico, said we had to have. The agent came out and looked first at the truck with Duluth's pink chair sitting in the back, then at the trailer covered with graffiti.

"How much insurance do you want?"

"What do you think?" I said.

"Minimum," the agent answered.

Two hours later, we were camped on this beach just north of Ensenada, well over the border.

The sea made so much noise during the night that I hardly slept, and in the morning we all moved slowly, as if exhausted by our rapid flight. The first thing Duluth did when he woke up was to put his pink chair on the sand. Then he sat in it and watched the sun rise.

"Shoot," Christobel said. I felt her fingernail running around the flesh of my toenail, scraping some wayward polish off my skin. A slight wind was blowing. Already I could feel how the grains of sand were sticking to the wet polish on my toenails.

"I got a little messy," she said. "I went outside the lines a little."

"That sounds like you're coloring in a coloring book."

"It's very difficult," she said, frowning at me.

"I can see your Mom and Duluth. They're way, way down the beach, almost to the rocks now."

"What do I care," she said.

Sometimes she was like that, very contrary. I'd noticed that Christobel didn't have much patience. Anger rose in her quickly and came out in fitful little bursts, childish tantrums. Earlier this morning she had thrown a knife in the sand, as if playing mumblety-peg, when her mother begged her to finish her breakfast. The knife had landed near Duluth's bare foot. It was only a table knife; still, it had been disturbing because it happened so suddenly. She had a violent side to her, I could see that.

A young Mexican man, riding a horse that was so skinny its head look oversized, came ambling down the dirt path behind our camp. He rode right up to us. The man was very thin himself and had an acne-scarred face; but when I looked at his eyes, I saw how gentle they were. He was riding one horse, and leading another.

"*¿Les gustaria montar a caballo?*" He motioned that I could climb up behind him and he would ride me up and down the beach. I shook my head. He pointed to the other horse and tried to give me the reins.

"No," I said. I shook my head again. He shrugged, and I watched him ride off, back up the road, leading the second horse. It was unshod, and its hooves were so long in front that they'd begun to curl up, like a genie's slippers.

"Do you want to get into the water and go wading?" I asked Christobel, who was just finishing with my toes.

"You can't move until your polish is dry!" she said sharply.

"I mean *afterwards,* after my polish is dry."

She looked over her shoulder at the surf. "No," she said. "I think it's too cold."

"Feel it—it's warm."

She walked down to the ocean and put one foot in the water. "You're right, it's pretty warm." She gave me one of her goofy looks, a crooked smile, a gaping mouth; then, suddenly, her expression changed to seriousness and she said, "But I still don't want to go in."

I kept looking at Christobel, trying to find some shadow of my brother's face in her features; but I couldn't see that she looked anything like him, and neither did she look like her mother. She had a childish, round face, and although she wasn't a girl, really, it was hard to think of her as being over twenty-five, she was so soft and immature. And yet she had all this makeup on, and it made her look a little crazy or wild. She walked back toward me and sat down in the pink chair and gazed straight past me at the surf.

I looked down at my toes, which were startling, the red was so bright. I wasn't used to seeing any color like that on my feet. The flesh around my toenails was smeared with red, like Christobel's lipstick, which often wandered outside the lines of her lips—the color extending to surrounding areas, as if it were beginning to migrate to new places. The same was true of her eye shadow, which knew no boundaries.

Then suddenly, out of the blue, Christobel said, "I've been baptized."

"What religion?" I asked, although I figured it must have been Catholic.

"No religion. I did it myself."

"How did you do that?"

"I just said some words over myself."

"What did you say?"

"I don't think I want to tell you."

"Don't, then."

"I just said some words and then I went down in the water, and you know, I just dunked down and came up again."

"Where did this happen?"

"Lake Sherwood. It's this place that Jim used to take us on the weekends." She picked up a rock and threw it at the water. "He liked to fish. I didn't have nothing to do out there so I just made things up."

"And that's where you baptized yourself?"

"Yeah. Lake Sherwood."

Duluth and Inez were gone a long time. When they returned, Inez was holding her skirt in front of her, making a sack out of it. They had collected mussels from the rocks, and she was carrying them this way, in her skirt, which was now soiled and wet. The skirt was red, made out of a soft fabric that looked luxurious and pretty. The way she was lifting the material, you could see her legs beneath her skirt and how they were still shapely. Duluth looked happy. He was wearing one of Jim's shirts that he'd stolen from his closet. It was too big for him and hung loosely on his frame, but it made him look like he had more meat on him than he did, and it was an improvement on the suit jacket. He'd spent part of the morning swimming in the ocean, and he had a clean, fresh look.

"We're going to build a fire," he said, excited. "And Inez is going to show me how to steam these mussels."

"But shouldn't we be going?" I said. "Shouldn't we be getting on the road?"

"It's so late now," Duluth said. "We wouldn't get very far before it'd be dark, and one thing you can't do is drive at night in Mexico—there are too many animals on the road. We'd be better off just staying here another night and leaving in the morning."

I could see that things were going to move very slowly here and that it was going to take longer than two days to get to San Ignacio. I couldn't shake the feeling that we ought to be hurrying. It seemed as if Jim were behind us, hovering and watchful, an ominous presence, like a bad memory of something that you can't shake. But I didn't insist that we leave, as I probably should have.

I looked out at the stippled surface of the sea and decided just to let things happen.

We gathered wood, and while the mussels steamed, Inez

made flour tortillas and patted them into flat cakes to cook on the skillet. It made me think of the only other time I'd been to Mexico.

My brother Rodney had served a mission for the church in northern Mexico. When his mission was over, my family drove down there to bring him home. I was eleven years old.

We left in June, when it wasn't yet too hot, and crossed the border at Nogales. There were six children in the car. When we finally reached Mexico, I was surprised by the flat, boring landscape. I had expected so much more of my first trip to a foreign country. The desert was even more colorless than Arizona.

The second night we stopped in Hermosillo, a colonial town with a beautiful park. A police station across from our motel had pictures of bandits posted outside, dark and dangerous-looking men. We spoke no Spanish and kept to ourselves.

Four days after crossing the border, we came to the small village where Rodney had spent the last two years. The local church was a small stucco building with a basketball court out back. Two missionaries were playing ball when we drove up. There were no paved roads in this town. The people seemed very poor. The place had none of the charm and prettiness of Hermosillo. We parked in front of the church. Then we saw Rodney running toward us, his suitcoat flapping.

Before we left the next day, Rodney took us to a house to meet an old woman he'd converted, who sat making tortillas in front of a fire.

As we sat in her house, which had a dirt floor and wooden benches for furniture, Rodney explained how he'd converted the old woman, her two sons, and a daughter-in-law. He was sure her husband would eventually join, too; he'd been receiving the lessons. The Mormons, Rodney said, could offer these people care and comfort, visions of a better life. Mexicans are very spiritual, he said. "We are to these people now what the

Catholics were a couple of centuries ago. . . . We're the new religion for them, the new hope."

He spoke to the woman he'd converted, and she answered in Spanish, and then he translated what she'd said for us. "She says, 'My head was all confused and I didn't know what I was thinking. Then a friend told me about the Mormon church and I went there and I began to feel better. I'm a believer now. My son had a bad foot and doctors didn't know what he had, so I took him to the church and he was cured.'" As Rodney translated her words for us, she had looked away from us and continued to make her tortillas, forming the cornmeal into flat little cakes by patting the *masa* between her palms rapidly as if she were handling something hot.

The air smelled of wood fire and the aroma of mussels steaming in their own juices. The sun was just starting to set as we ate. From her stash of goods in the trailer, Inez found everything we needed—a tablecloth, plates, utensils, even a candle in a tall red glass, decorated with a picture of the Virgin. I read the words written on the glass: "Beloved Lady Mary, Queen of Mercy, be charitable to me and give me your advice. . . . Help us who travel, who are afflicted with illness, and who are pursued by our enemies. . . ."

She lit the candle, and we sat in a circle around it, eating the mussels, which tasted strongly of the sea, and the tortillas and some beans warmed over the fire. We made our beds as it grew dark, while we could still see, folding our blankets and laying them right on the sand; then we stayed up a while longer. It wasn't cold, although the wind carried a chill and it felt good to have a blanket around my shoulders. Duluth brought out a mattress for Inez. He seemed chivalrous and old-fashioned with her, like a real gentleman, and I thought, There are possibilities in each of us that we never imagine until somebody or something calls them out. The stars appeared, one by one. Inez began singing a song in Spanish.

"What do the words mean?" I asked her when the song ended.

She laughed. "My mother taught me this song. It's called 'Fulanita.' 'In you, my darling, I had such confidence, and in the end I remained unwed. And now I throw myself into forgetfulness—I get drunk, Fulanita—to see if I can forget. And if you want to marry, remember that I will not forget you. And now I throw myself to the vices—I get drunk, Fulanita—to see if I can forget. . . .' "

"I wish I had a drink," Duluth said, as if he'd just been reminded of something.

"Tomorrow, Paquito," Inez said. "Tomorrow we'll get some tequila, or mescal." She laughed. "Maybe some mescal with a leetle worm in it. *Mañana.*"

"*Mañana,*" Duluth said.

I walked down the beach by myself and looked at the night. There were lights from a few houses up in the hills, and they cast slivers of a pale silvery sheen on the water. And then, after a while, I went to bed, enfolding myself in the blankets on the sand.

Christobel was lying near me. I thought she was asleep but suddenly I heard her whisper, "Aunt Verna?"

"Yes?"

"Do you still want to know what I said when I baptized myself?"

"Yes."

"I said, 'Remove the bad thoughts from my head. Help me to not injure other people.' "

I waited for a moment to see if there was more, but that was it. "Remove the bad thoughts from my head. Help me not to injure other people."

"That's nice," I said. "That's very nice."

"Good night," she said.

"Good night," I replied.

17

I THINK THAT in some way I never could have imagined, the faithfulness of chinchillas colored my thinking for life.

When humans lose someone they love, they make their way back to ordinary conditions as soon as possible. Another mate is sought, and usually found. Alliances are re-formed. It doesn't even seem that difficult to forget, let alone replace, a former partner. My mother's cousin, for instance, married the twin brother of her dead husband, without waiting so much as a year after the funeral—and they were in their late seventies, an age when you might think you'd be able to finally accept a life alone. Some impulse seems to propel humans into immediate recoupling, replacing what's gone almost before we've understood what it is to miss it.

Not so with chinchillas, or snow geese. Sometimes, sheer pining for the lost loved one sends the mate to an early grave, as if there are pains so unconsolable that death is preferred to living.

What accounts for such loyalty? Do noble traits surface now and then, choosing as hosts the most unlikely candidates, like small rodents from the harsh world of the Andes, or tenacious birds consigned to a migratory life?

The unknowable: What impulse binds lives so irrevocably?

I knew I had to answer Leon's letters. It was time. In the end, I would give him his divorce, releasing him to form a new life with Pinky.

But I wondered, Should I bother getting a temple divorce from him? Should I petition the church, saying, "Separate us forever from our marriage vows?" If I didn't, and if what I'd been taught was right, I could be his wife in heaven. That was a somewhat frightening thought, since Pinky could be his wife, too. According to what Mormons believe, Leon could have seven wives in heaven, whereas I could have only one husband. It sounds complicated, but it's really very simple. It's just a kind of heavenly law, which allows men more of everything.

I had to move on; I understood this. I couldn't spend the rest of my life tethered to the memory of a lost mate. The prospect of being alone wasn't what worried me; it was the idea that I might never really know anyone again, the fear of losing some capacity for intimacy.

The only one I'd felt anything for since Leon was Vincent, and it seemed to me that we were so different from one another we might have come from separate, but somehow mildly related, species. Like he could have been a coyote and I a wolf. I might have been a salamander and he a lizard. Or he could be a rabbit and I could be a chinchilla. Things somehow similar and yet so unalike.

I remember a particular year, a time when it looked like Lawrence Bagley would go out of the chinchilla business. His chinchillas refused to breed. A female died, and the remaining male of that pair stayed huddled in the corner of the pen, shunning food. When James and I stood in front of its cage and looked at it, it shimmied with fear. Then a male died, and its mate went into mourning. Now there were two solitary chinchillas. A male and a female, who showed no interest in each other. There seemed to be no reason for these deaths. Mr. Bagley grew increasingly worried.

Mr. Bagley was always giving James and me lessons on the nature of chinchillas, as if we were his small apprentices, destined to inherit his business, such as it was. He lived in a community where people bred Holsteins and Clydesdales and hardy strains of sheep, and nobody much wanted to talk about an animal that wasn't even good to eat, let alone ride, milk, or rope, one that eventually ended up on the backs of distant rich

people. Who cared? This was the West, where things had a
certain practicality, and Mr. Bagley was alone in his apprecia-
tion of the exotic chinchillas. In such a climate, we must have
naturally filled some need for him to have an appreciative
audience.

Sometimes we worked alongside him, helping him clean
the pens or change the water in the containers; and as we
worked, he talked. He told us about other unusual qualities
that chinchillas have aside from mating for life. For instance,
the female is the dominant member of the pair. She is slightly
larger than the male, and if there's any fighting, she wins.

Courtship begins with the male or the female pulling tufts
of hair from the other's body. It sounded a little rough, pulling
each other's hair out like that; but it seemed fair, this kind of
thing, which either the male or the female could start and
which, after all, was only a sort of game, a part of mating. In
fact, we hardly ever saw the chinchillas fight. They were peace-
loving animals, shy and gentle, and grouped as they were, in
little family units, they seemed somehow more identifiable,
more domestic.

A chinchilla litter consisted of five or six young. Mating
took place a few minutes to a few days after a female had given
birth to a litter, so that several litters could be born each year.

During the period when Mr. Bagley's chinchillas refused
to breed and then started dying one by one, James and I visited
them more frequently. The animals seemed dispirited. They
stayed huddled in the corners of their pens and began shunning food. They grew weaker. Their coats turned dull. Their
eyes no longer looked so bright; they were fixed into stares.

One day we found Lawrence Bagley standing in front of
the pens. "I don't get it," he said. "I don't understand what's
wrong."

Ever since the chinchillas had escaped and we'd been
wrongfully blamed, Mr. Bagley had been trying to make it up
to us, going out of his way to be extra nice. It wasn't hard for
Lawrence Bagley to be nice. Actually, he was about the nicest

grown-up we knew. So James and I felt pretty bad for him when his chinchillas started giving up the ghost.

I said, "Why don't you put a pan of ice cubes in there with them?" It was August, and pretty hot. Maybe the animals were suffering from the heat.

James added, "Larry thinks it's a pretty good idea."

Mr. Bagley looked at us as if we were oracles. "You know, you might be right—it might just be the heat."

Whatever it was—the pans of ice, or just the added attention that the chinchillas got, or luck, or fate—things began to improve. The chinchillas began moving around. Their appetites improved. By fall, several females were expecting babies.

When the young were born, they arrived fully furred. They could run around within hours. In the space of a few weeks, dozens of new chinchillas were born—in the beginning, no bigger than your thumb. As the weather changed, the parents kept their young huddled between them, forming a little nest with their bodies, protecting the babies from the winds that came down out of the canyon. It felt as if snow could arrive at any time. Each day was suspenseful. When would the first storm come?

Although Mr. Bagley put them together in the same pen, the lone male and the lone female whose mates had died earlier stayed separate and did not look as healthy as the rest of the chinchillas. We gave them special attention. We brought the tenderest tops from the carrots from our own garden and tried to entice them to the wire. Occasionally they came to us, nibbled for a moment, and then withdrew.

The leaves on the oak brush up on the mountainside had almost completely dropped by the time the first storm came. The snow stuck to the ground next to our house but melted near the shores of the lake where it touched down on the salty earth. The days turned gray, one after another, and each afternoon cold winds blew down the canyon. It seemed early for that kind of harsh cold, but nonetheless it arrived, and the weather stayed bad for weeks. Mount Ogden and Ben Lo-

mond both turned solid white, though further down on the
cliff face the snow was as thin as powdered sugar.

School took up most of our time; but in the hours between
the bus delivering us home and the darkness coming, James
and I often put on warm play clothes and walked up the road
to see how the chinchillas were doing. We worried about the
babies especially, and of course the lone male and female.

At this time, I remember, there was an retarded girl in the
neighborhood, the daughter of Bill and Anna Lee Morley.
That was what she was called—"the Morley's retarded girl."
Her name was Mary Ann, and she developed a crush on my
brother Rodney and made herself a nuisance to him, and to
my mother as well, although everybody showed sympathy toward this girl and above all demonstrated forbearance for the
situation.

Her parents took her to church, and it was there we began
to notice her paying special attention to Rodney. She would
stand in the foyer before sacrament meeting started and wait
for Rodney to arrive. She was twenty years old, three years
older than Rodney, and she was large, with a bust that was
overdeveloped, which gave her a soft womanliness that con-
tradicted her childish ways.

"Hi, Rodney!" she would gush when she saw him. "How
are you, Rodney?" she would cry. Her voice was loud, inap-
propriate, and she seemed weird to us younger kids. Her re-
tardedness had given her loud, slow, incomprehensible ways,
an awkwardness that we couldn't understand and that made
her different, a person whom under normal circumstances we
would never have thought of knowing. And yet we could not
help knowing her, because the ward had enfolded her in its
collective life, and there wasn't a church member who didn't
treat her kindly and with what tried to pass for normal re-
sponses.

All through the fall and into the winter months Mary Ann
came to our house for visits. My mother was too kind to dis-

courage her, and so Mary Ann would sit on a stool, watching my mother roll out pastry dough or fry thin, curling pork chops, and ask her questions about Rodney.

Sometimes she would say "I love Rodney" and smile foolishly. "He's my boyfriend," she would say. My mother would try to change the subject. "What's your mother doing this afternoon?" she would ask Mary Ann. When I came into the kitchen, Mary Ann would say "Where's Rodney?" It was her favorite question; she asked it of everybody. And I would say "I don't know," although perhaps I did know but I didn't feel I should tell.

I associate her now with that cold winter when the snow came early while the chinchillas were still newborn, and with the yellow stool at the end of a warm kitchen where she always sat, and with the smell of dinner cooking, and with my mother's indulgent patience.

I remember one Sunday, a fast and testimony day, which fell on the first Sunday of every month, when Mary Ann, as usual, was waiting for our family to arrive for church, standing just inside the foyer, next to a long coat rack where people hung up their heavy winter coats before going into the chapel.

"Hi, Rodney!" she called as soon as we opened the door, and all nine of us, my entire family then since Willie wasn't yet born, came into the warm church. "Are you my boyfriend?" she cried.

Her parents, Bill and Anna Lee, were standing near her, and Anna Lee put her arm around her big daughter and squeezed her shoulders and laughed. My mother laughed, too, and said, "Oh, hi, Anna Lee." They were very good friends, Anna Lee and my mother.

Anna Lee said, "Hello, Marge dear."

My father took Mary Ann's hand and said, "How's my gal?" That's how people treated Mary Ann. They tried to make her feel she was special.

"Fine," Mary Ann said. "Where's Rodney?" She was staring at Rodney as she said this, but he was avoiding looking at her; and I felt that unless he answered her or paid her some attention, she would act like she didn't see him, as if ignoring somebody could work both ways—he did not exist for you until you existed for him.

My father said, "You don't want that no-good kid. I thought maybe I'd be your boyfriend today."

Bill Morley laughed, because he understood how my father was trying to help the situation by taking away the embarrassment we all felt about Mary Ann's obsession. Rodney, who was quietly hanging up his coat, didn't look at anybody but walked quickly into the chapel.

What was Rodney's response to all this? From the beginning he was not unkind to Mary Ann, nor did he take to ridiculing her, because he was naturally gentle, the one who always helped my mother with canning and, uncomplaining, took over babysitting whenever he was needed. It seemed he just wished that he could evaporate in her presence, that she would find him invisible. When we teased him about Mary Ann, he looked pained. He did not joke with us, and after a while we stopped joking with him.

Sometimes, sitting in church, my mother would make me a doll out of a hankie to keep me amused. Or she would save the tiny sacrament cup, made out of paper that had been pleated and joined at the rim, and I would pull the pleats apart one by one and make a flat, round circle out of the paper, and she would draw a face on it for me. She did this that Sunday. She drew a clown face on a used sacrament cup.

The sacrament consisted of small cubes of bread, usually very white and very light, like Wonder bread, which is what was often used, and little paper cups of water, passed on silver trays by twelve-year-old boys who walked the aisles in the same pattern week after week. First the bread was passed, then the water. Bread, water. If for whatever reason you considered yourself too sinful that week, or if you were a lapsed Mormon, or if you felt some other, hidden unworthiness, you weren't to take the sacrament but rather pass it to your neighbor, until the silver tray had made its way down the entire row, and the boys in the aisles received it.

After the sacrament had been passed, the bishop made the regular announcements about ward activities, and then he opened up the meeting for bearing testimonies and sat down. Everybody waited, to see who in the congregation would be the first person to stand up and bear testimony.

I don't remember who it was now, and it's not important. It might have been one of the regulars, somebody like Henrietta Bowen, who, as everybody knew, dyed her husband's hair black to make him look younger; or it might have been Delilah Wadman, an emotional woman who couldn't bear her testimony without crying, or Brother Stanfield, another regular, known for going on too long and taking time from other people. It could even have been a kid, because kids stood up, too, although they often said things that made people giggle, like thanking the Lord for rabbits and dogs, or telling embarrassing home incidents. Everything in these meetings seemed finally allowable, acceptable, though sometimes people squirmed—as, for instance, when Sister Malone, a particularly unhappy person, asked why the Lord was testing her so by giving her a daughter who disliked her so much and who had left the church. These things were almost too private to hear; and yet they were said anyway, and everybody just lowered his eyes and listened, momentarily exposed to Sister Malone's deepest grief.

When Mary Ann stood up that day, I think everyone was surprised, because she had never done that before.

"I'm so thankful for Rodney," she began, speaking loudly in a harsh voice that always sounded to me as if she were just recovering from a cold, and I felt my mother shift beside me, straightening herself up a little. Usually my family sat together, taking up a whole row, and that's what we'd done that day—we were sitting in a straight line, my mother and father in the middle of the row and the kids stretching out on either side of them. Rodney was sitting down at the end, and I leaned forward to try to see him; but I couldn't—he was pressed back against the seat. I could see other people in the church were rubber-necking, turning around in the seats, trying to look at either Mary Ann or Rodney.

"I love him," Mary Ann said, and it sounded like "I lawb him."

My father reached over and took hold of my mother's hand and they held on to each other, their hands resting right at the point where their bodies met, at the seam of their thighs; and then my mother put her free hand on top of their clasped hands, as if beginning some childhood game, and I saw her knuckles turn pale.

"I'm so thankful for my parents and for my boyfriend, Rodney," she said, and then she laughed. "Rodney Flake," she said, and there were other noises in the church, people either clearing their throats or whispering or laughing in a suppressed, low way. It was the children who laughed, I remember that now, not the adults.

"My boyfriend," she repeated quietly now, as if less sure of herself.

"I bear my testimony, I love Jesus, I love my mom and dad, and I love Rodney," she said. "I say these things in the name of Jesus Christ, Amen." She sat down. My mother and father wiggled their clasped hands for a second, and then they let go of one another and I heard my mother let out a little low sound, like "ssssss."

After that, I think it was decided that Mary Ann wouldn't be allowed to come to our house anymore, because she was never there, sitting on the yellow stool, when I came into the kitchen after school. I think it was something that Anna Lee and my mom decided together, and it was not an unkind act on their part; it was simply that a thing was going too far and wasn't doing anybody any good. There was harm done, in fact; and we all saw it that day when Rodney left fast and testimony meeting early and didn't come home for a long time. When he did appear, he looked scared and helpless, like the time the brakes on his car had failed and he'd run his Studebaker through the garage door and then stood on the porch, in the falling light, waiting for Dad to come home so he could tell him what he'd done. You could see how scared he was by looking at him; you could see that nothing could help him until he'd confronted Dad with the news and had the worst of it over. But, instead, he'd lost his nerve, and he took off and went hunting and didn't come back for three days.

For a long time we didn't see Mary Ann. "She's having a bad spell," I heard Bill tell my Dad. "She's gotten violent again."

On Easter she emerged, wearing a pretty lavender dress and a wide-brimmed hat to sacrament meeting. Anna Lee and Bill kept hold of her and steered her clear of Rodney; but just by looking at her then, when Rodney was standing in the same room, I could tell that she'd been cured of her feelings for him, and it seemed to me that she'd forgotten all about him and didn't even remember that things had happened the way they had.

Later that day, on Easter, one of the chinchillas, the lone male whose mate had died, was found dead in his cage. I was the one to find it. And after all that Easter talk at church, about death and resurrection, it seemed I couldn't separate one death from another, that it was just a dying day, although I knew that actually it was the day Christ got up. The tiny pelt, bluish gray with faint dusky markings, was salvaged for its worth. I know this only because I asked, not because I was there to witness the skinning. Mr. Bagley, though he looked awkward for a moment when he said it, told me that yes, he had saved the skin.

In my mind these things are connected: Easter; Mary Ann in her lavender dress; the death of the male chinchilla; and the way the snow was finally beginning to melt then, so that the very next week I could take my horse back up into the hills again and ride to my secret places, far from home and away from everything.

Summer came, and then it was gone and it was almost time to start school again when one day, during the middle of the week, Anna Lee Morley, who taught my Sunday-school class, stopped by my house to pick me up and take me to the farm, which was owned by the church. All the kids in the class were meeting to pick string beans. Mary Ann was in the car with her mother. I didn't know it then, I couldn't have known it, but that day would be the last time I would see Mary Ann alive before the boating accident in Pine View Reservoir that took her life late in August.

The church farm was in Uintah, at the bottom of the narrow valley where the Weber River flowed toward the lake. It was a hot day, and working down the long rows of beans, which had grown up and wound themselves around the runner strings, I felt the sun on my neck where the fuzz from the bean leaves had accumulated from all my bending and reaching down among the plants, and a certain kind of miserableness descended on me of the sort that just made me wish I were someplace else, *anywhere,* thinking that nothing could be quite as bad as this was. It was hard work, but everybody had to do it sooner or later; we all had to put some time in at the church farm, and there was no way out of it for me that day, especially since I'd come with Anna Lee and I had to wait until the very end of the day in order to get a ride home with her.

Mary Ann did not have a long concentration span, nor did she have a way with beans, pulling them harshly from the vines so that sometimes she brought the whole plant down from its stringers. She was finally told to do something else, and she brought us a jug of water, walking from person to person, pouring out paper cups full of water for each of us, and when she came to me, I was very happy to get a break and took the water greedily. She stood there watching me drink.

Suddenly, lifting her chin and looking around her, at the

rows of beans and the cows which were grazing just beyond
the bean field, and at a pair of workhorses standing in the
corral, she said, "I do not know what animal I am like, I do not
know what plant I am like!" And then she smiled, and for a
second you would never have thought that she was the way
she was, so different from everybody else. She repeated her
words, over and over, in a sing-song way, walking down the
rows: "I do not know what animal I am like, I do not know
what plant I am like. . . ."

I didn't think of this immediately; the connection only
came to me the second day we were in Mexico as I was looking
at Christobel, who was digging a hole in the sand with a spoon,
and suddenly her familiarity, the feeling I'd had for several
days that I had *known* her before, became a thing I could
understand. She was very much like Mary Ann, more like her
than anybody else I'd ever met. And that night when she told
me what she'd said when she baptized herself, I remembered
thinking of Mary Ann and her exact words in the bean field: "I
do not know what animal I am like, I do not know what plant I
am like. . . ."

The thing that Vincent had said, that each family had an
event that formed its central story, was something that I now
saw in terms of Carl, how his death had become that central
thing for my family, because it left us with Christobel and we
didn't know what to do with her, a half-Mexican girl who was
not like us and never would be, who grew more evidently
different the older she got. She was of our family, but she was
not in it. We could never enfold her, take her in as one of us,
not in a million years and that was our shame.

At different moments throughout the night, unused to the
sound of the surf, I awoke and found myself on a beach in
Mexico, lying under faint stars, next to Christobel. At one
point I thought I heard the small, soft whining of an animal,
and I thought, There's a dog nearby, and I sat up looking

around for it. I stared into the black night, listening alertly for
the sound, and then I realized it was only Christobel, making a
tiny whistling sound as she breathed. I laid back down and
moved my feet under the covers; and where my toes scraped
against the opposite foot, I felt the grit trapped in the polish,
brushing against my skin like sandpaper.

I couldn't sleep; and, as often happens in the night, when
things start coming to you and always look worse than they
are, I began worrying. I worried about all kinds of things:
about where my life would go from here; whether Jim would
figure out where Inez had gone and catch up with us; if the
truck would ever be able to make it back up the road from
the beach. A lot of unsettling thoughts stirred in me during the
night, until finally it started to get light, and I felt relieved just
to be able to get up.

18

DURING THE NIGHT, the tide came in. When I
awoke, the water was only a few feet away from us.
The sandy beach had disappeared; the water met the base of
the cliffs near the little shelf of land where we had camped. It
was windy, and a fine mist blew up each time a wave crashed.
The big pillar that had parted the water was gone, lost beneath
the sea.

I got up and took a towel out of the truck and walked up
the dirt road to the showers, which were in a low wooden
building set back between two trailers. Three dogs, tied up in
front, barked as I passed by, and I tried to stare them down
into silence, imagining that they might know I was friendly
through some kind of mental telepathy; but they lunged at
their ropes and bared their teeth as they snarled. Below me,
on a flat stretch of sand, a small shrine had been built; white
rocks lined a path leading to it. Inside the shrine, plastic flow-

ers lay at the feet of a statue of the Virgin of Guadalupe. I
wondered who prayed there and what they prayed for, kneeling out in the open in the little field at the edge of the sea.

Inside the shower room, everything was dirty. Broken toi-
lets were stacked up in a corner. A piece of jagged mirror had
been propped up in a sink that didn't have a faucet. It was hard
to find a place to put my clothes as I undressed, everything was
so dirty, and finally I set them next to the mirror in the sink. I
tried the shower. The water was cold. For a long time I let the
water run, but it didn't get warm, and the cold water splashed
against the cement and spattered up onto my legs. I could hear
the waves crashing outside. The cement was cold on my bare
feet. Naked, I stood shivering, waiting for the water to get
warm; and when I realized that it wasn't going to I threw some
cold water on my face and under my arms and dressed again
quickly. I stared at myself in the jagged mirror. I wondered
what it meant to be a muse. I tried to picture Vincent's face,
and I had a hard time doing that. Then I tried to picture Leon;
I had no difficulty seeing him.

When I got back to the campsite, Inez and Duluth were up
and dressed. They watched me approach, as if waiting for a
report on the showers, and when I told them there wasn't any
hot water, they looked disappointed.

"I could sure use a shower, Verna honey. Are you sure the
water doesn't get hot?"

"You can try it." I shrugged. "It didn't get hot for me."

"I say we just leave here," Duluth said. "We'll find some
place down the road to take a shower." He put the pink chair
back in the truck. We picked up our bedding. Inez leaned over
Christobel and shook her gently. Christobel began moaning,
and then whimpering.

"What would you do, Christobel," I said, "if you had a
million dollars?"

"Start a beauty parlor of my own."

"That's a pretty good idea." She was braiding my hair as

we talked. I thought she'd ask me, "What would *you* do with a million bucks?" But she didn't.

"Also," she said, "I'd get my mom a lot of stuff—you know, a house, a car, perfume, some shoes, everything she wanted." She laughed; it was a kind of hoarse bark. Then she hit her chest a couple of times.

"Are you getting a cold?"

"No. I can't breathe sometimes."

The day was just turning warm, and the sun was shining through the window of the truck, falling on my shoulders like a blessing. We were sitting in a Pemex station in Guerrero Negro. It was early afternoon.

"Also," Christobel said, "if I had a lot of money I'd get married."

"How would money help you get married?"

"Somebody would like me," she said.

I wanted to say "I don't think you should think that way," but it seemed to me that she was probably right. Money might make her attractive to somebody, but it would, of course, be all wrong. And yet I couldn't help wishing she were rich, because it might make her life easier. . . . *Things are most unfair; if I'd gold, I declare, I'd also have brains . . .*

Christobel pulled on my hair, struggling to make the braid lie right. "It isn't easy," she said. "It isn't easy at all."

"What?"

"Making this hair work right."

"Oh." I thought she meant her life.

For three days now, we had been driving. When I looked at the map, I could see how the road crossed from one side of the peninsula to the other, like a shoelace threading eyelets. So far we hadn't left the Pacific Ocean side of the peninsula. But now we were heading inland. This was the last stop. We were getting gas, filling our water jugs, preparing to start into the desert and cross over to the Gulf of California. A wind was blowing. Little eddies of sand rose up near a sign that said: SU

CASA NO TERMINA LA PUERTA. GUERRERO NEGRO ES SU CASA.

Right then, we were the only customers in the Pemex station. The attendant stood at the rear of the truck. Every once
in a while I glanced back at him. He avoided looking at me. I
couldn't figure out why it was taking so long to fill up the
truck. Inez and Duluth had gone across the street to try phoning her brother to tell him we were only a few hours away. We
hoped to be in San Ignacio before the sun went down.

The night before, we had camped near a place called San
Quintín. While we were alone, sitting on a bluff above a little
bay just as the sun was setting, I began thinking I'd like to ask
Inez something I had always wanted to know. I asked her how
she and Carl had met.

"You're not going to think this is so romantic, but I tell
you, Verna honey, it was. You know Chinatown in San Francisco? It's a big place, you know, and I used to take the bus
through there going to and from this beauty parlor where I
was working. They call the bus the Orient Express. You had to
fight for a seat. Sometimes I got off the bus and stopped in this
old church there in Chinatown, just for a few minutes—you
know, to light a candle and say a prayer. I like churches. I like
the feeling they give you—you know, that everything's gonna
be okay, even when it isn't. You go into a church and it feels
like it don't matter, nothing, because we're all the same
there—everybody wants the same thing, and money doesn't
make you better.

"In the front of this church, which is pretty big place,
Verna, and beautiful, so beautiful, is the rows of candles, and I
am lighting a candle when I look over and see a man. He's a
sailor—he's got his head bowed and he's lighting a candle,
too, and it's like everything is happening so slowly then. When
I look at him, I see the most beautiful face I think I've ever
seen, and I cannot stop looking, you know? I don't think I've
ever stared at a man like this, but I can't help it. I am so

surprised that he is next to me, and with the light from the
candles coming up on his face, he looks like a saint to me. He
could've come right out of a picture! His skin is so pale, except
for his cheeks, which are pink, and you know, his lips so full.
He is serene and handsome. His eyelashes are long like a
woman's. He's got dark hair that curls naturally. Such a rosy
face! Suddenly he looks at me, and I look away from him,
hoping he hasn't caught me staring. Then I go back and kneel
in one of the pews near the front, and I start saying a prayer—
always it's the same, a prayer for my family, my dead father,
my brothers who are still in Mexico, my sister who ran off with
a worker and who nobody's heard from since, and I also pray
for the husband I know I'm going to get pretty soon. The one I
want.

"Before long, I look up and there he is, the sailor. He
looks briefly at me and then he turns away and kneels down in
a pew across from me. I finish my prayer and get up to leave.
He looks at me again, and I see his face, his beautiful, saintly
face. And then I walk out.

"Next week, I see him in the church again. This time, we
smile at each other, like we've met before. Usually, I'm not
shy, but he makes me feel this way. Still, this time we both
finish our prayers at the same time, and as we're walking out, I
say to him 'Merry Christmas,' because, you know, it's Christmastime. In fact, it's almost Christmas Eve.

"Christmas Eve, I go to the church with my mother, and
who do you think is there? This time, he speaks to me and also
to my mother, greeting us, but my mother doesn't speak English, so she can't answer. Then I get an idea, and I say to him,
'What you doing for Christmas Eve?' and he says, 'Nothing,
I'm a long way from home.' I tell him we're having a dinner
and I tell him where it is, that it will just be relatives and
friends. No big deal! Why not come? I say. And he does. He
came with me that night."

I could see how some birds had landed in the mud where

the water receded from the shore. They were walking around
and leaving little tracks. On the slope below us, there were
hundreds of clam shells, as if somebody had had a feast sitting
right in the spot where we were, and then just thrown the
shells over the edge.

"He comes to dinner—you know, we're having tamales,
like we do every year at Christmas—and he sits right down
and starts helping us make them. My uncle is there, and a
cousin and her family, and some neighbors. He just sits right
down and says, 'Show me how to do it,' so my mother instructs
him, shows him how to put the *masa* on the corn husk and how
much meat to put in and how to fold it all over. He laughs—
you know, he's real happy making tamales like that, and I'm
happy because he seems to fit right in.

"My cousin says, 'So how did you two guys meet?' and I
say, 'We met in the church in Chinatown.' She says to Carl,
'Oh, so you are Catholic?' My mother smiles and nods, *'Sí, es
Católico.'* 'No, no,' Carl says, 'no, not really—I'm a Latter-day
Saint.' I laugh, because I think he's making a big joke—you
know, because he look so much like a saint to me! I think he's
kidding us about being such a good man, a saint. Only later he
explains to me that this is really a religion—LDS, Latter-day
Saint. *Los Mormones.* I never heard of this, to tell you the
truth."

She hesitated and looked away. When she looked back at
me, her eyes were moist. "So, that was the beginning, Verna.
We met in church."

"What was he doing in a Catholic church?"

"I don't know why he was in that church, you know.
Maybe he just felt like I did, that it's a good place for all the
nice feelings you can get in there. There are places in the
world like that, and you don't need no other reason to go
there than that feeling."

"I guess," I said, although I could not remember ever feeling that way in a church.

We were quiet for a time.
Inez began singing:

> *Rosy Malva*
> *the white carnation of this spring,*
> *Come closer, darling of my life.*
> *So we can talk Because I love you*
> *Come closer, darling of my life*
> *So we can talk . . .*

"Boy, do I miss him," she said, looking down at the mud, the geese, the open clam shells on the hill below us. "After all these years, you know, I still miss him."

Later in the evening, while we were eating some fish he had caught, Duluth said, "I could stay here for the rest of my life and be happy." He looked out at the ocean and wiped his mouth with the back of his hand. There were islands out in the bay, brown volcanic cones. He looked out at the islands, and then he turned and grinned foolishly and looked at each one of us, as if showing us his happiness. Then he coughed, and couldn't speak for a moment. "Do you think your brother would let me stay down in San Ignacio for a while, Inez?"

"I dunno about that, Duluth. I mean, I haven't seen Lorenzo for a long time. I don't know what kind of setup he has. He says he's got a little place, but you know, he might not have room for you—I don't know."

"I could be very happy down here, I think," Duluth said. "And I wouldn't ask for anything, either—I wouldn't mind working for this kind of life."

Duluth and Inez—I could see them staying on together. I figure anybody who'd been with them over the last few days would have noticed the liking they had for each other—not love, not romance, but something else. Maybe Duluth would stay with her and Christobel in San Ignacio. Who knew? It would be a better life than the one he had now, spending his nights in a horse trailer and his days sitting on the benches between the teachers' union and the liquor store, becoming dirtier and sicker every day. Maybe nobody ever got complete hold of anything, but only a small part of it that they could make something out of while they had a chance. I was feeling pretty confused these days, as if I, too, were in a certain sense homeless. I wasn't sure what I should do once I had dropped Christobel and Inez in San Ignacio. I had no picture of the future anymore. What was ahead for me? It seemed to me I could return to Los Angeles or just as easily go back to Utah. I could get a divorce from Leon, or I could go visit him in Evanston and see if maybe he hadn't changed his mind, or maybe I could even stay in San Ignacio with Inez and Duluth and Christobel and we'd make a family of sorts, spending the rest of our days together the way we'd spent these last few days, which wasn't so bad an idea, really. And then, of course, there was Vincent. What about him?

I was in suspension, sitting in a Pemex station in Guerrero Negro, where the dirt met the sea in an area of salty marshes and everything looked parched. I wondered how it was that I had come so far without intending this direction and how I could feel so uncertain about my future. It seemed to me I had lost control of something.

"You're wiggling too much," Christobel said. She pulled on my hair.

I had seen something out of the corner of my eye and turned my head, causing Christobel to lose hold of the braid she was making. A long, low white car, so clean and shiny it looked out of place in the little dusty town of Guerrero Negro, was cruising by. It was a Chrysler New Yorker, my father's dream car. That was the kind of car he'd always wanted, I remember; and to me when I was a kid, just the name of this car had sounded like it held within it all the things people who actually lived in New York must have, lots of comfort and luxury, a clean, sleek life with every convienence, luxury instead of thrift, glamorous things like coats made out of fur, and money to burn.

I knew I had seen that same white car before, but I couldn't place it immediately. Then it hit me, and I said, "Oh my God!" and pushed Christobel down on the seat.

It was too late. He'd seen us. I saw the brake lights go on, and then he started to back up.

"Don't get up," I said to Christobel, and I held her down firmly with my hand. He backed right up next to the truck and stopped the car and grinned at me.

"Well," he said. "Hello, Verna! You're just the one I was looking for. I figured it was you that gave Inez a ride."

"I'm by myself," I said.

"You bet you are."

"You can just kept driving, Jim. There isn't anybody I know of who's looking for your company."

"You wouldn't have stolen goods in that trailer, would you?" he said.

"No, I wouldn't."

"The funny thing is, that chair, the pink one there in the back of your truck, looks exactly like one that's missing from my living room."

"Communal property laws are good in California, and she didn't take any more than her share."

"What do you mean, 'communal property'? That's divorce talk. I don't know anybody around here who's getting a divorce, except maybe you. Where's Inez, Verna? Just tell me where she is. Then there won't be any trouble, not one little sliver of it—not from ol' Jimbo, anyway."

Christobel was crying. I could feel her back shaking. I didn't know exactly what to do. My mind was racing, and meanwhile I was trying to stare him down, to show him I wasn't afraid; but I had a hard time just looking at his awful face, that big nose with pores like holes in a kitchen strainer. A mean man, and evil in a particular way that women sometimes recognize more quickly than men.

"Look," I said, "you can't make somebody stay with you if they don't want to, and you can't go around terrorizing them, either. That's something they've got laws against. If Inez wants to leave you, you got to just back away from it, Jim."

"Where is Inez?" Jim said again, still smiling. I remembered his leg, how lame he was, and I knew he couldn't run fast, and I thought, If I grab Christobel and run into the desert, he won't be able to follow us. But what about Duluth and Inez?

I remembered his pleasure in shooting the lemons off the trees, and the bright little holes he'd put in the fence, and the way he'd said, 'Let's have a picnic tonight, hon, let's eat out-side—I believe that people ought to eat outside every chance they get.' How he made *everything,* even a picnic, sound sinis-ter.

"I guess I'm just going to have to have a look around here myself," Jim said. "Maybe she's gone to the toilet, huh? Maybe she's over there in that store across the way."

Just then Inez and Duluth came out of the building across the street and started walking toward the truck. It was a couple of seconds before Inez saw Jim, sitting in his car parked there beside the truck, and then she stopped. She just stared. Her face looked like Rodney's had the day the brakes failed and he'd run his Studebaker through the garage door, which was the same look he'd had on the day Mary Ann has testified to her love for him in church, a look that was sick and anguished and trapped. She whispered something to Duluth. He took hold of her arm and led her to the truck.

"Ah," Jim said. "How you doin', honey lamb?"

"Leave us alone," Inez said. "I don't want nothing more to do with you, Jim."

"I'm going to have you arrested," Jim said, "for stealing my property."

"What property? I didn't take nothing but what belonged to me."

"What's that man got on his back, then?" Jim said.

I realized Duluth was still wearing Jim's shirt. It looked bad, Duluth standing there in that shirt. If only he hadn't taken it; if only he'd just left it in the closet.

Duluth quietly unbuttoned the shirt and tried to throw it into the car where Jim was sitting.

Jim batted it away so that it fell on the ground in the dust. "You think I want this shirt back after you've had it on?" Jim shouted. "Who the hell are you, anyway?"

I saw Duluth standing there, so vulnerable and thin, naked from the waist up, his ribs so prominent you could count them; he was breathing hard, and without his shirt on he couldn't hide that he was shaken up and afraid.

"That's my boyfriend," I said quickly, "Duluth Wing, but that's as much as I intend to tell you about things that aren't any of your business. Now we're leaving."

All this time Christobel had been lying down on the seat, but now, when her mother opened the door, she sat up and slid over close to me.

"Well, Christobel, nice to see you," Jim said. "How you doing? It looks like it's going to be a little crowded in there in that truck. Don't you want to come over and ride with Jim in his car? Let your mama and your auntie and her thief of a boyfriend cozy up to one another in the truck all alone, and you and me will just ride in comfort in my nice car? Come over here with Jim, Christobel. You know Jim will take care of you."

Christobel started to cry. "Mom," she said. And then she started to lose it and screamed "Maawwwmmmm!" Inez turned and stared at Jim. They glared at each other.

"Just get in the car," Jim said. "Both of you." Three Mexican women who were walking by looked at us, and I could see that while no one in the world, even if she spoke the same language, could ever begin to understand exactly what was going on between us, everybody would have guessed it was something bad.

"You bastard!" I said. "Stop scaring her."

Inez climbed in.

"Get in with us," I said to Duluth. I didn't want him riding there in the back, sitting in the pink chair, unprotected. I don't know what I thought was going to happen. I just wanted us all to be together.

"I'll just follow you, then," Jim said. He smiled at us.

Inez pushed over close to Christobel and then raised her hips up, arching herself against the seat, so Duluth could get in the front seat next to us, and when he was in and had closed the door, she lowered herself, so that part of her was sitting on top of one of his legs. I started the truck and drove off. None of us said a word. But I was thinking, Oh, God . . . Oh, God, what next?

In front of us lay a hundred miles of empty country. I knew that. We were headed into the Vizcaino Desert, a flat, dry land where there was only one road, narrow and winding. The sun shone in my eyes. The wind that came rushing in the windows was warm.

"If only we weren't in Mexico," Duluth said some time later, "we'd go right to the police, you know. But he can probably make it look like we took his stuff, accuse us of theft, and that's bad for us."

"It's my stuff!"

"They might not see it that way, the police. You just don't want any kind of trouble down here with the Mexican police."

"How did he follow us, anyway?" I asked.

"I dunno," Inez said. "Listen, I swear I don't know how he figured out where I was going."

"You didn't ever tell him about your brother in San Ignacio?"

"Sure, I told him. I talk about Lorenzo all the time, and sometimes, you know, I got letters from him."

"Letters with his address on them, right?"

"I guess," Inez said wearily.

After a while Duluth began drinking. He'd bought a bottle in Guerrero Negro. He drank tequila straight, and Inez joined right in to help him. Christobel seemed to be in some sort of trance. Her mouth sagged and she stared straight ahead. I just kept driving. We drove for a long time that way. He was never far behind us, following us in his sleek Chrysler New Yorker, my father's dream car.

"Well," I said after a long while when nobody had spoken, "did you get hold of Lorenzo at least? Is he expecting us tonight?"

Inez looked at me. "He doesn't have a phone. But you know, it's going to be all right. He'll be there, I know it. You'll see. He'll be there, it's gonna be okay."

19

WE DROVE through the desert all afternoon, past tall stands of cactus, and dead animals lying on the side of the road, their hides stretched taut over an empty web of bones and sun-dried as if already tanned. Once, a man appeared out of nowhere, weaving down the road on an old bicycle. Another time, dozens of birds circled slowly against the blue sky, and I looked out to see a field of rotting melons, pink and green, lying in the middle of the parched land.

As we drove on and on through the afternoon, I thought about the events that had brought me to Mexico, and I wished for a lot of things. I wished Inez hadn't married Jim. I wished Carl hadn't died. I wished Christobel was not a person with so many problems. I wished Duluth were a little more competent, as all he'd been doing since we left the Pemex station in Guerrero Negro was drinking tequila, and now he seemed quite far gone. Most of all, I wished Jim weren't following us. The hope I had was that we'd all be okay, and it seemed to me as long as we were together, we might be. Strength in numbers. But then I saw all of us—Christobel and Duluth and Inez and myself—as people with broken lives. Life had been a series of separations from those we loved, and I could not see what anybody was moving toward, how we could escape these broken pasts, and I wondered if we were kidding ourselves that there was such a thing as starting over.

When the sun set, fanning pink over the horizon, we still hadn't come to San Ignacio. The desert was all around us, empty and colorless, endlessly rolling toward the edges of the world. And then it was dark, and even the desert was lost.

"Are you tired, baby? Are you all tired out?" Who was Inez talking to? Me? Christobel? "We shouldn't be driving in the dark."

"I know that," I said. "You got another idea?"

"We don't really have a choice."

"Is he still behind us?"

"He's still there."

"I can't see his lights."

"He's coming. He just hasn't made it around that last curve yet."

"There he is." His headlights appeared again, two yellow points, looking oddly cheerful in the night.

Christobel spoke up. "I only ever did one thing wrong," she said.

Nobody asked her what it was. She had been talking in disconnected sentences for the last hour, and every time we asked her about something in order to try to understand better what she was saying, she came back with another disconnected thought.

"Why aren't there more women dentists?" Christobel asked. "Every dentist I ever been to is a man."

"*Hija,*" Inez said, taking Christobel's hands in her own and then stroking the hair away from her forehead. "We're almost there." *Hija*—daughter. It sounded like "eee-haw," that stupid television show; and yet coming out of Inez's mouth, it was a beautiful word.

Suddenly we saw some lights ahead, down in a little valley, and I knew we'd made it. In the bottom of the valley lay San Ignacio.

"You'd better get out those directions to Lorenzo's place so we know where we're going."

The directions were simple: Turn left at the shrine of the Virgin of Guadalupe before you reach town. Go past three sheds. Turn left again. When you come to the goat pens, bear left.

The goats looked menacing in the lights of the truck, like little bearded devils. Dust rose so thickly behind us that the headlights of the white car disappeared from sight, and it was possible to believe Jim had just vanished and was no longer following us.

"I shouldn't have taken Carla's brush," Christobel said. "I shouldn't have stolen her brush. I didn't mean to take it, but I did."

"Honey," Inez said, "just be quiet."

Duluth said, "I sure hope your brother's got other people there. I don't know why, but I think it just might help if he's got about ten big guys working for him, and every one of 'em walks out to greet us."

A house came into view. It was surrounded by rocky hills, and you could never have said it was anything but a poor place. I don't know what I expected, but this wasn't it. I guess I had thought of ranches in Utah and I had imagined Lorenzo's house would look something like that. I supposed it would have a couple of barns and be surrounded by fields of green pasture or crops. But the house here was what you would call a kind of shack, long and irregular, surrounded by a herd of goats and a lot of junk, including at least a dozen wrecked cars. Our headlights shone on a few poor buildings and a fence made out of old tires painted white and a dump site littered with tin cans and bottles. There was a shelter made out of palm fronds, just a roof held up by four poles, and under this roof, right beneath the palm thatch, a woman was cooking something over a fire in big black pots, and I thought, Well, there's the kitchen. Propane lanterns were hung from the beams and threw soft light on the woman. When we stopped, I could smell she was cooking pinto beans, a certain odor that to me is both familiar and slightly sickening, a heavy, starchy smell. We parked the truck but didn't get out. I left the truck lights on and the dust caught up with us, moving in the headlights like smoke. A tall man came out of the house. Two other men followed him.

"Lorenzo?" Inez said, and climbed down out of the truck to meet him.

But it wasn't Lorenzo. He spoke to Inez and identified himself. He was Lorenzo's wife's brother, a thin man who was missing his lower front teeth. His beard was a white stubble, and he looked too old to me to be the husband of the woman who was cooking, but it turned out that he was. Lorenzo, the man told Inez, had gone up to Bahía de los Angeles, a little fishing village on the gulf. He was helping his son dig a well up there, and he wasn't expected to come back. He was going into business with his son, up in Bahía de los Angeles. He'd moved up there some months ago.

When Inez told me this, I couldn't believe it.

"Didn't he know we were coming? Wasn't he expecting us?"

"I don't know," she said, agitated. "I didn't know he wasn't going to be here."

"You mean, you never really talked to him and told him you were coming down here to live with him?"

"I couldn't, Verna honey. There wasn't time, you know? I mean I had to go, okay? You know, I just figured he would be here, okay? That's what I figured on."

I looked at Duluth. He smiled a little and shrugged.

"Well, what we going to do?" I asked.

"I dunno," Duluth said in a slurred voice. "I really don't know."

It was a few minutes before Jim arrived. He didn't pull his car up close to us, but parked back behind the goat pens. Inez began speaking to her brother's brother-in-law rapidly in Spanish. I knew she was explaining the situation to him. He listened with a serious expression on his face. The other two men were listening, too. Only once did the man look over at Jim, sitting in his car, and even then his expression did not change. Only his eyes moved. Pretty soon he came over to the truck and opened the door and motioned for all of us to come inside.

Duluth stayed outside for a little while with the men. There was a woman inside the little house, and when I said hello to her, she said "Hello," very prettily, and it sounded to me like "yellow." Inez sat down in a wooden chair and put her face in her hands.

Christobel moved as if still in the trance. I sat her down in a chair and then turned to look out the window. Duluth and the other men started walking toward Jim, who was still sitting in his car.

Suddenly Jim put the car in reverse and began backing up. Then he skidded to a stop, turned the New Yorker around, and headed back down the road, disappearing into the dark before anyone had said a word to him.

That night, we slept in the house of Lorenzo's brother-in-law. It was made of tin and boards and planks, a house of many colors and materials. Some parts were painted pink, others turquoise. One outside wall was made of car hoods, beaten until they were flattened out, and then nailed into place. The refrigerator, run by propane, sat on the porch next to a twenty-gallon container for water. The fridge had leaked and rotted the boards around it. Several beds were outside right next to the house. The younger men and boys slept there, covering themselves with bright woven blankets, not far from the bodies of the old, rusty automobiles. The chickens that were running loose everywhere flew up into the trees to roost for the night. I slept on a narrow bed in a small room with Inez and Christobel beside me.

At three in the morning, the roosters began to crow. It was a very comforting sound to me. I thought, We've come through this, surely we have, and waited for the morning.

As soon as I could see a little light coming through a space between the curtains, I got up and went outside. Jim wasn't anywhere to be seen. Although day hadn't really broken yet, someone was up before me. In the half-light I could see a heavyset man, wearing an old hooded sweatshirt, working near some pens. He had the hood up on his sweatshirt, covering his head, and he looked like an elf. For a while I watched him. He took a rooster from a cage and smoothed its feathers. He seemed to be talking to it. He dangled it upside down by its feet and shook it. Then he gathered it up against his stomach. He took it over to where a table had been made of boards and he flopped it on its side and waited for it to get up. Then he flopped it over again, on the other side. He did this over and over. Then he took it to his chest again, and spoke to it, stroking its head.

The goats were moving in their enclosure, which was made of thin, irregular sticks. Everywhere there were broken and abandoned things, and wreckage; occasionally a dog or a cat emerged from among the different piles of junk, skinny, wary animals who looked sideways at me and avoided coming near.

Then the women got up, and I began to smell breakfast cooking. Someone brought me coffee.

Inez came out, smiling and looking happy. "Verna honey," she said. "You are up like the roosters." She was wearing a purple bathrobe. Her skin looked pretty against the bright color. She stretched and yawned, opening her mouth wide, and I could see some of the gold covering her back teeth.

I pointed to the man who was still playing with the rooster and asked her what he was doing. She went over and talked to him and came back.

"He's training those roosters for a big cockfight next week. He's got seven roosters he's training. He says the fight is up in Vizcaino and everybody comes from all around. That rooster he's holding now, he's a big champion."

"Oh."

"It's beautiful here, huh? Look at that river." The river was a dull, opaque green, its surface oily in places, but it slid tranquilly past banks lined with grass.

"It is nice," I said. The woman in the palm-thatched kitchen rang a bell, and some men came out of a small shack near the goat pens and sat down on benches at a long table. They were young men, and they glanced sideways at me.

"I like it by the water," she said. "The worst place I think I ever lived was Fresno—there was no water there. We moved down there for a while after my father died, but nothing was happening for us in Fresno. Then we went to Tulare County— you know, my mother got a job in a canning plant, and for a while things were pretty good. I even went to school. I didn't ever go to school before that. Lorenzo and I went to the ele- mentary there called Horace Mann and we were the only Mexicans in our class. We didn't know any English, but a teacher named Mary Douglas took time with us and we learned so quickly that by Christmas we were reading from some books. With Lorenzo and me, it was always a contest to see who could do better, you know? I haven't thought about Mary Douglas for a long time. I don't know why I think of her now. *Recuerdos,* eh? You don't ask for memories, but they come anyway, like mosquitoes."

The cook called to us. *"Ya está listo el desayuno. ¡Vengan a sentarse a la mesa!"*

"Sí, sí. Let's go eat, kiddo."

Breakfast was ham and eggs, tortillas and beans, and salsa. Inez said, "When we first got to the United States, nobody knew what anything was. I remember my father ordered ham and eggs in a cafe—he just pointed to something on the menu, you know, and it just happened to be ham and eggs. The waitress says 'Ham and eggs?' and he nods. That's how he learns what ham and eggs is, and after that, that's all he ever orders because that's all he knows how to say!"

Inez laughed. Lorenzo's brother-in-law, a very shy man, and his family all smiled, but they seemed uncertain of us. It seemed to me that our presence in their house had them confused, especially since Christobel wasn't doing too well. She had begun pacing back and forth, walking the same pattern over and over, looking at the ground, and she asked repeatedly when everybody's birthday was, sometimes shouting in your face. Even if you told her, she asked again. She sat and stared at people and chewed on the ends of her hair.

This, Inez said, wasn't a good sign. This was what she did before she had that breakdown, that one other time, when things got pretty bad. She had become obsessed with birthdays.

Duluth rose late and missed breakfast. He found coffee and tortillas and salsa waiting on the table for him. Inez was sitting next to me, talking to the woman who'd fixed our breakfast, when Duluth walked up. He looked hung over as he stood in the sunlight, squinting.

Inez glanced up at him. "You don't look so good, Paquito."

"Yeah, well."

He scratched his ribs. "What are we doing? Are we going back to L.A. or what?"

I looked at Inez. Suddenly, she seemed to take charge, as if she'd already thought everything out.

"This is what I think we should do." Inez looked first at me, then Duluth. "We leave here and go up to Bahía de los Angeles and find Lorenzo."

"How far is it to this place?"

"I dunno."

"Show me the map."

It was eighty-eight miles back to Guerrero Negro, and another eighty across open desert to the turnoff to Bahía de los Angeles. The village was forty-two miles from the main road. I shook my head. Almost two hundred miles. It would be a long day of driving on bad roads across the deserted country.

The goats bleated. I looked out toward the pens, where the road disappeared into the desert. Jim hadn't come back. Maybe he'd given up. The cock trainer, who had stopped for breakfast, had now gone back to his work. He was once more flopping roosters on their sides, waiting for them to get to their feet, and flopping them over again. Champions, I thought, on their way to Vizcaino to have razors strapped to their legs and fight to their death. Over breakfast, Inez had asked the man how many times in one night a rooster had to fight, and he said, "Seven. Seven fights in one night." It seemed impossible to me that anything or anyone could be so lucky as to win a life-or-death battle seven times in one night, only to have to face another such night. But his roosters had. One cock, he said, had been fighting many nights—many, many nights. "Do the roosters have names?" I asked him, and when Inez translated this, he laughed. Of course they didn't. He found it a very funny idea, a rooster having a name. They were known only as Manuel's roosters.

After breakfast we packed up the truck and said goodbye, then drove into the town of San Ignacio to get some gas. The village was nestled in the middle of a thick stand of palm trees, which stretched up an arroyo where the river ran. We drove past a green lagoon and wound through a forest of palms where men were collecting thatch in the dappled light, until the road suddenly brought us into the little town. Everything was clean and shady and pretty. It looked as if the dirt roads in the town had been swept smooth. The little adobe buildings had been painted pink and blue and green. An old stone church faced a park in the town square. We filled the truck with gas, then parked near the square. Inez wanted to stop at the church, and I walked inside with her. Duluth and Christo-

bel stayed outside where there was a garden and an old cemetery, and a small, cobbled courtyard.

Inez knelt down and began praying near a statue of Christ
on a pedestal at the front of the church. The church was a very
old place. I felt the chill of stone walls. Birds darted from a
nest in the rafters and chirped overhead. Pink cloth had been
hung from the ceiling in two long drapes, which met at the
altar piece amid a profusion of flowers and carved figures. I sat
down on a bench behind Inez. The ceilings were high and
arched, and that feeling of lofty space, the stone walls, the very
age of things impressed me immediately. They do that, I
thought, make the roof so high, in order that you'll feel drawn
upward, toward the big rounded ceiling, and imagine that
you're already being lifted up to heaven, on your way to a
better place.

Everything was still and cool in the dim light. Candles
flickered at the altar, where a young man was kneeling. He
had his head bowed and his hands were clasped, and I
thought, He's awfully young to be praying so hard. He didn't
stir at all, and as I watched him I grew very calm. I thought of
Carl.

Something came over me then. I felt a transforming lightness, as if I were not only myself but of the same substance as
all that was around me, encased in something that was the
same as the young man up in front, the same as Inez, the same
as the flame of the candle and the waxy flowers, the wooden
Christ. It was a good feeling of not being separate and alone
anymore. For a long time I simply felt these things. What if it
were possible to believe, I thought, in something other than
the random and fateful sequence of events?

After a while I stood up and walked outside. Duluth was
standing in the courtyard, talking to a small girl. She held up a
package of dates and turned them in front of her. Everything—the pink and blue and aqua paint on the adobe walls of
the little stores, the small grassy park with the great leafy trees,
the bright dresses worn by two women sweeping the court-

yard, the statue of the Virgin in the shaded recess of the garden, the little girl with her basket of dates, a stone stairway
leading to an ancient wooden door—everything seemed in-
fused with the age and spirit of the place, and the clear shim-
mering light, a colorful, shining intensity; these sights lifted
me, as though my body weighed nothing. From Utah to Los
Angeles to Mexico I had come. The farther south, the clearer
the light, the brighter the color, the more the feeling of age-
old mystery settled on everything like a subtle vibration.

The child, who had thick black hair hanging straight to her
waist like a beautifully draped headdress, lifted the plump
dates in the air and turned them in front of Duluth. I could
hear her small, singsongy voice:

"*¿Quiere comprar unos dátiles? Son riquísimos y tan baratos.
¿Por favor? ¿No quiere comprar unos dátiles? Ve que buenos están.*"

I knew Duluth would buy dates from her, that he wouldn't
be able to resist. I turned my face up and looked at the blue sky
and the brilliant scarlet bougainvillea cascading over a wall. I
thought, If there were a church like this near me, I might go to
it often. Wouldn't that be funny, if I got religious again one
day?

Then I realized that it wasn't that; I would never become a
Catholic, or anything else. It was simply this: I saw the truth of
what Inez had said, about how in church you could get a feeling that everything was going to be okay even when it wasn't.
What a lovely, beautiful deception! I thought I understood
why Carl had gone to the church in Chinatown where Inez had
first seen him kneeling in the dim candlelight. We are drawn
to the flickering hope, imagining that within these reverent
spheres something might be mended.

I thought of Carl, and then of Leon, and then I thought of
Frank, who felt suddenly very near—and it seemed to me that
as you grew older and time and travel and deaths separated
you from your past, someone's presence was composed largely
of memory and was destined to arise at will and either fill or
vacate your mind at odd moments. Dear old Frank, dying, and

leaving neither chick nor child. Dear beautiful Carl. Dear lost ones.

Duluth walked over to me. He was holding a package of dates.

"What are you going to do with those?"

"I don't know," he said. "I don't even like dates."

"Neither do I."

Then I turned and saw him. The white Chrysler was parked under the big trees whose branches extended beyond the small central square. Somebody was playing an accordion in the square, and the music, festive and tinny, floated on the air. Sitting in the car, his eyes hidden by dark glasses, Jim faced us. He smiled, then held up his hand and waved.

"Shit," Duluth said.

"Go into the church and get Inez," I said. "Tell her it's time to go."

Duluth hurried inside the church. I looked around for Christobel and saw her sitting on some steps in front of a door at the side of the church. She stood up as I walked toward her.

"We have to leave now, Christobel," I said. "Come with me and we'll go to the truck."

"I want to know something," she said. Her voice was unusually high, and her eyes were dark and troubled.

"What's that?"

"What day were you born?" she asked in a loud, angry tone. It was as if she were yelling at me in an effort to air some long-outstanding grievance.

"April twenty-third," I said quietly.

"Oh," she said.

"Come on, Christobel."

She rose slowly and I took her hand and she allowed me to lead her away, following me in a stumbly sort of way, like someone who is playing a game in which she has been chosen, on the basis of some previous loss, as the one to be temporarily blindfolded.

20

IT WAS STILL LIGHT when we finally reached the crest of the hill and looked down at the blue waters of the Sea of Cortez and the town of Bahía de los Angeles. You never would have thought this town was nice, that was for sure, you could see that it wasn't going to be anything, you could see how it was just as poor as every other place we'd passed that day—a jumbled collection of shacks and broken rusty automobiles—and I felt let down because I'd hoped for something better, something that looked friendlier and more familiar and less raw. We drove down the hill toward the cluster of buildings at the water's edge as the sun glistened on the water, and I thought, Why does everything have to be so disappointing?

For a long while now, he'd stayed out of sight. But I knew he was still following us. There was only one road. It led only one place, Bahía de los Angeles. Anybody who looked at a map could tell that the road dead-ended there. It was as though we were being driven toward the sea, and there wouldn't be any place left to go once we got there.

After so many hours of driving through the desert it was nice to see the waters of the gulf. Big islands rose up out of the bay, bare and purplish-colored humps. The bright blue water was unreal, like a dream.

Lorenzo was right where he was supposed to be, at his son's café. It was windy outside, and a sign in front of the cafe swung back and forth and banged against a post. The cafe stood on a hill overlooking the water and the narrow road. Small, colorful lights had been strung across the front of the restaurant, and even though it was still daylight, they were blinking merrily. Christmas lights in May. As we drove up, she saw him standing outside.

"There's he is," Inez said softly. "Lorenzo."

I hadn't expected Lorenzo would be such an old man, although he might not have been old so much as aged from a life of hard work. Still, he had a nice face. He had a beautiful face. In it, you saw kindness and honesty, and something else—a great openness and strength.

He was hauling rocks in a wheelbarrow when we drove up. Three other men were helping him. One of these men, I later learned, was Jesse, his youngest son, whose big, smiling wife stood in the doorway of the restaurant, holding a baby only a few weeks old to her breast.

"Buenas tardes!" Lorenzo called in a friendly way when we all got out of the truck, thinking we were customers for his son's restaurant. Then he recognized Inez, who was rushing toward him, and he cried *"Madre de Dios!"* and stopped what he was doing.

They embraced each other. I don't know what they said; they spoke only in Spanish. But it was clear what they felt. They were brother and sister, finally reunited, and they were very happy to see one another again.

After a while everyone was introduced, and we all went inside the little cafe. Jesse, who owned this place as well as another restaurant up nearer the border, spoke a little English, and he kept saying, "This is surprise, eh? This is real big surprise!" He brought us beers. In the kitchen the baby sat in a plastic carrier, crying, his mother said, from colic. She kept pushing a pacifier into his mouth; he kept spitting it out and crying ever louder. There were women cooking, bustling around a big stove. The place was filled with good odors—pungent, warm, and rich. Three men came in and sat down and ordered something. Then another couple arrived. Where was Jim? I kept wondering. Everything suddenly seemed confused and noisy, and I couldn't relax. I kept looking out the window, again and again, waiting for the white Chrysler to pull in next to the truck; but it didn't show up, not even after we'd been there for a long while.

Lorenzo and Inez hadn't seen each other in over twenty

years. She told us he was very happy she had come. They talked so fast in Spanish I couldn't believe they could understand anything. Sometimes they talked right over each other. It was nice to see them this way, and I thought, Maybe it's going to work out for her, maybe this will be okay, he'll help her out.

Christobel sat twisting a hank of her hair into a thin, ropy strand which she pulled across her face, rubbing it over her lips and nose and eyes. She seemed lost inside herself.

Some time later, I walked down the dirt road to the beach and stood and looked out over the bay.

The wind was blowing so hard that the water all moved in one direction and curled over on itself in white little crescents that rose and disappeared like bits of bobbing paper. There was a strip of black rocks on the beach, and on either side of this dark strip the rocks paled into a colorless gray, like the sand itself. The islands were also a muted purplish-gray color, as was the desert that surrounded the town, through which we had driven for hours and hours to come to where we were. Far out on a spit of sand stood a little white lighthouse, trimmed in red.

I thought, I've got to give Leon his divorce, it's time now. I imagined writing him a postcard saying this thing in several different ways. The water crested and blew off the top of the waves in a fine spray. Just keep up my health insurance, and that includes my teeth. I'd tell him that.

Then I imagined writing Vincent a card from this place. What would I say to him? "I miss you"? "Having a good time"? None of this was true. I didn't know what I could put on a card, and after a while I gave up thinking about it.

I sat down on the rocks. I saw that among the gray stones there were were pink shells lying near me and also spotted ones with fluted edges. There were shards of rainbow-colored pearly shells, black and ugly on the one side, fantastically beautiful on the other. Suddenly, amid all that grayness, I saw how the rocks themselves were also subtly colored, stippled with gold and green and rust. I looked at the ground and I saw clearly how colorful everything really was. I remembered the day the chinchillas escaped how James and Mom and I had walked through the woods and looked at the ground. Everything had appeared distinct to me then, too, as if I were really *seeing* for the first time. Now I felt that I was seeing things that way again, and each rock appeared distinct and colorful, each shell a marvel of form and intricacy which could be looked at for a long time, and things weren't only gray now. . . .

You could have just said "I really like you." You could have said something like that. . . .

Every once in a while I looked up at the road to see if the white car was coming. There was just the road, empty and black, snaking up the hill through the tall slender cactus.

I felt a fear of going back to Los Angeles, but I couldn't see myself in any other place at the moment. I kept trying to picture myself back in Willard, and I could not place myself there. I saw that I was a person of no distinct location anymore. I belonged nowhere.

I hardly recognized myself now, I appeared so strange and familiar at once. I remembered something Vincent said one night when he'd come to visit me: "Of all the things in the world, only one is presented to a person in two ways, and that is the person himself: he knows himself externally as a body, as appearance, and internally, directly as part of the primary essence of all things. This makes us strange creatures, doesn't it?" he said. "We are both strange and familiar to ourselves."

This was how I felt.

I never thought I would be a person whose future was so uncertain she couldn't imagine what was coming next. I'd always foreseen something of a future—a place, some persons, a particular life, even in its shadowiest form, ahead of me. Now, well, I could hardly call up anything except myself, a woman with poorly braided hair and a windburned face and rumpled clothes, sitting alone on a strange beach.

I looked at an island shaped like a horse's head and it

stirred a memory of something in me: the barn next to my father-in-law's place that succumbed to the lake's rising waters. It sat out there in the water, a thing totally out of place. I never actually saw that barn; I mean, I didn't *really* look at it when it was on dry land. Not until Leon and I circled it in the rowboat, peering into what would have been the hayloft had it been on dry ground, when it had already become a cavernous chamber of salt water, useless and pitiful, did it seem interesting to me.

"You have to lose-ed something before you are ready to change enough to do what you need to do in order to keep it," Frank once said to me. "If you're lucky, you find it again."

And then I lost Frank, who slept his way to death on a train headed for Tonapah. And I lost Leon. I was far from my family. I had few real friends. I didn't know exactly what I had kept anymore.

When I finally walked back to the restaurant, it was dark; everyone was sitting inside and getting ready to eat dinner. The kitchen was next to the dining room; there wasn't a wall between the the two rooms, and you could see four or five people moving between the stove, a sink, and large refrigerator. Jesse was waiting on tables. Lorenzo and Inez, Duluth and Christobel, and Jesse's wife and baby were all sitting at one long table, and I sat down with them. There was a warm, happy feeling at the table. At another table there were some Americans, an older couple and a younger couple, who were all dressed up, like they were at a country club in America instead of a little cafe in a remote Mexican village. Their voices were a little too loud. I heard the younger woman say, "This is the best abalone I have had in a long, long time."

"And so cheap."

"How much was it, Arthur? How much did they say this abalone cost?"

"Three dollars."

The woman laughed. "Can you imagine getting this back home?"

"Look at that dear little kitten. What's the word for 'cat'? *Gato?* Here, *gato gato* . . . here little *gato.* Give him a bite of your lobster, dear."

Dinner was brought to our table and we all ate eagerly, hungry because we hadn't had any food since breakfast. I looked across the table at Christobel to see how she was doing. Her eyes were dull glass beads. Inez, however, looked happy, and so did Duluth. I kept looking out the window for the headlights. Where was he?

Before we went to bed that night, Inez said to me, "I told Lorenzo everything. He said not to worry. He's not afraid of Jim. We can stay here as long as we want. He's got a house he just built over the hill, and there's room for us there. He said from now on we're safe with him. He said not to worry about anything, okay? He told me to tell you he appreciates you helping me and you got nothing to worry about now."

"Okay."

"And you know what else, Verna honey?"

"What?"

"I don't think he's going to come. Just a feeling I got. I think he's given up now. He knows there's no hope."

Jim did not come until late the next morning.

We were all out in front of the restaurant, looking at Lorenzo's well, which in three days, he said, would be giving water. He said he had dug other wells in other parts of Mexico. He knew something about wells. He knew by the trees and the way the land sloped that there would be water here, and he'd hired some local men to help him start digging. There had never been a well in Bahia de los Angeles, and nobody believed he'd find water. For years and years all the water for the village had been trucked in from Guerrero Negro, ever since the first people had settled here. If he did find water, he would be the first to do so, and he'd be a rich man.

For weeks Lorenzo and Jesse had dug the well by hand

alongside the workers they hired, until they'd gone down forty-seven feet and hit a layer of large rocks. The workers walked away, telling Lorenzo he was crazy. There was no way to dig through the rocks, they said, and they no longer believed there was water in this place, anyway. Lorenzo and Jesse kept working until they'd hauled the boulders up out of the shaft, using ropes tied to the bumper of a truck to pull them up. Then they dug two more feet and hit water.

Lorenzo explained all this to us while we were standing around his new well. I looked down the shaft, which had been lined with concrete blocks. A crude ladder led to the bottom, almost fifty feet below. What looked like a small silvery circle of mirror was really the oily surface of the water, reflecting the sky. I dropped a rock and it went *plop* and the mirror broke up. All around the well, covering the holes that hadn't been filled in, were boards, which wiggled when I stepped on them. It seemed like somebody could easily slip and fall into the unfilled crevice, and I backed away, feeling suddenly nervous.

We all turned at the sound of a car door closing and saw him at the same time. Inez spoke to Lorenzo quickly and Lorenzo nodded his head and assumed a sterner look. Jim stepped out of his car. He wore a brightly colored sport shirt and a pair of blue pants. His hair was wet and slicked back against his scalp, as if he'd just come from the shower. His face appeared large and ruddy—reddened, perhaps, by days of driving in the bright sun. Inez went over to him, but they didn't say anything right away. She put her hands on her hips and stared at him.

Then she said, "I thought you gave up."

In the sunlight, I could see how her hair was thinning, how the roots were gray. Jesse and Lorenzo and three of the workers who were helping them build a fence with the boulders taken from the well walked over and stood behind Inez. They were small men, but they looked hard from their work. Duluth joined them. He appeared very frail next to the workers, and he seemed agitated. He was the first to speak up.

"I think you'd better leave," Duluth said.

"I ain't leaving without talking to Inez, and you can tell that to the goons, too." He made a mistake then. He shoved Duluth, pushing him back against the others, hitting him on his chest.

And then, swiftly, Lorenzo had Jim by the neck, and he was working him down toward the ground, as if he were going to choke him to death there on the spot. But just as suddenly he pulled him back up and pressed him against his car, the white New Yorker, my father's dream car. He lifted his fist and hit him. A bright trickle of blood appeared at the corner of Jim's mouth, and he made a gurgling sound. All this happened so fast that everyone standing there under the bright sun didn't have time to move before it was over and something else happened, something I could not have predicted. Inez moved over to Jim's side. She went to him and put her arms around him.

"Don't hit him!" she said.

Jim started begging and crying, pleading with Inez to go home with him. I could not have told what was going to happen, which was that Inez started comforting Jim in order to try to get him to stop crying, and then he put his arms around her and cried all the harder and begged her to please, please give him another chance. He told her he did not know what he would do without her; he said he needed her. Inez said, "It's going to be okay, Jim," repeating this over and over to him, and then she spoke to Lorenzo in Spanish. There were sharp words between them. They began arguing.

Finally Inez turned back to Jim.

Jim said, "Just give me a chance, Inez—honest to God, I can be a good husband to you. I can and I will."

I did not believe that he would be, but I knew it was not a thing that needed me to believe in it. Inez was going to do what she was going to do. Jim reached up to her, and Inez knelt down beside him.

Inez and Jim clung to each other, sitting on the ground.

Nobody said anything except Jim and Inez, and they were talking to each other in voices so low we couldn't hear what they said.

Pretty soon Duluth and Lorenzo and the others came away. We all went into the restaurant, embarrassed, I think, to just stand there and watch two people pouring out so much emotion on each other. We left Jim and Inez huddled close together, sitting on the ground next to the white New Yorker, where they stayed, talking for a long time.

"Have you had enough to eat?"

Christobel nodded.

"And what about you?"

"Stuffed," Duluth said. He patted the front of his shirt.

"And what about you?"

"I've had plenty, too, thanks," I said.

Marta, the woman who was married to Jesse, could speak English, and she did most of the talking to us. The men who had been making the rock fence, working all afternoon outside in the yard with Lorenzo, sat at the table, silently finishing their meal. Marta had told us that normally the women serve the men first, and then afterwards they sit down and eat by themselves. But because we were here, because visitors were present, we were all eating together, men and women.

I understood why it would be hard for Inez to live here. But it was not so easy to understand how she could have gone back to Jim.

They didn't even bother to take much from the trailer, just a few boxes of her clothes. Jim didn't come into the restaurant. He stayed out in the car while Inez came inside and talked to us. She cried and asked us to understand, if we could, that he really did love her and that they needed each other and they wouldn't be happy apart.

Lorenzo argued with Inez. He threw his hands in the air and shook his head. He slapped the palm of one hand with the back of the other and talked some more to her. Inez looked down, away from him, and kept repeating something. Then he shook his head, turned away, and went back to work.

Inez looked at me. "Verna? You understand?" She took my hands and stared into my eyes.

"No," I said. "I don't. I wouldn't go back with somebody who hit me all the time. I don't believe it's going to get better. I wish you would stay here with Lorenzo."

Suddenly Inez slumped down on a chair. She put her head down. "I don't know what to do. What can I do? It don't matter no more, does it? I mean, after a while it just don't seem to matter. You know, in my life, it never seemed to matter much what I did, it all turned out the same bad way, like somebody else was deciding things."

Inez turned to Christobel and asked her what she wanted to do: Did she want to stay here or go back to L.A. with them?

Christobel, seeming more lucid and calm than she had for a few days, said, "I want to stay here." Inez asked Jesse's wife if Christobel could stay with them for a while; she was a good girl and also a good worker. When things settled down with Jim, maybe she could come back for Christobel. After speaking to her husband briefly, Jesse's wife said yes, of course Christobel could stay.

Finally Inez turned to Duluth. "You gonna stay, too?"

"Don't go with him," Duluth said. "You don't have to do that, even if he does say he needs you."

"Oh, Paquito," Inez said, "you don't understand anything about it, I'm afraid."

But I thought he did. I thought way back to that day outside Vegas when he'd told me the story of his wife at the party and how the man had unbuttoned her blouse and she had just let him do that and how Duluth said he knew from that point on that she was always going to be cheering men up. I thought he understood the terrible tragedy of some women's lives, how they don't ever see the possibility of having something for themselves but only imagine themselves endlessly serving somebody, offering up the cheapest sort of cheer, and all the while denying their pain.

"I'm going to come back soon," Inez said, even then trying to be cheerful, "for a visit, so this is not really goodbye, huh, 'cause I'm going to visit again soon."

She hugged Christobel, who was quiet, and said, *"Hija,* honey, be good, and I'll write to you soon." And then she hugged me and thanked me and said again how she had always liked me. She hugged Duluth and started for the door, then hesitated and said, "I better use the bathroom before we go," and disappeared through a door at the back of the room.

I don't think we thought anything about it when Christobel got up. Duluth and I just sat there and watched her. She stood up so quietly. Her manner was calm. Nothing seemed different. There was no indication that anything was going to happen. But later I realized we should have known. We just should have known.

She walked outside, down the steps, and crossed the dirt to where Jim was standing, looking down the well. He had no premonition, I'm sure, of what was going to happen, unless in those few seconds between when he turned and saw her standing next to him and the first blows fell on his face, he had time to think, and then he might have known. He might have thought, My God, here it is.

He lost his balance. That's what everyone said, and a part of that was true. He was caught off-balance. He was standing on those shaky boards. He really did fall back, or, rather, he stepped back. She really didn't push him. He just took one step, tumbled backward, and his body folded over as he struck the rim of the well, and before he could utter a word he was gone, falling as effortlessly as laundry sliding down a chute, falling down fifty feet, past the welts of fresh mortar holding all the carefully laid cinder blocks in place, past the crude ladder—so useless to him now—falling into the small pool of oily water, hitting the surface loudly, landing in the bottom of the first well in Bahia de los Angeles, his neck instantly broken.

21

IN THE MOONLIGHT, the horse swayed from side to side as it carefully picked its way down the steep hill. The trail was rocky. Ahead of me, I could see Lorenzo on his horse. He was leading a mule, and Christobel was riding on the mule. Duluth was behind me. He was singing a song that I had taught him, a Patsy Cline song: "I can see an angel walking, someone else is by his side. . . ." I turned around and looked at him and he said, "That's right, Verna."

"What's right, Duluth?"

He didn't answer; he just began singing again.

It was almost a full moon, and the whole landscape was lit up and bluish white. To me, the color around us was like moonlight on snow. The pale sand of the desert was almost as light as snow.

Lorenzo said that he lived in a new house, one he had built himself, although the road hadn't yet been completed all the way to his door. In order to reach his house, we had to go by horseback, following a trail through the hills, because it was easier than walking. We did not start out until after dark, when the police and the doctor had left, and yet we could see, we could see a long way by the clear light of the moon.

We arrived just before midnight. It was a nice house, just as Lorenzo said—three rooms, very small, but cozy and neat and freshly whitewashed. There wasn't any junk around Lorenzo's house. Instead, a small garden had been laid out in furrowed rows. The house was built around a central courtyard, where an old cactus grew straight into the air. Lights were shining in the small windows as we rode down into the valley. When we got closer, I could see how the desert came right up to the walls, except for the garden area. Olive trees had been planted around the house. In the distance, on the hillsides, what had first looked like white boulders were really pale goats, bedded down for the night and lying still in the moonlight. On the wind, you could smell the goats and others odors, including a wood fire.

Lorenzo's wife, Juanita, was waiting for us. She served us hot chocolate and sweet buns. None of us spoke while we ate. I think we all felt the need for silence. I thought of Inez, who was spending the night elsewhere—with Jesse and Marta, in the rooms beneath the restaurant. She was heavily sedated. The doctor, an old friend of Lorenzo's who had come all the way from Guerrero Negro, had given her a small dose of morphine, the drug that had made Carl's own dreadful end somewhat more bearable, and left some sleeping pills.

"She will recover," the doctor said. "It's the shock of it. But she will recover, though you must keep the daughter out of her sight for a while. Just keep them apart."

That night I dreamed of Leon. We were standing in the stalls beneath the bleachers at the rodeo grounds. He was wearing some yellow leather chaps and a shirt that matched. Someone called his name for the bull-riding event. I said, "Leon, you be careful out there." And then he just rose up and, without walking, moved across the ground, about a foot above it, as if he wanted to show me his powers, and settled on the back of a bull that was made out of mother-of-pearl, like the seashells on the beach.

Three mornings later, we got back onto the horses and rode over the hill to the little restaurant, where I'd left the truck and trailer. The goats were climbing the trails threading through the hills. Some of the goats had bells tied around their necks, and as we passed by, they ran from us and their bells tinkled, making a pretty sound.

Christobel said, "I like this, Verna."

"What do you like?"

"I like this horse." She was holding on to the saddle horn with both hands. She stayed close to Duluth, and sometimes she rode up beside him and, letting go of the horn for a moment, took his hand and held it. Once I heard him say, "It's okay that things are turning out the way they are, Christobel. Nothing is your fault." Then he reached over and brushed the hair back from her face.

Lorenzo rode ahead to make sure things were all right. He came back and said, "Inez is sleeping. Marta thinks it's a good time to come in."

As soon as we arrived at the restaurant, Christobel took out her brush and asked Jesse's wife if she could style her hair. Jesse's wife was breast-feeding the baby. She looked up and said, "Sí" and turned around in her chair. Christobel touched her heavy black hair.

"How would you like some French braids? I think that'd look good."

Duluth helped me unload everything from the trailer and the back of the truck. "She doesn't want to see these things again," Lorenzo said. "She said to give it all away. Just leave everything out. People here can use things—they'll come and take them away." Some of the women came out of the kitchen. Lorenzo explained to them in Spanish that I meant to leave all these things and for them to take whatever they wanted.

The women approached the pile of belongings, shy and serious at first. Then, as they began picking things up, their expressions changed, and they began to speak to each other— one or two words, uttered quickly. One of them held a Mister Coffee machine up and looked at it. Someone else looked at a tin tray stamped BUDWEISER. Another woman picked up a picture in a gold frame. I realized it was a photograph of Carl.

"I'll take that," I said. Later, I'd send it to her. I was sure she'd want it.

I stayed in Bahía de los Angeles three weeks. During that time I read *Faust*. I read it slowly, and still I could not understand it. The words seemed too different from the way people spoke now. My mind wandered as I read.

I took long walks alone. I rode Lorenzo's horses into the

hills in the evening when the heat of the day had died down. I found I enjoyed being alone; it no longer seemed difficult the way it had before. I didn't feel lonely; I felt peaceful being by myself.

One night, Jesse and Marta and Duluth and I went to see the movies that had just arrived, brought to town by traveling gypsies, who drove from village to village showing their films in a round canvas tent. The tent had no roof. It was a circular drape, suspended on posts, open to the sky. Inside, a screen had been set up, and wooden benches were placed in rows. The projector sat on the bed of a truck backed up to the tent and ran off a small generator. I didn't know what the story was about, and it didn't matter. People laughed a lot during the film. It was a windy night. With the stars above us, the picture flickered on the screen. The tent flaps were lifted by the wind and flapped wildly; and gazing down once, I saw children, lying on the ground outside, looking between our legs, staring up at the screen. Later, we left the movie and walked slowly back up the hill to the restaurant. In the morning I went back to see if the gypsies were still there, but they had vanished without leaving a trace, as if the wind had borne them away.

Jim's sister arrived, and also a brother. They spent the night at the nicest motel in Bahía de los Angeles, the Villa Vitta, which had electricity during certain hours of the day. They both came from Texas and spoke in soft voices about their brother. Not being close to Jim, they said, they didn't know what to say. But they wanted to know more details. The man, Richard, walked over and looked down the well. Monty was the woman's name—short, she said, for Margaret.

"I can't understand a thing like this happening," she said. "What was he doing in this godforsaken place?"

Lorenzo spoke to them at length, using Jesse as an interpreter, explaining how Jim had fallen to his death, and they seemed to accept his version of things, that this was an accident, sudden and fateful, like all acts of God.

Lorenzo arranged for a coffin to be brought in from an-

other town and asked one of the Americans who lived at the
trailer court down by the water to drive the body to the small
airport outside town. Less than twenty-four hours after they
arrived, Richard and Monty flew off with Jim's body in a small
Piper Cub plane, on an afternoon when everything was unusually calm.

I came to see that the wind blew almost constantly in Bahía
de los Angeles, and the sand got into everything—sheets,
shoes, hair, even your teeth. The wind wore me down, and I
spent hours sitting idly in the restaurant just to be away from
it. One afternoon Duluth and I walked all the way out to the
lighthouse at the end of the spit and sat battling the fierceness
of the wind, trying to talk. Some Americans arrived, a young
couple, and attempted to put up a tent on the beach, but it
blew away, and they had to chase it down the sand. I was tired
of this place by now, and I told Duluth that.

"So are you going back soon?"

"I think so."

We were quiet for a while. I looked at Duluth and saw how
much better he appeared. He was washing dishes and cleaning
up in the restaurant now in exchange for his room and board
and a little money. He still drank, but only at night, when he
walked down to Guillermo's Bar, near the turtle pens at the
water's edge, and sat with his friends from the trailer court.

"I was sure scared by that man," he said, picking up a stone
and skipping over the water. "I'll tell you that. When he saw
me standing there in his shirt, I thought, Oh, shit, Duluth,
you're a cooked chicken."

"I wish I could say I was sorrier to see him go."

"I just wish Inez wasn't taking it so bad," he said.

One night I called my parents from a phone in the office of
the motel nearby. I told them where I was and what had happened.

"Oh dear," my mom said.

"When did this happen?" Dad asked.

"A few weeks ago," I said.

"And you were there when he was killed?"

"Yes," I said. "I was."

"What an awful thing," Mom said.

"That's a real tragedy," Dad added. The line was full of static.

"How's Inez?"

"She's still pretty shook up."

"Will you tell her we're sorry?"

"Yes."

"Will you give us her brother's address down there so we can write to her?"

"Yes," I said again, and gave them an address for the restaurant.

I suppose at some point later a letter did arrive. I can't imagine that they didn't write if they said they were going to. I'm sure they would have done that—expressed their condolences, tried to offer Inez their support, asked if there was anything they could do. They would certainly have wanted Inez and Christobel to know how sorry they were.

They had to go to Guerrero Negro one afternoon for an appointment with the *policía*, and Lorenzo drove them in his old truck. Christobel came out of the restaurant and stood looking warily at her mother. It was the first day since the accident that Inez had gotten out of bed. It was also the first day she stopped taking sedatives and seemed at all alert. They just looked at each other and didn't say anything. And then Lorenzo put his arm around Inez and walked her over to Christobel and put his arm around her, too, and then he just took them both to the truck and helped them get in. They came back very late at night. Everybody came inside together. Inez said, "Well, that's over." Later, through Jesse, we learned that there wouldn't be any investigation or charges. Everyone accepted that it was an accident, and everyone was free now to do whatever they wanted to.

Duluth stood by the well, talking to Lorenzo. His skin was tanned; he'd begun to look like one of those western men who easily could be mistaken for a Mexican. A little mustache had appeared on his upper lip, just some dark hairs in a thin and straying pattern. He even had a different way of walking these days, a looser and more confident gait.

I went inside to say goodbye to Christobel.

"This is so hard," she said. "Her hair is *so* thick." She was braiding the cook's daughter's hair, a young girl of about twelve.

"I'm leaving now, Christobel," I said. "I'm going back."

"What do I care," she said.

"Well, not much, I guess."

I looked down at her fingers, working to place the hairs into the separate strands that she held in her fingers. I thought of her father, Carl, the most beautiful of all my parents' children, perhaps the gentlest, and the first of us to die. I saw his casket, suspended above his grave, and remembered how I could look beneath it and see all the way across the valley, where the lake met the Oquirrh Mountains. *It's a lovely view . . . a beautiful spot.*

I took Christobel and put my arms around her and held her. I felt sorry for all the losses everyone had suffered. Christobel didn't resist when I hugged her, but neither did she respond; she was suspended, waiting for me to finish, like somebody holding a breath, so she could go on with things that mattered to her.

I said, "Christobel . . . goodbye."

"Goodbye," she said, looking down at her hands, which had resumed their weaving. I walked outside to where Duluth was waiting for me.

"Lorenzo says I can stay for a while, so that's what I'm going to do," Duluth said.

"I'm glad," I said. "I think this is a good place for you."

"I think she might need me, too."

"Well," I said, "I don't know about that. I don't know what she'll do."

"Anyway, I'm staying."

"It's a good idea," I said. We both looked over in the direction of the women from the village who continued to come each day and were still going through what was left of the pile of goods. A younger woman had put on a sequined beret and was strutting around, and the other women were laughing, covering their mouths with their hands.

I looked at the trailer and I realized I didn't want it anymore. It had moved enough people around, and it looked so dilapidated that I couldn't imagine selling it now. My worldly goods had devalued, and I thought I might as well cut it loose. So I gave the trailer to Lorenzo, who was very happy to get it and could not thank me enough.

Duluth and I hugged each other and said goodbye.

Then I went to the door leading to the rooms beneath the restaurant, where Jesse and his family lived. I opened it and stepped inside quietly. Inez was still sleeping, her dark hair spread out on the pillow. I stood there for a long time looking at her. But I didn't wake her. I didn't have to. She opened her eyes and she said, "You're leaving now, aren't you."

I said, "Yes."

"I always liked you," she said.

"I always liked you, too." I said.

Then I turned and left.

There was only this, the past that you carried in your memory, and the present, which was undecipherable, and the unknowable future, which might already be inside you, leaking out in unreadable script but which you could never in a million years guess. It was these things I thought about, driving toward home.

Home at that point was just an idea. Home was fields of newly mown hay, wet from a fresh rain. Home was a valley so broad you couldn't walk it in a day. Home was two people sitting in a small house where nothing changed except a few things that faded in the sun, red plastic geraniums muting to a pearly pink, where people watched the TV for news of the world and tried to out-guess game-show contestants. Home was a future unknown. Home was a set of things, a past and a present and a future, all quite inseparable at that moment, as if time had stopped going forward and backward and was rising and falling, up and down, like mercury in one grand column.

22

IT'S A perfectly fine day. I can see them out the window, walking across the lawn below me.

Years are upon us. It's almost the end of a century. As I write this, it's New Year's Day. Last night, on New Year's Eve, we celebrated and became reflective, the way people do on that particular night, which is so unlike any other night of the year. We tried to sum up our lives. We pledged ourselves to the future. He said, "To clear days ahead," and raised his glass. Just then, the baby woke up and cried, and I said, "Your turn," which it was.

Yesterday, we received a letter from Christobel:

Dear Verna and Vincent,
    I am writing to thank you for the lovely calendar you sent me. It was wonderful. I enjoy it very much. Mom and Duluth are back. I may go to their house on New Year's day. It was nice writing to you, so please remember me.

Christobel Flake
The Park Vista Guest House
1771 Walter St.
San Francisco, Calif.

The summer before my father died, I spent quite a bit of time with him. I remember once he lifted his head from his bed and he said, "What's the best time to see trees?"

"Trees?"

"I don't know, but I think it must be the fall, when there's a tapestry laying on the land. I don't know, though. I liked things bare. I've always liked the look of a bare tree. I believe that's what I'm becoming. I'm getting stark-bare for death.

"Sometimes I used to walk out and look at things in the winter—you know, after the snow was melted but when things were still pretty much dead. I did like the look of it then. I liked just seeing the bare trees."

Toward the end, when he could no longer bend over to tie his shoes or pull at the tall weeds that began to take over his garden, my mother dressed him each day according to his instructions.

"That blue shirt," he'd say, "and those checked yellow pants, I think."

He lay in bed, in these colorful clothes, usually wearing his silver bola tie with its great turquoise stone. He was so thin that the stone seemed to hold him in place and keep him from floating up off the sheets like a piece of paper ash.

When Vincent met him, my father said, "What size shoe have you got on there, son?" He made Vincent lift his foot to his bedside table, and firmly, with his same old concern, he turned on his side and felt the leather around Vincent's toes.

"They're too wide," he said. "I'd go to about a ten-and-a-half triple-A if I were you."

I miss him very much, although there's still my mom, who is close to us.

Last night, when Vincent had taken Silvia in his arms and rocked her back to sleep, we settled down again, resuming our New Year's talk. He said he had high hopes for his new work, a concerto that has taken up most of his time during the last winter. He also said that I have never stopped being his muse.

He said, "The muse has always been a sanctifying woman, God help her." Then he laughed. Of course, with Vincent there are still many things I don't always understand. As for me and my outcome—well, I am writing this book, aren't I?

And finally I have come to understand *Faust*—a little bit, anyway. It is a book, above all, about evil and desire and the fateful bargainings on behalf of love. This is how I explained it to Vincent last night.

We touched our glasses and took another sip of wine.

I thought of funny things last night. I thought of Ab Jenkins and the Mormon Meteor—I could almost hear the voice of the KSL sportscaster, announcing his name: "There he goes . . . Ab Jenkins in the Mormon Meteor!" I remembered finding pages of *Peyton Place* up in the hills one time, and how I was thrilled by some descriptions in that book. I saw thin garments flapping on a clothesline, chickens running around with their heads cut off, my father holding up one glove he'd just found, a fire in the center of a frozen pond, the view from the property in Layton where the house had never been built, and Leon kneeling in the thin snow and proposing to me. I remembered how completely wet and helpless and tiny a newborn chinchilla looks. Frank appeared to me too, smoothing back his thinning hair, eyes shining bright. Also I saw Carl. He was healed and well and stood smiling at me.

It's four o'clock now. I am sitting at the window overlooking the sea. It's winter. As I say, New Year's Day. The sunlight is patchy on my clothes. Below me, the little river flows out of the channel into the ocean. Vincent and the baby have just walked out onto the lawn. He raises his arm and points to the sky.

They walk down farther toward the water, passing beneath a willow tree, and emerge into the fast-fading light. Vincent is gesturing, pointing something out to the baby. Silvia lifts her chubby hand and pats his face. The water beyond them is coming in in fanciful rows, small, lacy waves. They just keep coming, row after row of flowing ripples, these endless waves. The Pacific is such a wide, fathomless ocean, and here we are, still on the rim.

THE CHINCHILLA FARM

Judith Freeman

DISCUSSION QUESTIONS

1. The book is divided into three parts: Utah, Los Angeles, and Mexico. How do these three very different places shape Verna's understanding of herself and the world? At the end of the book, why does she decide to return to Los Angeles?

2. The Church of Latter-Day Saints is a rather secretive world, and Verna opens a window into the day-to-day lives of Mormons in Utah. It is an all-enveloping world, and we see how the members of the church built their lives around its principles and community. Why did Verna and Leon decide to leave the church, and what impact did that have on their future decisions? What did you learn about Mormonism that you didn't know before, and how did this affect your understanding of the characters?

3. Author Judith Freeman does not present a rosy view of marriage in this book; from infidelity to violence to simple disillusionment, couples find reasons to tear apart. Verna says that Leon left her and that there was nothing she could do to stop it. Is this true? Why does Vincent say that Jolene left him? Inez's marriage to Carl is the most loving and positive in the book, and it remains the defining relationship of her life. Do you think it could have endured in the face of all the problems couples eventually confront?

4. The Mormons in the book strive to demonstrate the good qualities of the church: forgiveness, tolerance, and acceptance among them. But Verna's family has trouble accepting Carl's wife, Inez. Is this racism, or is it merely the result of the remoteness and insularity of small-town life? Similarly, Verna says that Christobel "was of our

family, but not in it. We could never enfold her, take her in as one of us, not in a million years, and that was our shame." There seems to be a paradox of simultaneous exclusion and acceptance in the Mormon church. How does this paradox play out in the characters' lives?

5. Vincent is an odd character—he is cold to Verna when they first meet, then he befriends her, then he rebuffs her advance, and finally he declares that she is his muse. Freeman portrays him as an uptight, rich, fragile intellectual. What is the attraction between them? They see the world in such different ways. What could make Verna decide to return to him in the end? Do you think it was the right decision?

6. Inez and Jim have the most obviously disastrous marriage—his jealousy and violence make him dangerous for her. She makes a difficult choice in deciding to leave him. Do you think she could have done it if Verna hadn't come back into her life? Her decision to leave for Mexico changes the lives of many other people: How are Verna, Christobel, Duluth, and Jim affected?

7. Vincent says that every family has a central story and that one or two events will act as defining points, collecting about them emotions and a sense of common identity. What are these events in Verna's life? How do they act to pull people in her family together? Sometimes other people, like Duluth, are involved—does this make them family in some sense, for having shared in the family's story of itself?

8. Verna is a remarkable narrator, because she seems innocent of the pretensions and egotism that other characters have. She is almost transparent, giving the reader a clear view of the events and people in her life, while being hard to decipher herself. How does Verna's first-person narration shape the novel? And how does her innocence as a character affect her decisions?

9. The escape at the chinchilla farm seems to be one of the defining events in Verna's childhood. Verna and her brother Stanley had loved tending to the exotic little animals, and they were terrified of being accused of letting them escape. Why is Verna so fascinated by them? What is it about the farm that lends itself to the title of the book?